LOVE
&
OBITS

ALSO BY JOHN ED BRADLEY

Tupelo Nights
The Best There Ever Was

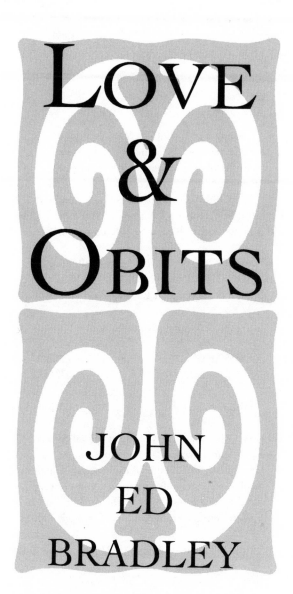

LOVE & OBITS

JOHN ED BRADLEY

A John Macrae Book
Henry Holt and Company   New York

Published by Henry Holt and Company, Inc.,
115 West 18th Street, New York, New York 10011.
Published in Canada by Fitzhenry & Whiteside Limited,
91 Granton Drive, Richmond Hill, Ontario L4B 2N5.

Library of Congress Cataloging-in-Publication Data
Bradley, John Ed.
Love & obits / John Ed Bradley. — 1st ed.
p.   cm.
"A John Macrae book."
I. Title.   II. Title: Love and obits.
PS3552.R2275L68   1992
813'.54—dc20   91-27714

ISBN 0-8050-1680-5   CIP

Henry Holt books are available at special discounts
for bulk purchases for sales promotions, premiums,
fund-raising, or educational use. Special editions
or book excerpts can also be created to specification.
For details contact: Special Sales Director, Henry Holt and Company, Inc.,
115 West 18th Street, New York, New York 10011.

First Edition—1992

Book design by Claire Vaccaro
Printed in the United States of America
Recognizing the importance of preserving
the written word, Henry Holt and Company, Inc.,
by policy, prints all of its first editions
on acid-free paper. ∞

10 9 8 7 6 5 4 3 2 1

To Mom,
Gina, Donna,
Bobby and Brent,
and to Uncle Dave and Mere,
and to Miss Connie, of course

LOVE
&
OBITS

⚑ *One* ⚑

The assignment editor, a woman named Jennifer Eugene, had walked over from Lifestyle. She was an old friend of Joseph's, but they rarely talked anymore, not since his demotion to the Obituary desk. Joseph put down the sandwich he'd been eating and wiped the corners of his mouth with a paper napkin. "Something wrong?" he said.

"Louie Vannoy died. They wanted me to tell you."

"Me or Alfred?"

"Well, Alfred . . . anyone in Obits. Where is he, by the way?"

"He's at lunch, then goes for a two o'clock interview. He said to expect him back no later than three."

"Then you write it, Joseph. Someone in Lifestyle will do an appreciation. You can go forty inches with this one."

"Forty? You're kidding."

"I checked with Mr. Yates and he wants it for A-1."

"Since when does a restaurateur land on A-1?"

"Since Mr. Yates says so. Just write it, all right?"

"Nobel Prize winners don't rate A-1, but Mr. Big puts Louie Vannoy there. I don't get it."

"He ran a nice restaurant, the most popular in town."

"Yes, he did."

"He threw those famous parties where everyone got drunk and

arm-wrestled and farted and did whatever it is men do. Haven't you ever heard Mr. Yates talk about those days?"

"I can't say that I have."

"Louie'd invite all the top brass from the Pentagon, the Hill, the White House—all men, sometimes a bimbo or two for show. They'd eat and drink and tell stories about each other. Back during Watergate, guess who went to Louie Vannoy when Deep Throat refused to talk?"

"Ah, the recipe for good reporting. A matzo ball soup salesman with a big mouth."

"Whatever works," Jennifer said. "You know that." She pointed to a notebook on his desk and Joseph picked it up and began to take notes. "Apparent heart attack," she said. "He was glad-handing a table of K Street lawyers when it hit. Two men tried to revive him. One blew into his mouth, the other pumped his chest. From what Mr. Yates says, there were screams from the kitchen, people running for the exits. It was absolute pandemonium. Louie never got up."

"What about funeral arrangements?"

"None yet. This happened maybe half an hour ago."

"All right, then. Let me get on it."

"And Joseph?"

He put the pad down and turned his face to her again.

"You look like shit."

Since he had not written a major story in many months, the prospect of appearing on the front page frightened Joseph as much as it exhilarated him. Forty column inches amounted to about sixteen hundred words, not an easy task considering the 7 P.M. deadline, and Joseph wasn't in much of a writing mood. The night before, he'd gotten drunk at a Georgetown pub with his friend Leander McNeese, and he had yet to shake the feeling that his eyeballs weren't set right in their sockets, his tongue a dull, sticky lump at the back of his throat.

So as not to waste any time, Joseph called Louie Vannoy's Restaurant on Connecticut Avenue, identified himself, and asked if anyone there could assist him with the obit.

"I'll leave a message with the wife," a man with a flat, Greek-sounding accent said. "She's at the funeral home picking out big oak casket like he like."

Joseph made a note of this. "Like who likes?" he said.

"Mr. Louie. He always say put him in oak casket. So she go pick one out. You understand?"

After the call Joseph walked over to the newsroom library and stood before the clerks seated at big iron desks. There were six of them, all women, clipping articles from today's paper and filing the stories by byline and subject matter, and none seemed inclined to help Joseph. After a few minutes a reporter with the National section stepped up, and in no time two of the librarians were digging through the stacks, trying to find the material he wanted. Joseph cleared his throat and rapped on a desk, but still no one acknowledged him.

"Louie Vannoy just died," he finally announced. "I was wondering if one of you workaholics might round up his clips."

A woman in front slapped her metal ruler against her desk, producing a deep, hollow bang, then shuffled toward the back. She returned with two bundles of clippings and, ignoring Joseph's outstretched hands, deposited them in an in/out tray next to the Nexis news-service terminal. "Sign the card and have them back by the end of the day," she said.

"You think I don't know the rules around here? What the heck's wrong with you, lady?"

She didn't answer, but then she didn't have to. Joseph Burke was assigned to Death Row, and in a newsroom crowded with more than two hundred people of greater standing than herself, he was one of a few staff members at whom she could vent her displeasure.

Back in Obits, Joseph was reading through the files when the telephone rang. "This is the front desk," a voice said. "A woman down here to see someone about her husband."

"Who is it?"

In the background the guard said, "Who are you?" And Joseph heard the answer: "Laura Vannoy. I've come to talk about Louie."

"I'll be right down," Joseph told the guard.

It was rare for the survivor of a decedent to visit the office, but Joseph preferred a personal interview to one on the phone. Plus, he welcomed a break from the newsroom. The Obit desk, situated next to the ever-hectic copy aide station and the men's and women's toilets, occupied the least desirable bit of real estate on the entire fifth floor. Rather than banish the section to a far, dark corner, Cameron Yates, the paper's executive editor, stuck it a short distance from the elevators, as if to warn anyone entering the *Washington Herald* that this was the fate of those who failed him. Since noon the activity around Joseph had been loud and dizzying—reporters playing microcassette recorders at peak volume, tapping at computer keyboards, shouting into phones; editors swarming about, issuing orders and booting trash cans; mail clerks pushing dilapidated buggies filled with interoffice memos. Probably because he was hung over, the grid of fluorescent lights overhead was an additional torment to Joseph. With the white rectangular tiles of the suspended ceiling they formed a brilliant checkerboard, most oppressive; he didn't dare look up.

Joseph regretted not having dressed better or used a comb this morning. He was wearing a dark winter suit and blue shoes, and his tie was a yellow polyester that reached all the way down to his crotch. In the elevator, alone, he tried to tidy up. He tucked the tie into his pants and attempted to mat down his distressed hair. He checked his breath and found it more sweet than sour—remarkable considering last night.

In the lobby he offered his hand to the widow and introduced himself. "I'm very sorry," he said. "Please accept my condolences and those of this newspaper."

She shrugged and laughed to herself a little sadly. "We'd been separated for eight months. I suppose I should feel guilty for not feeling worse, but I don't. So there."

To this Joseph had no idea how to respond.

"Louie thought he was immortal. He never took his heart pills or exercised. Did you know him, Joseph? Fifty-four years old and completely covered with baby fat. The angina, they're saying, is what got him."

Joseph led her outside, across Fifteenth Street, and into the lobby of the Madison Hotel. She was a handsome woman—a beauty, in fact—and far from the type he ever would have imagined Louie Vannoy married to. They sat at a table in the front lounge and ordered hot tea and toast.

"Is it Laurie or Laura?" he said. "I want to make sure I spell your name right."

"It's Laura. Though I do suspect that some people back home in Mississippi—if you were to ask them—would tell you I'm Laurie Jane, Roy and Tina Cobb's child. They'd also tell you I had no business marrying someone the age and what all of Louie Vannoy, and now, seeing what a mess the man made of my life, I guess I'd have to agree with them."

Joseph wrote her name down in his notebook and, though he knew he would never use it, a brief description of the widow. She had thick brown hair that fell in flips and waves to the middle of her back, lips coated pink, and large gray eyes not unlike those of Joseph's ex-wife. Her figure, he noted, was long, narrow, and dramatically fleshy. With respect to this last observation, Joseph wrote: "Glorious."

"I come from pretty simple stock," she was saying. "All my family's Yugoslavs who came over in boats, landed at Biloxi, and stayed there, over at Point Cadet on the east end of town. Did you by chance notice the accent?"

"I did. Yes."

"I suppose this bores you. I suppose what you really want to know about is Louie, the facts and such."

"All that you can tell me will help."

"Are you married, Joseph?"

He tried not to appear befuddled. "Was" was all he said.

The waiter arrived and poured the tea from a big silver-plated pot. He left a small ceramic dish ringed with lemon slices and another with cleverly decorated sugar cookies. No toast.

"Garçon," she said. "Might you consider bringing me a screwdriver, extra heavy on the juice?" She turned to Joseph. "Anything for you, darling?"

"Excuse me?"

"Would you like a drink?"

"No, thank you."

The waiter left and Laura Vannoy nibbled on one of the cookies. "Father was a card mechanic," she said. "Mother was a cocktail waitress. They're both dead now."

"These are Louie's parents?"

"No, Joseph. Mine. Roy and Tina." She put the cookie back on the plate and brushed some crumbs off her blouse. "Do you know what a card mechanic is, Joseph?"

"It's someone who repairs automobile engines."

"That's what everybody thinks I'm saying. But it's not *car* mechanic, it's *card* mechanic. As in card shark. He worked at one of those titty clubs down on the beach. He suckered people. Tourists, mainly. Poker players. I remember how at home he'd always do magic tricks. There was this one where he'd tell you to pick a card out of the deck and then to put it back in anywhere. He would tap the top and say some magic words and no matter what card you chose, the whole deck would become the card you'd picked. Fifty-two queens of diamonds, for example. It always seemed to me a miracle that he could do this. And I wondered if he could transform me as he did that deck of cards. 'Make me rich,' I'd tell him. 'Make me famous. Make me a beauty queen.' He would tap the top of my head and say his magic words but it never happened. He said I wasn't believing hard enough."

Joseph waited, wondering if there was more. Finally he said, "But what about Louie, Mrs. Vannoy?"

"Louie?"

"I'm writing his obituary. I need to know the kind of person he was. If you could help me build a picture of the man . . ."

She was staring out the window as if at something far away. "I was only seventeen when I met him," she began wearily. "He must've been thirty-seven, thirty-eight. I was lying there on the beach and he walked up and said, 'Young lady, I'd like you to meet someone.' I looked up and there he was, standing in the sun. To see him I had to shield my face with my hand. 'All right,' I told him. 'And who might that be?' He made a big production of bowing and swinging his arms out wide. And then he said, 'Me.' "

Joseph was beginning to feel uncomfortable. None of this was newsworthy, and he wasn't sure how to steer her toward a more specific discussion of Louie Vannoy's past. "He had a flair for theatrics, your husband?"

"He had a flair for a lot of things. In the beginning he was a person of real appetite. And I enjoyed that about him. Myself, I too believed life was to be spontaneous . . . *combustible* is a word I always liked. In the beginning he used to tell me that he wanted to burn fast and gold, like a Roman candle."

"Did your husband have any children or grandchildren? What about brothers and sisters?"

"I used to believe the worst thing a person could do was to deny himself. When you were hungry, you ate; thirsty, you drank."

The waiter approached with her drink.

"What timing," she said, lifting the frothy screwdriver off his tray. She offered Joseph a silent toast, then gulped down half the drink. "It's delicious. Would you like some, darling?"

Joseph dropped his pen. "Did you call me darling?"

"I wondered if you wanted some of this."

"No. I really shouldn't. This is my work."

She was smiling now. "Does this happen to you often? Do you meet women who've just lost their husbands and who immediately start telling you all about themselves?"

"Never."

"I'm only thirty-three years old, Joseph. And you?"

"The same," he answered, turning a page of his notebook. He cleared his throat and sat up tall in his chair. "One thing I couldn't find in the clips was where your husband went to high school and college. Did he win any honors there? Was he in any clubs or on sporting teams or anything like that?"

She turned back to the window. "Louie and I always sort of pawed at marriage, Joseph, we never really grabbed it. He'd taken a room in a hotel downtown and I kept an apartment in the Dresden—me and Amelia, that is. Have I mentioned Amelia?"

"Was she his daughter?" Joseph wrote the name down.

"She's mine, darling, by a previous relationship—previous to Louie, I should say. I was a child, only fifteen, when it happened. A boy from Keesler Air Force Base there in Biloxi took advantage of that wild, unfettered spirit of mine. I don't regret it." She put away the rest of the drink. "Would a woman with a child scare off a person like yourself? Not all men can handle that type of situation."

"Would a woman . . . ?"

"Oh, don't be so timid, darling."

"Timid?"

She stood and patted her mouth with a napkin, leaving a creamy pink smudge nearly identical to the one on the rim of her glass. "I'll excuse myself now, Joseph. Good luck with your story. I'll be looking for it."

"But you haven't told me about your husband." He rose to his feet and followed her to the door. "Mrs. Vannoy?"

"Laura," she said. "And make it all up."

"Make what all up?"

They were standing in the shade of a dark blue canopy that extended as far as the curb. She reached up to pat his cowlick, and to his surprise he didn't stop her.

"Make Louie's life all up," she said. "And this time keep me out of it, will you please?"

She left and Joseph went back into the lounge, paid the bill, and gathered up his pen and notebook. His flesh was pebbled with goosebumps and he felt a hot, electric tingling at the base of his skull. His groin stirred as well.

The waiter walked up. "Everything okay, sir?"

Joseph was studying the mark her mouth had made on the napkin. "Did you hear that woman? She called me darling."

ᔑ *Two* ᖶ

Of the few dozen photographs Joseph owned of his ex-wife, none was less flattering than the one he had chosen to enlarge, frame, and hang on the wall. It showed Naomi in bed, hugging a pillow to her belly, her right breast brown and peaked against the fluffy globe of eiderdown. The viewer saw a splash of hair covering her nose and mouth, eyes colored pink by the camera flash. On Naomi's suggestion, Joseph had taken the picture—along with several others—a week or two after their wedding, and she herself had choreographed the pose.

"We'll keep them around for when we're old," she had told him. "That way when you give me hell for getting fat and flabby I can always show you how pretty I once was."

Tonight, when he returned to his apartment after work, Joseph removed the picture from the wall and held it at arm's length. "I'm still not impressed," he said aloud. "You look cheap, Mimi."

In the bathroom, he propped the picture on the lip of the tub and urinated before it, watching the pink eyes instead of taking aim. "And let's never forget what a shit you are. You're one of the worst shits that ever lived."

Since moving into the apartment more than a year ago, Joseph's bitter monologue had become a near-daily affair. The reason for it, once solidly fixed in his mind, eluded him now, and he recognized his behavior as being juvenile and not a little odd. "You're a fucking nut," he told himself as he put the picture back on the wall. "This isn't you, Burke. This isn't you at all." Then, glaring at the image of Naomi again: "See what you've gone and done to me, Mimi?"

A few minutes later, as Joseph stood before the window in his studio watching the lights of Connecticut Avenue down below, the telephone rang and nearly sent him diving into the glass. Blood roared in his ears, and he had to brace himself against the wall to regain his composure.

"I was hungry," his father said. "I was hungry for some of that fish your mother used to fry."

Joseph, still reeling, sat down and rubbed his eyes. He listened as Woody explained that since the nurse had left several hours ago, there was no one to cook for him.

"You wouldn't come over and surprise your poor old pappy, would you, son?"

"No," Joseph said. "I wouldn't." And then he hung up.

Tired of watching the street, he put on a hat and overcoat, left the apartment, and started in the direction of Adams Morgan, the eccentric little neighborhood where Leander McNeese lived. At the foot of the Duke Ellington Memorial Bridge, he encountered two women standing beneath a streetlight, their starched yellow hair powdered with snow, lips painted the color of aluminum. He figured they were working girls trying to score new territory, and examined their faces more closely to see if he recognized them. The taller one wore a heavy, ribbed ski coat over a metallic blouse; the other a white cardigan sweater, tight-fitting jeans, and buckskin boots. They waved at each passing car and bounced on stiletto heels.

"Are you lost, honey?" the taller one said.

Joseph tipped his hat back and lighted a cigarette. "What are you girls doing out here on Connecticut Avenue? This is supposed to be a nice neighborhood."

"You don't think we're nice?"

"I didn't mean that. I thought you only worked downtown."

"See what you get for thinking?" the short one said. "You want a date or not?"

"I only sleep with people I love," Joseph answered, sounding far more serious than he'd intended.

"Who's talking about *sleep?*"

"You ladies want some coffee? How 'bout a piece of pie?" He was backpedaling now, hands in pockets, showing his best smile. "Café Lautrec sound good?"

"Café this," the short one answered, and grabbed her crotch.

"I'd love to," Joseph said. "But we just met. And I have this rule about not doing that sort of thing with strangers." He lowered the brim of his hat and started forward again.

"Hey," one of them shouted after him. "Take that goddamn shit off your head. Nobody wears a hat anymore."

Joseph nodded and straightened his shoulders. "Precisely," he muttered under his breath.

At Eighteenth Street he stopped at a couple of bookshops and cruised the quiet aisles. In the first he stayed long enough to hear de Falla's *Nights in the Gardens of Spain*, and to melt the numbing cold from his nose and hands. In the second, a rare and used shop, he considered charging a reissue of Liebling's *Sweet Science* to one of his accounts but feared a credit check by the cashier. As much as Joseph, a former sportswriter, admired the book, the lone ten-dollar bill in his pocket was marked for a café au lait and an éclair at Lautrec, and maybe a tip for the energetic little man who sometimes tap-danced on top of the bar.

It was almost one o'clock now and because traffic was scarce snow had begun to accumulate on the street and sidewalks. Stacked on the outdoor tables of the cafés were upturned chairs secured by link chains and combination locks; Japanese lanterns burned brightly in the elm and ginkgo trees. Through the frost on the windows of the Belmont Kitchen Joseph saw a party of diners huddled over deep bowls of soup and platters of charred ribs. Candlelight shone on their faces and fell on the red-checked cloths covering hunks of bread. Joseph paused for a moment and admired the scene, hunger driving a wedge in his throat.

At last he crossed the street, stepping carefully to keep from slipping in the slush. Above the café's striped canopy a mural of Toulouse-Lautrec stood two stories high, a red shawl coiled around the artist's neck and hanging down his chest. Like the wings of a great bird, the brim of his hat spanned three windows east to west.

"You look about as lost as I do," Joseph said, then tossed the smoldering stub of his cigarette into the icy snow.

Inside, a tabby cat lay atop one of the barstools, mewling for attention. Only a few couples sat at the tables, the late hour having sent the dinner crowd home. Joseph removed his hat and coat, stamped his feet on the tiled floor, and followed a waitress to a table near the piano. Here a woman was delivering a proud but undernourished rendition of Cole Porter's "Ev'ry Time We Say Goodbye."

The waitress handed him a menu.

"I won't need it," he said.

Somewhere between the door and the table he had changed his mind: he ordered cheesecake instead of the éclair.

"Aren't you Joseph?" the waitress said. She didn't look up from her notepad. "Leander's friend?"

"That's me."

"He was here earlier. He said if you come in to tell you to give him a call."

Joseph lighted another cigarette and took a long drag. Leander lived above La Fourchette, the restaurant next door. "You didn't notice if he was alone, did you?"

"At first he was and then he met someone."

"Did he say to give him a call before or after he met this someone?" Joseph wrapped his hands around the glass candle dish.

"I honestly don't remember," she said.

"I'll call anyway."

As he deposited a coin into the pay phone at the end of the bar, the cat stretched and yawned, then stepped quickly across the stools to meet him. "Come here, little kitty," he said, rubbing its neck. "Come see Uncle Joseph."

Leander answered quickly.

"I catch you in the middle of something?" Joseph said.

"More like the end."

"A lady here said to call you."

"You're at Lautrec?"

"Waiting for cheesecake." Joseph heard a woman speak Leander's name, followed by inane murmuring.

"Guess what?"

"Don't make me."

"My goddamn rubber just broke."

The woman laughed and so did Leander.

"I'll let you go," Joseph said.

Joseph had first met Naomi here at Lautrec. That was five years ago, the same spring Woody had told him he was working too hard and needed to relax, to find someone and fall in love. She was sitting at a table in the back with friends from work, and for the better part of an hour she did nothing more than look at him, her head tilted, her mouth fixed in a lascivious grin. The others drank wine, ate buttered chips of French bread, smoked cigarettes, and exchanged office gossip. "You want to look at someone else?" Joseph finally said, tired of her staring. It was the first thing he had ever said to her. Someone introduced them. She was new to the Lifestyle staff, a movie critic. You spelled her last name R-i-c-h-a-r-d, and pronounced it the French way: *Ree-shar!* "Will you let me have your babies?" she asked him later, as they were riding the elevator up to her apartment in the Kennedy-Warren. "And I want them all to be boys and look just like you. Wouldn't that be fun, Joseph?" The next week he was on assignment in Reno, Nevada, covering a fight for Sports. It was Mancini-Bramble, their first. The desert air made him light-headed, giddy; Joseph had never felt better. He called her three times a day and in detail she described what she would most like to do to him. She wanted to go down on him in full view of the mirror on her closet door. And she wanted to screw him on the floor of the newsroom after the final edition had been shipped and everything was dark save the spinach-green faces of the video display terminals. As she spoke he masturbated. "Come for me. Do it, Joseph ..." A few days later she mailed him a small jewelry box filled with pubic hair. She had shaved herself with a double-edged razor, she explained in the letter that accompanied the Federal Express package; no one but they would ever know. "Who are you, where did you come from?" she wrote. "And what is it you plan to do with me now that I'm yours?" On the flight home he had sat rubbing a swatch of her mousy brown hair between his fingers.

"Not plain coffee," he told the waitress.

"Au lait?"

"Please," he said.

"It's warm milk is the difference, that's all."

"I know. But it does something to the coffee."

"It makes it au lait," she said.

"It makes it soft, and that makes it less bitter."

"Whatever you say, Joseph."

Now Naomi lived in New York. After leaving Joseph, she'd dated around before marrying someone named Hans Verdooth, the publisher of a movie magazine. They owned sailboats and sports cars, a house in the Hamptons. For her thirtieth birthday he'd given her a film collection that included several hundred titles. She was expecting a child in June, their first. "You and me," she'd once said to Joseph on the phone, "it really wasn't so nice as it seemed at the time, was it?" She was working on a screenplay and considering augmentation after the baby came. "Augmentation to what?" he had wondered aloud. That was their problem, she'd told him. During the eighteen months they'd been married he'd never looked at her long enough to see that one of her breasts was smaller than the other. And he was supposed to be such a goddamned great reporter!

"When it's slow like tonight I make more mistakes than when we're busy." The waitress placed the cup on the table.

"Don't worry about it," he said.

With a finger he stirred the drippings in the saucer. He leaned over the cup and inhaled the rich aroma. Along the length of the street the bars and restaurants were beginning to close. Through the front window he saw neons fade to black, awnings being folded into neat accordions. In the trees the lanterns blinked to darkness.

He motioned to the waitress. "Would you by chance have today's paper anywhere handy?"

"Today's or yesterday's?" she said.

He glared at her and smiled. "Tomorrow's, actually."

"Hang on a minute." She walked behind the bar and stooped to check the shelves. "What section?" she called to Joseph. "Any one in particular?"

"The whole thing if you have it."

She gave him the paper and disappeared behind the swinging kitchen doors. It was the Sunday "Gold Star," the *Herald*'s first of six editions and the only one to hit the streets by midnight. Joseph studied the A section, the lead story stretching above the fold. LOUIE VANNOY, RESTAURATEUR, DIES AT 54. He read closely, checking for any changes his editors might have made. When space was tight, the copy desk often lopped whole paragraphs off the end of a piece, discarding a kicker the reporter had spent long hours working to perfect. "Vannoy," to his delight, appeared almost exactly as he'd written it. Editors at the *Herald* seldom were that kind, least of all to him.

At the pay phone, he deposited a quarter and dialed information. "Louie Vannoy," he said, and spelled the name.

The cat nuzzled his arm. "Are you a lonesome kitty?" he said. "Come to Uncle Joseph."

The phone rang six times before she picked up.

"Mrs. Vannoy . . . ?"

"Yes, this is Laura. Who's calling?"

The waitress was refilling his cup. Over the line Joseph could hear music, loud and jazzy, and people talking. There was laughter. "It's the fellow who interviewed you about your husband. Joseph Burke?"

"Yes, darling. Of course."

"Forgive me for calling so late."

"No, we were just waking here."

"I beg your pardon?"

"I had the restaurant cater it. We're all eating and drinking and trying to console one another, but Monday we bury him. Are you coming, Joseph?"

"To the funeral, you mean?"

"Yes. Of course. What else?"

"I have to work Monday."

"I'm sure everyone'll cry then and feel just awful about tonight."

"Look," Joseph said, "I just got a copy of the paper and was wondering if you had a chance to see my story."

"I don't think you're telling the truth, darling. That's not what you were wondering at all." Someone was calling her name and for a moment it seemed to Joseph that she was no longer there. At last she said, "Let's promise always to be honest with each other. If we're going to do this, darling, let's do it right."

"Do what right?" Joseph said. And now he was certain that she was gone, that someone had pulled her away from the phone.

"Hello," a man said.

"Yes, I was speaking with Mrs. Vannoy."

"Isn't it horrible?" The man sounded drunk.

"Yes, well . . ."

"I was there, you know. I saw him fall."

The receiver changed hands again. "I'm back, darling. Hello? Are you still holding?"

"Would you like to have a drink sometime?"

"But I'm having one now."

"With me, I should say."

"Yes," she answered, shouting above the racket. "Do you know Cities on Eighteenth Street? Look for me. I'll be the grieving widow in black."

"When? What time?"

"What about next Saturday? Is ten o'clock okay?"

"Fine."

"And darling?"

"I'm still here."

"Run a comb through your hair, will you? And leave that silly little notebook of yours at home."

6 In the morning Joseph took a cab to his father's house at Logan Circle in downtown D.C. The grand but poorly kept Victorian, a rental, was at the heart of what real estate agents liked to call a changing neighborhood. Of late only a handful of stout-hearted urban pioneers had dared move here with their futons, espresso machines, and compact disc collections, while peddlers in both the flesh and drug trades, periodically forced by police from the Fourteenth Street corridor, were using it on weekends as an open-air market. Woody and Cleo, both retired schoolteachers, had moved into the neighborhood about ten years ago, when three-story houses such as this one were renting for the same price as a one-bedroom apartment in Georgetown, and before anyone had ever heard of crack cocaine. They probably would have left the area long ago if not for Woody's stubbornness: he was unwilling to admit he'd been had by a fast-talking realtor, to whom he had referred ever since as "that frigging jerk Marco."

After dodging a couple of wine-ruined beggars on the sidewalk, Joseph let himself in through the front door, into a den crowded with cheap furniture, burning torchères, and his father's hospital bed. Woody, generally propped against a huddle of pillows, TV remote control in hand, was nowhere to be seen.

Joseph was alarmed by his father's absence, but then it occurred to him that perhaps Woody had risen to his feet and walked away from this place, finally overcoming the guilt that had put him on his back for the last nine weeks.

Ever since that morning in October when he'd driven into a culvert off the George Washington Parkway, "fatally injuring" Cleo, as a colleague of Joseph's at the *Herald* had reported, Woody had been pretending to be paralyzed from the waist down, and doing so with an actor's cunning and guile. Except for a curious latticework of cuts across his neck and chest, which had since healed, he had survived the wreck unscathed.

Joseph checked the dining and sewing rooms and found his father lying in a puddle of grease and flour in the kitchen, his wheelchair tipped over on its side. Both refrigerator doors were open, cooling the wide, shining room.

"I wanted to fry some fish," Woody explained. "All night long, I could think of nothing else."

"Where's Marissa?"

"It's Sunday, remember? She's off. I'm afraid you're stuck with me all day today, son."

Joseph stepped over his father and checked the freezer compartment of the refrigerator. "There's no fish," he said. "I could cook up some toast and scrambled eggs."

"You can cook them but I won't necessarily eat them. Like I said, I've got my heart stuck on fish."

Joseph set the wheelchair upright and lifted Woody into it. He handed him a dish towel. "Why do you keep torturing yourself, Father? When is it going to stop?"

"It's funny," Woody said, staring down at his legs, "but I'll get an itch and when I scratch I don't feel anything. You'd think my legs had turned to air or rubber or something."

Joseph removed a skillet from the cabinet and put it on top of the stove. "Since you're all out of fish, I'll just make a normal breakfast, okay? Whaddaya say we be normal today, Father? It would make me happy."

"I bet I never do it again," Woody said. "I bet I never make love to a woman again as long as I live."

Joseph had heard it before and knew better than to respond. He poured some oil into the skillet and turned up the fire beneath it, then cracked a half dozen eggs into a bowl and stabbed the yolks with a barbecue fork. "Is it milk you add or water to make them fluffy?"

"The insurance might pay for a nurse and a bed and a wheelchair, but there're a few things they can't give me back."

Now that they had turned a glowing, uniform yellow, Joseph poured the eggs into the sputtering oil and stirred them around with a wooden spoon. "Do you think my fire's too hot?"

"They can't give me back my wife, and they can't give me back what most made me a man."

Joseph ignored him, and Woody pounded his chest and roared his once-famous Tarzan imitation.

"Haven't heard you do that since before Mother died," Joseph said. "You must be feeling better." He put four slices of bread into the toaster. "I'll grant you that all this ain't fried fish, but it should hold you over until lunch. Then we can get a pizza or something."

"I don't want it," Woody said. "I just want my legs back."

"Your legs are fine, and you know it. All the doctors say you've got the kick of a long-distance runner."

"Then how come I can't walk?"

Joseph spooned the steaming eggs onto a couple of plates and added the toast and dollops of fruit jelly. "But you can walk, Father. You can run, you can do anything I can do." He paused before adding, "The doctors say you can even make love if you feel so inclined."

"Did I cry out when they stuck needles in my toe? Shit no, I didn't cry out. I didn't say a word."

"You felt it, though. I was watching when Marissa poked you the other day. You were lying there pretending to sleep and you pulled your foot up—you pulled it right up!"

Woody snorted and went back to cleaning himself off. "It's like dead meat down there, son."

"Then why is it that whenever you sleep, you move your legs under the sheets? Explain how that seems to happen every night."

Woody considered this. "You cut off a frog's legs and they jump all over the place, right?"

"I've heard of frog's legs doing that, of course I have. Just never people's." Joseph went to the refrigerator and poured a couple of glasses of milk. "Did I tell you I started work on Nixon's obit?" he said.

"Nixon? When did Nixon die?" Woody rolled over and positioned himself at the head of the table.

"He didn't, Father, but he's getting up there, you know. So I wrote him a letter. It's gentler than a phone call, and I thought I could better finesse the situation and keep from coming off like a kook. And if I was lucky enough to get him on the phone, what would I say? 'Mr. President, this is Joseph Burke. I'm writing your obituary and I was hoping you might share with me the details of your calamitous life.' If he agrees to be interviewed it'll be on the condition that what he says will appear only after he's dead."

"You should show more respect, son." Woody was studying the toast now. "At least wait till the man's sick."

"With a lot of famous people we write them beforehand. Somebody had written Greta Garbo nearly twenty years before she died. And when it happened all we had to do was call it up from the computer files and update the first few paragraphs. That's why I've started on Tricky Dick—just in case it comes all of a sudden, we won't be unprepared."

Woody took a sip of the milk and spilled some, leaving a trail along the outside of the glass. "What do you mean by 'it'?"

"Death, Father. Death is it."

"Did you write your mother's beforehand?"

"You know I didn't. Alfred Giddings wrote it the day it happened. I would've been glad to but I ended up spending the whole day in the hospital with you."

"I've suddenly lost my appetite," Woody said.

"If you don't eat I'll take it out to the people in the park. That's what Mother would've done."

Woody rolled over to the trash can and deposited his plate in it. "You can go ahead and take yours, son. I just finished mine."

Later that morning, after cleaning the dishes and scrubbing the kitchen floor, Joseph piloted his father into the den, hoisted him out of the chair, and put him in bed. Once a powerfully built, athletic man who spent his afternoons either fishing the Anacostia and Potomac rivers or jogging the cinder paths at the Mall, Woody of late had become as thin and underweight as Joseph, whose own physique had suffered in the time since Naomi left. Although Joseph chose to believe he'd inherited his mother's dark good looks, in fact he more resembled his father, a blue-eyed blond with long, thin hands and feet and an annoyingly prominent Adam's apple. Today Woody was wearing a faded flannel shirt and a pair of jeans worn at the knees and seat—his uniform of choice since graduating from paper-thin hospital gowns.

"Will you do me a favor?" Woody said.

"Name it."

"Go out on the veranda and see what's going on across the street. Suddenly I feel like I need to know."

Joseph did as he was told, standing at the threshold with the door slightly ajar.

"What's there?" Woody said.

"Nothing. Not a thing."

"I don't believe it."

"Maybe it's still too early yet. And it's Sunday. What could possibly go on out there on a Sunday?"

"You'd be surprised," Woody said. "Aren't there any bums? Look over at the benches that circle the statue."

"I see one or two, that's it."

"Doesn't count, son. They're always there."

"That's what I mean," Joseph replied, then stepped back into the house and closed the door behind him.

"Those people out there," Woody said, suddenly sounding as if he were about to cry, "without you I'd be like them, son. I'd be all alone, I'd have nothing."

Joseph accepted the rare praise without comment. He sat on the couch and flicked on the television set with Woody's remote, and he made certain not to look over at his father, lest he embarrass them both. "The Redskins game is getting ready to start," he said. "You feel up to watching it?"

Woody didn't answer. He'd covered his face with a pillow to keep Joseph from seeing him weep.

6 At work on Monday no one was dying. The telephones rang but all of the calls were for Book World and Washington Home, departments in far-flung areas of the cavernous fifth-floor newsroom. Convinced that other sections were experiencing the same problem, Alfred Giddings dialed the switchboard and complained about the screwups, and one of the operators, after explaining that a new employee was being trained, told him to go to hell, and added, "I know all about you, fatso. You've got no authority here."

Rattled by the exchange, Alfred quickly ingested two bagels and as many candy bars. Even Joseph, hard at work researching "Nixon," paused briefly to watch his friend attempt to either revive or destroy himself by gluttony.

"Want anything else?" Joseph said, when Alfred appeared to be finished. "I could run down to the cafeteria and get you some cheeseburgers and fries."

"No. I'm feeling much better now, thank you."

In the past, this time of year had always been the most frantic at the Obit desk. Deep winter was when people died—you could set your watch by it, Alfred liked to say. Drunks lost control of their cars, geriatrics forgot to wake up in the morning, the depressed found relief in sleeping pills and handguns. Not everyone suffered, though. Funeral homes flourished, cemeteries advertised reduced rates on burial sites, limousine fleets and vehicular escort services ran from dawn till dusk. Obituary writers wrote and wrote.

"I don't trust a winter morning without corpses," Alfred said, "especially one that's beginning to freeze my lips shut. It's not a good sign, Mr. Burke."

"I like it," Joseph said, leaning back in his chair. "I like it just fine."

"Not me. It bodes trouble ahead. Something awful's coming, something really bad."

"Give it a rest, pal. Nothing could possibly be more awful than what the two of us have already been through."

Like Joseph, Nate Thompson and Tinker Schwartz seemed to be enjoying the lull. Nate indulged his obsession with crossword puzzles, while Tinker, the victim of a personality disorder that manifested itself in periodic cleaning jags, tidied up around her desk. She was scrubbing the face of her computer monitor with a sponge and ice-blue cleansing fluid.

"The quiet makes me think they've found a cure for all the ills of the earth," Alfred told Joseph. "They come up with cures for all the ills of the earth and we're flat out of work."

"Did you hear what I said, Alfred? Relax, goddammit."

"I love death, I love what it does."

"Alfred—"

"Oh, Joseph, what in heaven's sake is going on out there?" And suddenly he stood and raised a pair of fists to the ceiling.

For more than a decade Alfred had been slot editor on the Obit desk, time spent checking for grammatical errors and misspelled words and writing headlines that refused to offend: ORVILLE RAY, 81, DIES; WAS ACTIVE IN CIVIC GROUPS. Alfred was once a celebrated arts-and-entertainment critic, a Pulitzer Prize winner favored by most *Herald* insiders to succeed Cameron Yates as the paper's executive editor. His slide to obscurity was unrivaled until Joseph Burke, formerly of Sports, Lifestyle, and the Magazine, joined him on Death Row. Tired of writing criticism, Alfred had matriculated to the National desk, where after contributing only half a dozen stories he was sued twice for libel. Charged, in both instances, with fabricating quotes, Alfred had found his confidence so undermined that he no longer trusted his reporting skills and instincts. Writing on any subject, no matter how trivial, he fully expected incendiary calls from libel lawyers—accusations that his facts were all wrong, his tone condescending, his point of view prejudiced. Although both suits against him were eventually dismissed by the courts, Alfred had stumbled into a depression. He had blocked so severely that every attempt at writing produced only gibberish: he could build neither complete nor coherent sentences. "All these words are interesting," Yates had told him once, handling some copy, "but thrown together like this ... I mean, *slapped* together, what the god-damn hell are you trying to say here, Giddings?" To further aggravate his situation, Alfred had developed a nervous stutter, begun to eat compulsively, and nearly pulled out all his hair. Months with a therapist produced no improvement, nor did a salary hike that made him one of the highest-paid reporters on staff. Finally Yates, acting on Alfred's request for reassignment, introduced him to a section where no subjects sued because all of them were dead. Now, some twelve years later, most of the staff continued to steer clear of him, fearing that his bad luck would rub off or that some higher-up with a pipeline to Yates would see them gabbing together and squeal. Even Nate and Tinker, themselves longtime failures without hope of ever being assigned to another section, did their best to ignore him.

Joseph had always regarded Alfred as one might a three-legged animal, part of the carnival of misfits the paper either attracted or engendered. But then when he himself joined the list of reporters who'd screwed up so badly that Mr. Big had no choice but to bury them, Joseph learned that with three legs or two, the leash for an obit writer was short and murderous.

Since losing his Magazine slot, Joseph had scribbled story ideas on slips of paper and stored them in his desk drawer, hoping that one day he might be allowed to report them, though aware that such a turn was highly unlikely. Yates had never pardoned anyone on Death Row, and although he had not ruled out the possibility, his thinking was well known among staff members: Let the hack grow frustrated, let him bitch and moan all he wants, let him threaten to walk out, and then help him to the door when he finally does—anything to avoid another brawl with the Reporters Guild, the union whose primary purpose seemed to be to stick it to management while ostensibly protecting the rights of has-beens like Alfred and Joseph.

At noon today, when Joseph broke for lunch, Alfred appeared to be feeling better. The switchboard, at last, had straightened out its problems, and all was fairly quiet in Obits. Kicked back in his chair, Alfred read from a batch of files on Ronald Reagan's years in the White House, his small black eyes darting from line to line. "For all that was written about him," he said, "and all the pictures taken, when I close my eyes I still can't see him."

"He looked like his son. Remember the ballerina?"

"Okay. I see him now." Alfred studied the yellowed clipping a moment longer, then said, "There was something I was hoping we might talk about, Joseph." He looked over the divider to make sure Nate and Tinker weren't listening. "It's concerning Jennifer Eugene. I was wondering if perhaps I should ask her out . . . what you thought about it."

"You mean a date?"

"If she said no, Joseph, I'm afraid it'd kill me."

"She's a fine girl, Jennifer, but I really don't think she's one to die for, Alfred."

"You don't think she's worth the trouble?"

"It isn't that. *She* doesn't think she's worth the trouble."

Alfred stood and leaned in closer to Joseph. A look of fear and dread had come over his face. "If you were a woman, Joseph, would you consider going out with someone like me? And be honest."

"Sure I would," Joseph replied, hoping to sound cheerful and not at all surprised by the question. "I'd buy you chocolates and roses. I'd take you dancing. And if you let me, I'd probably even sleep with you."

"You'd sleep with me?"

Joseph put his hands on Alfred's shoulders, his mouth close to his ear. "I'd probably do it to you, Alfred."

"You'd . . . ?"

"I would. I swear it."

A few minutes later Joseph left the office and walked along Fifteenth Street to Rhode Island Avenue, the cold, gusting wind at his back, and half jogged to Logan Circle. He hoped to get his blood pumping, to drive the numbness from his hands. People watched from apartment windows: this well-dressed man in saddle oxfords running spastically, as if new to the experience. He wished he were an athlete, at least then he could show top form. He began to remind himself how old he was—thirty-three, as of a few weeks ago. But instead he said, "My lord, Joseph, you still haven't learned how to run."

Woody was sitting in his wheelchair on the veranda, wrapped in a Scotch-plaid wool blanket, his Baltimore Orioles cap pushed back on his head. A stack of newspapers and fishing magazines lay at his side. He was studying the dictionary, plastic-frame reading glasses poised on the tip of his nose.

"What's it today?" Joseph said.

"Misogyny," Woody answered, his eyes glued to the page. "The hatred of women."

Marissa, the nurse, was watching from the window, waiting to learn the day's word. A native of El Salvador, she had recently immigrated to the States with her husband and two young children and settled in the jungle of low-rent housing complexes in southern Maryland. After the accident, Joseph had tried to get round-the-clock nursing, but the insurance company, acting on the doctors' conclusion that Woody had suffered far less trauma to his body than to his head, had agreed to pay for only twelve hours of daily care. Marissa's duties were little more demanding than those of a baby-sitter, and perhaps to convince herself that she was earning her daily wages, she also did housework and cooked Woody's meals. Through the glass, now, Marissa looked dark and smoky, a smear of black cherry at her lips. Woody had taken it upon himself to help her learn the English language. "A word a day keeps the bozos away," he had told her once. "Bozos," she'd repeated, thoroughly confused. Sometimes he dropped a blind finger onto the page of his dictionary, but more often he focused on a particular letter and sought a peculiar entry. If the word he chose was familiar, he tried again. Marissa knew few of them.

"A misogynist," Woody was saying now. "I must be one of those.

At last a word that was invented for the Wood man." He traced a finger over the page. "At least since your mother died I must be. Because frankly I can't stand a one."

It was January—nights of snow and rain, days spent indoors. Joseph watched a couple of bums sitting at the foot of the monument across the street. They were new to the neighborhood, dressed in rags and stocking caps. At night they would cross the street and flop in an abandoned apartment building, sleep under sheets of plastic or newspaper, and wake to the prattle of rats as big as dogs.

"Hey, Father," Joseph said. "How're you feeling today?" He sat on the steps and unbuttoned his coat.

Woody closed the book and dropped it to the floor. "The Mason-Dixon line," he said, "begins here, my friend." And he pointed to the spot.

Joseph propped his elbows on his knees and rubbed his face. His stubble, peppered gray along the jawline, had the reverse effect of making him look younger than his years. He could see his breath in the air. He reached back and patted Woody's blanket. "How're those legs? You still paralyzed down there?"

"The central nerves in my spinal cord have been damaged, perhaps severed. I will never walk again."

Joseph lighted a cigarette. "Nobody's dying today," he said. "But watch, tomorrow we'll be swamped. I prefer it when they spread their departure times out evenly."

"Like at the airport?" Woody said.

"Exactly." Joseph took in a lungful of smoke and exhaled slowly. "If somebody important doesn't die by five o'clock, Alfred Giddings is going to lose his mind."

Woody sat shaking his head. He smelled of analgesic balm, Marissa's morning massage. Suddenly he raised his hand. "I volunteer, son. Take me."

"Nope. You'd make too ordinary an obit. Giddings wants someone famous. He's counting on a politician." Joseph leaned back against the banister and lifted the cigarette to his mouth. "And besides, if you volunteered who would I have left to pick on? And what would Marissa do?"

"You're absolutely right," Woody said. "Because I think she's fallen in love with me, son. In fact, I know she has."

"Marissa's married, Father."

"That never stopped anybody. Look at your wife."

Joseph flicked his cigarette out onto the lawn. "You want a sandwich? I'm going inside now."

"A what?"

"Lunch, Father. Can I make you something?"

As Joseph headed for the door, Woody clutched the arms of his chair and began to shout in a voice that hardly sounded human. From the slate rooftops of the houses next door, pigeons broke into flight, moving toward the trees in the park. The outburst lasted no more than thirty seconds, time enough to wind him and drain the blood from his face. Across the street the men leaning against the statue didn't stir, they didn't appear to have heard.

Marissa stepped through the door and Joseph put his hand out, stopping her. "Everything's okay," he said. "Let him get rid of it." But she brushed by him and knelt beside the wheelchair.

"I'm going to make a sandwich. Are you hungry, Marissa?"

She mumbled a reply in Spanish, then laced her fingers through Woody's. "Woodrow," she said, enunciating carefully, "you are a sick man, my friend."

He reached down, picked up the dictionary, and started flipping through it. "Motherfucking sonofabitch," he said, pointing at a page.

"Very, very sick," she added.

Later that evening, after Marissa left, Woody soiled the bed as Joseph stood staring out the front bay window, watching for activity in the park. The sour odor made Joseph cough, and he could almost taste it on his tongue. "You find this funny?" he said.

A wet mound ran like a cloud down the sheet, and when Joseph turned Woody over on his side, the sight made him gag. He spat into his handkerchief and coughed from deep within his chest.

"I didn't feel it coming," Woody said. "I would've warned you otherwise. I promise."

Joseph, working quickly, cleaned the mess with a rag and sponge. Woody's buttocks were still firm and muscular and showed no sign of atrophy. Joseph wrung the rag out in soapy water, then dried his father off with a bath towel and sprinkled baby powder between his legs.

"How'd it go down there?" Woody said. "Was it bad? It sure smelled awful bad."

"I'd rather not talk about it, if you don't mind."

Joseph placed the dirty sheets in a laundry bag and put some fresh ones on the bed. Woody was naked now, waiting to be fitted into clean clothes. He held his arms out in front of him, hands limp at the wrists.

"You would rather degrade yourself than get up and walk to the bathroom," Joseph said. "I find that disgusting, Father."

"What kind of a world is it when a man can't take an accidental shit without getting reprimanded by his son?"

"You can walk, Father. I know you can."

"Your mother, now, she was the lucky one."

"Okay, here we go again. Mother was the lucky one."

"She felt nothing. All I am is feel."

Early the next morning Marissa grabbed Joseph by the arm and walked with him back to the kitchen. "Please," she said in a strained whisper, "if ever these happens again let me know. I write on Woodrow chart." She was leaning against the table, still clutching Joseph's arm. "Then the insurance see how sick he is."

"Maybe we should just be honest with each other, Marissa. You're a fine person, very pleasant, but I don't know if your being here is what Father needs. He isn't getting better."

As she let go of his arm, a stricken look filled her face, and Joseph thought she might cry. "He always use pan before," she said. "I promise, Joseph. Always."

"Yes, but you haven't helped. If anything you've complicated matters. He's beginning to depend upon you for his every happiness. And he attempts to punish me when you're not around."

"I am a good nurse, I tell you I am."

Joseph put his hands on her shoulders and tried to calm her down. He'd been out of line, he knew that. And maybe Woody had been right. What sort of world was it when a man couldn't take an accidental shit in front of his son?

"Marissa. Forgive me."

"Yes, Joseph."

"I'm troubled is all. I'm hardly myself."

"You are hardly . . . ?" Clearly she didn't understand him.

"Hardly myself," he answered. "I've changed, I'm different, I'm not who I used to be."

She shrugged and looked away and he knew she had no idea what he was talking about.

◨ *Three* ◧

It was a little after eleven when Joseph arrived at Cities on Eighteenth Street, more than an hour late for the drink he'd arranged with Laura Vannoy. Woody had kept him occupied with insurance papers and medical bills until eight-fifteen, and by the time he was able to take a cab back to his apartment and change clothes, he was already behind schedule.

To reach the Adams Morgan restaurant, he had run the mile or so with one hand clutching his necktie and the other the change in his pants pocket. To his relief, Laura had chosen to wait at the bar. He spotted her as he entered: she was reading a folded section of the newspaper and eating from a bowl of goldfish crackers.

"Sorry I'm late," he said, claiming the stool beside her, "but I had to go over to my father's and help him out with something. It took longer than I thought."

She drummed her teeth with her fingernails. "I'll forgive you, Joseph, if you promise to answer a question."

"I promise."

"Why don't they always say who wrote what when you get to the obituaries? They do on all the other pages."

The bartender stepped up and Joseph ordered Sambuca over ice. "Is the kitchen still open?" he said.

The man shook his head. "Sorry."

"Hey"—she was punching Joseph's forearm with a finger—"I asked you a question, and you promised to answer it."

"You mean why don't I get a byline?"

She nodded and put her glass to her lips.

"I never asked because I suppose I never cared."

"Then when I read the paper in the morning how do I know what's yours?"

"Just read them all and chances are at least one of them'll be mine." The waiter returned with his drink. "You like licorice?" Joseph said. "That's what Sambuca tastes like."

"Can I ask you something else?" she said.

"Anything."

"Do you like your work?"

"Love it." He leaned forward against the bar.

"Do you really?"

"No," he said.

"Well, everybody said your story on Louie was very nicely done. Even Amelia liked it."

"And what did you think?"

"I'm afraid I didn't get past the first paragraph. All that celebrity restaurateur, businessman-of-the-year stuff. It had nothing to do with the writing, darling. It was Louie."

Joseph picked up their drinks and led her to a table near the door. It was Saturday night, the crowd was young and noisy.

"The other day at the Madison, could you tell I was tipsy?"

"I suspected, yes."

"They'd given me whiskey before breaking the news. I suppose they thought it would anesthetize the pain. But like I told them later, you should've gotten me drunk a few years ago when he first started his foolishness. That's when it hurt." She laughed quietly to herself and traced a finger around the rim of her glass. "I was thinking how fast and loose you must've thought I was, blowing into your office like that—and Louie hardly even dead yet. And then on the phone with all that music and everybody cutting up. The truth is, Joseph, I'm not fast at all. And all that noise and whatnot was just friends of Louie's commiserating. I suppose people in Washington wake the same way they do back home in Mississippi, only here they do it without the blood and grit under their nails."

"You forgot your paper on the bar."

"What?"

"Your paper. It's over on the bar. Want me to get it?"

"Oh, no. That's okay. I just brought it for you, really. Because I had those questions." She was staring into his eyes, or through them, at something just on the other side. "There's a story, Joseph, that I think you might want to write."

He nodded, waiting for more.

"Between you and me, or at least for now between you and me, we're considering selling our share of the restaurant, me and Amelia are. Louie had a couple of partners, these are buddies of his, and they've offered to buy us out. The place is worth pretty much, but it's been in a little trouble lately—running in the red, as they say. Or is it the black? I get those two mixed up."

"Red is losing money."

"In the red, then. And today they tell me the lease renewal's coming up. I really don't know if I want to worry about all that, now that it's me and Amelia with our butts on the line. Forgive me for sounding irreverent, but I've never been very fond of the place."

"If you sold out, what would you do?"

"Well, with Amelia's share I'd send her to college and set up a trust. And with mine I'd use what all I learned about the business and open a café somewhere—maybe here in Adams Morgan or over in Georgetown if I could afford it. This would be my own place, and nothing like Louie's. All that ever mattered to him was who sat at what table, but at mine you could sit wherever you liked. I'd have real flowers on all the tables and creaky old ceiling fans and the food'd be all the things I grew up eating. None of this nouvelle cuisine routine. This is my dream, you might say. I'd work in the kitchen, because I like to cook. I'd even wait tables just to make sure everyone was happy."

A young woman wearing an ankle-length apron approached the table. "The bartender wanted me to tell you that he was wrong about the kitchen. We're still serving."

"Nothing, thank you," Joseph said.

"What about an appetizer—how about tapas?"

"No," Joseph said. "Thanks, though."

After the waitress left, Laura said, "What on earth is a tapa? Is that what she called it?"

"It's an appetizer. You don't get much."

"Makes me feel so old. Amelia always says I'm like that person who slept all those years and woke up and found the world had changed."

"You mean the woman . . . Sleeping Beauty, don't you?"

"No, silly, not her." She slapped his arm. "I mean the old guy with the beard. I can see him but can't remember his name."

"Give it a minute. It'll come to you."

She settled back in her chair. "Can I ask you another question? You don't have to answer if you don't want to."

He didn't say anything.

"Why is it you write about dead people?"

With the tip of his finger Joseph wiped the lipstick stain off her glass. He could hear the music more clearly now—something Spanish, coming from speakers in the ceiling. "Do you want the real reason or the one I usually tell people?"

"The real. And don't even think about lying to me."

He could feel his heart beating in his chest. "Back when I was on the Magazine, I had an affair with a source, a woman who was married to someone I was writing a story about."

"Is that so out of the ordinary?"

"It only happens every day. But not with the wife of Royston Peden."

"You mean Peden from New York? The senator?"

"Formerly betrothed to Mary," he replied. "The blonde."

She leaned forward, inches from Joseph.

"The worst part was when somebody tipped off a gossip columnist about it. It wasn't clear to me at the time, but now I'm almost certain it was the distinguished senator himself who put the story out."

"Pretty rotten, that guy."

"Apparently he'd been screwing around for years and they were getting ready to go through a nasty divorce. He thought this would help him out. And guess what?"

"Not me."

"It did."

She took a drink of his Sambuca. "Tastes like medicine, darling. Like something for diarrhea." She wiped her mouth with the back of her hand. "Any time you're ready to continue."

"At first some of the editors and reporters at work joked about it. They punched me on the arm and asked how it was. Then Cameron Yates—he's the editor of the paper . . . Yates calls me into his office and sits there staring at me with his hands folded on top of his head."

"Sickening, isn't it? I remember he came to the restaurant a few times and tried that. But Louie'd slap his elbows and make him stop."

"As it turns out he's an old family friend of the Pedens. And apparently he'd spent the morning on the phone with Royston. The lawyer for the *Herald* was also in the office with us, and he did most of the talking. He said my involvement with the woman was unethical, a breach—I'd compromised the paper's integrity and violated the trust it had worked to build with the community. Yates didn't move. Even now I can see the sweat stains under his arms." Joseph paused to regain his breath. "Still listening?" he said.

"Yep."

"Finally this lawyer—I'm in Yates's office, remember . . ." Joseph grabbed a handful of crackers and tossed them into his mouth. "Finally he gives me a letter of resignation and tells me to sign it. It's a sentence is all, saying I hereby surrendered my position as a staff writer for the *Washington Herald*. In my hand, though, it felt like my wrist was going to break, it was that heavy. When I tore it up and dumped it in the trash Yates dropped his hands and pointed two fingers at me. He told me that as of that moment I was reassigned to the Metro copy desk. In other words, I was being booted from one of the best writing slots on the paper to pushing copy about crap like dog shows at the D.C. Armory."

"They were trying to break you," Laura said.

"Yes. But after a few weeks they seemed to figure I didn't mind the demotion, so they moved me over to Obits. We call it Death Row because everybody who works there—as far as Mr. Big and the *Herald* are concerned—we're dead."

Laura reached over and lifted his chin, forcing him to look at her. "Did you love her?" she said.

"Did I love Mary Peden?"

She nodded.

"Of course I didn't love her." He was whispering. "And to be honest with you, Laura, I don't know if I found her particularly attractive."

"Then was it part of the arrangement?"

"If you mean was it necessary for me to go to bed with her in order to get the information I wanted, no, it wasn't. At least I never got the impression that it was. I guess I can't really say what got into me. My wife had left . . ." He inhaled deeply. "I did it because I could, I guess."

The table nearest theirs grew louder. "I'll have to include that one on my list of all-time sad stories," Laura said. "Right up there with mine and Louie's."

She reached out to take his hand but Joseph pulled away.

"I'd better be going back to my father's now."

"Going back where?"

"My father's. I guess I didn't tell you about him."

"Another sad story, is it?"

"He's paralyzed from the waist down as the result of an automobile accident. Or he's pretending to be."

"How . . . what do you mean? He's faking like he can't walk?"

"I should go now."

"Fine, Joseph. If that's what you want."

He left some money on the table and she followed him outside. He waved a cab over.

"What a pair you and your father must make," she said. "Him pretending to be a cripple and you there pretending to help him. Him with his lower lip hanging and you with yours. I bet you two have a good old time." She laughed. "Tell me something, Joseph. Why is it I can't feel sorry for you?"

"Did I ask you to feel sorry for me?"

"Not in so many words you didn't."

The wind was cold against Joseph's face, but if anything he felt a dark kind of heat. "I really should be going," he said.

"Then hop to it. Nobody's stopping you." She got into the car and pulled the door shut. "Hey, I just remembered something." She rolled down the window and thrust her head out. "It was Rip van Winkle. The old fellow who fell asleep."

"Call about the restaurant," he said, "and I'll forward you to Mr. Yates. I'm sure he'll assign somebody who'll do a good job with it."

"You too busy with all your dead people to write it yourself?"

"It's my job, Laura."

"Now that . . . that's absolutely the most pitiful thing I've ever heard." And she waved as the driver slowly pulled away.

When Naomi first started seeing the boy from work, Joseph tried to determine what he'd done to drive her there. He knew that he was a moody person, a little intense perhaps, but so was she. He wondered if his failure was as a lover: Had he not been attentive enough? Was his equipment not up to par? He asked her to list her reasons for leaving, and she began by saying that she was no longer in love with him, it was as simple as that. A few months into the marriage she had become bored by him, she said, bored by his impassivity and lack of humor. Before, she had regarded his stoicism as a heroic trait, but now she saw it as a flaw. He was too serious. He was beautiful, yes, but being beautiful didn't mean much when you forgot he was even there.

Where had the passion gone, she wanted to know. Work was what he cared about most. He was less interested in the details of her daily existence than in those of the people he wrote about. It was far easier, for example, for him to ask the subject of an interview about the regularity of his or her bowel movements than to ask the same of his own wife. What she needed, she said, was to be frightened by love, not appeased by it. She needed this above all else, and she would never have it with him.

"I suppose she stopped loving me because I wasn't curious about how many times a day she visited the toilet," Joseph had told Jennifer Eugene one afternoon in the *Herald* cafeteria. And Jennifer had nodded wearily and said, "You insensitive brute. You selfish snob. I'm surprised it took her this long to find a copy aide to fuck."

Now, on the sidewalk in front of Cities, Joseph reminded himself that he was better off without her. He remembered how she never liked to cook or eat at home and how she often complained that the smell of food in the apartment nauseated her, clung to her clothes, stank up the upholstered furniture. He remembered how slow she was to dress in the morning and how at night she often read with the bedside lamp on while he tried to sleep. The hours she spent talking with friends on the telephone, how critical she could be of even great films, the hard Midwestern way she pronounced certain words—these things he remembered. And yet other moments came to him. He recalled, for example, how she looked in a summer dress with the sun in her hair and her lips parted to reveal the whitest, loveliest teeth on earth. He recalled how he slept with his left arm thrown around her, his hand cupping her breast, and how in the morning they woke that way. And of all things he recalled how wet she got. They used to make jokes about it. "I'd like to crawl in there and live for a while," he had said once. He might've drowned but that was the point. To love and then to die.

Finally he crossed Eighteenth Street and entered Lautrec. A waitress asked him to wait a second, she was cleaning a table just then.
But another ten minutes went by before she led him to a place near
the window. "Sorry," she said. "It's a real zoo here tonight. I almost
forgot you were standing there."

The crowd was young and handsome, a twin to the one at Cities,
only more lively and animated. A jazz band was stationed in the middle
of the room, three gray-haired black men playing bebop with their
eyes closed. No one seemed to be listening to the music, not even the
musicians.

On Joseph's orders, the waitress—Leander's friend, the one who
had served him last week—brought over two shots of tequila, a shaker
of salt, and some lemon slices.

"Are we getting drunk tonight?" she said.

"Don't know about you," he replied, toasting the girl, "but I sure
the hell am."

She was small and dark, no more than twenty. He thought her
eyebrows needed plucking, and that the pockmarks on her forehead
were unfortunate; otherwise she was lovely.

"I wish I didn't have to work," she said, looking back in frustration
at the smoky room.

"Me too," he said.

"Do you mean you wish I wasn't working or do you mean you're
working now and wish you didn't have to?"

"Both."

In one hand she was holding a round serving tray, in the other a
pen and notepad. "I got some great news yesterday. And tonight I feel
like celebrating, like doing something."

"Here's to news," Joseph said and offered another toast.

"I'm negative, can you believe?"

He put some salt on his finger and licked it.

"I was part of the cattle call at the Red Cross down the street.
Seemed like almost everybody else had track marks on their arms or
was full of sores. I tried to hold my breath so as not to inhale the air."
With the point of her pen she beat the cork lining of the tray. "It was

kind of sad, though, seeing some of those people come out of the back rooms crying like it was a funeral."

"Congratulations," he told her. "Now go get me another shot. And don't bring any lemons this time."

When she returned she leaned over and whispered in his ear, "Can you tell I'm not wearing any panties?"

"No."

"Good," she said. "Because for a minute there I was starting to worry."

Her name was Charlotte; he heard the woman working behind the bar say it. He sat and drank tequila and after the restaurant closed they walked to Calvert Street and crossed the Duke Ellington Bridge. His head hurt from all the smoke and noise. The lamps rising high above the suicide rails shone yellow and clear, dropping bouquets of incandescent fire on the pavement. He couldn't hear the creek down below for the wind and traffic, the late-night roar of the city. He looked for the women he'd seen here the other night.

"Have you been tested?" she said.

"Not for what you're talking about."

"We can't do it, then. From here on out I'm not taking any chances, not even with a sweetie like you."

He didn't respond and she said, "I like you a lot, Joseph. So please don't take this personal."

He'd been wrong about her age: she was twenty-two, a dance student at George Washington University. She lived with two other girls in the Alwyn, an apartment building in the neighborhood. Leander, she said, was always trying to get her to pose nude for him. He was the only artist she'd ever known, and she hoped the last. She thought he would be a lot better-looking if only he'd shave his beard and cut his hair. One night she was having dinner at La Fourchette, and she could hear him in his apartment up above, hammering and sawing wood.

"Did you know he made furniture?"

"I used to have one of his menageries," Joseph said. "It was really quite elegant, and probably worth a lot."

"What happened to it?"

He thought better of telling her the truth, that Naomi had taken it when she'd left him. "Somebody stole it," he said, staring at the ground.

They walked on for another hundred feet.

"You think Leander's been tested yet?" she said.

"I have no idea."

"No telling what that boy's caught over the years."

The Calvert House elevators weren't operating so they took the stairs. At each elbow in the well they stopped and kissed. Her hair smelled of sweat and fried food, but inexplicably he found it intoxicating. He put his hands on her breasts and discovered she wasn't wearing a brassiere.

She pushed him away and pulled up her shirt. "Do you think my nipples are too small? My dad had little ones." She circled a pale aureole with the tip of her thumb. "I got these from him, I guess."

The air in the apartment was stale, the bed unmade, the floor covered with dust and the sun-faded pages of old newspapers. Cheap ceramic-base lamps, a couple without shades, stood on cardboard boxes and pressboard tables. Joseph had come to regard the studio as the place to which he retreated each night; he didn't really live here.

"What a dump," she said.

"Thank you, thank you very much."

He had leased the apartment after Naomi left, and although she had never set foot in it, he could feel her presence in every inch of living space. She was a ghost and he was her prey. At night she hovered over his bed, crept into his head, and monopolized his dreams. In the bathroom she lived in the soap and shaving cream and shampoo. He could taste her in his morning coffee.

"This is depressing," Charlotte said.

He pointed to the stereo. "Why don't you put on some music. Play anything you like."

She chose Bill Evans, his concert at the Montreux Jazz Festival. Someone was introducing the band members to an excited crowd.

In the kitchen Joseph poured wine into two ceramic cups, both showing coffee stains on their bottoms. "I need to go to Conran's," he said through the open door. "Buy some glasses."

"Spend your money on a maid first."

"Yes," he said, laughing.

"Or a shrink. I don't know how you can stand it here, Joseph. If I didn't know better I'd think you were trying to punish yourself."

He walked with the cups back into the room. She was studying the framed photograph of Naomi on the wall, her mouth open, her eyes wide in disbelief. "Who's the girl, Joseph?"

"Some people call her Mimi—short for Naomi, Naomi Richard. We were married once, a long time ago."

"Did Leander take this?"

"Nope. I did."

"Did she know you were taking it?"

"She was the one who wanted it."

He removed the picture from the wall and wiped the dust off the glass with his shirtsleeve. "What do you think?" he said, handing it to her. "Isn't she something?"

"You can't really see her face to tell. But I'll give her this much, Joseph: her tits're nice."

He shuffled over to the bed and sat watching as she put the photograph back. She spent more time than necessary making sure it was hanging straight.

"I might let a man take my picture," she said, "but I'd never want anyone but the two of us to see it."

"That was my deal with Naomi," he said. "But after she left I figured all promises were off."

She sat next to him on the bed, took the cup from his hand, and put it on the floor. "Let's talk about now, Joseph—about you and me alone in this room together."

"Fine."

"Can we cut our own deal? Can we do everything but the real thing? Can we just kind of play with each other and try to get off?" She put her mouth against his neck and traced her tongue up to his ear. "Sometimes I wish I was like Rema and Cardin at work. Believe me, they never had to go to the Red Cross and wait in line to find out whether they were going to die."

"And why's that?"

"Because they're lesbians, you big dumb ox." Charlotte lifted her face and stared into his eyes. "You should be grateful she left, Joseph. Just look at her."

She started kissing his neck and ear. The high, hard cheekbones, the fat lips, the bowl of thick, dark hair—these were like Naomi's. He started to speak, then decided not to.

"Even if you do get excited," she said, "we can't do it—not until they come up with a vaccine."

The window blinds were open and he could see the lights of the avenue. Red and green canopies in front of the bars and cafés flapped in the breeze.

"If I take my clothes off, Joseph, will you promise to tell me a story?"

"I don't know any stories," he said. He reached for the cup of wine and drank it all in a gulp.

"Then make one up," she said. "It has to be sexy, though."

She removed her shirt and let it drop to the floor, then she unzipped her skirt and drew her legs out of it. Her smell was like a weight on his chest. From between her legs a downy stream of hair climbed to her navel.

"Once upon a time," he said, "there was a man and a woman and they were very much in love."

"Call them something," she said. "If they don't have names I can't see them. I need to see them."

"Joseph and Mimi," he said without hesitation.

She seemed to consider this. "Go ahead."

"They were the kind of people who as a pair are doomed from the start, they really have no chance in the world."

"Why?"

"Just listen," he said, and closed his eyes. He rested a hand on her leg. "They meet after work at crowded restaurants and bars. They've been married for a few months, but she still likes to talk about other men, those she's been with. And she counts them like coins. One, two, three, four—she's always counting. Five, six, seven, eight—"

"I know some girls like that."

"Her pockets, her purse, are full of them. One night Joseph waits at Paolo's thinking she won't come. She's half an hour late and he worries that something has kept her at the office. It's cool out, all the leaves have turned, and the streets are busy. When she arrives she sits next to him as if he were a stranger. This is how they've planned it. They don't speak. 'Go take your hose off,' he finally tells her. Nearly half an hour goes by. When she gets up and walks to the toilet, he orders something—to the bartender, at least, he wants to look normal."

"Yes," Charlotte muttered.

"Joseph can see her walking between the tables, her head down, trying not to draw attention to herself. In her hand she's holding what looks like a small black rag. Her stockings knotted up in a ball."

Charlotte suddenly grabbed his hand and pressed it against her. He felt his fingers stiffen, her dense, wet web of hair. "Joseph," she said, "can we just forget what I said earlier about the vaccine. I think this is ridiculous. I mean, if I have to die over something, why not this? Why not happy?"

"Listen to the story. Mimi has removed her stockings."

She lay back down. "It isn't fair," she said. "You're not getting off. If I get off, you should too."

"I'll get off. Just let me finish first."

She exhaled heavily and started rubbing herself again.

"So she reaches the bar and sits back down on the stool and he puts his hand on her thigh. 'You are so fucking beautiful,' he tells her. 'Now go take off your panties. I want to see what the rest of you looks like.' "

"You stole that from me," Charlotte said, sitting up again. "Because I wasn't wearing any at work tonight."

"This happened," Joseph insisted. "All of it. I swear."

"No, it didn't." She picked her clothes off the floor and put them back on. "You're a thief, Joseph. You plagiarized."

She went into the bathroom and washed her hands. He stood in the open doorway and watched her in the mirrored door of the medicine cabinet. "I must be a fool," she said. "I must. I lie there playing with myself while you fantasize about your ex-wife." The fluorescent lights made the pockmarks on her forehead appear as deep as craters, they illuminated the face of a woman who now looked less like his wife than he'd thought.

"I can't compete with a picture on a wall," she said. "You're just not ready yet."

He was quiet, examining her face in the glass. "You're right," he said. "I apologize."

"Will you call me when you're ready?"

"I'll call you," he said.

After she left, slamming the door behind her, Joseph sat at the window drinking what remained of the wine and watching the street. The phone rang, startling him, but he didn't get up to answer it. He compiled a mental list of who might be calling at this hour. Charlotte would probably never speak to him again. Naomi and Hans were off vacationing in Europe, and she usually called him at the office, where, surrounded by people, he couldn't raise his voice and tell her to fuck off. Laura was home by now, and why would she want to hear another of his depressing little stories? Leander was in New York, there to shoot a fight at Madison Square Garden. *Alfred* ... Alfred wouldn't call. He, too, was asleep, dreaming of dead presidents and movie stars.

Finally Joseph said, "Father, is that you?" But by then the ringing had stopped.

Several hours later, at around nine o'clock, Joseph was descending Connecticut Avenue, striding against the wind that tunneled between the rows of apartment buildings. By the time he reached Dupont Circle he was numb and exhausted, ready for more coffee, anything to clear the ache in his head. His lips were chapped, his hair mussed, and he was still wearing his suit from the night before. Sunlight reflected off the morning snow and drove needles into his chest, leaving him slightly breathless. He was scheduled to work today but he decided to stay away from the office. In his mood he half believed he'd never go there again. Tomorrow he would just up and quit, as they say. Up and walk. Fuck you, Mr. Yates, he would say. And fuck you and fuck you and fuck you, he would tell anyone else who got in his way.

He considered stopping for a coffee and a blueberry muffin at Suzanne's Bakery but decided instead to spend the money on a cab. He leaned against a light standard and watched the customers inside the little shop. They were staring into the smoky red light that bathed the trays of pastries.

At Logan Circle his father was sitting up in bed, pillows fitted behind his neck. The sun pouring in from the window made his face look small and pale.

"Good morning," Joseph said, plopping down on the couch.

"Your skin looks like raw biscuit dough," Woody said.

Marissa, dressed all in white save a porcupine of multicolored bows in her hair, entered with a tray loaded with cups of coffee and choco-late-iced doughnuts. "Not to be mean," she said, winking at Joseph, "but you no feel so well?"

"Must've picked up a flu bug or something," he replied.

"Something," she said.

Woody was pointing at the dictionary on the coffee table. "Marissa, honey, why don't you take my Bible there and go in the kitchen for a minute. Look up some words for Uncle Woody."

"Begs pardon," she said.

"Joseph and I have something very important to talk about. It's of a private nature."

"Okay," she said. "I acquiesce." She picked up the Webster's and left the room.

"Joseph," Woody said directly, his reading spectacles balanced on his nose, "how are we doing on the money end? And be honest. It's time we formulated a plan."

Joseph closed his eyes and bit into a doughnut. "I was up late," he said, "all night, to be honest. I don't know if I'm prepared to discuss any of this now, Father." He tapped his temples. "My brain isn't working as it should."

"But this is important to me. I need to get it off my chest. And so do you. Let's discuss it like the adults that we are."

Joseph dipped the doughnut into the coffee and took another bite. "We've run into some problems," he said.

"Okay."

"We've got two households when we can hardly afford one. Rent at this address alone is nearly triple what you and Mother paid when you first moved here."

"Is it really?"

"It's fifteen hundred dollars."

"Fifteen? I had no idea, son. Your mother always took care of those things."

"It's the same as what you receive each month in retirement pay."

"Yes," Woody said, "we do have a problem, then, don't we?"

"I was thinking about breaking the lease on my apartment. I have only a little left in savings, hardly enough to make a difference. If I moved in here it would cut both our expenses in half."

"You don't want to spend the rest of your life minding after an old cripple. Even if it did save us from financial ruin, I wouldn't do that to you, son."

This, Joseph knew, was entirely untrue, but he lacked the spirit to argue. He poured his father another cup of coffee and said, "We have Marissa for only thirty more days. The insurance won't provide for anything more. If you plan on keeping her around—well, as things now stand, Father, I just don't see how we can afford to."

"Marissa stays," Woody insisted. "Hear me, Joseph?"

"I know you like her, Father, I do too. But practically all she does is watch you read the dictionary and repeat new words. 'Acquiesce,' Father? Did you hear her say that? Once the insurance company drops the case, it'll be impossible for me to justify the expense of keeping her around."

"It would break her apart to leave us," he said. "Tear her to pieces. Here it is Sunday, her day off, and she came over to make sure I'm fed and happy. She's in love with me, Joseph, deeply in love."

"I remember hearing you say that."

"Then what do you propose? How do we resolve this?"

"If you don't start walking again," Joseph said, pausing to let the words register, "then the only solution, as I said earlier, is to live together, to share a place."

Tired of discussing problems that were beginning to seem insurmountable, Joseph sat on the couch and opened the newspaper to Classifieds. He was curious to see the listings for rentals in Northwest D.C., still the most desirable of the city's four quadrants. When Woody and Cleo had first moved to Logan Circle, they had announced that it was a temporary assignment until they could save enough money to buy a house in Friendship Heights or the Palisades. This had proved to be mere talk, however. All of their retirement pay had gone to the necessities of living, which, in their case, included regular fishing trips for Woody and painting supplies for Cleo. Although they had made periodic drives through the neighborhoods they coveted, the truth was they had never opened a savings account. Joseph put the paper down. Rentals in Logan Circle were still a bargain compared to most other Northwest neighborhoods, and the prospect of buying a place anywhere in the metropolitan area was nil.

"Here's something," he announced. "A row house on California Street, just around the corner from where Mac lives. Two bedrooms. Utilities included. Twelve hundred dollars, Father. Look at this, it even has a view."

Woody shook his head in disgust. "I thought you wanted to move in here. What's this about a view?"

"It's a place we could rent."

Marissa had returned to the den and was sitting on a stool next to the bed. "Let's find a word for Joseph," Woody told her, taking up the dictionary again. "Check the *A*'s here. See if asshole's listed."

Joseph didn't respond, and Woody said, "Apologize. Apologize to me and Marissa here."

"Sorry," Joseph said. "You're right. I guess I'm so tired I'm no longer thinking straight."

Later that morning, after napping on the couch, Joseph called the Obituary desk and told Alfred he wasn't feeling well and wouldn't be reporting to work today. "The hours'll have to go against any remaining vacation time," he said. "Because when Cleo died I used up all my sick leave." Joseph could hear clattering keyboards in the background. "You have any problem with that, Mr. Giddings?"

"None. None at all. But I don't think I'll report your absence today, Joseph. You need your vacation days as we all do, and besides, I truly doubt anyone here will miss you." He laughed and added, "I know when I'm sick and take time off, no one misses me."

There was a moment when neither spoke, then Alfred said, "If you're sick, does that mean we're off?"

"I beg your pardon."

"We were supposed to go to I Matti, Joseph—with Mac, remember? That party he's been talking about for days now?"

"No," Joseph said. "I mean sure, Alfred. I'll make it."

Joseph could see his father through the bay window. He was sitting in the wheelchair, watching the park through a pair of binoculars, his black cap pushed back on his head.

"Marissa," Joseph said, pointing outside. "Get him back in here. Someone'll shoot him, for crying out loud."

"Did someone get shot? Somebody dead at Logan Circle?" Alfred was saying on the other end.

Joseph pulled the front door open and, covering the mouthpiece, mumbled, "For heaven's sake, Father."

"We're to meet him at nine in the dining room on the second floor," Alfred said now. "Mac says to wear a suit and clean underwear and to bring lots of raincoats."

"Raincoats . . . ?"

"Condoms, I think some people call them."

Joseph said goodbye and put the phone down.

"My lord," Woody muttered, as Marissa rolled him into the den. "A monster. Look at the big, ugly monster." He had lifted the binoculars to his face and turned them on Joseph.

"It's not polite spying on people, Father. And it's dangerous. They may think you're a cop or something." He pointed to the bay window again. "Think of this, Father. Think how easy it would be for one of those people to kill an old man in a wheelchair. They kill kids for their sneakers every day."

Woody pushed himself over to the window and turned the binoculars on the park. "If it's shoes they want, then they can have mine. I'm paralyzed, in case you've forgotten. Sneakers on Woodrow Burke are about as useless as tits on a bull."

"God, Father, what's happened to you?"

Marissa crouched in front of his chair, put her hands on his knee, and began to stroke it. But Woody, laughing as if at his own joke, continued his watch.

At I Matti that night, Alfred Giddings and Leander McNeese joined Joseph at the end of an elaborately dressed banquet table, near the platters of white pizza, fried mozzarella, and pickled olives. A young woman named Mara was throwing the party in honor of her own twenty-fifth birthday, and doing so in a style generally reserved for golden wedding anniversaries. At the moment she was standing on a chair in the center of the room, performing for an audience that included, among other celebrities, a young liberal congressman and his glamorous wife, a seven-foot-tall professional basketball star who twice now had leapt upward and scraped his nails on the ceiling, delighting everyone, and an elderly stage actor and his teenage girlfriend.

In one hand Mara held a chalice brimming with champagne, in the other a near-empty bottle. Applause and laughter shook the yellow lights.

"Somebody said she was Persian," Alfred mused.

"The last Persian I knew," Joseph said, "was a cat of my poor mother's that shed hair all over the place. Since when did Persians become people again?"

"Since they left Iran with all the money," Leander replied. "They're the ones who can never go home again."

The basketball star placed a paper crown on Mara's head. Everyone cheered.

Alfred said, "She may be a little thick upstairs, but Mara does have amazing breasts. You have to give her that much."

"It's the way they're all hiked up," Joseph said, surprised by his friend's enthusiasm. "It's a trick."

"Yeah," Leander added. "You'd know about that sort of thing if ever you got serious about something besides food."

"What are you saying, Mac?"

Leander took his time cleaning the lens of his camera with the tail of his sock tie. "I'm saying you're a pig, Alfred. I'm saying it seems every time you see something with a little garlic on it you've got to go and put it in your mouth. I'm saying that one of these days you're going to bust wide open and it'll be too bad for whoever's standing nearby."

"Why's that?"

"Because they're going to get splattered with all kinds of guts and shit."

Alfred turned to Joseph and smiled. "The man's a real wordsmith. Did you hear what he just said?"

At around midnight Mara began to open her gifts, and Joseph and Alfred each took a bottle of champagne from the bar and sat by themselves near a closet door. Leander was standing on a stepladder in the middle of the room, shooting pictures and announcing "Marvelous, darlings" to convince the partygoers that they'd been duly immortalized.

"That's a word I've always loved," Alfred said.

"Which one?"

"Marvelous. I love the sound of it, and I love what it means. Are you ready for a history lesson, Joseph?"

"Just a small one," he answered.

"Back in the twenties all these American flunkies were moving to Paris, running from their memories of the war or just running. They probably never would've admitted it but what they were really trying to do was to find themselves—to discover the meaning of life, of all the silly damned things—and so they drank and danced and fornicated and ate and slept and fornicated some more. The French artists of the time had a word for all this. They said their young friends had come looking for The Marvelous. And they'd never been more right."

"Where'd you learn that, Alfred?"

"I was once an art critic, remember?"

"You won the Pulitzer Prize for it."

"You're goddamn right I did."

In addition to the champagne, Alfred was holding several pieces of bread topped with stewed white beans and onion chips, and he bit into one now. "If I could be anyone in the world," he said, "I think it would be Mac. He's gregarious and not unattractive, he knows a lot of interesting people. At work there isn't a more respected photographer. He travels the world over taking pictures. He speaks French, Spanish, and Japanese fluently, and, when he's sober, a fair approximation of English. All those things, and yet he doesn't give a good goddamn. He's our best going example of one pursuing The Marvelous, Joseph. And that's why I wish I were he—to be at once so extraordinarily ignorant and blessed, to have everything and need nothing."

"You're doing fine, Alfred."

"No, I'm not," he said. "I'm not doing fine at all. I'm ridiculously overweight—you might even say I'm obese—and I've pulled all but a few strands of my hair out." He touched a barren spot on his scalp, over an ear. "I wear glasses so thick light can hardly penetrate them. And I've never in all my life had anything more than a professional relationship with a woman. Did I ever tell you I was a virgin, Joseph?"

Joseph took another swallow from the bottle. He was starting to feel drunk. "Even for a virgin you're doing fine, pal, you're doing great. So try to relax, okay?"

"Don't tell me to relax, Joseph. Because I *can't* relax. I don't even masturbate anymore. Last time I gave it the old college try I thought it would kill me. I had this picture of me and Jennifer and some others—it was a snapshot from a Christmas party a few years ago—and I put it on top of the bed, and I was standing there doing it, you know, looking at Jennifer in this red and green holiday dress and her hair slightly beehived and her mouth a-red with lipstick. And next thing I know I'm lying on the floor, staring into this horrible, spinning whiteness." He drank some of the champagne. "I'd fainted, I guess."

"Sounds more like you came real hard."

"No, I'd fainted. If I'd come I'd have seen some stuff on the floor. But I looked everywhere and there was nothing. Also, if I'd come I think it would've been my last act."

"Not a bad way to go, Alfred."

"No sir," he said. "I suppose not."

Leander had gotten down from the stepladder, but he was no less occupied with his camera. He was pretending to shoot a woman who had joined the party only a few minutes ago. She was tall and thin, no beauty, a blonde with dark roots. She raised a hand to everyone except Mara, who rated a blown kiss and a curtsy. The padded shoulders of her red herringbone jacket reached as high as her earrings, and she was in the habit of touching them every few minutes, to confirm their exact placement. Before Leander's camera she was entirely comfortable; she might have been gazing into the face of a trusted friend. Leander threw bolts of light at her, shouts of approval.

The basketball player, standing all alone, watched with a sad mix of lust and longing.

"You recognize her, of course," Alfred said.

"No. Should I?"

Alfred clutched Joseph's wrist and pulled him close. "You mean you don't ... You've got to be kidding, Joseph. Tell me you're kidding."

Joseph didn't answer.

"Andrea Troy," he said, squeezing harder. "You mean you don't remember the gossip columnist who broke the story about you and Mary Peden?"

"Shut up about it, all right?"

Alfred pinched his nose as he laughed, trying to keep from making too much noise. His face turned pink at the center, purple along the edges. "Don't dare pretend you don't know who Andrea Troy is. Because I know better."

" 'Estranged wife of the distinguished senator from New York,' " Joseph said. "That's what she called her."

"I read it. You don't have to remind me."

Joseph unloaded more of the champagne. "And do you remember what she called me, Alfred?"

" 'Recent former husband of sexy *Herald* film commentator Naomi Richard.' Who could forget such sterling prose?"

Joseph was staring, and when the woman did the same he was certain she recognized him. His name was right there, on the tip of her tongue; she was anxious to say it. But in her eyes he saw something else, something familiar. She liked him. She was whispering now, to Leander, and pointing a finger. Joseph smiled, then nervously lifted the bottle to his lips. She wanted to meet him. Joseph threw his head back and drank.

"Fucking McNeese," Alfred said, hurrying to his feet. "He's bringing her over here."

Joseph stood and wiped his mouth with the back of his hand. "Andy Troy, meet a couple of friends of mine—Joseph Burke and Alfred Giddings."

Alfred went first. "Pleasure," he said, bowing at the waist. "I know your work."

"You've got an admirer," Leander said. "How 'bout that?"

"I said I *know* it," Alfred replied. "Hold your horses there, Mac."

Joseph pressed his mouth against her cool, powdery flesh. "An honor," he muttered. "Really, Miss Troy."

She smelled brand-new, he thought, like something wrapped in plastic, a toy.

"Burke, is it?"

"Yes," he said, then spelled it.

Her eyes were green. No, they were brown.

"Are those tinted contacts?" Joseph said, drawing close to get a better look. "Of course they are."

"No," she said.

"Yes, they are. My ex-wife had a pair. They made her eyes look green when all along they were brown."

The woman's cheeks filled with blood, her neck splotched purple. She put her hand on Joseph's chest and lightly nudged him away. "If you don't mind . . ."

"Don't worry about it," Joseph said, taking a step back. "If my eyes were the color of shit I might want to change them, too. How 'bout you, Alfred?"

Alfred spit a mouthful of champagne onto the carpet. Andrea Troy pivoted sharply and strode away.

"Goddammit, Joseph," Leander said, punching the floor with the heel of his shoe. "What the hell was that all about?"

"Nothing you would understand," he replied, and rocked back until his shoulders touched the closet door. "An old debt to settle. Something I've eagerly anticipated for more than a year now."

"Believe me, Mac," Alfred said. "She had it coming, she really did."

"The poor girl was just looking to score," Leander said, and glanced back to where she was standing. "I'm just over there taking her picture and she opens her mouth and says, 'My libido's always out of control this time of the month, Mac.' Just like she was commenting on the weather. 'It is, is it?' I say. And she says, 'I'm ovulating. It always gets that way when I'm ovulating.' Then she turns and sees you, and you smile and seem interested. So I say, 'My friend Joseph. Maybe he's ovulating, too.' She asks if her earrings are balanced and her shoulders are okay. Before I can say anything she's walking over here."

"I take it back," Alfred said. "If I could be anybody, it'd be you, Joseph."

"Maybe you should apologize," Leander said. "Not wanting to

fuck her is one thing, Joseph, but it don't seem right you had to go shit all over her eyes."

Joseph drank more champagne and ate yet another finger sandwich, then walked across the room and tapped Andrea Troy's padded shoulder.

"I'm thirty-three years old," he said, trying to sound as contrite as possible, "and I still haven't learned how to behave around a beautiful woman." Imitating Alfred, he bowed at the waist. "Please forgive me, Miss Troy."

She looked at the basketball player, then back at Joseph. "Apology accepted," she said. "But I'll have you know these contacts are just for fun—like costume jewelry, Joseph, they're not to be taken seriously."

"Of course," he said, bowing again.

"Then let's not talk about it . . . never again."

Joseph shook Sammy Polaski's hand. "I'm a fan," he lied. "From all the way back to the days when you first started playing at the Capital Centre. My father, when my mother was still alive, had season tickets. He loved the Bullets."

"You look familiar," Polaski said, stooping even lower. Joseph could smell garlic on his breath, and saw crumbs of parsley pebbling his lower lip. "I'm sure I know you. I saw you when you walked in and a light went off."

"How flattering," Joseph said.

"Come on," the man said. He thrust his hands into his pockets and rattled his keys and change. "Help me out here."

Joseph took a drink, a martini, from a waiter with a tray poised on the tips of his fingers.

"What kind of work do you do?" Andrea Troy said. "Maybe that'll help solve the mystery."

"I'm a schoolteacher in Montgomery County. Ninth grade."

"Lot of glands exploding around that age," Andrea Troy remarked with an idle yawn. Had she been any less impressed, Joseph thought, she might have fallen asleep while standing. "I don't envy you, Mr. Burke." She studied her nails. "Kids these days are different from when we were growing up."

Someone was calling Sammy Polaski's name: it was Mara, perched at the top of Leander's stepladder. She wanted him to jump once again and touch the ceiling. "Watch, everybody. Sammy's going to dunk the invisible basketball."

Leander, suddenly called to arms, sprawled out in the middle of the floor, his handy Leica aimed upward as Sammy Polaski, a ten-year veteran of the National Basketball Association, the idol of millions, leapt high into the air and touched the ceiling. Leander's strobe sneezed and flashed. People clapped, whistled, and raised their glasses. "Like a gazelle," Mara shouted to the crowd. "What an athlete!"

Sammy Polaski's return to earth had sent several unattended champagne glasses crashing to the floor, and Mara now added her own, tossing it against the wall.

"Do something else," she cried. "Come on, Sam!"

As most of the crowd watched in silence, Joseph turned to Andrea Troy and said, "My first job out of college was writing sports stories for a newspaper. That's how Sammy knows me—from about ten years ago, when everyone thought he was going to be a star."

She checked her shoulder pads. "But you said you taught school in Montgomery County—ninth grade."

"I was lying," he replied, sipping the martini. "I didn't want him to remember me. I once wrote some unflattering things about him. He's big and good-looking—just check out the size of those hands—but he didn't turn out to be as good as we'd all hoped. These days he's a marginal player, rarely off the bench. I'm afraid he's got white man's disease."

She looked Polaski over, her eyebrows furrowed, trying to detect symptoms of his problem.

"He's too slow," Joseph explained. "He can't run and he can't jump. He's spastic as they come."

"So this is what you wrote? About our Sammy here."

Joseph nodded. "Long, long time ago." He waved his free hand, as if to show the distance. "It was another life. That's why he doesn't remember."

Hoping to please those who wanted more, Sammy Polaski balled up some of the wrapping paper that had been torn from Mara's gifts, spun high and hard off his left foot, and hooked the colorful arrangement into a punch bowl. When he came down, more glasses crashed and everyone cheered, including Joseph, who felt an odd twinge of pity for the man.

"Do you still write for the Sports page?" Andrea Troy said, above the rowdy din. She was leaning into his ear. "And what paper is it? Something in the suburbs?"

"The *Washington Herald*," Joseph said. "But I write about the sadly departed now. I cover them like the goddamn dew."

She started to ask what he meant, but he placed a finger on her lips and spoke up quickly, "I'm an obituary writer, Andy—have been for the last year or so."

6 Most of the guests had already left when Joseph found Alfred still sitting alone near the closet. "Andrea Troy and I are leaving together," he said, squatting to look Alfred square in the face. "We're going for a nightcap at her place." When Alfred didn't reply, Joseph whispered, "Time for the big payback, my friend. Wait till I get her alone."

Alfred was holding a plate stacked high with Italian sausages, peppers, and meatballs. A fresh bottle of champagne was wedged between his legs. White sauce had stained the front of his shirt, and the corners of his mouth were colored red, brown, and green. Although it was cool in the restaurant, sweat dampened his scalp and dripped down the corrugated slats of his forehead.

"Hey, pal, you gonna make it?"

"A little indigestion," Alfred mumbled, chewing his lips. "Burns, though." The wine had deadened his eyes to such a degree that he could hardly keep them open. "Food never killed nobody," he added with a pained chuckle. " 'Cept maybe me, you know."

Joseph slapped his shoulder, hoping to knock some life into him. "Want a cab? Let's get moving."

"I'm going, I'm going." Alfred raised his chin, revealing sweat and stains and rolls of bleached flesh. "Where's Mac?"

"He left with Mara and the basketball star. Said they were going to Georgetown for some eggs and fries."

"Mac's taking me home," he grumbled, and then shouted: "*Mac! Time to go, Mac!*"

Joseph helped Alfred to his feet and walked him outside, Andrea Troy following close behind.

"Did you bring a coat?" Joseph said. "Alfred, is your coat inside?"

"No coat. Fat people don't need coats."

A cab pulled up. "Tell him where you live," Joseph said to Alfred. He handed the driver some money. "Take him home, please. I can't remember the address."

"I love you," Alfred mumbled.

"I love you, too, pal," Joseph said, and shut the door.

Andrea waved another cab over. "So, Mr. Burke," she said, sitting first and then swinging her legs into the car, "do you always go home with strange women?"

"Not always," he said. "But lately, yes."

She leaned forward in the seat and looked over the driver's shoulder, checking herself in the rearview mirror. "The Chastleton, please. On Sixteenth Street." Something about her gloss wasn't right; she picked at the corners of her mouth with a fingernail. "Basil makes my lips swell. I knew I shouldn't've eaten tonight."

At a street corner near Meridian Hill Park he watched the lights of a traffic signal play across her face. Her skin was beginning to go, her hands to wrinkle. The airbrushed photograph they ran each month with her column was at least ten years old.

"Do you lie compulsively?" she said, still looking at herself in the mirror. "Or were you just playing around in there tonight, with Sammy and all?"

"I lie only to people who might know me."

"I don't recognize you, do I, Joseph?" Her voice rose in volume yet managed to retain some of its inherent huskiness. She finally turned to look at him, and he saw that, yes, her lips did look a little swollen at the edges. "I mean, Joseph, you would tell me if I did. Wouldn't you?"

"A person walks into a room," he said, "and a light goes on. That's how memory works, remember? Ask your friend Sammy."

"I guess you're right. But I meet so many people, I can't tell you. All these names and faces dancing around inside my head. When you write 'Don't Ask Andy . . .' for the city's most popular magazine, you never know whose life you'll brush against next. I've been doing this for fifteen years, and I'm still often amazed. The *people!*"

The car bounced along. The driver was listening to Erroll Garner on the radio, his famous concert by the sea. On the back of the headrest there was a NO SMOKING sign, but as if to show who was boss, the man smoked anyway, a cheap cigar that sent smoke curling back toward Andrea's face.

"You don't smoke, do you, Joseph?"

"I do," he said, feeling his coat pocket for his package of cigarettes.

"Too bad," she said. "That means we can't get married."

She removed her shoes and rubbed the bottoms of her feet. The designs on her hose resembled paper cutouts of snowflakes, one starry point attached to another.

"Leander tells me you're ovulating," Joseph said directly.

She shook her head, laughing to herself. "You're a strange one, aren't you, Joseph?"

"It's all those kids."

"All what kids? Do you have kids? Are you married, Joseph?"

"The ninth graders," he said. "In Montgomery County."

She punched him with the heel of her shoe. "You told me you were lying about that! You said you wrote obituaries!"

He slid across the seat and kissed the side of her face. "I was lying about having lied. I really am a teacher. American and world history."

"So Sammy didn't recognize you, after all?"

"If he did," Joseph said, "I don't know how. Because as far as I can recall, I never saw the guy before in my life."

"Then until your mother died, your father didn't have season tickets to the Bullets games? That was made up, too."

"It was," Joseph answered. "I don't even have a father."

6 She lived with Balls, an immaculately groomed French poodle named after Honoré de Balzac. Theirs was a two-bedroom flat on the eighth floor of an old Beaux Arts building.

"Hope you don't mind another man in my life," she said, dodging the dog as she reached to switch on a table lamp. "If he acts weird it's because he hardly ever sees anybody."

"Antisocial, is he?" Joseph leaned over and ruffled the animal's fur.

"Quite the opposite," she said. "He just rarely meets people." She was kneeling now, before the dog bowl in the kitchen, filling it with dry food that smelled of vitamins. Copper-bottomed pots and pans hung from a web of ceiling tackle, casting shadows on the black-and-white checkerboard floor. Joseph watched from the doorway.

"Sometimes I bring friends over," she said, "but not very often. When I do, Balls pees on the rugs. He wants attention, I guess. And he hates the competition."

The dog circled Joseph's feet as he stepped back into the front room. "Maybe he's just jealous," Joseph said, studying some of the photographs hanging on the walls. "From what I hear, poodles can be awfully possessive."

"If he's purring like a cat, he likes you. If not, be warned. He'll nip at your ankles."

"I hear him purring."

"Good."

The pictures climbed from the baseboards to the crown molding, in no particular order, each about an inch apart.

"Are these friends?" he said.

"Hardly," she replied. "They're mostly famous people I met at parties over the years." She put the box of dog food in the cupboard under the sink. "Your buddy McNeese took a few of them. He's the best party-pic man in town, and the sweetest."

Joseph recognized some of the people in the pictures: Elizabeth Taylor, Gerald Ford, Kurt Vonnegut, Barry Goldwater, Jane Fonda. In a few of the earlier photographs Andrea's hair was a kinky brown mass stacked high on her head. "Any of these include members of your family?" he said.

"Those're all in photo albums," she said. "I can show them to you later if you like." Now she was pouring Perrier into the second of Balls's bowls. "Red or white?" she said.

"Pardon?"

"Wine . . . red or white wine?"

"Neither," he replied. "I changed my mind about that nightcap. I think I passed my limit about three hours ago."

"You don't mind if I have one, do you?"

"Not at all," he said. "You knew Truman Capote?" He pointed to a picture of the late writer looking fat and smug, a pair of dark, round glasses hiding his eyes.

"Poor Tru," she said, her mouth tightening. "What a tragedy, that one. And such an artist. He stood in this very room, Joseph, right where you're standing now. He was so full of pills and when he spoke he sounded just like a woman—he had this spooky old grandmother's voice. I actually walked in on him while he was using the bathroom. He was teetering over the commode with his thing out, splashing all over." She laughed and shook her head. "Everyone likes that story."

As he had hoped, there was a photograph of Andrea Troy with Royston Peden. He found it hanging in a dimly lit corner, next to a brass sconce holding two white candles wrapped in cellophane. In it her dress was cut low, and her hair was shorter, whiter than it was now; even the roots were yellow. The senator wore a tuxedo with wide, satiny lapels and a diver's Rolex that reflected a star of light from the photographer's strobe. His wavy brown hair needed trimming. His face was red and meaty.

"I poured you one anyway," she said, entering the room. "If it's too tart tell me."

He accepted the glass and pointed to the picture. "You know everybody, don't you, Andy?"

"*Him* I know. Maybe too well." She walked to the couch. "How 'bout let's sit, Joseph."

Without the shoes she was about a foot shorter than he. On the polished oak floor her footing was loose and unsure.

"What do you mean you may know him too well?" Joseph said.

"Who, love?"

"Peden. You said you may know him too well."

She sipped her drink and picked stray threads from the seat of the couch. "Can I tell you something in confidence, Joseph? Promise you won't repeat it."

"Who do I know that'd be interested anyway?"

"For years he was one of my very best sources," she announced, and with a haughty air flipped her hair off her shoulders. She was nodding as if to convince him, as if he had somehow suggested she wasn't telling the truth. "He would tell me virtually everything, Joseph. It was amazing." She laughed and scratched her scalp. "If only there were more like him on the Hill, my job would be a cinch."

"I'm impressed."

"His wife, too—she was always good for a quote. But what a story there. An alcoholic, Mary. The only person she hated more than him was herself. She would call, and then he would. Ring, ring, ring. Those two nearly drove me batty." She sipped the wine and patted the seat beside her. "I'm cold. Come here, sit."

Joseph glanced back at the picture. "Why is it everybody calls him distinguished? I hear that all the time in the news, see it in the papers. 'Distinguished' Senator Peden."

"I guess because he's been in office so long," she said. "From what I hear, though, the only things actually distinguished about him are his family name and the length of his you-know-what. He's bedded every single and divorced woman in this city, it seems, except yours truly." She yawned into the back of her hand, then scratched her scalp again. "Not that he didn't try, of course. At La Brasserie one night, in a private dining room. He was on the floor, trying to get me, when our waiter walked in."

For some reason the dog barked.

"Is this confession time?" Joseph said.

"Only if you swear everything dies here."

"I swear." He placed a hand over his heart. "Now can I tell you something, Andy?"

"You can tell me anything in the world you want, Joseph. I may make my living off people's secrets, but that doesn't mean I don't know how to keep one."

He considered telling her who he was and being done with it. He considered starting over and showing restraint, and not hurting her when the time came. Instead he said, "I've been wanting to sleep with you since the moment I saw you."

Her eyes brightened and a smile formed on her lips. She put the wineglass down and reached for something on the coffee table—a small brass paperweight shaped like an elephant.

"I want to make love to you," he said.

"I've always hated the way that sounds. I want to fuck you. Now that's music to my ears. That's how a man should say it."

"I want to fuck you," he said quietly, as if it were language utterly unknown to him.

"Then let's fuck," she said, standing now and reaching for his hand. She led him into her bedroom, Balls nipping at his heels. "If you don't behave," she told the dog, "I'll lock you outside. Be quiet, Balls, you're making Mama mad."

The dog's yelps diminished to a whimper as it scurried to an armchair in the corner and jumped on the seat.

"I lived with a guy for a few years," she said. "Balls used to like to watch. I hope you don't mind."

"Certainly not."

"That guy I lived with was really into it—showing off for a dog. He used to say there was a man trapped in Balls's body."

"Of course there was. Honoré de Balzac."

"He never got specific about it. But if I had to guess, it was the Marquis de Sade or someone like that. Because he was pretty kinky, this guy, although I must say I learned a lot from him. He introduced me to a part of myself that I didn't know existed. He was liberating in the truest sense of the word. And for a long time I thought he had ruined me for everybody else."

Joseph, watching her undress, could only think to say, "That's too bad, Andy."

"He ruined me because after him everything seemed mundane, nothing frightened or charmed. I felt ruined for sex."

"Did he like to do it outside or something?"

"It wasn't where we did it, Joseph, it was how."

He nodded because he understood; he had been married to Naomi Richard, after all.

"If you'll check my bureau there"—she was pointing to a chest of drawers—"you'll find a report containing some information that may be of interest to you."

"What kind of information?"

Stripped down to a bra and hose now, she walked across the room and took a slip of paper from the top drawer. "Go on," she said. "Read it. You'll like what it says."

"You read it."

She glanced at the paper, then up at Joseph. "It's from my gynecologist. Look, Joseph, my medical report—it's all right here in black and white." She held the paper out to him.

"But I trust you, Andy."

"Did you bring any protection?"

"Any . . . ?"

"The second drawer," she said, pointing. "I'll get a rubber and even put it on if you can stand me to. Some men can't."

She placed the foil-wrapped condom on a pillow at the head of the bed, rather like a hotel chocolate, he thought. Then she removed the hose and bra. Her breasts were full and hanging, her buttocks as thick and dimpled as Sunday hams. He saw the red line, a millimeter above the navel, where the elastic waistband had pinched her. She might have been alone in the room, she was that uninhibited. She might have been young and beautiful.

"Will you ruin me, Joseph?"

"I'll do it with you, Andy. I don't know about any ruining."

"Here," she said, holding her hands out in front of her, fingers dancing, "let me see you."

He stepped up to where she was sitting. She unbuckled his belt, unzipped his slacks, unbuttoned his shorts. Her hands, every inch of them, were warm and safe. He watched as she turned him left, then right, examining every angle. "This is what they're telling single girls to do now. It's the age we're living in. You've got to play it safe."

"Sure you do."

"I've got this girlfriend at work, she's pretty cute, about our age. She says she knows this girl who picked up a guy once at a bar and took him home. They had sex and everything, and then during the night the guy kisses her goodbye and leaves. She wakes up in the morning and goes to the bathroom and sees he's written, in lipstick, 'Welcome to the AIDS Generation,' all across her mirror. My girlfriend swears this happened."

"It sounds made up—like something I read in a magazine once."

"I don't know why you'd say that. I've never known my girlfriend to lie."

"Well, maybe her friend lied."

For some reason Joseph kept thinking of a time with Naomi, perhaps because he had felt then as he did now—afraid of being discovered, astonished by his behavior. This was before they were married, one night when they had worked late and watched the newsroom empty out except for a handful of copy editors snoozing at their desks. She had led him into the stairwell just off the copy aide station, locked the door behind them, and told him to sit down. In her gray pin-striped suit and heels, a rope of pearls encircling her neck, she had gone down on him and made him come, the sound of her sucking echoing to the ceiling high above. "Protein is good for you. Come on,

Joseph. Wanna taste?" She had opened her mouth to show him, and in the midnight gloom of the well, leaning against the iron balustrade, they had kissed long and soft and deep. He had worried that at any second the door would open and his name would be called, and that he would be asked to explain himself: *Who in blazes do you think you are, Burke? Just who?* And yet he had remained there, sprawled on the steps, and become aroused again. In minutes he was pulling her down on him for more, watching her performance, making more noise than was safe. Now, with Andrea Troy, he experienced the same combination of fear and excitement—fear because if a door swung open in the next few moments, it would be to her memory, and excitement because he alone held the key.

"Can I use the bathroom first?" he said, stepping back from the bed.

She laughed and drummed her feet against the mattress. "If you can piss with a hard-on, you can. I didn't know guys could."

He waited a moment before turning on the light. A poster over the toilet showed a small boy standing in an outhouse, his back to the viewer, his attention directed at a black hole in the seat. WE AIM TO PLEASE, it said. YOU AIM, TOO, PLEASE. At the lavatory Joseph splashed water on his face, then dried himself with a towel scented with lilac. In the mirror he watched his prick soften, the odd ticking of it, the balls beginning to descend. He saw a single drop of semen poised at the head, white and glistening. And then he found himself grasping a tube of lipstick and writing, in his best hand, "And Who Has the Estranged Wife of the Distinguished Senator from New York Been Seeing These Last Few Weeks?" across the polished face of the glass. The result was a mess but at least it was readable.

"Joseph," she called from the room. "Are you okay in there? Everything all right?"

"Just a second."

In the bedroom he found that something had changed. "Balls got bored and left," she said, climbing out of bed. "My turn now, okay? I'll just be a minute."

"A minute?"

"What's the matter, honey? Can't you wait that long?"

While she was gone he put his clothes back on. He tried to settle down but his heart was racing and he felt himself getting hard again. She returned carrying a hairbrush in one hand, the used lipstick in the other. She looked confused. "What is it supposed to mean, Joseph?"

"I was trying to be funny."

"You use up my best color, you write all over my mirror, and that's supposed to be funny?"

"After what happened to that friend of your friend I thought it would be. I thought you would appreciate it."

"I don't. And what does it mean?"

He was working the knot of his tie tight and square against his collar. He looked up and met her gaze. "It means you fucking ruined my life, lady."

"I've ruined . . . *what did you say?*"

"I'm none other than 'the recent former husband of sexy *Herald* film commentator Naomi Richard.' And you ruined my life."

"Get out," she said. "Get out before I call the cops." She flung the brush to the floor at his feet, the lipstick high over his head. "You sonofabitch! You lousy sonofabitch! Get out!"

A tightness spread across his chest and into his arms and shoulders. "Joseph Burke is my name," he continued, "and sources say I'm quite the dandy."

She slammed the bathroom door shut and locked it. "I've got a gun in here," she cried. "Get out! Get out of here! I mean it!"

In the living room he put on his hat and coat and took another look at the pictures on the walls. He was ashamed of himself but he figured that would pass in a day or two. Balls, yapping, weaved around his ankles and rubbed against his pants, dusting the cuffs with flea powder.

"I'll shoot you," Andrea Troy shouted, her voice thick and muffled now. "I'll kill you, Burke! I swear I'll kill you!"

When he left he closed the door behind him, and made sure the dog had not gotten out. It was three o'clock in the morning, and he wasn't tired at all. Tubes of fluorescent light flickered on the ceiling, and music was coming from down the hall—Caruso on a phonograph. The elevator car arrived, banging to a stop. He waited a long moment before entering.

◀ *Four* ▶

Joseph had designated this blustery morning in March as moving day, and both Woody and Marissa insisted on giving him a hand. Marissa reported to the house at Logan Circle wearing bib overalls and athletic shoes and carrying her graphs and charts in a rainproof backpack. She had fitted some work gloves into her side pocket. A faded red bandanna covered the top of her head.

Balanced on the edge of the hospital bed, Woody put on his cap and sunglasses, and then Marissa helped him slip into the leather boots he'd favored during his days as a fisherman.

"I appreciate your wanting to help," Joseph said. "But it's really a job for two. Why don't you stay home, Father?"

"So what if I won't be able to carry anything," Woody said. "I'll just sit around and give orders."

Joseph was too preoccupied with the task at hand to protest more. He had borrowed a pickup truck from a delivery man at work and had promised to return it by noon. That left him with only a few hours to load and unload his belongings and drive the truck back to a parking garage near the *Herald* building.

"No worry, Joseph," Marissa said. "Everything go fine."

"If only he'd walk we could do it all in about an hour."

"He won't walk."

"But if only," he said. "Everything would be so simple."

To Woody, Joseph's concern seemed irrational because there was so little to move. Over the last few days, Joseph had put all of his clothes, bath towels, and bedding into large trash bags. Except for a coffee pot and a few ceramic cups, he didn't own any kitchenware. The bed, the chair, and some books—that was about it. With Naomi he had bought living-room furniture, a bedroom suite, original art for the walls, a Seth Willard clock, an oak dining table, and chairs hand-crafted by the Amish of Lancaster, Pennsylvania, but they had all disappeared the same day she had. "Hope you don't mind," she'd told him during one of her phone calls, "but Hans put them in storage. He thought they were . . . well, *plebeian* is the word he used." Joseph hadn't known how to respond. He'd sat listening to the waves of static on the line. "If you want them back they're yours. Only thing, Joseph, they're up here in New York. At a U-Hide-It locker in Pleasantville. And I've got the only key."

Because the cab of the borrowed pickup truck contained bucket seats, with a five-speed column on the floor, Marissa had to sit in the back, squatting in the corner, both hands clutching the wheelchair to keep it from bouncing around. Every few minutes Woody rapped the glass and she flashed the okay sign. "If you break that window," Joseph warned, "you pay for it." Woody snickered and tapped even harder, then pressed his lips against it, leaving the thick shadow of a kiss.

Joseph was surprised when Marissa returned the gesture, covering Woody's print with one of her own. Stopping at a traffic light, Joseph reached back and wiped the glass with his sleeve.

"You're gonna give yourself a coronary," Woody said, "all worked up like this."

"Big deal. Who'd care anyway?"

At the apartment building, they took the freight elevator up to the seventh floor, all eyes on the numbered panel in front. When the door opened, Woody quickly pushed himself through it, nearly knocking Marissa down, and cut a wheelie before racing down the corridor. He was mimicking the sound of a tortured automobile engine, and Marissa had to run to keep up.

Joseph opened the apartment door and Marissa rolled Woody across the threshold.

"What the hell?" Woody said. "Smells like somebody had a turd party in here, son."

Joseph was prepared to argue that there was no odor but Marissa removed her bandanna and covered her mouth and nose with it.

"It may smell bad," Joseph said, "but at least I haven't been living in the middle of a goddamn combat zone." His defiant grin disappeared the moment it occurred to him that as of today he would be. "Is it really necessary to be so critical, Father?"

"Stop squawking," Woody said, "and tell me what stinks."

"It's the books. It smells like old books in here."

"The books stink, all right, but that's not the stench I mean. It's something else."

"If there's a smell, it came with the place when I rented it. It's always been here."

"Well," Woody said, moving to the window, "I hope to God they didn't charge you extra for it."

Joseph and Marissa searched the kitchen for the source of the odor. They looked behind the range and the refrigerator and in the cupboard. Having failed to find anything, Marissa said, "I know it now, Joseph. Woodrow, listen, I know this smell."

As both men waited for the answer, Marissa's expression suddenly changed to despair. Her face was a white mask and her hands trembled. Finally she caught her breath and said, "Like when my brother Armentor dies. It smell like death here."

Woody laughed and rocked back in his chair, nearly flipping over. Joseph, however, wasn't amused. Naomi had never visited the apartment, but he knew that Marissa was right.

"Time to go," Woody said, beating the spokes of his steel wheels. "You people are starting to act up, and I've got to get ready for my card game tonight."

"What card game tonight?" Joseph said.

"Friends from the clinic," Marissa explained. "The boys, he calls them, and no one under fifty."

"Thank you," Woody told her. Then he looked up at Joseph. "Bunch of sick puppies like me, son. I invited them over. Beer and poker, dips and chips, cigars and cigarettes. You're more than welcome to join us."

"I think I'll pass."

"Fine," Woody said, rolling out into the hall. "That way I won't have to share my matchsticks."

Back at Logan Circle, Joseph and Marissa unloaded the truck while Woody watched from the sidewalk. They assembled the bags and boxes on the veranda, then carried them into the house. In the park across the street, a couple of men caressing wine bottles stood on a bench and shouted instructions: "Don't scratch my walls"; "Watch your step, white boy"; "Look out for the banana peels, sweetie pie."

Joseph and Marissa ignored the pair, but Woody spun around in his chair and addressed them with a cocked hand. "Bang-bang," he said. "You're dead." The pistol turned into a semiautomatic rifle, and he was spraying them left to right. "Now you're ground meat, assholes! All of you!"

In little more than half an hour Joseph and Marissa finished carrying everything into the house, and they retired to the kitchen for glasses of lemonade. While Marissa cracked an ice tray in the sink, Joseph pulled out his wallet and thumbed through it. "What do I owe you? Twenty dollars enough?"

Marissa sat at the table and shook her head. "I no do this for you, Joseph. Woodrow needs you here. I do it for him."

He put the wallet back in his pocket and then poured another glass of lemonade. Only yesterday Marissa had stocked the refrigerator with more fresh food and drinks than Cleo had ever brought home. Was it possible, Joseph wondered now, that she really had fallen in love with

Woody, that she desired his company as much as he did hers? It was Saturday, in any case, and why wasn't she home with her husband and children? Why weren't they making breakfast in the kitchen, watching television, planning a day crowded with shows on the Mall and exhibits at the Smithsonian?

"Thanks for the help," Joseph said, meeting her eyes. "Woody and I couldn't have done it without you."

"Welcome," she answered, her smile showing the glistening lemon pulp that clung to her teeth.

A few minutes later he said, "Want to drive the truck back with me to the *Herald*? It won't take long."

"No," she said. "If it's okay with you, Joseph, I rather stay here and look after Woodrow."

6 From the day his mother and father had first moved to Logan Circle, they had designated the room next to theirs as the guest room. But as far as Joseph could recall, no guest had ever slept in it, himself included. Those times he'd stayed over, he had preferred the couch downstairs in the den, mainly because the guest room was small and stuffy, like a mop closet. It had no windows, and the chocolate-brown ceiling paint was peeling in jagged strips. The wallpaper, too, was cheap and tacky. Decorated with heroic-looking knights, bosomy dames, and horses snorting steam, it was peeling along the baseboards and warped where pipes had leaked. A few of his mother's better efforts with a paintbrush were hanging above the bed: bluejays sitting on a tree limb, October haystacks, antebellum mansions ruined by neglect. Now the room didn't seem so uninhabitable. In fact, Joseph thought he might feel more at ease here than he had in the apartment. With his father restricted to the bottom floor, the top belonged to him. If he so chose, he could sit on the john with the door open. He could walk around naked, displaying an energetic hard-on, symbol of his liberation.

To make room for his bed, Joseph had placed his box spring on top of the one already in the room, then sandwiched his mattress under the guest mattress. The arrangement, rising several inches above the top of the tarnished brass headboard, looked awkward, but Joseph had never before lain in a more comfortable setting.

"Your nose will bleed," Marissa said, watching as he dressed the bed with sheets and a blanket.

"I beg your pardon."

"So high. Better be careful, okay?"

Joseph didn't know whether to laugh or thank her for the warning. "How nice, Marissa. You made a joke."

The compliment brought a rosy flame to her cheeks. "You fall," she said, "you break your neck." Then she made a terrible cracking sound and twisted her small, knotted hands against each other. "You dead on the floor."

Joseph offered a restrained round of applause, although a few minutes earlier the scenario she'd described had crossed his own mind. "Two jokes in a row by Marissa Christiani," he said. "Nicely done."

While Joseph unpacked boxes in his new room, Marissa sat downstairs with Woody until mid-afternoon. They played dictionary games and she told stories about her friends and family in El Salvador. In the kitchen she fried bologna and made sandwiches dripping with mayonnaise, onions, and grease. They sat on the veranda and she sang songs in Spanish while Woody studied the neighborhood derelicts through his binoculars. Then at dusk, as Joseph was trying to nap in the guest room, laughter rocked the house, jarring drifts of dust from the ceiling, rattling the lamps and picture frames. Joseph opened and closed his door, temporarily quieting things. But soon the racket started up again, and covering his head with a pillow couldn't shut it out.

As Joseph lay there, it occurred to him that he had never heard his father laugh as hard or as passionately, not even when Cleo was alive—not even when he, Joseph, was a child.

Before she left, Marissa climbed the stairs and knocked on Joseph's door. "Sorry so loud," she said. "But I cut Woodrow's hair and we laugh."

Joseph chose not to answer, and she descended the creaky steps. Only after he was certain she was gone did he relax and let himself breathe again.

6 At around seven o'clock the poker players began to arrive. Footsteps sounded like tribal drums, echoing up the stairs and down the hall. In under ten minutes the front door opened and closed four times. Joseph sat at the edge of his bed, feet dangling inches from the ground, and listened to the riot of furniture being shoved around. Woody was barking commands, and phlegmy voices barked back.

"My lord, Finney, didn't recognize you with your pants on!"

"Watch your tongue, Woody, and hand me a beer!"

"Hey, Baines, what's wrong, old boy, can't talk when there ain't some fat-assed nurse poking you in the skull?"

"Hey, Woody, I'm talking, all right! I'm talking!"

The exchange was so loud they might have been seated right outside Joseph's door. In a moment of terror he wondered what he was doing in his father's house, and whether the sacrifice he was making was too great.

"Joseph! Oh, Joseph!"

"This the son?"

"Why'n't you leave him alone, Peters?"

"Is he the one who painted all this shit on the walls? Hey, Big Wood, who painted all this weird shit on the walls?"

"Pete, you're a dick, you know that?"

"Come on down here, son! Meet the boys!"

In the bathroom Joseph brushed and flossed his teeth. He might have taken a shower had it not involved removing his clothes; Joseph was in no mood to remove his clothes. And if not for the party downstairs, he probably would've gone to bed with his clothes on and slept until church bells or the cries of bums and whores forced him awake.

Joseph stepped into the den just as the one named Peters was returning from the kitchen. He was a tall, slender man with a prominent nose and a military-style haircut. The others were seated at a folding table in the middle of the den. Already the imitation-wood top was littered with crushed beer cans, matchsticks, bags of potato chips, and ashtrays full of smoldering cigar butts. The table's aluminum legs bent under the weight of their forearms, threatening to buckle. Smoke swirled above their heads in a tumultuous cloud. Everyone had placed his coat on the hospital bed, and except for Woody, who wore his cap, they had lined the top of the radiator with their hats.

Peters shook Joseph's hand. "I'm honored," he said. "You are truly a gifted artist. You possess what some might call a vision." He turned to face one of Cleo's paintings hanging over the fireplace. Entitled *Eating Flies and Bugs*, it depicted snowy egrets standing on the backs of Charolais cattle. "These cowbirds look so friendly," Peters remarked.

"Thank you," Joseph said. "But my mother was the artist. All her animals looked like people." He pointed to the face of one of the birds. "This little fellow, for example, resembles the delivery boy for a Chinese restaurant on Fourteenth Street."

Joseph walked to the table and the other poker players greeted him, in unison, by removing the tobacco from their mouths and nodding pleasantly. "Welcome to the land of the living," Woody said, tipping his cap. "These boys may look ugly and walk kind of crooked but at least they're clean, Joseph, which I'm sorry I can't say for you."

Joseph tugged at his shirt and mumbled something even he didn't understand, then sat down.

"Since Woody told me what you do," Peters said, "I never miss Obits. It first, then Sports. I see there's an art to it. Like painting or music's an art."

"I'll have to remember that," Joseph said.

"Or dancing's an art."

Woody slapped the table. "You gonna sit there and name all the arts, Pete? Shut up and deal, for Chrisake."

Working clockwise, Peters flipped cards to each of the men. "Poker's an art," he said.

"Not the way you play it," Woody groaned.

Each matchstick was worth a thousand dollars, and for a reason that went unexplained one cut in half was worth a hundred. The man named Trussell handed Joseph the equivalent of fifty thousand dollars and recorded the grant on a legal pad.

"Oh, I'm not playing," Joseph said. "I'd rather watch."

"Only players at the table," Woody said. "House rules."

Joseph moved over to the couch and sat reading one of his father's fishing magazines. The men played with furious resolve, pockets of sweat spreading over their clothes, ashes dribbling into their laps. After a while Peters said, "Did you know I'm a writer myself? I mean, I'm retired Navy, but I've been working on this book set on board a nuclear submarine. It's the turn of the century, you see, and the feds're experimenting with both sexes underseas. War breaks out on land, and of course down below everyone gets to fucking and sucking. Although I haven't gotten that far yet, I see orgies and whatnot."

"If there's plenty of fucking and sucking in it," Woody said, "you've got yourself a bestseller, Pete."

Peters leaned back in his chair and chewed hungrily on his cigar. He seemed proud of himself. About a dozen empty beer cans stood in front of him, more than any other player. "Not to exaggerate or anything," he said, "but I do believe it's got potential. Maybe one day I can get you to read some pages, Joseph, and tell me honestly what you think. From what I've been seeing in the paper, I really admire your style."

"I have no style," Joseph said. "No one in Obits does. We're strictly discouraged from having a style."

Woody was concentrating on his cards. "Joseph started out wanting to write novels, then this newspaper got a hold of him. After that, a woman who went to movies for a living talked him into getting married and lord knows he hasn't been the same since." Woody sipped his beer and swallowed a belch. "Nowadays you wouldn't think about reading a book much less writing one, isn't that right, son?"

"Right," Joseph said. "You couldn't pay me to read a book."

Presently Peters decided to reveal his illnesses: he had a hip that tended to slip out of joint and he also suffered from shingles, a painful skin ailment that "comes and goes of its own mind, leaving my butt and back all blistered." The enormity of his glassy black eyes suggested a hyperactive thyroid as well, but this he did not mention.

"I have Paget's disease," the man named Trussell said to Joseph. "Ever hear of it?"

Joseph said he hadn't, and Trussell looked disappointed.

"Me, it's a deformed spine," announced Finney, drawing a picture of it in the air with his left hand.

Everyone stared at Baines.

"Club feet," he said meekly.

By the time they broke for turns in the bathroom Woody was a matchstick millionaire. He wheeled himself over to the couch and dropped his winnings into Joseph's lap.

"Your inheritance," he said, flashing a smile. "Don't say I never gave you anything."

Peters braced his hip with the flat of his hand and dragged a leg over to the open door beneath the stairway. "Only be a second," he said. "Don't start the second half without me."

"Take your time," Woody grumbled. To the other poker players he said, "Shit, take forever if you like."

From the bathroom came the sound of Peters urinating in starts and stops. The toilet flushed and water ran in the sink, then something hit the wall with terrifying force.

"I can promise that Sheetrock in there won't take a grown man beating on it," Woody said.

They listened for more; nothing came.

"Maybe his hip gave out again," Finney said, dropping his hand of cards. "You think he fell?"

"Nah," Trussell said. "He'd of screamed bloody murder."

None of them moved from the table until Joseph, fearing the worst, walked over and knocked on the door. "Mr. Peters," he called. "Oh, Mr. Peters. You okay in there?"

Although the door wasn't locked, Joseph had a hard time pushing it open. Peters had fallen to the floor and his body was blocking the way.

"Dumb sonofabitch," Woody muttered. He wheeled in close to get a better look. "I told him not to drink so much."

With Baines lending a shoulder, Joseph was able to force a crack in the door wide enough to accommodate him. Peters was lying flat on his back, one arm draped over the open toilet, the tips of his fingers touching the blue water. His legs were as twisted as the cords of a distressed parachute, and he looked dead. There was an open wound on his chin and blood fanned down his shirt front.

"Pull him out of there," Woody said. "Let him breathe. Let him get some air, for crying out loud!"

Joseph and Baines clutched Peters under the arms and Trussell and Finney each grabbed a leg. They carried him across the room and dropped him on the hospital bed. Peters still wasn't moving. Joseph checked for a pulse but found none. He put his ear to Peters's nose, hoping to detect the sound of breathing.

"Anybody know CPR?" he said.

For half a minute no one moved, then Woody rolled up to the bed and yanked the seat of Joseph's pants. "Hit him in the chest, goddammit. Arrest his heart. Get it pumping."

Joseph reared back and with the side of his fist punched Peters in the sternum. "Do it again," Woody said when Peters didn't respond. "Harder this time."

As Joseph was preparing to deliver a second blow, Peters sat up and spit up a mouthful of blood, coloring the sheets. "Oh man," he muttered. "Shit."

For a while everyone was elated, then it suddenly occurred to them that Peters might have been faking all along. Joseph nearly added his voice to the outcry, then got another look at his chin and bloody shirt and knew this was no joke.

"You bastard," Woody said. "You phony bastard."

Peters folded his hands over the place on his chest where Joseph had hit him. "God, that hurts," he said, pulling the bedsheet up to his chin. "I must've fainted."

"My, how this card game has deteriorated," Finney said.

Joseph got some gauze pads from the bathroom upstairs and instructed Peters to hold a couple against the wound on his face. "This'll need stitches," he said. "Any volunteers to drive Mr. Peters to the emergency room?"

"I can drive myself," Peters said. His voice was stronger and his eyes had cleared, but as he headed for the door he fell down again, knocking the coffee table on its side. More blood ran from his chin, and as before, his eyes bulged black and glassy. Trussell and Baines helped him back to his feet.

"I must really be drunk," he murmured. "I must—"

"You're not drunk," Woody said. "You're fucking pickled. You're like something green and warty in a jar."

Finney, standing by the radiator, put on his hat and coat. "I'll take him to Georgetown Hospital," he said. "I live near there." He wrapped a scarf around his neck.

"I'd drive him," Woody said, "if only I could."

Everybody turned to look at Woody's legs. It was plain to Joseph that no one believed him.

"What're you staring at?" Woody said, then abruptly wheeled himself to the kitchen.

Finney grabbed Joseph by the wrist and drove his nails in deep. "I want you to know we all admire what you've done," he said, nearly whispering. "Not everyone would come back home, Joseph, particularly to live with someone in your father's state of mind."

Joseph wasn't quite sure how to respond, whether to dismiss his presence here as dutiful service to family or to be honest and admit that his move to Logan Circle was selfish, a way of saving money and hiding from his ex-wife.

"Thank you," he finally said. "You fellows come again. The door here is always open."

Baines and Trussell helped Peters walk outside and the cool air seemed to revive him. In the rear of an abandoned apartment building at the far end of the circle a huddle of bums had started a fire in a wire trash can. The flames whipped in the wind, nearly reaching the columns on the back porch.

"I'll take a cab back from the hospital," Peters told Joseph, "and come pick up my truck. Will you still be here?"

They shook hands and patted each other on the back.

Joseph said, "Me and Woody, we both will," and watched as the men left, each taking a different street.

6 At one o'clock in the morning, awakened by police sirens, Woody called for Joseph to get dressed and come downstairs, there was trouble for the whores and dealers. Joseph had been in the upstairs bathroom studying his mother's watercolor of hummingbirds, which hung over the toilet. The painting was as primitive as something a preschooler might sketch with his first crayon, and that, of course, was the charm, the beauty, of it. The faces of the birds looked human: noses, lips, eyes and eyebrows, ears big enough to support rings. On gossamer wings they hovered over white and yellow honeysuckle blossoms.

Joseph dried off, put on cloth slippers and a robe, and hurried down the stairs, taking two at a time. Woody was sitting up in bed, bobbing his head left and right as he strained to see through a small part in the curtains.

"Let's go!" he was shouting. "Come on, son. Step on it! We're gonna miss everything!"

Joseph lowered Woody into his chair and wheeled him out onto the veranda, into the colorful blaze. Three patrol cars had jumped the curb and were parked fewer than ten yards from the statue. A group of police officers stood under the trees, facing in the opposite direction. A couple wore uniforms, a couple heavy overcoats, a couple khaki pants and windbreakers pulled over sweatshirts. They were in no hurry to do anything, probably because whatever they'd come to police had already happened.

"A bust," Woody said. "They're finally cleaning it up."

"No," Joseph said. "They'd have a paddy wagon, there'd be more going on. It's too dead out there."

A few minutes later the uniformed cops silenced their sirens, and a basso rumbling could be heard.

"Can you make out what they're saying?" Joseph said.

"If you shut your mouth maybe I could."

For a Saturday, the circle was uncommonly free of traffic. The purveyors of flesh and drugs, generally busy on weekend nights, were nowhere to be seen, and their customers had scattered. Even the homeless were gone.

Joseph went back into the house and got the binoculars. By the time he returned outside, however, Woody knew why the police had come. "Someone's been murdered," he said.

It was another hour before the body was placed in a bag, laid on a gurney, and shoved into the back of an ambulance.

"He was a black youth," Woody said, squinting into the binoculars. "Short hair, light-complected. A lot of blood came out of the back of his head, so you figure it was a bullet here. . . ." He raised his arm and touched the base of his skull.

The ambulance left with its interior lights on, two sober-faced medics seated in front and one crouched in back at the head of the gurney. Woody said, "What's our average so far this year? Two murders a day, or is it two and a half?"

"I think it's more like one and three quarters."

In less than half an hour after the cops left, everything returned to normal. The heady aroma of marijuana smoke drifted in the air, and a new fire started in the drum behind the abandoned apartment building. People laughed and the bronzed figure of John A. Logan, saber drawn to strike, lorded over it all.

Pete Peters pulled up in a cab as Joseph was backing Woody through the front door. A patch covered his chin, studded in the center with a gummy red diamond. He strode quickly down the walk, favoring his right side, and in a single athletic leap conquered the steps. "Five stitches," he announced. "Doctor says I'll have a scar like a cleft."

"We're glad to hear it," Woody said.

"I've always wanted a cleft."

"Then we should charge you. Plastic surgeons probably take a lot for what my bathroom sink gave you free."

Peters said he couldn't stay long. He needed to call his wife and explain why he was running late, and he wondered if Joseph wouldn't mind corroborating his story if she happened to get suspicious.

"Wouldn't mind lying for you at all," Joseph said.

The two men helped put Woody back into bed, then Peters went upstairs to use the phone in the hallway.

"When I meet people like Pete Peters," Woody said, "or when I sit on the porch watching all the deadbeats drift in and out of the park, I wonder why your mother had to die and all of them get to live. I wonder what's the point."

About twenty minutes passed before Peters came back downstairs. Woody, by now, had fallen asleep.

"Everything okay?" Joseph said.

"Fine," Peters said. "You get a woman on a phone, no matter the hour, and it's Katie-bar-the-door. She talked and talked."

Joseph watched at the window as Peters walked to his pickup truck parked at the other end of the traffic circle. Some of the women trailed him, and from under one of the maples a man wearing a topcoat stepped forward to make his acquaintance. Peters turned to address the group. He peeled the patch off his chin, and everyone crowded around him. One of the women tried to help him put his patch back on, but the adhesive strip didn't hold. Another took some Band-Aids from her purse and fitted them on his chin, and yet another, this one about half Peters's height, leaned close to him and either whispered something in his ear or kissed him. Finally Peters and the woman got into the cab of the truck and drove off together.

"Hard to believe, isn't it?" Woody said, waking up. "I was beginning to hope Peters had caught something dreadful and died, and then I got to thinking that you, Joseph, were the one who would replace him at my poker table."

Joseph closed the curtains and turned off the light in the foyer, then chain-locked the front door. He had started back up the stairs when Woody said, "Poker ain't your game, is it, son? Never was, never will be."

6 Later that night—it must have been around four o'clock—Joseph woke to the sound of footsteps coming from the first floor. He put on his slippers and descended the stairs, careful to make as little noise as possible, certain that at last he would catch his father walking.

The moment he cleared the ceiling he dropped to his haunches and positioned himself behind the banister to take in the entire view of the den. To his dismay, however, Woody appeared to be asleep in the hospital bed. Covered by sheets and his blanket, he was lying on his side, snoring loudly. His wheelchair stood in the middle of the room, framed by the light shining through the bay window.

As he climbed back up the stairs, it occurred to Joseph that before he'd retired for the night he'd pulled the curtains closed. He considered nudging Woody awake—if he wasn't already—and informing him that he was on to his pathetic little game; but the lateness of the hour defeated his spirit for argument.

A few minutes later Joseph was settling back into bed when the footsteps sounded again, even louder than before, loud enough to shake Cleo's pictures hanging above the headboard. He knew this time that his father was moving about, but when he hurried downstairs Woody still lay in bed sleeping, positioned exactly as before. The sheets and blanket were as he had last seen them, and the chair had not been moved. A night-light near the fireplace cut shadows across the scratched and dusty floor. The curtains in the front window now hid the view of the street, the park, and the pale winter moon.

"Have it your way," Joseph said. "I honestly don't care anymore."

In response his father quickened the rate of his snores.

"We'll talk about this later," Joseph said.

He took a few more steps, then stopped and wheeled back around, hoping to discover movement under the sheets, eyes open, a grin that said it all. But Woody was asleep and Joseph now wondered if he hadn't imagined the footsteps and the opening and closing of the curtains. Maybe he was hearing and seeing things. Maybe it was he who was playing games.

6 On Monday morning, as Joseph and Alfred were having lunch in the cafeteria on the second floor of the *Herald* building, Cameron Yates walked by and interrupted their conversation. "I happen to have overheard you two discussing the murder of an unnamed youth in the park at Logan Circle," he said, pointing to a table nearby where he and a group of editors had been sitting. "My ears didn't deceive me, did they, Joey?"

"No sir," Joseph replied. "You heard correctly."

"And you were thinking about writing it, were you?"

"Not at all, Mr. Yates. It's not my department. I'm in Obits now, assigned to less sensational stuff."

Yates tugged at the lapels of his rotten tweed jacket and rocked back on his heels. He cut a quick glance at Alfred. "You taught him well, fat man."

"Thank you, sir."

"Because all but the rare homicide belongs to the beat reporter covering cops. Isn't that right?"

"That's right," Alfred said, swallowing hard.

"Perhaps the present situation in the city—namely, the rash of homicides—has bent the letter of the law somewhat, but check the *Herald Deskbook on Style* and see for yourself. It's all there."

"Yes sir," Alfred said. "Thank you for the reminder. We'll check it as soon as we get back upstairs."

"Very good, men. Carry on."

Yates took one step back, pivoted sharply on his heels, and left leading the band of underlings who'd joined him at lunch.

"What the hell was that all about?" Alfred said.

"I don't know, but did you catch a whiff of his breath?"

"A whiff of what? Liquor?"

"No," Joseph said. "Not liquor—sex, Alfred. I swear to God, pal, it smelled like a woman on his breath."

"What do you mean, like a woman?"

"I mean he smelled like . . ." Joseph bit into his sandwich. "It's true, isn't it? You've never been with one."

"Not with a woman," Alfred replied. "And certainly not the way you mean."

The cafeteria was crowded with reporters reading *The New York Times* and *USA Today* over coffee, cigarettes, and today's lunch plate of steak fries, boiled vegetables, and a stewed meat of dubious origin. In a corner alcove, several staff members were playing video games. Now that Yates and his subordinates had left, some felt free to curse their performance, others to shout with joy about theirs.

For a reason he preferred not to consider, Joseph no longer felt comfortable dining in the cafeteria. As a rule, he ate there only when the weather was too stormy to go elsewhere or when things were so busy at the Obituary desk, as they were today, that lunch was restricted to no more than half an hour.

It was while seated at a table near the bank of windows fronting L Street that Joseph had learned of his wife's infidelity. Said Jennifer Eugene, then his assignment editor on the Magazine: "She's screwing a copy aide, Joseph. A kid maybe twenty-one years old. I'd investigate if I were you."

"I wanted you to see something I wrote," Alfred was saying now. He reached into the briefcase at his feet and withdrew a manila folder. "But with this caveat, my friend: If any eyes but yours see this I will strangle you until blood leaks from every orifice on your person. Will you be able to abide by that?"

Joseph nodded. "No problem."

The folder contained a single sheet of onionskin paper, on which five perfectly drawn paragraphs detailed the death of Alfred Charles Giddings III, who, at the age of forty-one, had died of a broken heart.

The decedent, the story said, was a prize-winning reporter on the staff of the *Washington Herald*, now assigned to the Obituary section. He had no survivors.

"It's a rough draft," Alfred said. "So please overlook any misspellings."

"How'd your heart break?"

"She turned me down is how."

"Who did?"

"Jennifer declined to have dinner with me."

Joseph squeezed the paper into a ball. "I should make you eat this," he said.

"You mean I should make *you* eat it. You're the one who put me up to asking her out, Joseph."

"And how'd I do that?"

"You said if you were a woman you'd go out with me"—he paused to make sure no one else was listening—"and you also said you'd fuck me, Joseph."

"And I meant it—every word."

"The way she looked at me, I've seen it before. It's the way people look when they catch a fat person eating an ice cream cone. As if to say, 'You think he needs that?' But in this case it was 'Do you really need another dinner? And why should I be a party to it?' "

Before Alfred there had been others—men who had desired Jennifer's company and pursued it to no avail. Some years ago Joseph had observed a layout artist on the Magazine staff hustle her attentions over a period of several months. The man had seemed, to Joseph in any case, a winning catch. But one morning at work Jennifer informed him before a gallery of onlookers that he lacked the heroic qualities she was looking for in a man, and then asked him to please leave her alone. For years gossips had pegged her as a lesbian, then as the concubine of various celebrity politicians, then as a waif whose only home was the office. Although she seemed loath to attract suitors, Jennifer remained one of the most beautiful women to occupy a desk and claim a nameplate on the fifth floor. Her reputation as an aggressive and brilliant editor was well earned. If her performance ever drew criticism from staffers it was for her tendency to toe the company line. She had, it was said, a real genius for kissing ass. She'd once confided to Joseph that she'd donate her ovaries to charity for the chance to be an assistant managing editor in charge of either Lifestyle or the Magazine. And yet for all her allegiance to the paper, her late hours and weekends, the slot had eluded her. She now found herself working for someone with half her talent—and a man.

"I bet Yates would really love this," Joseph said now, and tossed Alfred's obituary into a planter near the door.

"Yates would make me go to the company psychiatrist again, the one I went to first for writer's block and then for my eating disorder. See how much she helped. I haven't written a real story in twelve years and I haven't been hungry in at least"—he looked at his empty plate—"well, however long it's been since I polished off today's mystery meat."

They carried their empty trays up to the trash cans in front, then walked to the service elevators.

"What you really need," Joseph said, "is to get laid, Alfred. I promise it'll change your life."

"Tell me what it feels like."

"It's like being a boy again with everything new."

"But I didn't like being a boy."

Back on the fifth floor, they walked through the Sports department, assaulted by a malnourished copy editor who yelled something about "life over yonder on Death Row," and through Metro, where everyone looked tired and bleary-eyed, ready to call it a day. As they neared Obits, Joseph spotted a cluster of reporters engaged in conversation with Cameron Yates. Alfred immediately joined the crowd, claiming a spot on the periphery, and Joseph followed. Yates was questioning the credentials of the president's recent nomination to the U.S. Supreme Court. He promised to continue the barrage of editorials criticizing the choice, and to show, once and for all, who in town had bigger balls—the man in the White House or the one up the street in the

Herald building. Applause erupted and swept around the circle, followed by a nervous lull. The trucklers and sycophants tittered, some repeating Yates's pledge, others shifting from foot to foot as if they suddenly needed to pee. Finally a sadly misguided intern stepped forward and made her pitch for glory.

"I'm going to repeat a joke I heard earlier that is terribly racist," Rachel Smith said, sounding a bit too sure of herself, "but in point of fact a young Negro courier—a good friend of mine, his name is Brock—told it to me only minutes ago in the copy aide station."

"Brock?" Yates said, hooking a hand around his ear.

The group stopped in its tracks, drew in closer to its leader, and waited for the young woman to continue.

"Why do Negroes have flat noses?" she said.

"You said Negro again, Rachel. Is that what you said?"

"Yes, Mr. Yates."

"But you mean black, don't you?"

"Yes."

"That or African-American, no?"

"Either, Mr. Yates."

"Then refer to them as such. Negro is an archaic term. You should know that, daughter. It's in our *Deskbook on Style.*"

"... I dunno ... well, sure ... yes, of course it is, Mr. Yates." Her confidence vanquished, Rachel Smith appeared to be on the verge of coming apart. Her lips paled as her face reddened, and her hands began to tremble.

"And what is this you were saying about their noses?"

"I was saying ... I was asking ... I mean, why is it they have flat noses ... why do black people have them?" And she lifted a hand and pressed her perky little Irish nose flat.

"Rachel?"

"Yes sir?"

"I'm married to a woman of color. Have you forgotten?"

"To a woman—"

"Do you plan to finish?"

It was all over for Rachel Smith. She had upset the most powerful newspaper editor in the world, thus sacrificing any hope of landing on the fast track. Joseph recognized her first mistake as being a failure to speak in complete declarative sentences, her second as not having made Cameron Yates laugh, her third and most serious as showing a lack of sensitivity and joking about blacks. The District of Columbia was 70 percent black, and Yates was married to an Asian—a "woman of color," as he obsessively referred to her, formerly employed by the *Herald* as a writer for the Food section. As Joseph himself and most veteran reporters knew, it was perfectly acceptable to tell dirty jokes in the office, the meatier the better, but ones about race were strictly prohibited. Rachel Smith, having begun her internship some six weeks ago after graduating magna cum laude from Sarah Lawrence College, apparently had not been apprised of this. Tomorrow, then, somewhere on the fifth floor aglow with fluorescent and cathode-ray tubes, Rachel would be introduced to her oblivion, to her very own Obits.

"They have flat noses . . . black people . . . the reason they have them is because that's where God put his foot when he yanked their tails off."

"And someone named Brock told you this?"

"Brock is black. He's black and he told me this. We were sitting in the copy aide station and he said it and I remembered it because he's black and I thought—"

"Tell Brock he doesn't amuse me."

If not for Joseph's own supportive hand Rachel might have collapsed to the floor. The group surrounding Yates suddenly became aware of ringing telephones, awaiting interviews, deadlines. Everybody scrambled in different directions, eyes cast either upward or downward. As for Joseph, after finding a chair for Rachel, he had escaped with the others, and now he and Alfred were dashing toward Obits like Olympian hurdlers.

Two telephone lines were ringing when they reached their desks, and neither Nate nor Tinker, notorious for disappearing at lunch for as many as three hours, was around to answer them. Alfred took one call, Joseph the other.

"Obits," Joseph said, breathing hard.

It was an assignment editor in Lifestyle reporting the death of a silent film star Joseph had never heard of. The movie critic planned an appreciation piece; Joseph had the obit. "How nice of you to call," he said and hung up.

Joseph had signed on to the house computer system and was trying to locate a wire-service story on the actress when Alfred sidled next to him. "What is it?" Joseph said.

"Your father. That was the nurse on five-one. She says he's missing."

"He's *missing?*" Joseph rose from the chair and put his jacket on. "How the hell can he be *missing?*"

"One moment about an hour ago he was on the porch with his binoculars, the next he's missing." Alfred punched the digital face of Joseph's telephone. "She says to call."

"You call," Joseph said, starting for the elevators. "Tell her I'm on my way. I'll be back as soon as I find him."

"Which means whenever, right?"

"Which means you get to write Tanya Golden."

"Did Tanya Golden die today? Really?"

But Joseph was already gone.

6 As Joseph was rushing home, running along Fifteenth Street and Rhode Island Avenue, Marissa found Woody seated in his wheelchair at the boarded entrance of the ramshackle apartment building across the circle. A chain link fence had recently been erected around the property to discourage vagrants from using it as a flophouse, and NO TRESPASSING signs had been posted on the weathered facade. The place, however, was no more secure. A week before, Joseph and Woody had watched from the veranda as people scaled the ten-foot-

tall fence—smack and crack addicts, for the most part, seeking sanctuary from the street. Later Woody had sighted a gang of leather-clad teenagers.

When Joseph rounded the corner he saw them immediately —Woody and Marissa in front of the building, holding hands.

"Oh, hello, son," Woody said, his face soured by the sight of Joseph. "Coming by for a late lunch?"

Joseph was too winded to speak. He rested with his hands on his knees, pulling at the cool air.

"All my fault," Marissa said, still holding Woody's hand. "I get excited and call but nothing wrong. He was here."

"I had gas," Woody announced.

Marissa smiled. She didn't seem to mind. "False alarms," she told Joseph. "Go back to work now."

"But you called me at the office, Marissa."

"We make mistake. Woodrow stomach hurt. This happen sometimes."

Woody pressed the back of her hand against his cheek, then rubbed it over his lips. "Must have been all the fish she cooked this morning. What a breakfast, Joseph! What a feast!"

"A going-away present," she said. "Leftovers in box."

Joseph turned to Woody. "I'm confused all of a sudden. Who's going away? It isn't you, is it?"

"Not me, son. This is the end for Marissa. From now on, when she comes to Logan Circle, it's a personal call. Everything's friendly. There's no business about it."

The insurance company was dropping Woody's case. Joseph hadn't forgotten about it, but he had been reluctant to bring it up and incite more debate. He was relieved to learn that the two of them had settled the matter without him.

"We'll miss you," Joseph said to Marissa.

"I come back. Every day almost. You see, Joseph. This place feels like home. I like it here."

"She sure does," Woody said. "And we like having her here.

Joseph, she cooked . . . it was the way your mother used to make it, only better."

"I bought some fillets this morning at the market on Maine Avenue," she said. "In the kitchen I added very secret ingredient."

"And guess what it was, son."

Joseph shrugged.

"It was love," Woody said. "It was an extra helping of love."

Joseph kept his mouth shut on the walk back to the house. If his father wanted to make a fool of himself, then let him. If he wanted to desecrate his mother's memory . . . well, he wouldn't have Joseph as an accomplice. As they crossed the park, Woody briefed Marissa on the history of the neighborhood and she listened as if spellbound, nodding to show her appreciation. "John Logan was a Union general," he was saying, pointing to the equestrian monument. "See how his saber's drawn? I always liked that. I used to wish he could come alive upon his horse and attack the people in the park. But no more. With you here, Marissa, they don't bother me. They have as much right to this place as I do."

They strolled by a vagrant singing to the statue of Logan. The man was leaning against the short iron fence that encircled the monument, and he smelled, Joseph thought, as if he could use a bath and some time alone with a stick of deodorant. He was wearing faded Army-issue attire, plastic shoes made to resemble leather, and gloves with the fingertips cut off. Joseph recognized the tune as belonging to his childhood, something by the Four Tops or the Temptations. Despite the man's apparent drunkenness, his voice had a quicksilver quality that suggested deep, clean lungs and a trained ear. His quavering tenor filled the park.

"Very beautiful," Woody said. "That was very beautiful, friend. Bravo!"

This was precisely the sort of person Woody generally avoided, one he never paid any mind to except through the lenses of his binoculars. A moment passed before Joseph was able to mark the importance of what he was witnessing.

"Bravo!" Marissa said. "Bravo, bravo!"

Woody rifled through the pockets of his shirt and pants, searching for money. "I'm broke," he told Joseph. "How 'bout helping this poor old singing star out?"

Joseph reached for his wallet, but Marissa had already removed some wadded cash from her coat.

"Here," Woody said, holding out a dollar bill. "Keep singing. Sing and be happy."

The man took the offering and Woody and Marissa continued ahead, Joseph following a few steps behind. Pigeons swirled above them and scattered in all directions. At the convergence of Vermont and Rhode Island avenues, Woody said, "Ready to learn something, Marissa?"

"I am ready, Woodrow."

"Ulysses S. Grant built that mansion there."

"Ulysses?" she asked.

"Ulysses S. Grant. Former president of these United States. He had a big black beard and they say he drank a lot."

"Who say?"

"Oh, I don't know, girl. Everybody."

Red bricks showed through the faded white face of the three-story building and the shutters were rotted and hanging at all angles. The side yard needed cutting and who could guess when the hedges, a durable redtop privet, had last been trimmed. As with so many of the other homes in the neighborhood, graffiti spoiled the cement walkways bordering the property.

"And the house there," Woody said, pointing to another great home in need of repair.

"I remember this young couple that lived in an upstairs unit, and they were very athletic, always jogging in tight shirts and shorts. At night they would screw with their bedroom windows open and all the lights on. Joseph's mother in particular enjoyed watching them. That's how we came to purchase those binoculars—"

"That's a lie," Joseph said, stepping in front of Woody's chair. "That's a lie and you know it."

"No lie, son. It's the truth. Your mother liked to peep."

"My mother . . ." He could find no words to defend her.

"You'd never know it, but she was an extremely sexual person, Cleo was. We had our secret life as I'm sure Marissa here has her secret life. And I don't know what's wrong with it, I honestly don't." He paused, then added, "Maybe if you and that wife of yours had built a secret life . . ."

Joseph didn't respond. A nervous itch had raised a ruddy spot on his neck, and he scratched it vigorously.

"Let's no be mean, Woodrow," Marissa said, kissing him on top of the head again. "This our last day, remember."

As soon as they entered the house Joseph sensed something different about the den, and only after a minute did it come to him that the hospital bed had been removed.

"We put in sewing room by kitchen," Marissa said. "Come look. I show you." She reached for Joseph's hand.

"But that was Mother's art room," he said. "That's where she kept everything. Her paints and her brushes are in there. All her canvases . . ." Joseph was glaring at his father. "She kept her easel and her drawing pads in there."

"Up on the third floor now," Woody said. "I wanted my own room. It's hard, Joseph, trying to sleep where everyone tramps through. Please understand. I had no peace anymore."

Woody rolled to where the bed had been. He leaned forward in his chair, removed a slipper, and scratched between his toes.

Joseph watched with as much amusement as disbelief. "Got an itch?" he finally said.

"Not quite an itch," Woody said. "More like a tingle."

"Then you're not paralyzed anymore."

"Everywhere but between my toes, son. And like I said, the only thing I feel there is a tingle."

"No one scratches a tingle, Father."

"I do," Woody answered. "And Marissa here."

Joseph waited for a response from the nurse, challenging her with a hard stare. "Tingle makes me crazy, too," she said after a while, then bent over and started scratching between her own toes.

6 At the office later that day, Joseph rendezvoused with Leander McNeese in the men's room.

"So why the long face?" Leander said.

"Suddenly my father's changed. He's kind and considerate, he talks to homeless people. I think he's happy."

"Yeah?"

Joseph unzipped his pants. "The problem is he's fallen in love with his nurse."

"The nurse, huh?"

"My mother wouldn't like it."

Leander smiled and rubbed his goatee against his shoulder. "Cleo's dead, squire. She died about five months ago."

"She still wouldn't like it."

They were both standing before porcelain urinals, relieving themselves in energetic streams. Joseph had a pencil fitted over one ear and a fountain pen over the other, and Leander had four or five cameras hanging from his shoulders.

"So I hear you know Charlotte," Leander said, somewhat timidly, which was completely out of character.

At the bank of lavatories now, they were washing their hands with squirts of pink industrial soap.

"The waitress at Lautrec, you mean?"

Leander was avoiding Joseph's eyes in the mirror. "How well do you know her, Joseph? Real well, very well, or extremely well? Pick one of the above. And be square with me."

"Not well at all," he said.

Leander yanked several sheets of brown paper from the dispenser and walked from one end of the room to the other, checking under the stall doors to make sure no one was seated there. "Tonight," he said, "she takes me to the Red Cross shelter for a blood test. Tuesday and Wednesday she gives me the hand jobs she's promised. Then on

Thursday night, after we get my results, I figure one of two things'll happen." He held up two fingers. "One, I take her home and get incredibly naked. Or two, I give you boys in Obits the story of my life in all its wicked splendor."

"Count on getting naked," Joseph said.

"Come by my place sometime Friday, okay? We'll have drinks on the roof and then I'll show you the pictures."

"What pictures?"

"That's another part of the deal. I take the test and Charlotte spreads her legs for my camera."

"That's quite a bargain, Mac."

"Show business, Joseph. What can I tell you?"

At the Obit desk, Alfred was finishing up his piece on Tanya Golden. Because it was a slow news day, Yates had decided to bump the story to A-1, giving Alfred his first byline this week and making him deliriously happy.

"Maybe that dyke Jennifer didn't break my heart, after all," he said.

"Then we shouldn't budget in your obit?"

"Maybe I want to be like Tanya Golden and live until I'm so old everyone says, 'Oh, did he just die? I thought he'd kicked the bucket forty years ago.' "

"Forty years ago you were still nursing at your mother's breast."

"My mother, . . ." Alfred said, then abruptly rose to his feet and started in the direction of the canteen, moving as quickly as Joseph had ever seen him.

"Did I say something wrong?"

Nate Thompson looked up from the crossword puzzle he was working on, and Tinker stood to look over the divider.

"Did either of you happen to overhear what we were talking about? I think I must've said something wrong."

"You were talking about breast-feeding," Tinker said.

"Was it particularly offensive, did you find?"

Nate shrugged his hefty shoulders. "Not to me, Joseph. But Alfred's sensitive about that kind of thing."

"He never had a mother," Tinker said.

Nate tapped a pen against his desk and shook his head. "Hey, Joseph. Weren't you the one who told us that?"

Joseph walked hurriedly to the canteen, where Alfred was standing before a vending machine, staring at the candies and potato chips through a sheet of smudged glass. "Hard to choose," he said.

"Then let me help you." Joseph joined Alfred in front of the wide case, removed two quarters from his pocket, and put them in the slot. "First off," he said, "you're too goddamned sensitive. I forgot, all right."

"Of course you did." Alfred reached forward and pulled a lever. "Baby Ruth," he said. "Wasn't he a ballplayer?"

"It was Babe, Babe Ruth. He was with the Yankees."

"Babe, Baby," Alfred said, unwrapping the candy. "It all tastes the same to me." And then he left the room tugging at his suspenders and smiling as if he owned the place.

Before leaving the office, Joseph called home and Marissa answered. It was almost seven o'clock, more than an hour past her normal quitting time. Feeling tired and petulant, he identified himself as "Woodrow's son, the other guy who lives there."

"I know who you are," Marissa said.

Woody got on and cleared his throat. "We were just in the dining room taking some of Cleo's paintings down," he said.

"You were what?"

"Taking some of your mother's pictures down and putting them in a room on the third floor. Does that pose a problem?"

"Don't you think we should've discussed this first?"

"Well, maybe. But I sort of figured you were as tired of looking at them as I was. Am I wrong, son?"

Joseph thought about it. "No," he said. "I guess you weren't."

6 Cleo had always believed that one day her artwork would find an audience, that although she'd never sold a painting during her lifetime, she would be discovered posthumously and live on for future

generations. Although Joseph had doubted that a market for animals and flowers with human faces would ever exist, he had hoped that perhaps her innocent view of the world would catch someone's fancy and at worst end up in a church recreation hall or a minor gallery dedicated to primitives.

Now, as he walked to Logan Circle, dodging beggars with tin cans and homeless people sleeping on the sidewalks, Joseph thought of his mother's paintings as one might a dark family secret. They were what he had to deal with instead of an alcoholic uncle, a psychopathic aunt, a sister who'd go to bed with anyone. They engendered shame, not pride. And as far as he was concerned, it was a miracle the paintings had survived this long.

But when he stepped through the front door and saw a few of her favorites still hanging on the walls of the den, he felt as if he'd defamed her. How could he have belittled her achievement? How wrong he had been: Cleo really was an artist, she would live forever. As long as people saw her work, she would be around.

From the sewing room, Woody called, "Welcome home, son. I was hoping that was you."

Before leaving for the evening, Marissa had placed a battered wing chair in the corner, and Joseph sat in it now. "Who else would it be?" he said.

"Well ..." Woody lowered the mail-order catalogue he'd been reading. "It could've been any number of people."

"Name them. Name any number."

Woody crossed his arms and turned to look out the window that addressed the back alley. "It could have been Marissa. She could've left something and was coming back for it."

"That's one," Joseph said. "Who else?"

"Could've been Pete Peters. He called earlier. He said he'd drop by sometime and tell me about the other night."

"Two."

"Maybe a detective investigating the murder in the park. They usually do that, you know."

"That's three," Joseph said. "Keep going."

Woody extended his arms above his head, stretching. There was something about his gaze that indicated an absence of ill will, a lightening up. Woody was truly changing for the better. He somehow looked younger, more like the man Joseph had known before Cleo died. "Can we talk about something?" he said.

"I guess it depends on the subject matter."

"I want to talk about Marissa."

Joseph squeezed his eyes with his thumb and forefinger. "Marissa has two children and a husband at home."

"For the record," Woody said, "Marissa got married when she was very young, a teenager. She meets this character Fred, son of wealthy people, just returned from two years of study in American schools, owns his own car. . . . Tell me, what poor peasant girl wouldn't fall head over heels? I happen to know for a fact that there's no more love there. She told me so herself. They don't even share the same bed."

"How, then, do you explain the children?"

Woody cupped his chin with his hands. "A good question," he allowed, "but these things happen. People aren't yet smart enough to explain their brief and mindless passions. Can you?"

The room still smelled of Cleo's oils. A bold rainbow of colors streaked across the wall behind Woody's head, and Joseph found the collection of drips and strokes strangely beautiful. Here was her masterpiece. He determined never to let anyone paint over it.

"On the way home I was thinking maybe we were being hasty in taking down Mother's pictures."

"But on the phone you agreed it was time."

"Well, Father, I guess I've changed my mind."

"They're where they belong now, son. Let them rest."

"This matters to me."

"No, it doesn't," Woody said. "You only think it would matter to her."

"We told her we loved them when she was still alive and we seemed to mean it. I don't know why now that she's dead they're no longer worth anything."

Woody leaned back and rested his head on the wall, partially covering the spot where Cleo had tested paints. "I've been wanting to ask a favor," he said. "And I want you to say yes before you even hear the request."

"Is it something about the paintings?"

"No. Something else."

They were staring at each other. "Okay," Joseph said. "The answer is yes."

"Will you take me fishing, son?"

"Oh, God."

"That's right. That's right. I knew you wouldn't let me down."

That night Joseph dreamed he was paralyzed, sitting in his father's wheelchair, and someone was pushing him along the cinder track at the East Mall. They passed in front of the Hirshhorn Museum and Sculpture Garden and the National Air and Space Museum, moving toward the Capitol, huge and white up ahead. The Capitol was being renovated, and in front of it scaffolding rose many stories high. Everywhere the winter grass was tall and green and shifting in the cool breeze. Joseph could hear a calliope, the ancient music lifting clear above the shouts and laughter of children. They veered right and started along Independence Avenue, past the Botanic Garden with its great glass roof flashing in the sun, past enormous gray office buildings and the Library of Congress.

Finally they stopped in the middle of a Capitol Hill street. In the place of row houses and apartment buildings, fields of green and gold now stretched as far as he could see.

"Why have we stopped?" he said.

For some reason he had thought Naomi was pushing him, or perhaps his mother, but then Laura Vannoy stepped around the chair and stood in front of him. She held her hands out. "It's time now, darling."

"Time for what?"

"It's time. Trust me."

"But I can't. I'm not ready."

"Walk," she commanded. "You can do it. Come to me."

Joseph strained to push himself out of the chair. His chest hurt and his legs burned and tears washed down his cheeks.

"Come to me. You can do it."

He began to walk and she moved back, just out of his grasp. He strode forward and she retreated a pace. She walked faster and so did he. Soon they were running, Joseph lagging a short distance behind.

That was all there was to his dream—it lasted just a moment—but he woke suddenly and sat up in bed. Blood beat in his heart and he could still hear the calliope playing in his head. He'd had a wet dream, his first in many years, and the sticky white oyster clung to his shorts and the hair on his lower belly.

It was nearly seven o'clock in the morning, and although he'd been asleep for more than eight hours, he felt as if he'd been up all night. His limbs throbbed as if he had really been running, and his lungs burned for air. He also was crying, and that surprised him more than anything else.

Five

"Something terrible has happened. Something ... oh, God, Joseph!"
They were in the office, standing by the elevators on the fifth floor,
and Alfred's breathing was so labored that he appeared to be on the
verge of hyperventilating. His complexion was a milky purple and
sweat stained the collar of his white cotton shirt. Joseph, long accus-
tomed to seeing his friend behave this way, hardly gave him a second
look. One of the Metro copy aides, however, stopped and asked if
Alfred needed help.

"Can I get you an aspirin or something?"

Alfred shook his head and waved the man on, but seemed genuinely
touched by the offer. "He must be new here. Otherwise he'd have
known better than to talk to me."

If the news was bad, Joseph figured the cafeteria was the best place
to hear it, and so he led Alfred back to the elevators. As he'd often
pledged, one day he would bomb the entire second floor of the *Herald*
building, and every rotten bit of information he had ever gathered
there would vanish in the dust and rubble. "Is it really terrible?" Joseph
said now.

" 'Terrible' 's too nice a word" was the reply.

They might have begun their conversation on the way down had
Harry Delmore, the paper's managing editor, not been present. At the

second floor, as the doors slowly pulled open, Alfred beat his fists against the wall and yelled, "Hurry up, goddammit." Delmore, a genial man whose job was to shadow Cameron Yates and see that his orders were strictly obeyed, did not seem at all bothered. Newspaper reporters were famous for such conduct, and before fifteen years under Yates's thumb had turned him into a eunuch, Delmore had been known to vent his own share of rage. If his smile dissolved now, it was because something in the copy he was reading displeased him.

"Oh, hello, yes," Delmore chirped, stepping out of the car. "I think this is the place." He inhaled some air. "Quite a stench, eh, boys. Well, can't have everything, can we?"

Joseph led Alfred to the table where Jennifer Eugene had informed him of his wife's duplicity. "Sit there," he said, pointing to Jennifer's former seat. Joseph chose his own red plastic chair and fixed his stare on the bank of windows. Down below on L Street, cars were lined up awaiting their turn at a parking garage that promised low rates—$7.50 all day—for early-bird drivers who reported before noon.

"Do you want coffee and a doughnut?" Joseph asked.

"I've got no appetite, but thanks. I don't think you'll want anything either after you hear what I'm going to tell you." Alfred paused and wiped the sweat from his face with his shirtsleeve. "Mr. Big called me into his office this morning, not ten minutes before you got here. He wants me to write again."

"Yates wants you to write again?" Joseph reached over and slapped Alfred on the shoulder. "That's great news, pal—for all of us. Maybe there is hope of a reprieve, after all."

"But that's not why I had to see you. That's not the news."

Joseph sat up in his chair.

"The truth is, I'm afraid to write about anyone but dead people again. I'm afraid because of what happened twelve years ago. You've never been sued, have you, Joseph?"

"Not for libel."

"It isn't much fun, even less so when you've been unjustly charged. Do I look like the kind of person who would fabricate quotes . . . who would stick words in someone's mouth?"

"Not at all, but people file these suits against the *Herald* all the time. Listen, Alfred. Some people seem to think a big outfit like this one would rather settle quickly than get caught up in a long legal battle that'll end up costing it tens of thousands of dollars in attorney's fees alone. Only thing, the *Herald* doesn't settle. Management—and I use that term loosely, it might only be Yates—management wants the public to believe that we're above reproach, that everything we print is golden. It's part of the mystique this place has worked so hard to build over the years. But truth be told, half the time the writers on this staff can't even spell their own names right, let alone those of the people they happen to be writing about."

"You're only trying to make me feel better."

"Maybe I am. But it's also how things are around here. You got sued, so what? Forget about it."

"I got sued by two different parties in two totally unrelated stories I happened to write."

"Just a coincidence. And that was a long time ago. If Yates has asked you to write again, it's clear he hasn't forgotten your value to this place. And neither has anyone else."

"Well, I'm happy in Obits, Joseph. And I told him that. I said I wasn't ready for a transfer."

"The man finally opens your jail door, and you step in deeper."

"He said after twelve years he could no longer justify my salary for the work I was doing, and that he could hire two young reporters who'd interview a steaming pile of horse shit for the money I was making. Then he said something that left me absolutely pale, Joseph."

"What was that?"

"Not to harass the women here, and he was serious—even angry, I would say. And I said, 'What women, Mr. Yates?' He mumbled something I couldn't understand, and then said, 'I think you know.' I said, 'I don't think I do.' But by then I did. He was talking about Jennifer Eugene."

"Jennifer wouldn't—"

"And all I did was ask her out to dinner." He shrugged his shoulders and fingered the wire basket of sugar packets in the middle of the table. "So I told him to go ahead and fire me. But that first I'd like to take my grievance to the Reporters Guild."

"You shouldn't have threatened him with the Guild, Alfred."

"But that isn't even the *news*. That isn't the real reason I brought you here."

Alfred's hands were shaking and his color hadn't improved. Joseph fully expected him to fall over at any moment and perish beneath the glow of the parking-garage neon. Then there would be an obituary to write. No, Alfred had already done that. But there would be the headline: ALFRED CHARLES GIDDINGS I I I, ACE OBITUARIAN, SUCCUMBS AT 41.

"So if you can believe it Yates backed down. You know how he likes to kick his feet up on his typewriter stand and fold his hands on top of his head? Well, he does this for maybe a minute and stares up at the ceiling. He doesn't blink. Finally he leans forward and slaps his hands on the desk. 'Loved your Tanya Golden piece,' he says. 'See ya around, fatso.' And that was it. I told him goodbye and left."

"Brilliant," Joseph said.

"Yes, it was. It was one of my finer moments." But his face still looked desperate. Presently he reached into his pocket and removed an in-house letter addressed to the Obituary desk. He slid it across the table. "It's from Mac."

"Mac?" Joseph pulled the card out of the envelope. "Shall I read it aloud?"

"Yes. I want to hear it. . . . I want to hear the words."

Joseph hesitated, and studied the indelicate scribble. " 'Dear men,' " he began. " 'You are cordially invited to come over to my place tonight after work. We'll have a slide show and tell stories. I already have the projector set up and a sheet on the wall. We'll drink Calvados and smoke some Cubans and I'll entertain with a few nudie pics of women you might know. After the show we'll divide my estate right then and there, so please come in trucks and/or U-Haul trailers.

" 'Alfred, you get all my woodworking tools, Joseph gets what few books I have. If you squires decide to bring flowers, bring chrysanthemums, which everyone knows are most popular at funerals. Very truly yours, Leander McNeese.' "

Alfred yanked the card from Joseph's hands and put it back in his coat pocket. He was more angry than distraught. Joseph, recalling his meeting with Leander in the men's room a few days before, felt his own limbs begin to shake.

"You didn't read with enough emotion," Alfred said. "And you forgot the kicker."

Joseph closed his eyes against the glare of the windows. " 'Ain't nothing but a thang,' " he whispered, reciting the postscript from memory.

"He's talking about some serious shit, you know."

"Is he really, fat man?"

Alfred got up from the table and jogged to the service elevator, his rubber shoes squeaking on the highly polished floor. Joseph rested his face against the window and watched the cars down below on L Street.

It turned out to be a busy day, and of this Joseph was glad. He reported on the deaths of a retired secretary with the Government Printing Office and a Central Intelligence Agency logistics specialist—obits that rated a measly ten inches apiece. For lunch he ate honey-roasted peanuts, a bag of buttered popcorn, and a couple of chocolate bars.

Alfred spoke to him only once, to remind him to keep his stories within budget. Joseph had written several inches long yesterday on a piece about an armored-truck guard who suffered a massive coronary while hauling bags of cash to his vehicle. One of the decedent's co-workers had told Joseph an interesting anecdote relating to the tragedy, and although Joseph had anticipated Alfred's cutting it today, he had deemed the information too extraordinary to ignore.

After the driver slumped to the ground, Joseph had written, an unidentified teenager absconded with a money bag containing nearly five thousand dollars. Less than an hour later the boy was arrested at a sporting goods store in Georgetown after trying to buy merchandise for a gang of five friends, all students at an inner-city high school. Among the items they'd selected were sneakers that sold for a hundred and fifty dollars a pair, designer sunglasses, and sweatshirts with GEORGETOWN HOYAS stenciled in satin across the chest. Earlier the boy had bought several pieces of jewelry for his girlfriend and grandmother, and, for himself, a boom box, an Italian dress suit, and several dozen compact discs. Joseph had called a police captain he knew and had confirmed the report, but Alfred, pecking angrily now at his keyboard, cut these paragraphs and sent Joseph a message via the house computer. "The driver died a perfectly normal death," it said. "It's the thief who lived the abnormal life. We cover the dead, Joseph, not the living. How many times am I going to have to remind you of that?" In a postscript he'd added: "When you die how would you like it if some delinquent stole something of yours and *Herald* Obits gave more space to the theft than to the essential details of your life, i.e., general education, career history, church affiliation, surviving family members?"

Joseph wrote back: "If I were dead, Alfred, I suppose I wouldn't give a good goddamn one way or the other how the *Washington Herald* wrote about me."

Alfred snapped a couple of pencils in half and tossed them against the divider. "Also, Mr. Burke," he typed in reply, "if this business about the thief is so newsworthy, and I don't think it is, it belongs on the desk of a real reporter, not with a fucking *has-been* like yourself."

After reading the message, Joseph grabbed Alfred by the arm, pulled him out of his chair, and walked him back to the canteen.

"It wasn't me who wrote that card," he said. "It was Mac. And another thing, if he does have it, he didn't get it from me. Do you hear what I'm saying, you fat sonofabitch?"

Alfred put his face in his hands and sobbed. "It's all my fault. Forgive me, Joseph. Please."

"Just stop acting like a goddamned baby. I'm sick of it."

About an hour later Joseph received another computer message from Alfred: "Regarding tonight, comrade . . . Can we go together? I'd feel much more comfortable if you wouldn't mind."

6 That evening at around six o'clock, a security guard called Joseph and announced a visitor. On the list of names that immediately came to mind, none was more prominent than Andrea Troy. Since their night together, Joseph had expected her to show up one day at the office and shoot him dead in the middle of the newsroom, or, worse, camp in front of the *Herald* building and via bullhorn announce to the world his inadequacies as a lover.

"Who is it?"

"A Mrs. Vannoy," the guard said.

"Laura Vannoy?"

"That's the one."

Joseph promptly reported to the men's room and splashed water on his face, combed his hair, and pinched the pleat in his pants. The day had left him looking tired and haggard—like someone entirely strange to the sun, he thought, a recluse with no life beyond the confines of a single, windowless room. He drew in a lungful of air and began to jog in place, hoping to get his blood pumping. He lacked rhythm, however, and the pathetic sight of himself in the mirror was almost more than he could bear. After a minute he quit, feeling every bit the fool, and also quite exhausted.

He was walking toward the exit when Cameron Yates emerged from a stall, stuffing the tail of his shirt into his pants. "Saw you through the crack there," Yates said. "This where you usually report for exercise?"

Joseph was too stunned to speak; he merely nodded.

"You must have a date," Yates said. "I've never seen anyone primp so much in all my damn life." He tightened his belt and laughed to himself. "She'd better be worth it, son."

"No date," Joseph said. "I was just freshening up."

Yates stepped back toward the john, lifted his right foot, and kicked the handle. "Okay, Joey. Whatever you say."

After all these years a solo encounter with Yates could still make

Joseph sweat. But then he made everyone sweat. In another life he had been an amateur weight-lifting champion, the best in the world in his intermediate class. He wore smoke-ruined tweeds even in hottest summer, old black wingtips, and skinny belts of exotic animal hides. Yates spent most of the day in conference rooms presiding over meetings with his managing editor, deputy managing editors, assistant managing editors, and deputy assistant managing editors, and lounging in his expansive, glass-walled office crowded with antiques. In Yates's presence, some of his top staffers seemed to forget who they were, their importance, their inviolable place at the *Herald*. Until the Peden affair, Joseph himself was awed by the man everyone called Mr. Big, acknowledging Yates's place in history, his role in the shaping of modern American journalism. People, after all, wrote biographies and made documentary films about men like him; they carved their words into the facades of public buildings. At sixty-two, he had already enjoyed half a dozen wives and now looked ready for half a dozen more. He had partied with movie stars and foreign heads of state and counted former U.S. presidents among his closest friends. "The newsroom of the *Washington Herald* is not unlike a Las Vegas casino," he had once been quoted as saying. "The stakes here are high, folks. And the lights, goddamn them, never dim."

"I just hope she's under twenty-five," Yates was saying now. "Remember we have our reputations to uphold." He stepped forward and peered into Joseph's face. "You weren't planning on reminding me that Jakki's young enough to be my grandchild, were you, son?"

"No sir. I wasn't."

"People do that, meaning well, but it upsets me."

"I don't doubt that, Mr. Yates."

"Jakki can no more change the generation into which she was born than she can the color of her skin."

"No sir. She can't."

When she wasn't entertaining celebrities at their Chevy Chase mansion, Jakki Yates wrote cookbooks that always managed to land on the *Herald*'s list of bestselling nonfiction. In most cities the books barely sold enough copies to rate spots on the shelves, but in Washington booksellers could not keep enough in stock, thanks largely to front-page Book World reviews like the one that ran a few weeks ago. It referred to her latest as "a miraculous achievement . . . must reading for carnivores and herbivores alike . . . should revolutionize the art of the wok."

Yates leaned in closer, inches from Joseph. "My wife, son, you never went with her, did you?"

"I'm afraid I don't understand, Mr. Yates."

"Did you ever go the sweaty distance with my wife, Joey?"

"Sir?"

"Did you tweak her little red nipples?"

Joseph coughed and looked away. "I honestly never knew her, sir, not even to say hello."

"Because you're both very attractive people, and a newsroom is a small place. Things happen."

"I can assure you—"

"Now Mimi Richard, I understand she's moved to New York and married some movie magazine fellow. Whatever went wrong, son?"

Joseph didn't answer.

"Mimi was the kind you might take to the dance—she looked pretty smart with a drink in one hand and a smoke in the other—but she'd never fit in at home with Mama. Her thermostat, as they say, was set a few degrees hotter than the rest of ours."

"I think I get it."

"Not that she was cheap."

"Oh, no."

"She was just fast as a fucking racehorse is all, she liked to run." Yates rocked back on his heels and smiled. "Now answer me this one last question, young man, and speak from the heart. How do you like it over there in Obits?"

"Speaking from the heart, Mr. Yates"—Joseph tapped his chest—"I'd rather write for another section."

"Good. Still dreaming about life off Death Row, are you?"

"I have a few story ideas."

"After disgracing everyone associated with the *Washington Herald*, you're now saying you'd like to come back into the fold and make us proud. Is that what I'm to understand?"

"That's it exactly, sir."

"Glad to hear it. Well"—he clutched Joseph's upper arm, testing the muscularity—"I'm rooting for you all the way."

"I'd be willing to start all over again in Sports, Mr. Yates. I'd write up peewee-league football games, I'd do the monster truck shows at the speedway in Manassas. I'd take any assignment as long as the subject was a living, breathing thing. I'd cover cops, local school boards—I'd even volunteer to do the Capitol Hill party circuit for Lifestyle."

"Don't beg, son. It doesn't well suit a man of your intelligence. And besides, it wasn't me who couldn't keep his pecker in his pants." Yates glanced at himself in the mirror and seemed pleased. He was a newspaper lion and he knew it—he was everything great men were.

"Try to enjoy your present position at the *Herald*, my boy, and make the best of it. Because it looks to me like you've gone and gotten yourself stuck there."

Yates left tapping the walls with his knuckles and whistling "The Battle Hymn of the Republic." He bounced on the balls of his feet, his sinewy calves absorbing the shock, the plates of muscle in his chest lying as flat and hard as they had forty years ago. Joseph waited in the men's room until he could no longer stand the sight of himself in the mirror, then walked to the elevators, pausing for a moment to observe the shameless herd trailing Yates through the maze of desks and cubicles here at the largest-circulation daily the nation's capital had ever known.

"She left maybe a minute ago," the security guard said when Joseph reached the lobby. "Didn't leave no message, neither."

"Did she say anything?"

"Not that I heard."

"Was she walking? Maybe I can catch her."

"She walked in and then she walked out. But like I said, that was a minute ago, maybe two now."

Joseph looked through the glass wall fronting Fifteenth Street. A crush of pedestrians moved along the sidewalk, headed in the direction of the McPherson Square Metro station. Down the street several cabs were waiting in front of the Madison Hotel.

"So I guess I missed her," Joseph said.

"And I guess I'd have to agree with you," the guard said.

It was a long shot but Joseph decided to run outside and search for Laura anyway. Louie Vannoy's Restaurant was on the basement floor of a Connecticut Avenue office building, and she was probably coming from or going there. He took the alley that cut between the *Herald* building and a labyrinthine parking garage, running with his elbows held tight against his rib cage for better balance and locomotion. His tie looped over his shoulder and flapped in the breeze. Delivery trucks and long-bed trailers stood at the *Herald* loading bays, rent-a-cops waiting for trouble, the lazy odor of ink heavy in the air.

Joseph was approaching the rear of the Soviet Embassy when he spotted her up ahead, her tail of hair swinging left to right as she stepped lightly down the broken road. He slowed his pace and tried to straighten his clothes, conscious of the automobile parked near the back fence of the embassy, and the two grim-faced security guards —either Soviet agents or U.S. Secret Service—seated in front. They watched as he drew near, their sunglasses reflecting the fading afternoon light.

"Hello there," Joseph called. "Hey, Laura! Wait up!"

She wheeled around but kept moving, backpedaling. Joseph called out again and she stopped and leaned against the high iron fence that surrounded the embassy.

"Sorry I took so long," he said, catching up. "I ran into Yates in the bathroom and couldn't break away."

"Are you busy now?" she said.

"No, not terribly. But earlier we had quite a rush. My friend Alfred says it's the new spring weather—everybody running around outside, trying to shed the winter lard."

"I was wondering . . . I thought it might be nice to sit somewhere and talk. Have some tea."

"Sure."

"Let's hurry up and get out of this alley. I hate walking here. I have this creepy feeling someone's watching us."

Joseph glanced back at the guards in the car. "Those guys look pretty harmless to me, Laura."

"Not them," she said, then pointed to a camera fixed against the embassy wall, its lens directed at the alley. "The ones inside worry me more. They can probably hear every word we're saying, and I'll bet they're recording it, too."

Joseph stood at the fence and pressed his face against the bars. The tan bricks of the building were coated with dust and grime. All the windows were shuttered, some with missing slats, others supporting pigeon and squirrel nests. A riot of antennae and surveillance tackle rose from the roof.

"Darling, please." She turned to the camera. "He's only showing off for my sake. Joseph . . . *Joseph*, come along."

"*Pravda* on the Potomac," he said as they walked toward Sixteenth Street. "That's what people used to call the *Herald* before Gorbachev came to power."

She blew a wisp of hair from her face and shrugged her narrow shoulders. "I'm afraid you've lost me."

"As if the paper weren't liberal enough, its headquarters occupy the same city block as the Soviet Embassy."

"Oh, yes."

"Late at night, while the city sleeps, our editors meet with their policymakers and hammer out what'll be in tomorrow's paper—in keeping, always, with the old party line."

"Sometimes you newspaper people think too much," she said. "In fact, you think yourselves right out of being funny."

They crossed the street, jaywalking to keep from being hit by a produce truck hustling to make the traffic light.

"Want to stop by the Geographic first?" Joseph said. "We could tour the museum."

"I'm afraid I've already been there."

"You've been there today?"

"I've been everywhere today. I'm so tired of walking, my feet are beginning to feel like old meat." She stopped and adjusted her sandal straps. "Why don't we just go sit somewhere. Do you know the Tabard Inn? Over on N Street?"

"Heard of it."

"Right in the middle of the city, and they like to pretend it's rural Vermont or something."

He saw in her face a sadness that cut straight through him. He reached to hold her hand as they crossed the avenue.

"What's wrong?" he said.

"Nothing."

"Something's wrong, Laura."

She didn't speak for at least a minute. "I'll tell you when we get inside. I'm not up to saying just yet."

At the Tabard they crossed wooden floors that groaned beneath them and inhaled air rich with the fragrance of potpourri. The room was dark except for a single candle burning in a sconce and electric pin lights illuminating the oil paintings that crowded the walls.

They chose an antique settee in the middle of the room.

"Not to be critical," Laura said after they'd ordered coffee. "But some places strain too hard for atmosphere."

"Go ahead. Be critical."

"This couch, for example. I can feel the coils chewing at my backside. When I open my café everyone will be comfortable. How can you enjoy yourself otherwise?"

The waitress brought the coffee and poured two demitasse cups. On each saucer she placed a chocolate mint wrapped in fancy green foil.

"One thing about Louie's," Laura said, "when you went for dinner at least there was enough light to read the menu by. Of course, the meal might've been awful, but you could see it to get at it, know what I mean?"

Joseph was quiet.

"It's a done deal," she said. "We came to terms last night."

"On the restaurant, you mean?"

"Louie's partners want to keep the name and the menu, as if I care. The only thing I was worried about was the staff, and it's staying on, too. I guess I'll spend the next few weeks clearing out Louie's things and saying my goodbyes. As I told you that time at Cities, Joseph, it's yours to write—an exclusive, isn't that what you people call it?"

"I hope this doesn't insult you, Laura, but I doubt that the sale of Louie's will rate the kind of coverage you have in mind."

"Well, that's only partly why I came."

"And what's the other part?"

"To apologize. I was too eager the other night, it was all my fault. On the cab ride home it hit me how pushy I'd been, asking you all those personal questions. I should've just kept my big mouth shut. It's like I didn't know how to act or something."

"I wasn't so great either."

"No, you weren't, but I figure you had an excuse. You had your father to attend to. And you had this idea of yourself all alone in the world, and you had to live up to that."

"I don't remember saying anything about being alone."

She didn't seem to be listening. "Ever notice how many men walk around all by themselves at night? Men like you, darling. They're in trenchcoats, if you'll notice, hands in pockets, eyes cast downward, and they're just out on the streets, walking."

"To be honest, I haven't noticed that."

"They've lost something they know they'll never find and yet they're out looking for it anyway. Or at least that's my theory. They're out looking for the girlfriend who left with some other guy, or for the little-league pitch they struck out on half a lifetime ago, or for some general feeling they once had about themselves and can never have again."

"Maybe they just want some air."

"Maybe. Yes. But more likely not."

"Or maybe they need the exercise."

"You can make fun, darling. Feel free. I know where I come from, and I know how simple a place that is. I might be a little sort of person full of little ideas. But you need to think about something."

"Do I?"

"You need to think about how you got to where you are now, and why you're here and not someplace else."

"I'm here because you came to the office to see me."

"You're here because you ran out into the street to find me. But that's not the here I'm talking about, Joseph, and you good and well know it."

The waitress brought them a bowl of peanuts. "Enjoy," she said, bowing at the waist.

"I hate that," Laura said after the woman was gone. " 'Enjoy.' They're all saying it now. Some years ago they were saying 'Bon appétit.' It was when that Julia Child was all over the TV, that big woman."

Joseph was thinking about lonely men in trenchcoats, himself among them. "When they say what?"

" 'Enjoy.' That word."

Joseph's coffee had gone cold. He put some money on the table and followed Laura outside.

"Do you have to be in love with a woman to have a relationship with her?" she said. "And by relationship I mean go to bed. I mean sex."

"I don't even own a trenchcoat."

"Are we still on that?"

Joseph murmured, "But I wasn't in love with Mary Peden, re-member?"

"That's true. You weren't, were you?"

They walked on, quiet again except for the hollow clopping of Laura's heels on the pavement. They stopped at a street corner and he turned to her with a look of intense surprise. "So, no, Laura, I don't have to be in love. And if my recent behavior is any indication, I don't think I even have to like her very much."

She didn't respond, at least for another couple of blocks. "I guess I don't either," she said. "Because, Joseph, I'll tell you now, I've been with men. Ever since Louie moved out I have—yes, it's true. A number of them."

"That's okay. You're an adult, after all."

"Take a guess how many."

"I'd rather not."

"It's less than five."

He knew she wouldn't let it go until he gave her a number. "Three," he said at last.

"Two, darling. I've been with two, isn't that terrible? And afterward all I could think about was Amelia, getting back home to Amelia. She's mature enough to handle my wicked confessions, but it was being with her that I needed. To be comforted by someone who was mine."

They stopped at a busy intersection and waited for the light to change.

"Let's go get a room," she said.

He didn't answer and she said, "We could go to the Mayflower, it's just up the street a bit."

"The Mayflower, Laura?"

"Forgive me. I don't know why I said that."

"I thought you were being serious."

"I was. Are you disappointed?"

Joseph didn't answer.

"I need to say something here, Joseph, because I promised to always be honest with you. I would love to get a room but the truth is, I saw Santa Claus last night and I haven't been feeling so hot. Now I know that's not very romantic, and it may be an odd thing to say to someone I hardly know, but it's the truth and there's nothing—"

"Who did you see?"

"Is it only in Mississippi they say that? Santa Claus, darling. I started my period."

"Your menstrual period?"

She nodded. "Men are strange about things like that, or most are. They don't like to think that women have periods or go to the bathroom. They know it happens, but they don't want it to."

"I don't think I'm that way."

"I didn't say all men, darling. I said most."

He walked with her the rest of the way to the restaurant. "When you're ready you should call the Business desk and ask for Terry Orton," Joseph said. "Tell him I gave you his name."

"Ready for what?"

"To go public with the news about the restaurant."

She laughed and stepped closer, her face nearly touching his chest. "At first I thought you meant when my period was over and I was ready to be with somebody."

"Terry's a fine editor and a good man, Laura, but he might not be willing to comply. Office gossips say he's gay."

"Sorry, Joseph," she said, pushing through the revolving doors. "I guess I must just have it on the brain."

He stood staring at the building, waiting for her to come back outside and explain herself. "Have what on the brain?" he said, heedless of the people walking past. "You have what, Laura? You have what on the brain?"

She did not come back outside, however. After a few minutes he gave up and started on his way home, making sure to keep his hands out of his pockets, and his head up, lest someone think him lost and all alone in the world.

6 Leander's flat had two bedrooms: one in which he slept, the other in which he worked wood. Since he always dined out in the neighborhood, Leander had turned his kitchen into a darkroom and photo lab. Here he had produced some of the black-and-white images that had earned him more White House Press Awards than any other photojournalist in history. One citation honored a group of pictures he'd shot of Pennsylvania coal miners, another his work showing an archipelago of slums in Soweto, South Africa.

In the dining room, photo equipment lined the tops of work-benches and filled several thirty-five-gallon garbage cans. He brought to all this hardware no particular method of cataloging, and as a result often had difficulty finding something once he'd put it down. For years Joseph had failed to act on his promise to come over and help clean up the place. More than anything he had been daunted by the task, which in his estimation would have required a solid nine-to-five work-week. The few times Joseph had visited, he and Leander had sat on the roof and drunk cognac, smoked cigars, and searched the night sky for constellations.

In his living room, Leander displayed some of the furniture he had constructed himself: a ladder-back chair and church pew, an elaborately carved hutch and sideboard, a coffee table built with hundreds of children's alphabet blocks. In addition to his collection of motorized and hand tools, he had accumulated dozens of antique Stanley Tool Catalogues and Starrett Instructional Guides, some of which he'd framed in glass boxes and had hung on the apartment walls. Periodi-cally over the years, he had visited hardware stores in rural Maryland and Virginia and traded photographs for calipers and breast drills, wood lathes and band saws, miter boxes and drill presses.

He'd once boasted to Joseph that for a "beaver shot" of a television actress—a former girlfriend now residing in Southern California —he'd walked away with a spiral ratchet screwdriver, a file-and-rivet set, a sixteen-pound sledgehammer, and two milk pails galvanized in pure molten zinc.

Tonight, when Leander answered the knock on his door, Joseph was startled to find that he'd cut his hair. The fuzzy goatee had been shaved to reveal a weak chin and upper lip, and his ponytail, for years as thick and bristly as the tail of a fox, had been clipped at the base of the skull. As usual, he was wearing cargo pants and a silver-plated concha belt, a khaki correspondent's jacket, and a pair of black canvas tennis shoes over bare feet.

"Gentlemen," he said, greeting them with handshakes.

He took their coats and hung them on a pegboard. At the center of the room he had placed the alphabet coffee table, on top of which stood an open bottle of Calvados, three snifters, a projector, and a circular tray of Kodachrome slides. On one of the brick walls he had draped a white bedsheet, covering several of the framed catalogues.

"Hey, squires, I've got some shit in the box if you're hungry. Alfred, Joseph, can I get you anything?"

"Why don't you start by telling us what this is all about?" Joseph said.

Leander's demeanor remained as open and relaxed as ever. He laughed as he removed several Cuban cigars from a brown paper bag and clipped the ends. The lighting of the first required considerable concentration, and only after a plume of smoke had risen to the ceiling did he speak. "It's about friendship, I suppose. What the hell else would it be about?"

"Your note was strange, Mac," Alfred said, looking bewildered. "You really scared us."

"Didn't mean it to be strange," Leander said. He blew out his match and handed out cigars. "Promise I didn't."

Generally sedentary, Alfred now shuffled from foot to foot, hands fiddling with the coins in his pockets. "Good," he said, laughing nervously. "Because you really had us going there for a minute, Mac. You know how much I've always admired your tool collection, but *goddamn* . . ."

Leander ignited a match with his thumbnail and held the flame out to Joseph. "Ready?" he said.

Joseph clenched his teeth against the cigar and leaned into the fire, looking past the flame and into his friend's eyes. He was hoping to find a clue.

"Mac had you going, too, didn't he, Joseph?" Alfred said, pouring some of the amber-colored liquid into one of the snifters. His laughter had become so hard and idiotic that he was having trouble keeping his hands steady. "The tension . . . the tension in the office today, it was really high, Mac. I didn't . . . I mean, I really didn't think I'd make it."

Joseph puffed on his cigar. Had either he or Leander moved his head an inch to the left, the cherry-red tips of their smokes would have touched.

"Worst practical joke anyone ever pulled on me," Alfred was saying. "It just plain wasn't funny."

Leander took the cigar out of his mouth and flicked it against the side of a glass tray. "Why don't we order something from Young Chow?" He handed the telephone to Alfred. "I want steamed dumplings and orange beef."

Alfred looked at Joseph.

"Moo shu chicken for me. Two extra pancakes."

"Since you're treating, Mac, I guess I'll have to go with the Peking duck. That okay with you?"

"Fine," Leander said, rolling the cigar around in his mouth. "Anything in this world you want, fat man."

After Alfred ordered, Leander turned on the projector, throwing a square of light onto the sheet. "I thought we'd get started," he said. "For somebody just reaching middle age, it's been a relatively full life. I've got lots of pictures to show."

Unlike Alfred, Joseph was not yet sure about their friend, and although he'd considered asking him directly, he now decided against it. This was real life, after all, not newspapering. While real life required compassion and solicitude, newspapering called for fearlessness and indifference. Had Leander been the subject of a story Joseph was reporting, he would have had no choice but to pose the question unambiguously: Do you have it, Mac? And the effrontery would have been justified. One, he was a reporter with a deadline to make. Two, the public interest was being served. Three, it was newsworthy. Four, an assistant managing editor had assigned him the story and in order to stay employed he needed to get at the truth.

Leander put the Kodachrome tray in place and asked Alfred to turn off the lights. "If you squires want to take notes on any of this," he said, punching up an image of a naked baby, "you'll have to use the reflection or come sit closer to the projector. For point of record, I didn't shoot the family stuff—the ones of me as a kid and my family. Everything else, though, is mine."

In the picture, the infant was lying on a picnic blanket, looking perfectly ordinary. A straw basket lay open on the grass next to an old-time football with strings laced from one pointed end to the other. "My mother loved cameras," Leander began. "She took this when I was three months old. You can see the focus is off a little. But not bad for an amateur."

He flicked to a picture of his mother, a sickly looking woman with bags under her eyes. Her dress was a floral print, tight across the belly. "She died when I was six," he said. "I really can't remember her. Sometimes I try to get her voice back, but it won't come. Other times I try to get her smell back, but nothing. She had diabetes. Her pancreas just burned out, I suppose. They found her in a bathroom at work. She was a secretary for a liquor importer. She was of German stock, a Heinzen. In the basement of our house she brewed her own beer."

The next picture was of his father and only brother, Jim. The elder McNeese was a short man with black hair and a broad grin. He was standing in front of a ginkgo tree aflame with yellow leaves. Since both Jim and Mr. McNeese were squinting, Joseph figured the sun was behind the photographer. His curly hair notwithstanding, Jim bore an uncanny likeness to Leander. They had the same facial structure, the same chin and lip. And neither seemed to have a concern in the world.

"My father was an engineer. His area of expertise was nuclear power. When I was a boy we moved all over the country while he directed the construction of those plants that every few years show up in the news. He was a scientist, and I hated him."

Alfred interrupted. "You hated him?"

"I hated him," Leander said. "When I was thirteen—this was long after my mother died—we were living in Vermont. He had fallen in love with another woman, her name was Joan something, and me and my brother and the two of them were driving along this mountain road. It'd been snowing for days, a blizzard really, and we had no business being out there. I saw maybe two cars, not counting those that'd died up on the shoulder. All of a sudden this drift came down and hit the passenger side. We started to flip over, but then bounced back square. We had turned completely around, though, and were on the other side of the road. The car wouldn't start, so my father gave Jimmy five dollars and told him to walk with me up to town, which was several miles away. It took maybe two hours to get there, and then another thirty minutes to find help, a man who worked at a feed store."

Leander was staring at the picture of his father and brother. His jaw quivered and his eyes narrowed. He started to shake his head. "Am I boring you guys?"

"No," Alfred said. "Go on."

"This man, this fellow from the feed store . . . he drove us to his farm and saddled up a couple of horses. Me and Jim on one, him on the other. By the time we got up the road, more snow had slid down from the mountains. The place where the car had been was now a snowbank but you could make out an outline beneath it. Jimmy went crazy and ran to the spot and started digging. The man tried to pull him back but he wouldn't stop. I just stood and watched. To be honest, I really didn't feel anything. 'Ain't nothing but a thang,' this fellow from the feed store kept saying. I knew they couldn't be alive down there. 'Ain't nothing but a thang,' he said. Eventually some help came, and when they got through the snow they found them holding on to each other, my father and Joan, both sort of smiling. They were dead."

Leander flicked to a picture of a young man no more than twenty-five years old. He was wearing jeans and a letterman's jacket and his hair was cut short. "This is Jim," he said. "After my father died we went different ways—to foster homes. About ten years later I was shooting a college football game in Wisconsin, I was down on the sidelines, you know, and I kept hearing somebody call my name up in the stands. I turned to look and there he was, this guy you're seeing here. He said, 'Are you Leander McNeese?' And that surprised me. I didn't recognize him and kept trying to place him. 'Yeah,' I said. 'My name's McNeese. Who are you?' So the guy begins to laugh. You see that jacket he's wearing? He turns and wipes his nose on the sleeve, and if you look close you can see it in the frame." Leander stood and pointed to the place. "I say again, 'Who are you?' Because I really don't know. 'I'm Jim,' he finally says. 'Your brother.' And that's when I took the picture. I used the Leica. You can tell by the quality. But I never saw him again. I hollered that I had to get back to work, and that was it. Now whenever I'm assigned to shoot a game I look around thinking he'll be there."

By the time the food arrived Leander was deep into the photographs depicting his life and career as a general assignment news photographer. Alfred sorted out the paper cartons and chopsticks, and they ate while the slide show continued. There were pictures of Leander's travels around the world, of cities such as Addis Ababa, Cairo, Kuwait City, and Hong Kong, and of people rich and poor, corpulent and emaciated, dead and alive. Leander had found in Afghanistan, Nicaragua, and Washington, D.C., what others had looked for in Vietnam. There were also pictures of life in the United States—of football games and mountain ranges and space shuttle launches and marches for and against abortion. There were some of hurricanes and volcanoes and earthquakes and car crashes; and of arid deserts and smoky blue mountains, of back alleys and crack houses. And for each slide Leander had a story to tell. When with his remote control he punched up a dated picture of Alfred Giddings, for example, he said, "This is one of my best friends in the whole world. He comes from Pittsburgh, the son of a millionaire industrialist."

"Move on, move on," Alfred said.

Leander raised a hand to silence him. "His tale begins at his birth, which his mother did not survive—"

"Keep her out of it," Alfred interrupted.

"For years his father walked their great house, cursing God under his breath, kicking furniture—"

"Not furniture," Alfred said, "walls, he kicked the goddamn walls. And it was me he cursed, not God. If you're going to tell it, Mac, tell it right."

Leander cleared his throat. "When Alfred was six, his father sent him off to a tweedy New England prep school where everyone wore blazers and bow ties to class."

"Twelve years," Alfred said. "The only time he let me come home was at Christmas and a few weeks over the summer. Never at Easter or Thanksgiving. He didn't want me."

Leander was looking at the picture on the wall. "When Alfred quit law school to become a newspaperman, his father—"

"Disowned him," Alfred said. "But enough." He waved his chopsticks at the sheet. "Next slide."

Leander ate some rice. "I first met Alfred about fifteen years ago. I was new to the paper and had been assigned to shoot a picture of some artist freak Alfred was writing about for Lifestyle. Am I right, fat man?"

"Right."

"After the interview we went to Louie Vannoy's for an early dinner—"

"You went to Louie's?" Joseph said.

"I liked the pickles and bread there, and always got a good table. This was the late seventies, I think, and Alfred was into leisure suits. He had more leisure suits than anyone on the fifth floor. Back then the *Herald* had a dress code, and Yates used to ask him to trim his sideburns, which were cut like muttonchops. But our friend was a trendsetter and he refused to shave." Leander stood next to the sheet and pointed to the picture of Alfred. "As you can see, he still had hair and he hadn't gone soft yet. He was young and brilliant, and, like a lot of people who are young and brilliant, he thought he would stay that way forever."

Leander switched to a recent picture of Joseph typing at his keyboard. "Joseph Burke was too pretty to be a man," Leander said. "That's what the women at the office used to say. When he was writing for Sports he would walk into a press box and everything would go silent. That's because sportswriters are a bunch of slobs. Give them cold hot dogs and root beer and they think it's Sunday dinner at the Jockey Club. Joseph didn't fit in with the scribes, so they punted him over to Lifestyle. As Alfred can attest, the women there keep running counts of their orgasms and the men file their nails. They're insulted when you call them reporters. They think of themselves as *writers*—or, worse, *artists*—and news doesn't interest them. They do 'think pieces.'" Leander paused for a bite of one of the steamed dumplings. "Take the movie critic who would be Joseph's wife—"

"Ex-wife now," Joseph said. "And what the hell does she have to do with me anyway?"

"Let Mac say what he wants," Alfred said. "He didn't make me look so good, either."

"Joseph got a bum deal," Leander continued. "Remember where you heard it first." And before Joseph or Alfred could respond, he switched to a black-and-white picture of a nude woman lying on a rumpled bed, her face obscured by a blanket of hair. Her legs were bent, her knees pulled up against her chest, and from off camera someone was tickling the crack of her ass with either a goose or turkey feather. "Recognize her?" Leander said.

"It isn't Mimi, is it, Mac?"

"Why on earth would it be Mimi?"

Both Joseph and Alfred stood and stepped closer to the wall, but this only blurred the image. "Is this one eminently fuckable, boys?" Leander said. "Or am I just yanking my dick?"

"Who is she?" Alfred said.

"I'll give you a hint," he answered, and flicked to a color portrait of the woman, still nude. "Her first name is Jakki, and these days she's married to the executive editor of the paper you two hopeless fucks work for. But back when I knew her she was a nobody reporter for the Food section, still new to the wonders of the wok, but, as you might've guessed, a seasoned veteran at a few other things."

Joseph and Alfred shouted happily and pounded their feet on the floor, producing the kind of stupid noise Leander no doubt expected of them. He finally quieted them by advancing to a nude photograph of a man.

"This is a friend of mine I wanted you two fellows to meet."

The man was standing in front of a canvas screen covered with black and blue swirls. Fair-complected and neatly built, he appeared to be in his late twenties. Veins were visible on his chest and arms. His teeth were yellow and badly formed. His penis, long and gray, was a shade darker than the rest of his flesh.

"Move on," Alfred commanded.

The next slide showed the same man. In this pose he had cupped his hands over his penis, not to hide it but to lure the eyes of the viewer. It seemed an even more concupiscent portrait than the first. With clothes on, Joseph thought, this was someone he would pass on the street without noticing if not perhaps for the strength of his jaw, the confidence of his stride, the scent of his cologne.

"Next," said Alfred. "Come on, Mac. Move it."

Leander ate more rice. "Shall I tell you about him?"

"Tell us," Joseph said. "Tell us everything, Mac. Who is he? What's his name?"

"Name's Duane. I met him . . ." He paused to swallow. "I shot him for a Magazine piece. About this gay group at Georgetown University." He sounded winded, as if he'd just climbed a flight of stairs. "That was . . . what, Joseph, four years ago now."

"I remember the piece," Joseph said.

Alfred slapped his hands together. "Can we move on? I mean it, Mac."

"But he's a friend," Leander said. "I want to look at him."

"Fine," Alfred said. "But look at him after we've gone."

The next shot was of Leander sitting on the steps leading to the Northwest D.C. chapter of the American Red Cross. The yellow brick building stood between a restaurant called Bradshaw's and an antique lamp shop. A sign next to the door greeted visitors in Spanish. Seeing Leander as he'd looked only a few days ago disarmed Joseph for some reason. He could feel a quickened thudding in his chest and his face got hot. Leander's hair snaked over his shoulder and touched the mouth of his shirt pocket.

"I had Charlotte shoot me with the Rolleiflex," he said. " 'This is forever,' she kept saying." He stared at the image, studying it as if it were of someone else.

"You look good, Mac," Joseph said.

"Yeah."

Alfred reached over and took the remote control from Leander's hands. "Next slide," he said, and changed it himself, flashing a frame of cold white light onto the sheet.

"Too bad," Leander said. "All done."

Alfred punched up another square of light, then another. Finally, he came to the first of the images, the one showing Leander as an infant lying on a picnic blanket.

"I was thoroughly bored," Alfred said, hopping up off the floor. He put on his coat. "Thanks for the drinks and dinner, though." Joseph saw that he was about to cry. His eyes were glassy and his skin a chalky alabaster. He moved from foot to foot, his hands busily digging in his pockets. "I'll be seeing you, Mac. Come here and tell me goodbye."

Leander stepped up and Alfred threw his arms around him. They embraced for a moment and broke apart, then embraced again. "Goddammit," Alfred said, tears beginning to fall now. "Goddammit, goddammit, goddammit. I'll be seeing you, Mac."

"Okay. See you later, Alfred."

After he was gone, Leander asked Joseph if he wanted to finish off the cigars and the Calvados up on the roof. "The stars look good tonight. I've got this telescopic lens in a barrel somewhere. How about we take it with us?"

Joseph checked his watch and groaned. "The old man's alone. I really should be going."

"I'm glad you came," Leander said. "I had to tell you and the fat man sooner or later. I feel better now."

"Do you have it, Mac?"

"I don't know, to be honest. What I meant is Duane."

"Did you get your test results today?"

"Chickened out. Flat couldn't do it."

"Does Duane have it?"

"Don't know that, either. Haven't seen him in months."

"It was just something you tried, right?"

"Tried," he said, "and liked. But I only went with Duane, and only a few times."

"Maybe I should call Alfred and tell him not to worry. He won't sleep tonight thinking you're going to die."

"I'll call him. First thing in the morning." Leander opened the door and followed Joseph out onto the landing. "Will you remember what I told you, Joseph? And never forget it?"

"I won't forget it," he answered. "Never." But about halfway down the stairs, Joseph turned on his heels and was about to say something when Leander cut him off.

"You got a bum deal," he said, then slammed the door shut without another word.

Down on the street, a line of people had formed outside La Fourchette. Joseph gazed up at the windows of Leander McNeese's apartment and saw everything blink to darkness. A cab pulled up to the curb and an elderly couple got out. They were holding hands. The driver left the door open but Joseph waved him on.

It was a cool night, and Leander had been right about the stars. They were out in force, small darts above the haze.

W Woody was on the veranda when Joseph got home. "Someone's here to see you," he said, speaking quickly so as to get it over with. "She's in the den. I went ahead and told her to make herself comfortable."

Joseph climbed the steps and put his hands on his father's shoulders. "Is it Andrea Troy?"

"Who's Andrea Troy?" Woody leaned back in his chair and glanced out the bay window. "It's Mimi. She called and said it was urgent. I told her to come over right away."

Joseph closed his eyes and ran his hands through his hair. He wished he'd stayed over at Leander's. They could be on the roof now, getting drunk, blowing cigar smoke into the heavens.

"If I was wrong to let her come, Joseph, we can talk about it later. I'll apologize then."

"I don't expect you to apologize."

"Not now you don't. But you might after you see her."

They entered the den and Naomi rose from the couch and offered Joseph her hand. "Hans is in L.A. on business," she said. "I'm staying with Mom and Dad over at Highland Place."

"What's so urgent, Mimi?"

"Did I say something was urgent?"

"Father says you did."

She looked at Woody and laughed. "Why are you always putting lies into this boy's head, Woodrow?" She turned back to Joseph. "I did call to speak to you and when Woody invited me over—trust me, Joseph, he said you'd gone out for the night—I thought it might be nice to get some air. Plus, the Wood man and I had some catching up to do."

"I must've misunderstood what you were saying," Woody said. "I did think, though, that you used the word *urgent*."

"Hans'll be gone for a couple of weeks. And I thought, pregnant and all, I should be with family—in case of an *e-mer-gen-cy* or something. Maybe you got the words mixed up."

"Urgent and emergency. Since the wreck, it's not just my legs that've gone out of whack." Woody started rolling toward the sewing room. "If you two need anything," he said, "just holler."

"Thank you for being such a gracious host," Naomi called after him. "And so sorry again about Cleo." She blew him a kiss. "I hope your legs get better."

After Woody had disappeared into the sewing room, Joseph said, "He complains a lot, but he's never said a word about the accident. Did he tell you anything?"

"He talked about fishing, mostly."

"And what about Mother?"

"Only that he'd heard I didn't attend the funeral. I think it was his reason for inviting me over. He wanted to distribute some of the guilt that's kept him down all these months."

"The day we buried her," Joseph said, "he sat here at home, watching the park through his binoculars."

"Yes, well . . . I reminded him that at least I had an excuse—stuck up in New York and all—whereas from what I'd been told, the only reason he had for staying away was stuck up in his head."

"You never did mince words, did you, Mimi?"

"Words, no," she replied, and began to walk about the room in the fashion of certain runway models, her chin held down, arms akimbo. She spun around. "What do you think of Mimi in maternity clothes, Joseph? Can you believe I'm actually pregnant?"

"I can now."

"I tell you, I've never felt so alive."

Her every step suggested poise and not a little ballsiness. She was bad in the best sense, and good in the worst. Her limbs, he noted, were heavier than before. And her hair was shorter, her face fuller, her middle huge. A full six months into her pregnancy, however, and it was clear that she remained totally confident of her beauty. If she was unlike everybody else, he told himself now, it was only in that she believed herself superior to them. She would always win and never lose.

"I haven't told you about Europe yet, have I?"

"No. No, you haven't, Mimi."

"Hans and I got back last week and then he was off again."

"Well, I'm glad you had a good trip."

"Who said anything about a good trip? It was great." When he didn't respond, she said, "In London we stayed near Soho Square in this charming little hotel—Hazlitt's, it was called; Mrs. Newtigate's room—that was ours. Through the wall we could hear our neighbors making love." Her voice had suddenly gone British. "Hans and I cuddled in our bed, under all these wonderful down blankets, and when the guests next door said 'oh,' we said 'ah.' They said 'no,' and we said 'yes.' This went on for maybe thirty minutes, and then the woman, our neighbor . . . she started to blurt the word 'fuck' every few seconds. She was approaching climax, I presume. And guess how we answered?"

"I wouldn't know."

"We said 'you,' of course. Show some imagination." She giggled and sat back down on the couch. "Then later in Paris we were typical tourists. We ate baguettes and leeks and roasted chestnuts and drank café crèmes and aperitifs. We visited the museums and the bookstalls along the Seine. At night we took a taxi through Pigalle—that's the red-light district, Joseph, not unlike this part of D.C.—and yelled obscenities at the whores. It was all very Hemingway."

"I bet."

"Then in Spain we went to the bullfights—"

"Mimi?"

"I'm talking about my trip, Joseph."

"Yes, but I'm tired now."

She didn't seem to hear him. "Guess what I liked best about Europe. Or rather, what I remember most vividly."

"I'm sorry that Woody asked you to come here. I really think you should be going now."

"The *light*, the quality of the light. That's what."

He didn't respond.

"Did you and I ever have phone sex, Joseph? I can't remember."

". . . What?"

"Phone sex. I can't remember if we had it."

He waited a moment before answering. "You know we did."

"Because tonight when Hans called . . . well, it was pretty amazing. I kept thinking, though, that someone was listening. You know how sometimes conversations other people are having drift over the line and you can hear them?" Suddenly she was quiet, staring at the magazines on the coffee table. "You ever think about how we used to be, Joseph?"

"Why, Mimi? Why do this?"

"Just tell me, Joseph. Tell me how we used to be."

"My father's down the hall."

"What are you trying to say? Is it because I'm pregnant?"

"Mimi, you really should be going now."

"But Hans loves me like this and so do I. There's a human being inside of me, Joseph. And what . . . and what, I ask, could possibly be a greater thrill for a man than to see his wife like this?" She folded her hands over her belly.

"Can I walk you to the door?"

"Yes. You can walk me. And you can get me a cab. You, your father, this neighborhood, this house . . . God, it depresses."

He held the front door open and followed her out onto the veranda. The night was cool and breezy and he was glad to be outside again.

"I don't mean to screw up your head," she said. "I just get lonesome sometimes, I miss you."

"I see one coming."

"I'd almost forgotten how handsome you are. And seeing you, I guess, just stirs it all up again." She brushed back some hair from his face. "Oh, Joseph."

"I've met someone," he said. "Laura Vannoy. Do you know her? Her husband ran Louie's . . . he *was* Louie."

She thought about it. "Tall girl? Sort of talks like she's got gravel in her mouth?"

"She's from Mississippi."

"I remember her. I thought she was his daughter until someone told me different." She laughed. "I would think she'd be good for you, Joseph. A widow and an obit writer—my lord, I bet you two have lots of fun things to talk about." She kissed him and got into the cab. "The dead counseling the dead. Now isn't that the coziest arrangement I ever heard. . . ."

Back in the house, Woody had parked himself in the middle of the den and was practicing his cast with an imaginary rod and reel. His tackle box, cocked open, lay on the floor next to him.

"Why'd you do that to me?" Joseph said, locking the door behind him. "Why'd you ask her to come here?"

"I don't know. It was wrong. But I think about her a lot, too, you know." He was still holding his pretend pole, waiting for a strike. "Like I said earlier, son, I'm sorry."

Joseph picked up the binoculars from the coffee table and stood at the bay window. He focused on the park.

"From here on out," Woody said, "I call her Naomi. No more of this Mimi business. It's too personal."

"You can call her whatever you like. I don't care about that. Just don't ever invite her here again."

"Nope. It's Naomi—Naomi all the way." Woody pulled the blanket off his legs and threw it on the floor. "I wanted to show you something. You remember that little tingle I was having? Now get a load of this." And he began to wiggle his toes.

Joseph lowered the glasses and stared at him. "That's amazing, Father. When did they come back?"

"Earlier, when Marissa was here. She asked me to wait until tomorrow to show you. She wanted to see your response, but I just couldn't take it any longer. The anticipation was too much."

"I'm proud of you, Father. But I still won't be happy until I see you walk."

Woody clutched the sleeve of Joseph's shirt. "And I'm proud of you, son," he said.

Joseph offered the binoculars to Woody. "Here. Take them."

"Doesn't interest me anymore. But thanks."

"What do you mean it doesn't interest you?"

"Just that."

Joseph started to laugh.

"Want to know what does?" Woody said.

"Marissa. Marissa Christiani interests you."

"Yes, she does, Marissa most certainly does. But so does fishing. And you've promised me a trip. When do we go?"

"How about next week?"

"Let's make it Sunday. Pete Peters has a boat. A seventeen-footer with a hundred-horsepower Evinrude. It's one of those fancy bass rigs, has a live well, two casting decks, room for four. Says it's ours to borrow if ever we want it."

"I work tomorrow. And this week Sunday's my only day off."

"There's nothing better for a man than to fish on his day off. *Nothing.* I thought we'd hit Hains and Greenleaf and Buzzard points. Maybe skate on down the Washington Channel past the marina and try around this bridge I know. We can pack a lunch."

"Pardon me, Father. But I was thinking more along the lines of standing on a bridge or a roadside and casting from there."

"That's not fishing!" Woody roared. "That's baseball."

Joseph raised the glasses to his face and peered out at the park. Towering over the bums on benches he saw the figure of General Logan, a hundred years dead, green now with age.

"I'll go Sunday," Joseph said, "but only if you promise to let me sleep late. Don't set any alarms, either. Promise that. And if I feel like coffee and the paper don't rush me."

"We'll leave at noon."

"See there? You're already setting a time."

"We'll have to invite Marissa over," Woody said. "Get her to cook whatever we catch. Fry those babies up."

"Sounds grand," Joseph said, and watched as his father unleashed another imaginary cast toward the fireplace.

⟪ *Six* ⟫

Marissa called early the next morning when Joseph was in the guest room dressing for work. Woody picked up the phone in the den at the same time Joseph answered upstairs.

"I wonder will you be home in next hour?" she said. "I cook a surprise and bring it over."

"The boy may not be around," Woody said, "but I will. Look for me out on the veranda."

"Since when am I the boy?" Joseph said. He was standing in the hallway, a damp bath towel wrapped around his middle.

"I'm the man, you're the boy," Woody answered. "It's always been that way."

"You talk," Marissa said. "I will come later. This morning my husband Frederico fall and hurt his back."

"I hope it isn't serious," Joseph said.

"Not too much," she said, then added, "I can come but not stay long. Fred needs me very much."

"Another body to push around in a wheelchair," Woody remarked. "I'm sorry to hear that, my love."

"He walk fine. He only sprain it." Her voice became muffled as she covered the phone and spoke to someone in the room with her. "I need to go. Goodbye, Woodrow. Joseph."

"Maybe we should go into the wheelchair business," Woody said, laughing. "What do you think, Marissa?"

But she had already hung up.

About an hour later Marissa arrived carrying a large platter and immediately rushed back to the kitchen. Woody closed the front door and wheeled behind her, shouting, "Come on downstairs, son, before your breakfast gets cold."

Although Joseph had not grown up here, he felt as if he were a child again, getting ready for school—"the boy," as Woody had called him. When he'd go into the kitchen Woody would be at the table reading the newspaper and commenting on one world disaster or another. Cleo would be standing over a skillet, humming along to the radio as she watched strips of pork turn from pink to white to brown.

Suddenly the smell of cheese and seafood reached Joseph and a hollow ache struck at the pit of his stomach. He thought he might need the toilet again, but finally the sensation passed. When he entered the kitchen, Marissa was leaning over the sink, running cold water over her hands. "I burn them on the handles," she explained, greeting him with a smile.

Woody had tucked a paper napkin into the front of his pajama top and was brandishing a piece of cutlery in each hand. His triumphant grin discouraged Joseph from warning him against eating too heavily at this time of day. Marissa, filling a plate with enchiladas, took care to choose the meatiest of the bunch.

"When did you cook all this?" Joseph was peering over her shoulder at the platter. "They look like the real thing."

"I get up early, about five o'clock. Fred was up all night, no sleep. Me and my Sonny and Louise make them."

"Those're her kids," Woody said.

"I know who they are."

Marissa placed the plate on the plastic mat in front of Woody and added salt and a teaspoon of sour cream, then took Woody's knife and fork and cut up the food herself.

"King Farouk," Joseph said.

"That's me."

Marissa started to heap enchiladas onto another plate. "This is for you, Joseph. You eat now."

"Please," he said, patting his belly. "None for me. But I'd appreciate it if you saved some for when I get home tonight."

"Probably won't be any left by then," Woody remarked.

Marissa wiped her hands on a towel. "I go check on the kids now," she said. "Be right back. Two minutes."

"She left them in the car," Woody told Joseph.

"You should've brought them in," Joseph said. He chased after her to the front of the house. "Marissa, for heaven's sake, invite them in. I'll put on the television."

After conferring with the children, Marissa led them up the walk to the veranda. They were wearing knit sweaters and caps even though it was warm out.

"Make yourselves at home, kids," Joseph said at the door. "Sit back, take your shoes off. How 'bout an enchilada?"

"They full like ticks," Marissa said. "No way."

Joseph removed the mess of sporting magazines from the couch and the children sat next to each other with their hands folded in their laps, knees pressed together. In the sunlight from the bay window their hair shone thick and black.

Marissa returned to the kitchen and presently she and Woody plunged into an animated discussion about the origin of the enchilada recipe. Through the open doorway Joseph saw his father lean forward and lightly press his mouth against the side of her face. Marissa bowed her head, humbled by his show of affection.

Joseph, suddenly feeling queasy again, turned his head away.

"So what do you want to watch?" he said to the children. "You folks like Bugs Bunny?"

Sonny and Louise continued to stare at the floor, too timid or intimidated to look at him.

"How about Ninja Turtles? You want to watch the turtles?"

Neither said a word.

Joseph switched to a local station playing old Popeye cartoons and sat next to them on the couch. "This is wonderful stuff," he said. "They don't make 'em like this anymore. Everything here was drawn by hand, every last detail. These days it's all computerized."

A few minutes later Marissa pushed Woody into the room, and the children came alive. Joseph, too, sat up straight.

"Tell Mr. Joseph what you learn in first grade," Marissa said to Sonny, who covered his face with his hands. "He learn the pledge. He can say it all by himself, no help."

Woody cleared his throat and threw his right hand over the red-stained napkin hanging from his shirt. "I pledge allegiance to the flag," he began with his chin set forward, "of the United States of America. And to the republic for which it stands . . ."

Tears traced down Louise's face; Sonny's lips paled.

"They just shy," Marissa said in the middle of Woody's declaration. "Like their papa."

Woody finished and said, "Maybe Joseph spooked them. I know sometimes looking at him spooks me, too."

The kids started to giggle, but then stopped themselves. It was clear they had determined not to let their guard down.

"Okay!" Marissa said, clapping her hands. "To the car and wait. I right behind you." She pointed to the door and the children hopped to their feet and scrambled outside.

"Please, don't leave," Woody said, wheeling over to block the way. "You just got here. It's early yet."

"My Fred needs me," Marissa said.

Woody reached into his pocket and removed a wad of cash. "Here," he said, holding out the money. "Call and tell him to get his own nurse. I'll pay. Whatever you need, Marissa."

"Oh, Woodrow."

"Please, Father," Joseph said.

Woody tried to press the money into Marissa's hand, but she stepped back and stood behind a chair, creating a cushion between them. Through the window Joseph could see the children running circles around the car.

"What's that you're driving?" Joseph said.

She didn't answer.

"What kind of car, Marissa?"

"Blue with a white top," she mumbled. "No air-conditioning, though. It gets very hot."

"I meant the model."

"Lay off," Woody said. "The thing got her here, didn't it?"

She stepped in front of the chair and placed her hands on Woody's shoulders. "Save some food for Joseph. Okay?"

"Don't leave," Woody pleaded. "I need you here."

The children were yanking the door handle. "Their father fell and hurt his back. I see you next week." She leaned forward and brushed her cheek against Woody's. "Let's say Wednesday. I bring dough-nuts, okay?"

"Wednesday's too far away," Woody said. "Tomorrow." He pulled the napkin from his shirt, balled it up, and threw it at her. "Me and Joseph are going fishing in the morning and we want you to come."

"Tomorrow is Sunday. We have Mass and the children catechism. Next week, Woodrow. Please. If Fred is no better I will take him to emergency room."

"How can you leave me for him, Marissa?"

"Woodrow, I must go." Her voice sounded tired and weak. "He has hurt his back, not bad. But still—"

"Mine's worse. My legs are gone. I'm paralyzed, for Chrisake!" His face was red, angry. "Can he walk?"

She grasped the crucifix at her chest. "Bye, Joseph. See you later. Woodrow, goodbye, my friend."

She crossed the veranda and was descending the steps when Woody called after her, "*Tomorrow*, Marissa. We leave at noon." But she kept walking, eyes focused on the children.

After they were gone, Woody leaned back in his chair and screamed long and hard. Pigeons flew in every direction and a big stray cat, who'd been playing under the high bank of steps at the Grant house, darted into the traffic circle, barely avoiding an oncoming vehicle. The more Joseph tried to calm his father, the more noise he made. Finally Joseph gave up and returned to the guest room to finish dressing. By the time he came back down, everything in the neighborhood appeared to have returned to normal. The benighted were slouching under the maples and pin oaks, eyeing the pigeons hungrily. The cat was playing nearby in the weeds. Woody was now sitting quietly in his chair, wheeled close to the banister. And for the first time in days, he was staring through the binoculars.

"I should be home by six o'clock unless somebody important dies. Do you hear me, Father?"

Woody maintained his grip on the binoculars. "Death never takes a holiday, son. Remember that."

"I will," Joseph said, bounding down the steps. On the sidewalk he stopped and turned back around. "Hey, Father, the other day you said you weren't interested in those things anymore. Why'd you change your mind?"

"This neighborhood is what happened," Woody said. "Somebody's got to keep an eye on it."

"And that's the only reason, right?"

Woody's eyes remained hidden. "Just go to work, son."

For the most part, weekend mornings at the *Herald* were quiet and uneventful. Until noon only about a dozen editors inhabited the fifth floor, and they spent less time editing copy and watching the news wires for breaking stories than reading back issues of *Spy* magazine and planning lunch. Occasionally a staff writer appeared, there to call family and friends long-distance on the WATS line or to check if anyone dared change the lead or tinker with the narrative rhythm of his latest effort. The atmosphere was more relaxed now than during the week, mainly because Cameron Yates wasn't around to remind everyone that newspapering was the relentless search for truth, and that truth could only be found by charging into the day with fists clenched and raised.

Weekend mornings were Joseph's favorite time to work. Back in the days when he was regarded as a star, he had produced some of his best writing in the hours before the afternoon crowd showed up and kicked off its daily exercise of chronicling the adventures of the city's mayor, homicide detectives, sports teams, and, as Yates had once written in a memo to his assistant managing editors, "the one or two other things that seem to matter around Chocolate City these days."

This morning Joseph and Alfred arrived at the office at the same time, flashed their I.D. cards to the security guard, and rode up in an elevator together.

"Guess who called about half an hour ago," Alfred said.

"Leander McNeese."

"Never even got his test results, after all. Probably doesn't have it. Probably is as healthy as you and me."

"Don't sound so disappointed, Alfred."

The door opened and they walked to Obituaries.

"I started work on 'Frady' yesterday afternoon," Alfred said, "but I'm afraid it's yours now. I considered letting Nate and Tinker do it tomorrow, but they'd only screw it up."

"You're the boss," Joseph said.

Charles P. Frady of Rectortown, Virginia, was a retired diplomat with the U.S. State Department who accidentally shot himself while trying to scare a couple of groundhogs away from his broccoli patch. He'd missed the animals entirely but had managed to absorb a round from his .22-caliber pistol in the head.

"It's all here," Alfred said, handing Joseph a yellow legal pad full of notes. "I've done most of the reporting, I just won't be able to write it."

"I'll have a printout on your desk by noon."

Alfred ran his hands over his bare scalp. "Don't you want to know why I won't be able to write it?"

"I figured you'd tell me when you were ready."

"Urban rage," he said.

"Come again?"

"I'm writing a piece on urban rage for Perspective," he said, refer-ring to the Sunday-only section that included political essays, letters-to-the-editor, and cartoons. "I pitched the idea to Harry Delmore, who in turn ran it past Yates. Yates called me into his office and said rage was something he knew about, and then proceeded to shout at me for tracking up one of his goddamn antique rugs."

As Alfred sat at his desk and began to work, filling the otherwise quiet newsroom with the frenetic clicking of his keyboard, Joseph imagined himself ten years from now, still assigned to Obits, waiting for a celebrity or a high-ranking government official to succumb. In his vision, Alfred had succeeded Yates as executive editor, and Nate and Tinker had long since quit or retired. New meat, all of it dead, occupied the desks around him.

"Is something wrong?" It was Alfred. He had stopped typing. "I didn't think it was that tough a piece."

"It's not the piece," Joseph muttered.

"Keep trying, you'll find the lead."

"It's me, Alfred. It's my life, it's who I am."

Alfred gazed at him with neither shock nor sorrow, as if expecting such a statement.

"Okay," Joseph said. "Then how would you start 'Frady'?"

"I wouldn't. That's why I gave it to you." He folded his hands and placed them on top of his head, assuming the pose made famous by Cameron Yates. Then he kicked his feet up on the desktop and leaned as far back as his chair allowed. "But if I had to," he said, "this is how I'd do it." He cleared his throat and pointed to Joseph's keyboard, indicating he wanted to dictate. "Charles Percy Frady died yesterday at his country estate near Warrenton, Virginia. The seventy-three-year-old former diplomat and captain of industry suffered a self-inflicted gunshot wound in a hunting accident."

"I think you've got it," Joseph said. "Way to go, Alfred."

Alfred reached back and patted himself on the shoulder. "Yes," he said. "Way to go, *Alfred!*"

A few hours later, they walked to the Herald Pub on L Street, found a table in the lounge, and ordered beer and hamburger platters. This being Saturday noon, a large crowd had gathered, and the air was filled with laughter and cigarette smoke. An Orioles baseball game, one of the first of the new season, was playing on the television.

"Urban rage," Alfred said. "I'm absolutely suffocating beneath it, my friend."

The meal arrived and Joseph bit into his bloody sandwich. He considered telling Alfred about Naomi's visit last night, but instead found himself saying, "Urban rage, Alfred. What the hell is it, anyway?"

Alfred recoiled and let out a deep sigh. He mopped up some ketchup with one of his fries. "It's when you ask a colleague out to dinner and then get threatened by the boss."

"I think I understand now."

"And when the Metro stalls on the tracks and the conductor won't open the doors." Alfred was beginning to sound impatient. "You're stuck in a hot, crowded car for an hour, smelling armpits and sour breath and wishing there was an automatic rifle nearby so you could shoot somebody—*anybody*."

"Okay. Fine. I get it now."

"Or when you're at the Bureau of Motor Vehicle Services, and you've waited in line for two hours, and you finally get to the clerk and she says she'll need to see your birth certificate."

"But you've forgotten it at home."

Alfred nodded. "Now do you see why it's so important that somebody write this piece?"

The waitress returned and Joseph ordered a cup of coffee, Alfred another beer. Joseph figured the Orioles were winning because every few minutes a group in back cheered and the bartender rang a cowbell. At last there came a lull in the action, and Joseph said, "Alfred, have you ever interviewed a widow you later became interested in?"

"No."

"Why not?"

"The word's *necrophilia*, Joseph. You might look it up."

"I know what it means."

"That someone has sex with the dead?"

"That's it. But she's alive, Alfred. She's as alive as you and me. So explain, if you don't mind, how that would make me necrophilic."

"Not you," he said. "The widow. She might be lying there beside you, Joseph, but in her head she's really with him, the dead husband." Alfred drank more beer. "You aren't interested in a widow, are you, Joseph?"

"I might be."

"Is it the wife of that CIA guy, the logistics specialist?"

"It's Laura Vannoy."

"Ah. The cook's wife."

"He wasn't a cook. He ran a restaurant."

"He's a stiff nonetheless." Alfred pointed the neck of his beer bottle at Joseph. "Don't say the fat man didn't warn you."

Through the window Joseph could see fruit and flower vendors standing at their carts and, next to an automated banking machine, a man with a primitive cardboard sign around his neck. Then he saw Jennifer Eugene and Cameron Yates crossing the intersection of Fifteenth and L. Jennifer was a few steps behind Yates, who, dressed in a starched white tennis outfit, was nearly running. They were headed for the pub.

"Do you see what I see?" Joseph said.

"Oh, shit, I knew I shouldn't've had all that beer." Alfred gathered the empty bottles and put them on the table next to theirs, much to the surprise of the man sitting there. "My boss is coming," he explained. "He sees that I've been drinking and it's more ammunition. I could do without getting fired today."

"Don't sweat it," the man said, scattering the bottles.

Yates didn't bother to hold the door open for Jennifer. He entered with nostrils flaring, hair a mess, sweat moistening his jaw. "You were right," he said. "They are here."

"Hello, Mr. Yates," Joseph said, standing now. "Jen."

The crowd in back roared and the bartender rang his bell. Jennifer stepped forward and put her hand on Joseph's shoulder.

"What's wrong?" he said.

"Can you come with us to the office?" she said. "Mr. Yates needs a word with you, Joseph."

Yates pointed at Alfred. "You, too, if you don't mind."

"That's easy," Joseph said. "Let's go."

Alfred paid the check and they started for the door. "On second thought," Yates said, turning to Joseph, "you stay here. I'll need only Giddings."

"But if it involves me—"

"It doesn't," Yates said. "Forget it." He faced Alfred. "Come along, fat man. Jennifer."

Joseph watched as they crossed L Street and passed the beggar who spat and cursed when they ignored his pleadings. It was odd seeing Yates dressed in anything but tweeds. In athletic wear he looked older and less imposing. And without the newsroom to support his facade he wasn't as threatening. Joseph trailed them at a short distance, confused by the fuss but certain, though no one was saying anything, that it concerned him.

The elevators in the *Herald* lobby were tied up. Joseph cleared security and paused to avoid catching up with the others. He wondered why whatever had happened couldn't be discussed now. The dissolution of a U.S. presidency had been addressed here, as had a mayor's reckless abuse of drugs and alcohol, a congressman's obsessive pedophilia, and at least one staff writer's unauthorized fling with a source.

Now, in the early afternoon, reporters and editors crowded the fifth floor, and when Joseph entered, some cut quick, pitying glances his way. As he walked to Obituaries he sensed that he had lived this moment before, and remembered the afternoon when Leander and Alfred had informed him of his mother's death. He sat at his desk and signed on to the computer system. He called up "Frady" and read it again, glad to see that it looked as clean and polished as when he'd last checked it.

After waiting nearly half an hour, Joseph rose to his feet and stared in the direction of Yates's office. Alfred was standing in the doorway, nodding as Jennifer spoke to him. And through the wall of glass Joseph could see Yates seated in his tufted leather chair. One hand was resting on top of his head, the other holding a telephone receiver to his ear.

Joseph sat back down and wrote his byline above "Frady," figuring it wouldn't survive the Metro copy desk even if it did manage, by chance, to clear Alfred.

"Shall we go to the cafeteria now, Joseph?" It was Jennifer, standing a few feet away.

"Thanks," he said, "but I just ate."

"Don't make this difficult," Alfred said.

"Don't make *what* difficult?"

"We need some time with you, Joseph. All the conference rooms are occupied." Jennifer leaned in closer and lowered her voice. "We thought it might be more comfortable downstairs."

"It's bad, isn't it?"

Alfred and Jennifer looked at each other.

"Tell it to me here."

"Please, Joseph," Alfred said. "Come with us down to the cafeteria."

"Joseph?"

"I won't," he said. "Sorry, Jen, but I'm not going to the second floor, not ever again. You tell it to me *here*." And he beat his heels on the gray carpet.

Jennifer pulled up a chair. "Joseph . . ." She couldn't finish. Their eyes met and as quickly she looked away.

"Is it my father? Did something happen to Woody?"

She shook her head. "No, it isn't him."

Alfred cracked a pencil in half and threw it on Joseph's desk. "It's Mary Peden," he said. "They found her dead this morning in a room at the Willard Hotel."

"An overdose, apparently," Jennifer said. "Mr. Yates got the call while he was out playing tennis."

Alfred walked over to his desk and sat down. "You go home now, okay? I'll handle everything here."

"Can I write it, Alfred?"

"No, you can't write it. You've got to go home now."

"But I want to, I want to write it."

"It's mine, Joseph. Mr. Big's orders."

"I'm sorry, Joseph," Jennifer said.

"Don't be for me. I really didn't know her very well. You know that."

"Jakki Yates will do an appreciation for Lifestyle," Jennifer said. "She's writing it at home on her PC."

"Jakki Yates writes cookbooks," Joseph said.

"Mr. Big's orders," Alfred said. "Go home, Joseph."

"Don't fucking tell me that again, Alfred." But he was standing, filing the "Frady" notes into a desk drawer. When he started for the elevators, Jennifer followed close behind him. "This is bad news," he said, "but trust me, Jen, I'm fine. Me and Mary, I hardly knew her. It was just something that happened."

One of the elevator doors opened and the Sports editor stepped out. He was carrying a tray loaded with doughnuts and cups of coffee and his suspenders were off his shoulders and looping down to his knees. "Hello, Jennifer," he said.

"Hi, Bobby. How's life?"

"Still on deck, my love, swinging the leaded bat." Ignoring Joseph, he began to walk toward the newsroom.

"Something happen?" Jennifer said. "I thought the two of you were old friends."

"Something happened, all right," he said, boarding the car. He mouthed the words "Death Row" and pressed the down button.

6 By the time they had become involved, Mary was already beyond saving, she was gone. Or so Joseph liked to tell himself.

Once, at the Omni Shoreham, she had called him a mama's boy for ordering beer from room service. "I like my J.D.," she'd said, then had phoned downstairs for a bottle. Joseph remembered the smell of her breath, sour like a drunk's even when she hadn't been drinking, and how she sucked peppermints to cut it. One night she had apologized, and he had said, "I don't know what you're talking about." But she'd known better—she'd seen it in his eyes when they kissed. "I've soured inside," she'd told him later. Although they had rented a score of hotel rooms, he couldn't remember if they had ever spent an entire night in one. Before taking her clothes off, she would stand in front of the bathroom mirror, thrust her chin forward, and rub her fingers over the soft and wrinkled flesh. "Come look at what happens when you get old," she would say. In bed she was always quiet, nearly mute. And when they were done she would hold up her right hand, showing so many fingers—the number of times she had come. About her husband she had said little. "In your Magazine piece," she'd told Joseph, "just write that he turned me into the loneliest person ever. . . . Am I the loneliest person ever, Joseph?"

The affair had lasted less than two months. And all along he had figured she was marked for such an end, the smell of peppermint on her breath, a lousy thirty-column-inch appreciation piece, and an even shorter obit.

After leaving the office, Joseph spent the rest of the afternoon in the Herald Pub. Four glasses of scotch and he felt well enough to cheer with the crowd for its beloved Orioles; two more and he was wresting the cowbell from the bartender and clanging it with a fury that drew everyone to his feet. For a moment he felt like a genuine hero, and bowed to show his gratitude. Apparently no one here knew him, because otherwise, he decided, they would have spared him further embarrassment, dragged him outside, and ordered him home.

At the end of the game, the lounge cleared and a waitress turned off the television. Joseph paid his tab and left. It was dusk now, an overcast, wind-whipped afternoon, but in no way did it feel as if someone once close to him had died.

He considered returning to the newsroom and demanding that they assign him "Peden," as no doubt the obit was now being called, but in a moment of weakness he wondered if he could write it. He was drunk and the woman he remembered had no history save the one in which he'd shared. How, anyway, could he describe the look in her eyes when she ran her hands over her tired flesh, or the liquid shape of her mouth, or the awesome weight of her loneliness? None of this spoke of her Bryn Mawr education, her once all-consuming role as a Capitol Hill housewife, the names of those who survived her. And were he to write "Peden" as he remembered the woman, beginning with their first embrace in the backseat of a cab rolling along Pennsylvania Avenue and ending with a cool handshake in a hotel parking lot, Yates still would've shown him the page in the *Deskbook on Style* censuring such an approach to hard news, and there he'd be with an obit as dead as all the rest.

Joseph was now standing at the corner of Fourteenth and L, waiting for the traffic light to change. He was sleepy and needed a few minutes alone in the bathroom, a combination that struck him as being nearly intolerable. His clothes reeked of smoke and he wished he had not ventured into the pub.

As he crossed the street he found himself walking next to a woman who nearly matched him in height and who might have been lovely if not for her hair. It was brassy green, like the bell of a horn that needed cleaning. She was wearing a plain blue dress and white heels.

"Can I count on you?" she said, stopping him in the middle of the street.

"Depends on for what," he answered.

"Just answer the question. Can I count on you?"

"It depends on for what," he repeated, backpedaling toward the curb.

She joined him on the sidewalk and together they started in the direction of Logan Circle.

"I was wondering if you were looking for a date," she said.

Joseph started to laugh, then stopped short and wiped his mouth with the back of his hand. "I think I remember you," he said. "You and another girl were on Connecticut Avenue a while back. You said something ugly about the hat I was wearing."

"You must have me confused with somebody else."

"No, it was you, all right. Only your hair was different. It was yellow."

She ran an unsteady hand through it. "I got a bad rinse. That faggot Leon, I should sue him."

They reached Rhode Island Avenue and turned right. Up ahead he could see the statue of General Logan through the trees.

"So what's your name?"

"Mona."

"I'm Joseph."

"Joe or Joseph?"

"Joseph," he said. "But I don't date."

She seemed disappointed, and he guessed it had to do with the time she'd wasted on him. "Buy me something to eat," she said.

Joseph fingered his tie.

"I thought I'd be the early bird and get the worm," she said. "But, lord, there're no worms out. So let's eat, Joseph."

"I'm not hungry."

She stepped into the traffic circle and called a taxi over. "Let's go to Georgetown. I feel like some shrimp."

"Not me," he said.

"Oh, come on, *come on* . . ." She tugged at one of his belt loops, leading him toward the car.

"Food," he said, "but nothing more. You have to promise me that, Mona."

As Joseph was getting into the backseat he glanced in the direction of the house and clearly saw Woody standing on the veranda, the binoculars held up to his face. He was looking toward the opposite end of the circle.

"Let's move it," Mona said, pulling at his pants again.

Joseph shut the door and turned to peer through the back window. "Driver, make the circle, please."

They drove past a couple of connecting streets and approached the place Woody had been watching. It was the old boarded-up apartment building with the hurricane fence, weeds three feet high on the lawn. A couple of men were scrambling through the weeds and debris, headed for the rear entrance. Barefoot, they were wearing dark, loose-fitting rags. A fire was burning unattended in a barrel near the back porch.

"Nice neighborhood," Mona said.

Joseph slumped even lower as they passed in front of Woody. "See that old man?" he said.

She turned to get a better look. "Yeah, what about him?"

"What's he doing?"

"Standing there gawking at something."

"Still standing?"

"Standing *and* gawking. There's a wheelchair beside him."

"An empty wheelchair?"

"Empty except for a book. Looks like a Bible."

"That's his Webster's," he said. "A dictionary."

Soon they were climbing Rhode Island Avenue, out of view of Woody. "That old man can't walk," Joseph said, sitting up.

She looked surprised. "He can stand, though."

"This morning he couldn't even do that. He was paralyzed from the waist down. All he could do was wiggle his toes."

She put her hand on his leg. "Tell me how you know so much, Joseph. How'd you get so smart?"

"He's my father. I live with him."

There was a twenty-minute wait at Houston's on lower Wisconsin Avenue so they walked up M Street to a seafood place and claimed a couple of stools at the bar.

"What'll you have?" Joseph said.

"You decide. I like being the lady."

He ordered Coronas and two dozen boiled shrimp.

"Make 'em big," Mona said. "The beers, too."

The bartender served the drinks, then walked over to the raw bar and got the shrimp himself. A large picture window behind him had the name of the restaurant scripted in gold, and outside several tourists were looking in at the seafood lying on a bed of crushed ice. Joseph knew they were tourists from their washington, d.c. T-shirts and baseball caps displaying the likeness of George Bush on the crown. Out on the street behind them, a black BMW was idling in the fire lane, a driver seated behind the wheel. He was talking into a cellular telephone, his eyes fixed on the rearview mirror, watching, Joseph presumed, for the police.

"I bet that's a dealer's car out there," he said.

Mona didn't seem interested.

"They can kill a restaurant's reputation. People see their cars and a goon like that waiting outside and they're not likely to go in. People don't go in, the cook doesn't cook. The cook doesn't cook, nobody eats. Nobody eats, the business dies. I read about it once in the *Herald*."

"You believe everything you read in the newspaper?"

"Absolutely," he said.

Back when he was on the Magazine staff, Joseph himself had written the piece about how some drug dealers liked to frequent the city's best restaurants. While the dealer sat with his entourage at a prominent table and did business over expensive bottles of wine and platters of food, an armed driver guarded their illegally parked car and someone else tied up the restaurant's pay phone, securing it in the event the boss needed to call his street pushers. Everyone wore a beeper clipped to his belt, and the noise of all their remotes sounding at once often so upset diners that they got up and left in the middle of a meal, emptying the restaurant except for the huddle of overdressed teenagers pretending to be sons of Al Capone.

"The car's out there," Joseph said, "but nobody here looks very suspicious."

"Maybe they're in back."

"No. They never sit in back. They like being in the front of things. They like being seen."

Mona mixed some ketchup and horseradish in a saucer, then sprinkled salt and pepper on top. "You're a good conversationalist," she said. "Very entertaining."

"Coming from you that means a lot. I'm flattered."

"Then why won't you date me?" She dipped her finger into the sauce and tasted it. "I'm a lot of fun, Joseph." She licked more of the sauce, this time revealing her tongue.

"Forgive me, Mona, but I'm not even sure I know what you mean when you say 'date.' "

"It can mean any number of things. Whatever on this earth you want."

"What if I told you to go to the bathroom and take your stockings off? Could it mean that?"

"It could. But we might have a problem since I'm not wearing any."

He swallowed more beer. "Are you wearing panties?"

Although it was getting dark outside, few people were coming into the restaurant. The BMW was still idling at the curb, its headlights set on high beam, its emergency lights flashing. The driver had put the cellular phone away and he was staring in the front window.

She bit into another shrimp. "Do you want me to go to the bathroom and take my underwear off, Joseph?"

"Yes."

"To what end?" she said.

He considered a number of responses, then said after a moment, "I really don't know."

She got up, straightened her dress, and ran a hand through her discolored hair. "Save my seat. I'll be right back."

After she was gone, Joseph called the bartender over and ordered another Corona and more shrimp. "That's for the girl I'm with," he said. "And this is for you." He handed the man enough cash to cover the check and a large tip. "And when she comes back from the ladies' room," he said, "will you make sure she gets this?" He placed twenty dollars on the bar. "Tell her I'm sorry but I wasn't feeling well. Will you do that for me?"

The man put the empty bottles on top of the money. "I'll tell her," he said, nodding.

Outside Joseph stood in front of the BMW, waiting for a cab. He worried that Mona would return from the bathroom before he could slip away, but presently a taxi approached. The driver was leaning over to unlock the back door.

"Where the fuck do you think you're going?" came a voice. "I'm talking to you, asshole."

Joseph wheeled around and saw the man who'd been sitting at the wheel of the BMW. He had stepped into the street.

"I beg your pardon."

"I said where the fuck do you think you're going?"

Joseph opened the back door of the cab. "Home," he said, getting in. "And then to bed."

"Where's my lady, motherfucker?"

"Who?"

"My lady. Where is she?"

The cab driver beat his hand against the seat. "You coming or not? Let's go."

"Mona," the other man said. "Where the fuck is she?"

"You want *Mona?*"

A network of thick, crooked veins branched across the man's forehead. "You think you can run out on my lady, do you?"

"I left money on the bar," Joseph said.

"You left money?"

"Twenty dollars. Tell her I didn't feel well."

"Don't *you* tell *me* what to tell her," the man said. "Dumb motherfucker."

Joseph started to respond but the cab pulled away, moving east on M Street. "Where to?" the driver said.

"Logan Circle Northwest. The house with the old man sitting on the front porch looking through binoculars."

Joseph leaned back and thought what a fool he was. Mona probably would have talked him into renting a room and with her friend's help rolled him for everything he owned. He had written that story, too, back in the old days. And he'd marveled at the ignorance of people, the stupidity—men robbed while trying to get a nut.

They were in the heart of downtown now, the cab hot and dark
and rank with the odor of sweat. Joseph lowered the window and let
some air in.

"You say Logan Circle or Dupont?"

"Logan," he answered. "I know this is a bit out of the way, but I
was wondering if you might consider taking Connecticut Avenue."

"I don't know."

"I'll pay for it. Come on, pal."

"From K Street you want to go?"

"Yeah. There's a restaurant, Louie Vannoy's. Pass in front of it, if
you don't mind."

The driver slowed when they got there and pulled over to the curb.
Joseph stared at the building for a while, and then said, "Okay, that's
all." They started back up the avenue. When they approached the
apartment building where Laura lived, he said, "Would you mind
stopping again?"

The driver braked the car and turned onto a side street. He was
watching Joseph in the rearview mirror.

"I was hoping to see somebody," Joseph said.

"It's your money."

"A woman I know. She lives here."

"I'll wait as long as you like."

Joseph looked back at the Dresden, its rounded facade, the arched
windows set deep into limestone slabs along the first floor. "Thank
you," he told the driver.

"I don't mind waiting."

"No. I don't know why I'd want to see her anyway. I hardly even
know the woman."

When they reached Logan Circle, Woody was sitting on the veranda, the box of fishing tackle on his lap. He was counting artificial
worms. "Seventeen," he said as Joseph climbed the steps, "eighteen,
nineteen, twenty—"

"I know I promised but I can't go fishing tomorrow. Sorry, Father.
Maybe some other weekend."

Woody put the worms down and closed the lid of the box. "Yes. I heard about it on the kitchen radio."

"You understand, then?"

"I understand perfectly. You call it a night now, son. I'll keep watch. There's nothing to fear with me here."

Joseph went upstairs, took off all his clothes, and got into bed. He couldn't sleep, and an hour passed before he heard Woody come into the house, lock the door, and roll back to the sewing room. He tried to read one of the many paperbacks stacked on the nightstand, but he couldn't concentrate and tossed it aside. He also tried listening to the radio, and when this failed he put his clothes back on and went downstairs. He had decided to go out for a stroll, and was headed down the front steps when he remembered what Laura Vannoy had told him about lonely men in trenchcoats, walking alone. The night was wild with clouds and wind; sirens wailed in the east.

Joseph watched the sky for a few minutes, then returned to the house, climbed back up the stairs, and went to bed.

6 "Want some breakfast, Father? I was thinking about hiking over to the Korean deli for a fried egg sandwich."

"Fish sounds better."

"Forget it. And don't even think about starting that crap about fish again. No one wants to hear it."

They were in the sewing room. Woody, propped up against some pillows in bed, tore the photodegradable wrapping off the Sunday paper, and began to scan A-1. "I suppose you'll want to see this," he said. "Joseph?"

"I think I'll wait until later, if you don't mind."

"Your friend Alfred must be happy. They've got him spread all the way across the top of the page."

Joseph sat stiff and upright in the wing chair. "Okay, then, no egg sandwiches. But at lunch we should finish off Marissa's enchiladas. There's no point in wasting."

"What enchiladas?" Woody said, still reading. "I threw them out. They tasted worse than cardboard. And they gave me the runs, besides."

"But I thought you said they were great."

"Those enchiladas, you know what else they did?" Woody lowered the paper and pointed to his feet under the blankets. "I can't feel my toes anymore, Joseph. The wiggle's gone."

Woody turned to the jump page inside the section, and Joseph saw the headline stretching above the fold. EX-WIFE OF U.S. SENATOR FOUND DEAD IN HOTEL ROOM. And the tag line: MARY PEDEN, 46, APPARENT SUICIDE.

"You should be getting ready, son. Hard to believe they can have her body ready so soon. But that's what it says here." He put the paper down. "The visitation."

". . . What?"

"You're going, aren't you?"

"Sure I am," Joseph said, rising slowly to his feet. "You think I'd miss it?"

He went upstairs, changed into a suit and tie, and left the house. It was raining now, and he walked toward Fifteenth Street with a beach umbrella held over his head and parts of the *Herald* fitted under his right arm. By the time he reached the office his pants were wet and clinging to his shins, but he'd managed to keep the newspaper dry.

"Going to the funeral home, Joseph?" It was Jennifer Eugene, standing near the security desk.

"I was thinking about it."

"Did you read Jakki's piece?"

"Not yet." He pulled the wet pants away from his legs and wrung them as dry as possible.

"She showed a lot of discretion, I think. There was nothing about the scandal, so don't be afraid—"

"I'm not afraid," he said, then hurried through the glass doors, down the steps, and back into the rain.

Jennifer ran after him, calling his name. "Why does it seem you're blaming me? If you hate me so much, just tell me and get it over with."

He opened the umbrella. "I'm not blaming you for anything. And trust me, Jen, I don't hate you."

She stood next to him to get out of the weather. The only cabs on the street were idling in front of the Madison Hotel, waiting for the big-money fares to the airport.

"I should've called you at home last night," she said. "You might say it was nothing, but I know you too well, Joseph. I know it must have counted. If it would help I'll come with you."

"Jennifer . . ." He didn't know what to tell her.

"Can I come with you? I never met the woman, and yet I feel in part responsible for all that happened between the two of you. I'm the one who assigned you the Peden piece, remember? I was practically your . . ." She stopped herself and eyed the pavement. "I was like your matchmaker."

Finally a cab approached from K Street, moving slowly on the slick and shiny blacktop. "I'm not going to see Mary," he said.

"Joseph?"

"I just had to get out of the house. I started walking and this is where I ended up. Me and this place, it's like a dog and his vomit. I always come back."

"Let's go get a cup of coffee." She stepped closer, staring up at him. "Will you at least do that with me, Joseph? Sometimes now it's like you're a stranger and I don't know you anymore."

He motioned for the cab.

"We used to be like this," she said, and crossed her middle and index fingers.

"What do you want, Jen?"

"There's something I've been hoping to talk to you about. I've been keeping it secret for a long time but I don't think I can any longer."

"Is it about Alfred—about you ratting to Yates on Alfred? All he wanted was to take you out to dinner."

"It's not about Alfred. Joseph? Can I . . . ?"

"Are you going to say it or not?"

Tears shone in her eyes, and her nose began to run. "Go on. I'm sorry for everything."

He closed the umbrella and got into the car. "Me too," he said. "I'm sorry for everything, too." He put the newspaper beside him on the seat and pulled the door shut.

She remained standing in the street as the driver drove away. Joseph watched her through the back window, through ribbons of steam rising from the manhole covers. The rain was falling and she didn't move except to lift her face to the sky.

"Head west on Highway 66," Joseph said, dropping two twenty-dollar bills on the front seat. "I'll tell you where to turn once we start getting close."

They took K Street to the Whitehurst Freeway and crossed Key Bridge into Arlington. When they reached the interstate Joseph spread the papers on the seat and read by the light from passing traffic. A picture of Mary at a Capitol Hill cocktail party, taken five years ago by Leander McNeese, filled the front page of the Lifestyle section. Royston Peden stood next to her, his arm around her shoulders. Both were gazing at something just above the eye of the camera. The pose suggested—to Joseph, in any case—that whatever it was they were watching could be viewed on the next page, that when he turned to D-2 it would be there. But when he finally did, all he found were theater reviews, ads for furniture stores, and a few more pictures of the Pedens trying to look as if they really cared about each other.

⟁ *Seven* ⟁

The funeral home was on a newly paved industrial road near Warrenton, Virginia, a town some fifty miles from Washington. It stood
on a lot without trees, surrounded by acres of cement. Joseph thought
it looked like a family steak house and checked the roof for chimneys,
so certain was he that they'd arrived at the wrong place. The driver
maneuvered the car to the entrance and braked under the low-ceilinged
portico. A sign with plastic letters was standing in the window, announcing the dead. Only one was here today: Charles Percy Frady of
Rectortown. His body lay in Parlor B. Visiting hours were from noon
until ten. There would be a rosary tonight, tomorrow a Catholic Mass
before the burial.

"I'll be damned," Joseph said.

"Told you we'd find it."

It was two o'clock in the afternoon and the rain had turned into a
raw, swirling drizzle. In the far west the Blue Ridge Mountains were
shrouded in gray; they seemed as deep and impenetrable as the sky.
Joseph glanced back at the cars in the lot. "Not many people here. I
thought for a man of his station there'd be more."

"Maybe they all got lost like us," the driver said.

Joseph gave him another twenty, placing it squarely on top of the
first two. "I'd appreciate it if you waited. I shouldn't be long. And I'd
hate to be left stranded."

"Take your time," the man said.

The door to Parlor B was on Joseph's immediate right as he entered the building. This was his first trip to a funeral home since his mother had died, and he was uncomfortable and on edge. He signed the guest register, printing neatly and including his street address and city of origin. As Joseph had noted in the cab, Alfred Giddings and the copy desk had allowed his byline to remain above his story on Frady, and he now wondered if the Frady family would recognize his name. Who but a kind and well-meaning obituary writer would make an appearance at the wake of one of his subjects?

He walked to the front of the room, brushing by clusters of sniffling ladies and painfully nervous men. A moist heat enveloped him and drew beads of sweat to his cheeks and forehead. To everyone who turned to greet him he smiled apologetically and nodded. He made sure to keep his chin up, not an easy task in his present state of mind. He was feeling every bit the fraud and silently scolded himself for coming. He had no place here, and yet the mourners seemed to welcome him. It was as if they were expecting him. A couple of old women waved and hid their faces in frilly handkerchiefs, weeping noisily. And presently someone took his hand—a wiry, energetic man with a boutonniere pinned to his lapel. "When'd you get in, Bob?" the man said.

"What's that?"

"Did you just get in? I'm asking."

"Yes. A few minutes ago."

Joseph stopped a few feet from the coffin and folded his hands. Frady's face was caked with powder and rouge, and his hair was starched with too much spray. He was wearing a double-breasted suit and a red tie supported by a collar bar. His large, blocklike hands were folded over his midsection, a crystal-bead rosary between his fingers. He wore a wedding ring and a watch with a plain white face. His eyeglasses were crooked. There was a scar on his chin, but not a trace of the wound was visible.

An elderly man sidled up to Joseph, smelling of whiskey. "We've been waiting for you. Plane get in late?"

"I took a cab," Joseph said.

"From California?" The man laughed through his nose.

"Washington. I drove here from D.C."

"From National Airport, then. You should of flown into Dulles, Bob. It's closer and not so busy."

Joseph was both embarrassed and intrigued by the confusion. He might have identified himself, but if he told them who he was, it would've spoiled the pleasure of learning who it was they wished him to be.

"I can see the resemblance," the man said, taking in the decedent, then Joseph.

"I gather you two met." It was the first man, the small, wiry one. He had walked up behind them.

"Bob was talking about his trip."

"Yeah, what about it?"

"I took a cab from D.C.," Joseph said.

"You should've called. I'd've driven out to get you, me and the wife. You're with friends here."

"Well, thank you, thank you kindly. But I really wasn't certain I was coming. I didn't actually decide until I got into the cab and put some money on the seat."

"You were the only survivor, weren't you, Bob?" the first man said.

"As far as I know."

"Whaddaya mean, as far as you know?" The elderly man laughed.

"He means unless there were some other young uns out there we never heard about," the first one said. "If I'm to understand right, your papa was quite a stick man, back in his day."

"Be polite," said the second fellow.

Joseph studied Frady, trying to discover what there was about him that might have attracted women.

"Some doubted you'd come. But I told them if one thing'd get you home it was this." The man—the wiry one—blew his nose; his face reddened and his eyes watered. "Chuck always maintained that Bob was all for Bob. I suppose this disproves it."

Joseph reached into the coffin and picked a fleck of something off Frady's lapel. "What kind of a son wouldn't show up at his own father's funeral?" he said.

There was a kneeler next to the coffin, a spray of flowers on either side of it. Joseph said, "I think I'll say a prayer now, gentlemen." And he moved to kneel down.

"Don't think Chuck would've wanted any of that," one of the men said. "That rosary, either. But one of the women, a Roman Catholic, figured he should look the part of a God-fearing man even if he didn't live it."

"So he wasn't religious."

"No, he was too cantankerous for church, don't you remember? He was feisty for somebody his size. And usually it's your little man's feisty."

Joseph stepped back from the kneeler.

"I'm short and I ain't feisty," the wiry one said.

"You have your moments," remarked the other. He patted his friend on the back and led him toward the exit. "Let's leave Bob alone for a minute. We can always gossip later."

Joseph watched them walk away, then turned back to Frady. With Cleo they had kept the coffin closed, a bouquet of roses on the lid. At the head of the room they'd placed her most recent self-portrait on an antique music stand. People had touched the casket and spent a short time examining the picture. Everyone had said it seemed that at any moment Cleo would open her mouth and start talking, that was how real the picture was. But Joseph had thought it crude and insincere. In it his mother was leaning against a lamppost on a Georgetown street, a bunch of blooming mimosa trees in the background. She was thin and angular and looked at least twenty years younger than her actual age. Except for the fuzzy Polaroids that crowded a family photo album, it had been the only picture Joseph could find.

"Welcome home, Bob. Been a long time."

He wheeled around and saw a woman walking carefully on high heels that grabbed at the indoor/outdoor carpet. From her expression he could tell that she knew him to be an impostor, but she kissed him anyway. "I'm Carly, remember?"

"Yes, Carly. Of course. Nice to see you."

She was older than he, by about five years. Her hair was pulled up in a bun and she wore strings of pearls around her neck and wrists, rings on her fingers. Her eyes were sharp and intelligent, and Joseph took her to be the kind of person who exuded as much grace and confidence at a wake as at a wedding.

"We had talked about you only last week," she said. "I was trying to find your address. Our class reunion is coming up."

"Fifteenth?"

"No," she said. "Twentieth."

She was studying him closely, her eyes inspecting his face. Her perfume filled his head and nearly made him sneeze. "California's been good to you, Bob. I know we weren't close back in school but you do seem taller than I remember. Much more handsome, too, I might add."

He straightened his shoulders and forced a smile. "I've been through a lot of changes over the last few years, Carly. My wife left me and my mother died."

She seemed less disturbed by the statement than he was. "Didn't know you were married. But I do recall about your mom."

"Another thing," he continued, "I lost my job—well, not lost it exactly. Let's just say things at the office aren't what they used to be."

"How awful. And now this."

It felt good to say these things and he wanted to tell her more, but presently another woman joined them. She was also having difficulty with her heels on the floor.

"Bob, this is my mother, Dolores Hugo."

Joseph and the woman shook hands.

"Did you and your father reconcile before the end?" Mrs. Hugo said directly, one hand on Carly's shoulder. He thought the older woman looked like a dog. Her skin was red except for those areas she'd chosen to paint blue and silver. "Chuck was a hard person, wasn't he, Bob?"

"Yes, he was," Joseph replied, thinking of Woody. "I suppose it took my becoming an adult to see him for what he was."

Both women looked at Frady. A blue light was reflecting off the satin lining of the coffin. "And what was that?" Carly said.

Joseph could feel himself begin to tremble; he hid his hands in the pockets of his jacket. "A human being. Flawed somewhat. But not unlike the rest of us."

Another woman walked up to them, her purse beating musically against her belly. She was short and fat and wore a bright, floral-print dress that reached down to her ankles. "They tell me you're Bob," she said to Joseph.

He shook her hand. "How are you?"

"Not well," the woman said. "I've been sick."

The woman named Carly took Joseph by the arm. "Why don't we go get something to drink. Are you hungry?"

"I could eat."

"Try the carrot cake," the sick woman said. "I made it this morning from scratch."

Mrs. Hugo said, "And here you are sick, Peg. You're an enigma if ever there was one."

"I'm a what?"

"Tell her what an enigma is," Mrs. Hugo said to Carly.

"It's someone you can't quite figure out."

"Well," the woman named Peg said, "you learn something every day." She was shaking her head. "Never a dull moment."

Carly and Joseph walked into a large reception area. From a huge metal urn she poured two cups of coffee and they sat at a dinette table. "Would you like cream and sugar?"

"Please," he said. "Regular, if you don't mind."

"What about cake?"

"No, thank you. I seem to have lost my appetite."

Stirring his coffee, she nodded as if she understood. "Is it because you're afraid that I'll tell the others you're not Bob?"

"No. You can tell them."

She added more sugar to her cup. "Will you be attending the funeral tomorrow?"

"I'm going back to Washington this afternoon. I live there. My name's Joseph Burke."

"The real Bob, for your information, was a disagreeable person. I never liked him. In high school he had few friends. He sat behind me in homeroom, and he used to like to take his fingers and boot my earlobes, obnoxious things like that. He left Warrenton after graduation and as far as I know never came back. Even when Mrs. Frady died of cancer a few years back, he didn't show up. Mr. Frady never talked about him."

"I live with my father."

"Did he know Mr. Frady?"

"No, he didn't. He doesn't seem to know many people."

Joseph sipped his coffee and looked at the people gathered around a table at the other end of the room. Mrs. Hugo and her sick friend Peg were helping themselves to the various desserts. "I'm a newspaperman, Carly. I wrote the obituary on Mr. Frady for the *Washington Herald* —less than eight hundred words, it was, and then my kicker got cut. I should tell you, though, the real reason I came here was to avoid going somewhere else."

"Is that so?"

"It was because of a woman I once knew."

"Yes."

"Mary Peden. Ever hear of her?"

"Doesn't ring a bell."

"She's dead, she died just yesterday, and what I'm doing . . . I suppose it's a cowardly thing." He sipped the coffee and wondered how to continue. "I didn't have the heart to go and see her, and so I got in a cab and came here. You must think I'm crazy to show up at the wake of a man I never knew."

"It is odd, I admit. But some days I get in my car and take off for the store and end up in the chair of my beautician, telling her I need to be a blonde again. She's looking for the peroxide or whatever, and

I'm sitting there thinking how someone else must have his hands on my controls. What I started out for was a loaf of bread, and what I got was yellow hair."

"I'm not sure I follow," he said.

"Life tells you where to go, Joseph, you don't tell it. This I truly believe."

One of the men with whom Joseph had spoken earlier stepped up to the table. "The mortician wants to see you," he said to Joseph.

"Is it about the bill?" He had intended this as a joke, but neither of them laughed.

"No, it's about his window. Didn't you see it? It was added on maybe three weeks ago but no one wants to try it."

"What are you talking about?" Carly said.

"The one where you drive around and look from your car."

Carly Hugo wiped the corner of her mouth with a napkin. "Tell Mr. Miller that Bob would prefer a traditional visitation. Can't you see how upset he is?"

"It don't cost no extra," the man said. He looked at Joseph, and something in his eyes revealed that he recognized Joseph's pain. "I'll send the message."

Presently Mrs. Hugo and Peg joined them at the table. Each had cake and cookies stacked high on a paper plate.

"I should be going," Joseph said.

"But you just got here," Peg said, her mouth full of food.

"Bob's tired from all his travels," Carly said.

"Yes, I am. You can't imagine."

He stood and the two old women kissed him and patted him on the back. "Everything'll be all right," one said. And the other: "A good night's rest and you'll feel like new again."

Carly walked outside with Joseph and shook his hand before he got into the cab. The rain had stopped and the sky was beginning to clear. You could see the mountains now and the golden air above them, sunlight bright on the trees. "You were nicer than the real Bobby Frady ever was. And a better son."

"Thank you."

"I'm sorry about your friend Mary."

"It happens," Joseph said.

As the cab started to pull away, Joseph turned and waved to the woman. She returned the gesture, her hand held high.

"Let's go back to where we started," Joseph told the driver.

6 Back at Logan Circle, Joseph walked into the sewing room and found Woody sitting in the wing chair with his legs crossed, smoking as he scratched between his toes. The room was dark except for a dusky splash of light coming through the alley window and the beaming orange head of his cigarette.

"I guess you figure you've caught me at something," he remarked, then took a long drag and blew bullets at the ceiling.

Joseph sighed heavily and sat on the edge of the bed. "Even if the park wasn't busy," he said, "you should have locked the front door. I'm surprised. You're generally more cautious."

"Here I am with my legs hiked up and all you can say is I should've locked the door?"

"My worst fear is coming home and finding you strangled to death. I keep picturing you hanged by the strap of your binoculars. I tell you it's terrifying."

"The strangest thing happened," Woody said. "As soon as you left, my legs started to tingle. I lifted them up like this and they both froze hard as a board." He pointed to his knee. "Just help me with this. It's stuck, Joseph—like stone, I tell you."

Joseph ignored him. He lighted a cigarette of his own and inhaled a deep lungful.

"Then if you won't—" Woody slapped his knee a couple of times and knocked his leg back into place. Both feet were now resting on the floor. "There," he said, rubbing his thighs. "Boy, that sure feels better."

Joseph walked over to the window and stared outside. Cleo had forbidden them to smoke in the house, and yet there they were, filling it up. He turned back to Woody and said, "I'm tired of who I am, Father. I want to change my life."

"You're just down over what happened to this Peden woman. And I don't think Naomi's visit helped any."

"It has nothing to do with either of them."

"You only think it doesn't. You're in shock." Woody dropped the stub of his cigarette into a glass and started leafing through the newspaper stacked next to the chair. "I think I might have a solution," he said, sounding confident.

Joseph wasn't listening. "I want to feel as if I matter again. Did I tell you I met a woman?"

"There was a story in the *Herald* Travel section about Club Med. Maybe you should check it out."

"I'm lonely, Father. It only gets worse."

"Everybody's young and single. Bikinis all around. With your looks you could have your pick." Woody found what he was searching for and held it out to Joseph. "Come on, son. How do you know till you give it a try?"

When Joseph refused to take the paper, Woody started reading the copy himself, beginning with the headline.

"I want my own home and my own things," Joseph said. "I want to go to bed with the same woman every night and find her next to me when I wake up in the morning. I want a wife."

Woody stopped reading and put the paper down. He gazed up at Joseph. "Well, since you broached the subject, son, Mimi called while you were out. She said she couldn't stand it at Highland Place any longer, so she was going to rent a room."

Joseph turned on the bedside lamp.

"The Four Seasons. Or that's what she told me."

"Why didn't she just go back to New York if she was so unhappy? Why hang around here?"

Woody reached down and started scratching his toes again. "I didn't ask, because I didn't think it was any of my business. And I guess I figured you'd have the answer."

6 Joseph had always felt comfortable in the piano lounge of George-town's Four Seasons Hotel, once a favorite haunt of his. He'd often met subjects of interviews here, movie actors and authors passing through on publicity junkets. This evening, however, Joseph felt tense and self-conscious, and the lounge seemed entirely different from the place he had known years ago. It was empty except for a small group of Japanese businessmen arguing over a map of metropolitan D.C. He had a fleeting desire to grab the map, tear it to pieces, and toss it into the air like so much confetti. No, he wanted to make the men eat the map, dividing the bits evenly among them.

She had called and he had come running. And for this he despised himself.

"Is there a house phone?" Joseph asked the waiter.

"I can bring one over. Anything to drink?"

"Scotch and water, please."

Someone began playing the piano—a man wearing a faded black dress suit and dirty loafers, no socks. Long black hair fell in his face and the withered stub of a cigarette smoldered at his lips. He was typically undernourished—an *artiste manqué*, Joseph decided, whose real job was teaching music appreciation to impudent eighteen-year-olds at a suburban junior college. His glass tip jar was empty.

The waiter delivered the drink and the telephone. "Are you a guest of the hotel, sir?"

"Pardon?"

"I thought I'd bill your room."

"Oh, well, yes—Verdooth's the name."

"May I see your room key, Mr. Verdooth?"

"It's upstairs . . . with my wife."

"What number, sir?"

"I'm afraid I've forgotten."

"Very well. I'll check with the front desk."

"No. I don't mind paying with cash."

After he was gone, Joseph picked up the receiver and dialed the hotel operator. "Mrs. Verdooth's room, please."

It rang several times before she answered.

"Hello, Mimi," he said.

"Joseph?"

"For heaven's sake, we were married once."

She didn't say anything.

"Look," he said, "I'm downstairs in the lounge."

"What time is it?"

"Not yet eight o'clock."

"I was taking a nap and now there're lines all over my face from the bedspread. God, I hate that."

"Have you had dinner?"

"No. I'd have gone earlier but I wasn't feeling so hot after Mom and Dad's. I thought if my stomach ever settled down, I'd just call for room service."

"Why don't we walk across the street and get a pizza?"

"Not pizza. The thought nauseates me."

"Order anything, whatever you like."

"I'll get pasta."

"Fine. See you in a few minutes."

"Make it half an hour, Joseph—at least let me get these stupid lines off my face."

He was about to hang up, but then remembered something. "What room are you in, Mimi?"

"I beg your pardon?"

"Not that I would come up. It's just that the operator has a hard time with your husband's last name. I had to spell it a couple of times before she finally got it right."

After a long pause she gave him the number.

"Good, then. See you later."

In the next twenty minutes Joseph managed to drink three more glasses of scotch. He handed the waiter five dollars and said, "Give this to the maestro over there at the piano, will you, please?" Then he signed Hans Verdooth's name and room number on the bill and included a hefty tip for the waiter, bringing the total to nearly fifty dollars.

"I decided to charge my room, after all," he explained to the man. "Any problem?"

"None at all, Mr. Verdooth. Thank you very much."

"Still need to see my key?"

"That won't be necessary, sir."

On his way out of the lounge Joseph stopped at the table of Japanese businessmen. "I hope you fellows are enjoying your stay here in the nation's capital."

Apparently only one of the men spoke English. He translated what Joseph had said. Everyone looked confused.

"I was trying to be nice," Joseph said. "Tell them I was trying to be nice."

The man did as he was told and the others laughed and nodded and continued their noisy argument over the map.

"It's the last drink that always gets you," Joseph told the maître d' at the head of the room.

The man led him to a couch in the lobby. "I'll be fine now," Joseph said. But he wasn't so sure. His tongue felt thick and heavy; it barely seemed to fit in his mouth. And although the drinks had softened his hard edge, he still felt a bit irritable.

The elevator opened and Naomi walked out. She started talking long before she reached him. "I know you must think I'm crazy getting a hotel room, but I really couldn't take Highland Place another minute and I did want to see you again before I left. I thought I needed to explain my behavior the other night, and to apologize for it."

He took her by the arm and directed her through the lobby. "You weren't so bad," he said.

"Have you ever known a more difficult person in all your life? If I didn't know better, I'd think I was trying to seduce you, Joseph."

They were walking in front of the concierge's desk when someone called after them, "Mr. Verdooth ... Mr. *Verdooth!*"

Naomi spun around and Joseph spotted the waiter who'd served him in the lounge. He was dashing across the floor, waving Joseph's fountain pen in front of him. "You forgot this, Mr. Verdooth. Your Mont Blanc."

Naomi laughed. "Mr. Verdooth?"

"Thank you," Joseph told the man. He took the pen and put it in the inner pocket of his jacket.

"Why would that man think you were Hans?" she said, following Joseph through the door.

"I guess because I'm with you."

"But he doesn't know me."

"You'd be surprised. These people are sharp."

"Nothing sharp about that one," she said, and turned to get another glimpse of the waiter.

At the restaurant a waitress showed them to a table near the front window. The dining room was hot and crowded; cigarette smoke warmed the air. If there was music Joseph couldn't hear it. Everyone seemed determined to be heard over the other diners, and the result was near-bedlam.

Joseph was starting to feel the weight of the whiskey now, mostly in his head and legs.

"You okay?" he said to Naomi.

"Fine."

"If it's too much, tell me. We can leave."

"It's fine," she said again, studying the menu.

The couple at the table next to theirs was talking about a French film playing at the Biograph Theatre. The man complained that without his glasses he couldn't read the subtitles; the woman was critical of the cinematography.

"Would you mind if I put my hand on your belly?" Joseph said after a while. "Can I feel what it's like?"

Although the couple stopped momentarily to look at him, Naomi continued to examine the menu.

"Mimi?"

"No, Joseph."

"What's wrong with wanting to feel what it's like?"

"I can't believe you'd even ask that."

Hoping to appear unmoved, Joseph feigned interest in the objects that lined the shelf high up on the wall. Marionettes sat next to antique toys and artificial plants in brass pots. "Do you know who Geppetto was?" he said.

She shook her head.

"The old cobbler who either made or took care of Pinocchio, unfortunately I can't remember which at the present time." He winked at the woman seated at the next table. "And Pinocchio? Do you remember who he was, Mimi?"

"A puppet whose nose grew when he lied."

"There he is," Joseph said, pointing. He patted her arm until she looked up.

"You're drunk, aren't you, Joseph?"

The couple, leaning forward on their elbows, seemed more interested in hearing his response than Naomi was.

"Want to hear a story?" he said.

"I think I'm going to be sick, Joseph. I mean it."

He stared at her for a long time. "You want to hear my story, Mimi, or don't you?"

"Tell it."

"When Yates kicked me over to Obits, one of my first pieces involved an incident in this very room."

"Let me guess. Somebody had a coronary and keeled over dead with a mouthful of spaghetti."

"Wrong," he replied, then did his imitation of a buzzer going off. "A driver lost control of his car on M Street and came crashing through this window." He rapped the glass with a fist of knuckles. "Guy was killed right where we're sitting—pizza and beer everywhere. Of course, I thought it'd be a story for our cops writer but Yates said this kind of thing was fairly commonplace."

The couple stared at him in bewilderment; Naomi, looking bored, took a sip of ice water.

"Did you know," Joseph continued, "that in southern Florida, where they have all these retirement villages, geriatrics so often lose control of their cars, run into buildings, and kill people that the newspapers no longer even bother to cover it?"

The man and woman picked at the small chips of pepperoni that covered their deep-dish pie.

"Imagine being married to this for two years and hearing it every day," Naomi said to the couple.

Joseph cleared his throat. "I was only trying to make conversation, Mimi, since you weren't. And it wasn't two years. It was only eighteen months."

"At first it was sports heroes," she told the couple. "Then it was all these blowhards you read about in Lifestyle and the Magazine. Now it's dead people." She looked at the menu. "And speaking of dead people, Joseph, I was sorry to hear about Mary Peden. It was all so awful."

Joseph found it impossible to respond. He stared at her, then raised his hand and called the waitress over. "May I have the check, please?"

"But you haven't ordered yet."

"Not ours," he said. "Theirs." He indicated the couple next to them. "I'm afraid I've ruined their meal."

"Your story didn't bother me," the woman said.

Naomi stood and shoved the chair out from under her. "Excuse me, Joseph. But I need to be getting back to the hotel now."

Joseph left some money on the table and walked with her out into the street. They stood for a moment in front of the restaurant, jostled by passersby. In the lobby of the Biograph a crowd awaiting the next feature milled about under a chandelier burning cones of yellow light. Cars and buses crowded the near lanes leading to Wisconsin Avenue.

"It was really nothing you said in there," Naomi remarked at last. "I guess I'm just cranky these days."

He wished he hadn't called her, that he were still in the hotel's piano lounge drinking whiskey and feeling mad at himself and the world. "Is that an apology?" he said.

"It can be. Because I was wrong. And I was wrong to keep calling you all these months and to have gone over to your house the other day. We can't repeat the past, Joseph, even when it's one as screwed up as ours. It was cruel of me to say the things I did, and cruel to lead you on. I'm married to someone else now. And I've just decided it's time to end all this. That's really why I stayed over and took the room. I hated the way I felt after I left your house, and I wanted to say goodbye and do it without all the craziness."

"That's quite a mouthful, Mimi."

"Please, Joseph. It was tough for me to say those things. Let's not be sarcastic."

"Okay, then. Let's not." The couple inside the restaurant was still watching them through the window. "Mind if I go with you back to the hotel?" he said.

"No. But I'd prefer it if you didn't follow me inside."

"Wouldn't want to give anyone the wrong impression."

"We're being sarcastic again, aren't we, Joseph?"

They reached the corner and crossed the street, Joseph a few paces behind her. "This is good, thank you," she said when they reached the other side. She offered her hand. "We'll have to say our farewells now, Joseph."

"Farewell," he said. But he didn't leave.

They drifted beneath the colorful canopies of an upscale furniture store and a Vietnamese restaurant.

"You wouldn't want me this way, anyway," she said. "I have varicose veins, I have to wear these silly support hose. And like I told you, Joseph, there's this thing growing inside of me."

"A *thing?* Why would you call it a *thing?*"

She was walking faster now. "Let's just enjoy the night and not talk. Let's play the Quiet Game. You remember the Quiet Game, don't you? The first one to say anything loses."

He took out a cigarette. "I don't feel like playing."

"You talked," she said. "So you lose."

They moved on. In front of Bridge Street Books she stopped and scanned the titles featured in the window. "I'm just going to pretend you're not here, Joseph. Let's call this one the Invisible Game, but only I get to play."

"Will you have a drink with me at the hotel, Mimi?"

"No."

"Then will you sit with me in the lounge and watch me drink? I could use one right about now."

"No, Joseph. I won't. In the restaurant I kept thinking of all the secondary smoke getting in my baby's lungs. He hasn't even been born yet and already I'm giving him cancer."

"I won't smoke," Joseph said, stamping out his cigarette, "and we'll sit where no one's smoking. You don't have to have anything to drink, you don't even have to talk. All I want you to do is sit there and watch me."

"I don't think so."

"We'll watch each other. That's it."

"Joseph, I think you've already had more than enough to drink. You should go home and go to bed."

"I don't have a home."

"Oh, Jesus."

He stood between her and the window; she still wouldn't look at him. "I hate the way you make me feel," he said.

"Well, there you have it—the reason we didn't make it together. But you're not the only one who hates how he feels when we're together, Joseph. I do, too. You were always so busy being normal, just like you are now. Everything about you—every reaction, every word that ever came out of your mouth ... it's all so tiring and predictable. Why don't you surprise me now, Joseph, and be different from the way you've always been? Instead of pouting and threatening me, laugh it off, pretend you don't care. It just might shock me into thinking better of you."

She stayed a few yards in front of him all the way back to the hotel. At the entrance she tiptoed and brushed her cheek against his. "Have a good life," she said.

"Yeah."

"I said, have a good life, Joseph. I'm leaving now."

The doorman tipped his hat as she strode past him.

6 Joseph walked for what felt like hours, telling himself that the effects of the whiskey would diminish if only he kept moving. At Dupont Circle he stopped under the trees and sat on a bench. Men were playing chess at a nearby table; and over by the fountain at the center of the park, a gathering of teenage boys, laughing noisily, straddled ten-speed and all-terrain bicycles. Marijuana smoke drifted in the air.

He sat for about half an hour, then started on his way home, a warm, dusty breeze powdering his face. By the time he reached the intersection of Seventeenth and Massachusetts he could hear the sirens and horns of fire trucks, and at Fifteenth he could see the twisted orange light above the trees and buildings. It occurred to him that his father's house might be on fire, that everything they owned might be ablaze. And he began to run at a slow jog, testing his capacity for speed, then graduated to a hard sprint. Though fearful of what he might find when he reached the neighborhood, he was impressed by his effort at locomotion, how with whiskey in his bloodstream his stride seemed better and more efficient than ever before.

At every entrance to the traffic circle, police had set up barricades. Joseph raced through blue lights all the way to the middle of the park and watched as firefighters sent great arcing streams of water toward the old, dilapidated apartment building, which was now burning so furiously that except for an occasional glimpse of red brick all that could be seen were flames. The roof fell in, creating panic among many of the onlookers. While the firefighters were shouting to move back and clear the area, some of the people were drawn closer to the building, including, Joseph now saw, Leander McNeese, who was taking pictures from a spot no less than a hundred feet away.

Leander had stolen within the rim of firemen encircling the inferno, and water shooting from the barrels of long canvas hoses formed a brilliant, iridescent canopy above him. As Joseph watched, two firefighters in heavy black and yellow coats and aluminum hats ran out and each grabbed him by an arm. He resisted, swinging wildly, and managed to break away for a moment. But instead of heading to safety he started back toward the fire, closer now than he had been before, camera gunning. Finally two others raced in and overpowered him, and with the help of the first pair pulled him into the middle of the park.

"Stupid bastard! You wanna kill yourself?"

"Leave me alone!" he yelled back.

Presently several policemen stepped up and directed the crowd that had gathered around Leander to the other side of the park. Joseph showed his press card and explained that he was on assignment. When they left, he turned to his friend and said, "They're right, you know."

"I'd rather not talk about it now, if you don't mind."

"You might've killed yourself, Mac."

Leander was sweating and his hands trembled as he changed lenses on the camera. He popped out the used roll of film, stuffed it in a side pocket of his correspondent's jacket, and reloaded. "Do me a favor, Joseph, and don't tell me how to do my goddamned job, all right?"

"All right," Joseph said.

They were staring at each other. "I'm positive, remember. I got it."

"If you've got anything it's shit for brains. Because I'm telling you, Mac, you don't have it."

"I *might* have it!"

"Well, I *might* have it, too. And he *might* have it and he *might* have it!" Joseph was pointing at the firemen handling the hoses. "You don't have it, Mac."

Leander sat on the walk and leaned back against the short iron fence. Ash and grime covered his face and streaked down his neck, caking in the wiry hairs on his chest. "Somebody goes with somebody else," he said, laughing raucously, "and you die."

"You don't die."

He fell silent, gazing back at the fire. "What sort of time is it we're stuck being young in, Joseph? I wish someone would tell me."

Joseph closed his eyes. The whiskey, weakened now, was beginning to drive needles into his head. He wished he could just vomit and
get it over with. "I'll tell you what'll kill you," he said, nodding at the
blaze. "Fire will."

"Fire, my ass," Leander said, then stood and took a few more
pictures of the building. "You know what's crazy, Joseph? This is
what's crazy. Of all the shit I've covered—El Salvador, Nicaragua,
Iraq—and all the shit I've seen—the fires and bombs and plane and
car crashes . . . Of all that, nothing scares me more than the memory
of one skinny little fucker's arms in mine."

Joseph patted him on the back of the leg. "Relax."

"Relax, did you say?"

"That's right. But if you plan on winning another White House
Press Award you'd better take that film to the office in about"—he
paused to consult his watch—"five minutes ago. Otherwise you'll miss
deadline."

"Fuck deadline."

"I'll go with you," Joseph said. "We'll go together."

"Go where?"

"The Red Cross shelter. I'll go with you to get your results.
Tomorrow night, if you like. I'll even pretend to be you if you think
it'll make it any easier."

Leander stepped back and shot a picture of Joseph. "Let me think
about it," he said.

"Call or come by in the afternoon. I don't think I'll be going into
the office tomorrow."

Leander hustled off in the direction of the *Herald* building, and
Joseph walked over to the house. "Did you catch a glimpse of Mac in
the middle of all that?" he said to Woody, who'd been watching
through his binoculars.

"I saw him, all right, the big idiot. He looked like a live chicken
at a barbecue."

"How'd the fire start?"

"I couldn't tell you. I was inside reading about fish when the sirens
started."

For almost an hour they sat in silence, watching the firemen work, and then Woody mumbled, "The man with the cleft chin." Joseph spotted Pete Peters limping toward them.

Woody cupped his mouth and shouted, "Hey, Pete, did ya remember to bring your water pistol?"

Peters bowed his legs and pointed to his crotch. "Only pistol I know where it don't cost for the ammo." He climbed the steps and plopped down next to Joseph. "I went up close to see if they'd pull some crispy critters out, but it looks like everybody managed to get out."

"Whatever brings you back to the neighborhood, Mr. Peters?" Joseph said.

"Well, to be honest, there was a young lady I'd hoped to meet tonight over by the statue."

"A young lady or a prostitute?" Woody said.

"A prostitute."

"That's what I thought."

"It's all research," Peters said. "I don't actually penetrate anyone. What I do is sit in a room with the woman and ask questions. I want everything in my book at least semiauthentic, so I thought I'd put a whore with a heart of gold in it. People seem to like the type, though truth is, in all my research I've yet to stumble on one." Peters stood and held his head at such an angle that firelight splashed across his face. "Nobody's mentioned my chin," he said.

"I like it." Woody was watching Peters through the glasses, trying to focus. "From here, though, it could pass for a worm."

Peters started to protest but stopped himself and walked down the steps. "Since it looks like I won't be interviewing anyone tonight, I guess I oughta be getting back to the wife."

"You should go home and write," Woody said. "Put a fire like this one somewhere in your book—another flashback."

"It'd have to be," Peters remarked. "Because fire on board a nuclear sub would last maybe one nanosecond, then everyone's blown into a million kinds of shark bait."

After he left, Joseph and Woody returned to their quiet vigil. More than two hours passed before the blaze was brought under control and the firemen stopped flooding the building. In the meantime, Joseph had fallen asleep, his head resting on Woody's legs. When he awoke, the park had cleared and the streets running into the circle had been reopened. People were sitting on the benches under the trees, sharing bottles and smoking.

Joseph stood and stretched. His head ached and he needed to piss. "Father. Hey there. Time to get up now." But Woody was sound asleep.

Careful not to wake him, Joseph rolled him into the house to the sewing room. He pulled the sheets back and fluffed the pillows, then carried Woody from the chair to the bed, stepping over the many newspaper sections that lay on the floor. Woody mumbled unintelligibly, drivel dampening the stubble on his chin. Joseph knelt at the bedside and pulled the covers up to his chin, studying his face in the smoky light from the alley. It was still a good face, Woody's. It was firm at the jaw and not too weathered, and a lot like Joseph's, though of course not as clean and unmarked.

Joseph was swinging his legs around to get up when his knee bumped against something under the bed. He reached in and pulled out a painting of Cleo—the self-portrait he had chosen to display at her wake. It now seemed as inaccurate a rendering as it had then, but something about the painting struck Joseph hard and deep. And he decided to hang it on the wall directly across from Woody.

Come morning he would probably take it down. But for now it would stay here, Cleo's eyes staring at her husband, guarding him as he liked to guard the house.

Eight

The next day Joseph woke feeling exhausted. He'd had another wheelchair dream, almost identical to the first involving Laura Vannoy, and semen was caked all over his middle. He cleaned himself off at the bathroom sink, then went downstairs for a cup of coffee and something to eat. A radio was playing in the sewing room, the voice of a soprano issuing from the bottom of the closed door.

After breakfast Joseph reclined on the couch in the den with a stack of back issues of the *Herald* Magazine. He came upon several stories he had written a few years ago and found them almost painful to read. He discovered callow attempts at poetry where simple declarations would have been more affecting. The stories might have been written by another person, he thought, someone of middling talent. He could recall little about the interviews, the heat that had driven either the questions or the answers, the hours spent pecking at a computer keyboard, the joy he must have felt upon seeing his byline.

Had this really been the news, the things people wanted to read and know about? He could not believe it.

Time had devalued his work, as it had so many other things in his life. Books he had cherished a few years ago, for example, had recently lost their magic, and he now had trouble reading any small part of them. Logan Circle, a neighborhood he'd long feared to enter, had come to offer a roguish charm; it was even beginning to feel like home.

What in the past he had judged correct no longer was, and what had seemed wrong now wasn't. His father's make-believe was additional proof. Weeks ago it had been a source of great distress to Joseph, yet recently it had become perfectly acceptable. Another thing he found himself reconsidering was Naomi. Last night he had not seen in her eyes the fire that used to burn right through him. Where was the juicy wit he had so admired? Where were the qualities that had made her so desirable to him? And why lately had his body taken to purging itself while dreaming of another woman?

At around noon Woody emerged from the sewing room and rolled down the hall. "No work today?" he said, approaching the couch. "Is there a problem, son?"

"No problem."

"You want to talk about it?"

"Nothing to say, really, except that I don't feel like going." He returned to the lead paragraph of yet another story he could hardly recall having written.

"It's not about Mimi again, is it?"

"Didn't you say you were going to start calling her Naomi?"

Woody moved closer, the wheels of the chair bumping against the seat cushions. "What happened last night?"

"I don't want to talk about it." Joseph lowered the magazine and gazed into his father's eyes. "Leave me alone. Please."

"Are you down in the dumps, son?"

"Father, just don't talk, okay? I mean it."

The phone rang about ten minutes later, and Woody answered before Joseph could get up. " 'Darling,' did you say?" he asked, and uncorked a great peal of laughter.

Joseph yanked the receiver away and held it against his chest. "It's for me," he said.

"You're 'darling'?"

"Yes. Do you mind?" And he waited while Woody, smiling obnoxiously, piloted himself out of the room.

"Hello, Laura," Joseph finally said. "How are you?"

"Fine, considering."

He needed a moment to remember that her husband had died. "Oh, yes. I'm sure it must be difficult."

"I don't mean about Louie, Joseph. I mean about you."

As with their previous telephone conversation, Joseph could hear music in the background. This time it was a full symphony orchestra playing something dark and lugubrious. He wondered how she could stand it.

"Joseph, are you there?"

"Still here."

"I was wondering if you'd like to meet Amelia. She doesn't have school this afternoon and I thought we could all go looking at restaurants together."

"Not today, Laura. My father . . . he's not well, you know."

"He sounded good to me."

"I'm not up to anything today. Maybe later."

"That's been our latest project, looking at restaurants. First we take a Polaroid of the outside, then we go in and look to see how they've got everything arranged. We ask for a menu and if they refuse we just round up a copy and steal it. You should see our stash, darling. You could wallpaper the apartment with it."

He didn't say anything.

"What if I brought her over? Would that be okay?"

"No," he said, perhaps too abruptly. "I'm really not feeling well."

"Is it something you can tell me about?"

"It's nothing."

"Is it me?"

"No, Laura."

There was a pointed silence. The music on her end faded to a brassy whisper, then died altogether. At last she said, "I'm worried about you, Joseph. I'm worried one day you're just gonna trip over that big hanging lip of yours and hurt yourself."

"I think you already told me that."

"Well," she said, "then I'm telling you again."

After Joseph got off the phone, he invited Woody to join him in the den. He was feeling guilty for the way he'd treated Woody earlier and he regarded this as penance. They watched television and Joseph lured Woody into a discussion of the Baltimore Orioles, who were suffering through yet another frustrating spring campaign. Woody was of the opinion that the team needed new management, and he was saying as much when a knock was heard at the front door. Joseph started to get up, but Woody waved him back down and answered himself.

A courier, dressed in Day-Glo biking clothes, was standing on the veranda. "Mr. Burke?" he said. "Mr. Joseph Burke?"

Joseph rose from the couch and hurried over. "Yes," he said, pulling the door wide. "I'm Burke."

The man held out a slip of pink paper for Joseph to sign, then handed him a large manila envelope.

"What is it?" Woody said. "Something from the fat man?"

Joseph pried open the seal and removed a dinner menu from Cities, the restaurant where he and Laura had first met for drinks. He was about to see if there was a message inside when Woody jerked it out of his hands.

"What is this?" he said.

"It's from a friend."

"It's a menu."

"From a place in Adams Morgan. She and I went there once."

"What does it mean, son? Who would send this?"

"It doesn't mean anything, Father. And I couldn't guess why she sent it." He could tell that Woody did not believe him, so he muttered, "Maybe she thought it would pick me up."

"How would she know you needed picking up?"

"She called on the phone a while ago. We talked."

"I see," Woody said, nodding excitedly. "It's from 'darling.' Darling sent you this." He perused the menu, then handed it back to Joseph.

"A lot of food there, son. It makes me hungry. I think I'll run and have a snack. Want anything?"

"No, Father. Thank you."

Woody rolled back to the kitchen and Joseph sat on the couch, spreading the menu open on his lap. Beneath the listings for appetizers she had written:

> *My dearest darling,*
> *Next time we'll order tapas.*
> *Love,*
> *Laurie Jane*

A few minutes later Woody came zooming back into the den, his chariot clattering, wheels wobbling and streaking on the floor. He stopped a few feet from Joseph, his back to the television set. "What's a tapa?" he said.

"It's an appetizer. You don't get much."

"Why would she write that? What was she trying to say?"

"Don't ask me."

Woody slapped his hands against the wheels, startling Joseph. His face was aflame with color. "Well, I *am* asking. I'm asking what it means and I expect you to tell me."

Joseph tossed the menu on the coffee table. "It means—and I'm telling you only what I know for certain, Father, I'm not speculating here . . . it means that she thinks I'm a remarkable human being with qualities unlike any man she's ever met."

"You're turning this into a joke."

"She wants to eat tapas with me, Father, then marry me and devote herself to attending to my needs. She wants to trim my nails, brush and floss my teeth, and comb my hair. She wants to wash me and then dry me off. She wants to cook my food and clean my dishes and spoon fabulous dessert into my mouth. She also wants to hold my dick when I've got to take a piss, and yank it nice and proper when I'm done. Did I mention that she wants to give birth to my children? She does. A whole new nation of clinically depressed little people, all exactly like me."

Woody didn't seem amused. "I figured as much," he said, then hastily left the room.

At around five o'clock that afternoon Leander McNeese arrived wearing an Italian-cut double-breasted suit, a silk necktie, and alligator loafers. His hair was dark and oily, slicked straight back and neatly parted down the middle. He had shaved recently, probably before dressing, and his neck was raw and chafed. He smelled of soap and cigarettes.

"Going to church?" Joseph said, stepping up to greet him.

Leander didn't answer. He spun around and strode across the veranda, shoulders slumped, head down. Even in the shade Joseph could see the white flesh, peppered now with stubble, where he had shaved the hairline on his neck.

"Want to hoof it?" Joseph said.

"I'm sweating enough as it is. Let's walk up to the corner and grab a cab."

Later, when they reached Eighteenth Street, the driver slowed and squinted through the windshield at the buildings, looking for the Red Cross shelter. Leander offered no assistance, so Joseph spoke up. "It's there. By the lamp shop."

"Where?"

"By the lamp shop. See all the lights in the window?"

Leander paid and Joseph held the door open for him. "Let's stop by Millie and Al's first and get a drink," Leander said. "How about it?"

"We should just go in and get it over with."

Leander shoved his hands into his pants pockets. He was staring at the ground. "Answer me something, Joseph. Why aren't you at all worried that you have it?"

Joseph wondered if Leander was being serious. "Maybe I don't worry because in the last few years I haven't been with all that many people."

"That doesn't mean anything."

"To be honest, Mac, I could count them all on this one hand." And he held up five fingers, then folded them into a loosely clenched fist.

"You can still get it from a woman pretty easy, they say. Just one woman. When you sleep with her it's the same as sleeping with everyone she's ever been with. All those lives converging like that . . . it's got to scare you, Joseph." He paused and turned his back to the building. "Mimi wasn't so pure, if you recall."

"Tell me something I don't know."

Leander threw a quick glance at Joseph, then faced the street again. Joseph felt the blood grow hot in his face, and a tightness knot his groin. "Are you . . . ?" He was ashamed of the low, muddy timbre of his voice. He swallowed hard. "Are you trying to tell me something about you and Mimi, Mac?"

"It was a long time ago, Joseph. Before you ever knew her. And just a couple of times."

"Twice is all? Then you're saying I should dismiss it. Three times I can complain, but twice—"

"We weren't even serious about it. It was like fuck buddies, her and me, nothing more."

Joseph sat on the curb, drew his knees up, and wrapped his arms around them. "I don't know why I should care," he said.

Leander, careful not to soil the back of his slacks, crouched next to him and put his hand on Joseph's shoulder. "You've always looked at women and seen God, Joseph. That'll get you in trouble every time."

"What is that supposed to mean?"

"While I've seen whatever they could give me. A good time, for instance, some fun. I never expected much."

It was hot and Joseph could feel his shirt clinging to the perspiration that dampened his sides. He stood back up. "Well, Mac," he said, "shall I be you?"

"Whaddaya mean?"

"In there." He pointed to the door of the shelter. "I really don't mind. I'll go in and tell them I'm you."

"There's a word for people like me," Leander said.

"You're a coward."

Leander seemed stung by the charge. He placed a cigarette on his lips. "I was going to say 'asshole,' but coward'll do. Maybe that's why I'm always running into fires, huh, Joseph? To prove something to myself. Whaddaya think?"

It was clear to Joseph that he didn't really want an answer. "Follow me," he said, bounding up the steps to the entrance.

The walls of the waiting room were covered with posters and fliers warning against indiscriminate sexual behavior and announcing future blood drives and meetings of HIV-positive support groups. Along the scuffed and scarred baseboard at the rear of the room stood empty paper cups, many containing shallow pools of coffee and soggy cigarette butts. Except for a man sitting at a table in front, no one else was there.

"Can we sit for a minute?" Leander said, promptly settling into a chair. "I want to talk a minute longer."

"Talk about what?"

He was still pulling on the cigarette he had lit outside. "About the picture in the paper, for one. The fire."

"The angle was a little too severe. Everything was distorted."

"The angle was perfect," Leander shot back. He patted the seat of the chair beside him. "You'd better come sit. You're beginning to make me nervous."

"If you don't mind, I'd really like to get this over with."

"So what's the hurry?" When Joseph didn't answer quickly enough, Leander said, "Because I told you something you didn't like and now you want to get as far away from me as you can. That, or pound the crap out of me. Tell me which."

"First the pounding, then the getting away."

"I knew it," Leander said.

The man at the table in front stood and ambled toward them, a big manufactured smile on his face. Clipboard in hand, he was wearing a white lab coat with his name scripted in red thread across the left breast, and white shoes with corrugated rubber soles.

"Why couldn't he let us sit in peace?" Leander muttered.

"I assume you gentlemen are here for the test," the man said, stopping between the rows of chairs in the middle of the room. He had coarse black hair and wore eyeglasses. The frayed cuffs of his jeans were rolled halfway up his athletic socks. "You're early, though. It isn't until seven-thirty."

"I've come for my results," Joseph said.

"You mean the results of your HIV test? Which you've already had done here?"

"Yeah," Leander mumbled. "That's what he wants."

"My name's McNeese," Joseph said. "Could you get it for me?"

"I'm afraid you're out of luck, Mr. McNeese. The way it usually works here, the group tested on Monday gets its results on Thursday, the Tuesday group on Friday. It takes three days to do the lab work. When were you tested?"

"Last Monday," Leander said, before Joseph could respond.

"You can report either night—this coming Thursday or Friday. Someone can help you then." The man was speaking directly to Leander now. "It often happens that people can't come on time for whatever reason. But our policy is not to give them out individually during the day. Our staff of volunteer counselors isn't here then." He smiled. "Understand?"

"I was frightened," Joseph suddenly felt compelled to say.

"Oh, yes. As I was . . . as we all are." The man removed his glasses and cleaned them on his lab coat. "If you wouldn't mind not smoking, sir." He was talking to Leander, and pointing to a sign above the door.

"Sorry." Leander dropped the smoldering stub to the floor and ground it beneath the heel of his shoe. "I get nervous."

The man nodded. "We gave you an I.D. number, remember? Probably the last four digits of your social security number. This is anonymous testing. No one need know your name."

"Well," Joseph said, "it's McNeese, for your information. It's Leander McNeese."

"If I can show you any literature on the subject or help you with anything else, Mr. McNeese, feel free to come up front."

"Thank you," Joseph said.

The man left and Leander said, "Was it necessary to keep saying my name like that?"

Joseph checked his watch. It was still early, not yet six o'clock. "I think I'll go home now. Woody, you know?"

"No," Leander said, "I don't know at all, I don't know a goddamned thing." He removed a fresh cigarette and lighted it. "You're just pissed off because of what I told you."

"What do you expect, Mac? We were married."

"You're Mac. As long as we're in here, you're Mac."

"That doesn't change what you did."

"I don't think you even care what I did. From the beginning you should've known how she was."

Joseph laughed to himself. "That's just it. And still, I couldn't help myself."

The man in the lab coat came toward them again. "No smoking, sir. Please. I'm asking you for the last time."

Leander looked at the cigarette as if only just now noticing it. He held it out in front of him and watched the smoke curl toward the open window. "It's all going outside. Look at this. How can this bother anyone?"

"The sign says don't do it," the man said. He slapped his clipboard against the top of a chair, sending a hollow metallic sound through the room.

"All your signs say don't do something or other. Don't smoke. Don't use contaminated needles. Don't fuck without a condom. I'm getting a little tired of *don't*, you understand?"

"Don't . . ." But the man couldn't finish.

"Don't what? Don't sit here. Don't *live*. Look at all the cigarette butts in these cups." Leander pointed to the baseboard. "I'm not the only one sick of hearing 'don't.' "

"I was going to say don't talk to me like that."

"Like what?"

"I'm afraid I'm going to have to ask you to leave."

With his thumb and forefinger Leander flicked the burning cigarette to the floor and followed Joseph to the exit. "For the record," he said, glancing back, "it ain't him who's Leander McNeese, it's me. I'm the one." He slammed the door behind them and cursed as he descended the steps. "Can you believe that guy?" he said to Joseph.

"Yeah, I can believe him."

". . . such a faggot, such a fucking—"

"You're hardly qualified to call anyone a faggot," Joseph said. He waited until Leander turned to face him, and then added quietly, "Get a hold of yourself, Mac. I mean it."

Eighteenth Street was crowded with rush-hour traffic, and the noise drowned out whatever Leander muttered next. Joseph took a step closer, but Leander didn't say anything more.

"You still want a drink?" Joseph said.

Leander loosened his tie and undid the top few buttons of his shirt. "I don't want anything. I think I'll just go to my apartment and build something."

"Build what?"

"Something, all right. I'll build *something*."

They shook hands before parting. Joseph, upon releasing his grip, wiped his palm against his pants leg. "You and Mimi, Mac," he said. "What a match. You two deserved each other."

They started in opposite directions. Neither said goodbye.

6 The next morning Joseph slept until almost eleven o'clock, finally waking to the ticking of water in the plumbing overhead. He lay in bed an hour longer, drifting in and out of sleep, then got up and went downstairs. Woody was seated at the kitchen table, gazing bleary-eyed into a cup of coffee. He, too, appeared to have just gotten up. "You playing hooky from work again today?" he said.

"Looks like it."

"You know, of course, what happens to boys who play hooky—the ramifications?"

"I do and I welcome them."

"Fine, then. As long as you know."

After downing a glass of tomato juice spiked with hot sauce, Joseph padded back up the stairs and returned to bed. He slept nearly three more hours and then was awakened by the telephone. His father answered downstairs and chattered brightly when he learned who it was. Finally he called for Joseph to pick up. "Come on, son. Alfred says it's important." Joseph didn't move. He was staring at the wallpaper, counting the heroes astride horses snorting steam, and wondering at the grip of his depression. When Woody called again, Joseph started to get up, then told himself to lie back down. He had decided to quit his job, and he wasn't yet prepared to explain his reasons to Alfred or anyone else. After a minute Woody hung up the phone.

"The fat man says he's coming over. He'll be here shortly. Get up before I crawl up there and pull you out of bed myself!"

About half an hour later Alfred knocked on the front door. Joseph heard Woody's chair rattle across the floor, the door creak open, and the happy exchange between the two.

"Joseph!" Woody called.

Several seconds passed before Woody directed Alfred up the stairs to the guest room. Joseph pulled the covers up to his neck and feigned sleep. He found, though, that his eyelids moved even when he instructed them not to, and he couldn't seem to situate himself comfortably. As a last resort he turned over on his belly, and this, worse yet, left him feeling vulnerable.

Alfred's step was heavy, cloddish, on the stairs, and even heavier and more cloddish on the wooden hallway of the second floor. He entered the room breathing obstreperously, sweat dampening his face. There was a pencil poised over each ear, and several more crammed into his shirt pocket. Joseph raised a hand and greeted him warmly.

"You sick?" Alfred said.

"Worse than sick."

"What hurts?"

"Nothing hurts, really, though I have noticed I can't move my legs."

"Then you're paralyzed like your old man?"

"It must be going around."

Alfred sat in a bedside chair. His necktie reached only halfway down his shirtfront, and his sport coat was several sizes too small. "This isn't about Mac, by the way," he said.

Joseph didn't reply.

"That's not the news."

There was silence as Alfred chewed on one of the pencils. "Because Mac hasn't been seen or heard from all day today, just like you. I called Photo and they said he hadn't checked in. I called his apartment and got no answer. And to think that only yesterday in the office he'd been so delighted with himself, so pleased with his fuzzy fire picture." Alfred put the gnawed-up pencil in his pocket. "Did you see it, by chance?"

"Even better," Joseph said, "I was there when he shot it."

"I glimpsed the ruin when I walked over here. What a blaze."

Joseph fitted his pillow against the headboard and sat up straight. He had decided he would not tell Alfred about his and Leander's trip to the Red Cross shelter the night before. "So what's the news? I'm waiting."

Alfred kneaded his eyes with the heels of his hands. "I learned yesterday that Jennifer Eugene and Cameron Yates are having an affair."

Joseph didn't know how to respond because he couldn't tell whether Alfred was telling the truth. "Jennifer and Yates? Come on."

"And that isn't even the news." Alfred laughed.

"Then what is it, goddammit?"

"Yesterday morning I was going down to the cafeteria for a bagel, and who do I end up sharing the service elevator with but Jennifer Eugene? It was the two of us is all, and though she kept her eyes on the door and didn't seem interested in conversation, I started on something or other—the Orioles, I think it was, and how Washington deserved a major-league team of its own." Alfred paused and pulled out another pencil. "Then later in the cafeteria, I got behind her in the food line and asked if maybe tonight would be better for her."

"You asked her out again?"

"I thought we could go to Duke's or some place like that—a nice steak-and-potato dinner, some cheesecake, that's it."

"But she'd already turned you down, Alfred."

"Yes, but there we were, standing close enough for me to smell her delicately perfumed neck. I thought I should at least try. Anyway, she gives me her famous fat look, the one that says why should I expect her to contribute to my obesity. And then she says, 'Thank you, Alfred, but I'm seeing someone and we have plans tonight.' "

"Big deal," Joseph said. "So she's seeing someone."

"You haven't let me finish." He was pacing more frantically now, disturbing the pictures on the wall, shaking wisps of dust from the ceiling. "After work I followed her home, or, I should say, what I thought was going to be home. She was headed in the direction of Scott Circle, walking with a swing to her hips that I'd never noticed before. It was quite a performance on her part. Her lips were even puckered as if she were whistling, though, to be honest, I never got close enough to hear. I was playing it safe, keeping a distance of never less than fifty yards." He snapped the pencil in half and tossed it on the bed. "But then she walks into the Park Terrace Hotel. Fearing that I'd be found out, I chose not to enter and went over to some statue nearby and sat next to a couple of sleeping crackheads." Alfred stopped pacing. "Then along comes Mr. Big, stepping like the cock of the walk, and whistling, I recall now, exactly as Jennifer had. He carries himself this way straight into the hotel, stopping to speak to the doorman as if they were old comrades."

"Is that it?"

Alfred sat back down in the chair and wiped the sweat from his face with the edge of the bedsheet. Even the bald spot on the top of his head was dripping with perspiration. "Before a couple of frivolous lawsuits ruined everything, I was a reporter, remember? A real newspaperman."

"I remember."

"For fifty bucks the doorman told me everything. He said he and

Jennifer meet at the hotel at least twice a week. She comes first, he follows. It's been going on for months now."

"Not enough. If that were the only source you had it'd never make it into print. And do you know why?"

Alfred didn't answer.

"Because for fifty bucks the doorman's likely to tell you anything you want to hear. And because he's a doorman, not a clerk at the desk, not a maid. And because he probably never saw them enter the room together."

Alfred looked agitated. "May I finish?"

"Finish."

He took a deep breath and wiped his face again. "I was out of money now, so I walked over to First American on Fifteenth Street and withdrew a hundred more dollars from the money machine. The clerk, for that sum, confirmed the doorman's report. He even gave me the room number."

"You didn't?"

"Didn't what?"

"You didn't go up to their room, did you, Alfred?"

"No," he said. "I didn't. I waited awhile in the lounge, trying to get up the nerve to confront them when they came down. And I recalled something that had been bothering me for days. Why would Yates tell me to stop harassing the women in the office?" He waited for Joseph to answer, and when he didn't, Alfred said, "Because Jennifer told him I'd asked her out for dinner, and he was pissed off that I was trying to move in on his girl."

"Protecting his territory."

Alfred nodded. "I probably should've waited and told them something. But I thought of Jennifer, poor girl, and decided it wasn't worth embarrassing her. After my fifth whiskey and bowl of nuts I decided to go home."

"So you left?"

"So I left," he said. "But that still isn't the news."

Joseph waited.

"The news is Harry Delmore told me to tell you that Mr. Big wants to see you in his office as soon as you come in. You skipped work yesterday without calling in, and you've done the same today." Alfred shook his head sadly. One of his pencils fell clattering to the floor and rolled under the bed. "My guess is you're fired. . . . Are you going to come in?"

"Probably not until the feeling in my legs returns."

Alfred pulled at his fat face. "Is this supposed to be funny?"

"Before you leave," Joseph said, "please go into the sewing room and tell Woody I'll be needing to borrow his chair."

Alfred broke another pencil in half and flung it on the bed.

After he left, Joseph slept for another hour and woke feeling as if he'd been bludgeoned. His feet and hands were cold, his lips stiff, and he wondered if his heart was pumping hard enough.

Downstairs the television set was on, his father asleep on the couch with a fishing magazine open on his lap. The day was over, the light outside gone from the sky, and the park was crowded with people staring at the burned-out apartment building as if anxious to see it destroyed again.

Joseph sat in his father's wheelchair and rolled to the front door, opened it, and pushed himself out onto the veranda. To descend the steps he had to stand up and carry it—exactly, he told himself, as Woody had probably done all these months when no one was around to see him.

Joseph felt better now that he was out of the house. It was almost seven o'clock, and the air was beginning to cool. He enjoyed the quick ride up the sidewalk with the wind in his face, the way the leaves on the trees whirled in a lamplit blur. He crossed Fourteenth Street and wheeled by panhandlers begging change, indigents swigging wine bottles cloaked in paper sacks, and children of various and mixed breeding dancing to rap music from a boom box. At Fifteenth he turned left and rolled all the way to the *Herald* building, stopping only for traffic signals and slow-moving pedestrians. In the lobby, elevator cars were emptying loads of staffers from the fifth floor, most of whom walked past without acknowledging him. He spotted Nate and Tinker in the crowd and was relieved when they strode briskly by without speaking. The security guard inspected Joseph's I.D., tipped his hat back, and said, "What the heck happened to you, Mr. Burke?"

"Not a thing."

"Then why're you in that chair?"

Joseph thought hard on the question, framing a number of possible answers. "I really couldn't tell you," he finally said.

"You have a fall at home or something?"

"No. I didn't."

"What about a car wreck, hurt your back?"

"Nope."

The man checked someone else's credentials and let him through. "It's bad luck to sit in a wheelchair when there's nothing wrong with you. Anyone ever tell you that?"

"You're the first."

"Next week someone's apt to break your legs, Mr. Burke. Best to keep both eyes open at all times."

"I'll make sure to do just that."

"Don't ever say I didn't warn you," the man said.

Joseph took the elevator to the fifth floor and wheeled out into the newsroom. People dodged clear of his path, some staring in bewilderment. Harry Delmore stood in his way. "First your father and now you," he said, his voice thick with pity.

"But I'm fine," Joseph said. "This isn't even my chair."

"Then what are you doing in it?"

"I really couldn't say, Harry. Just thought I'd take it out for a ride."

"Oh, well. Steer clear of the potholes, Joseph."

"I'll do that, Harry. Thank you."

At Obituaries Alfred was working at his terminal. A legal pad filled with notes was on the desk in front of him, as were a couple of poppy seed bagels and a near-empty coffee cup. He stopped typing as soon as he saw Joseph.

"Urban rage," he said, "is when your best friend in the world makes an ass of himself and you feel powerless to do anything about it."

Joseph rolled up to his own desk and lay his head on the cool metal top. "I've come to see Mr. Big."

"You mean you've come for your walking papers."

"But I can't walk."

"Okay," Alfred conceded, "your rolling papers." He resumed typing, his eyes focused on the screen.

"So this is finally it," Joseph said, glancing over at Yates's office. He raked his hair with his fingers and straightened his tie. "How do I look?"

"Pretty damned pathetic."

"You wouldn't say that if you knew how I feel."

"I do know how you feel, I know precisely how you feel." His voice was strong and officious, less like the Alfred of Obits than the Giddings of National and Investigative. "You feel exactly the way you did before you got into that chair." He typed another sentence and stopped. "Which is to say you feel fine."

Joseph ignored him. "Why are all the lights out in the office of the silver-haired lion?"

"Because he left about an hour ago, trailing Jennifer, I'm sure, on her way to the Park Terrace. Looks like you'll have to wait until tomorrow morning to get slammed."

"Don't sound so disappointed." Joseph wheeled over to where Alfred was sitting and peered over his shoulder. The story's slug, "Urbanrage," was displayed at the bottom center of the screen. "When are you ever going to finish that thing?"

Alfred turned to Joseph and said, "They're probably fornicating as we speak."

"Don't think about it."

"Probably in the tub, lathered up, candles burning all around—the two of them slippery as seals."

"Yeah, but I wouldn't dwell on it."

Joseph went back outside and started up L Street in the direction of Connecticut Avenue, moving against the flow of one-way traffic crowding the three narrow lanes. The curbsides at each corner were cut for the handicapped, and he found the ride so smooth and easy that he was able to time the distance between traffic signals and to coast without once stopping for a red light. He knew now how his father had been able to keep up his facade all these months. Life in a wheelchair was not unbearable as long as you could stand at any time and walk away from it.

Joseph sped by a stationer's shop, several car rental agencies, clothing and computer stores, pubs and luncheonettes, and a multi-decked parking garage with a mechanical arm blocking the entrance, a woman seated in a glass booth guarding the exit. He turned right on Connecticut, weaved through the crowd milling around the mouth of the escalators at the Metro station, and parked across the avenue from Louie Vannoy's Restaurant. A menu card stood on a stand next to the entrance, unmoved by the breeze that stirred the canopy. Up the street he saw the Mayflower Hotel, porters unloading the trunks of gray airport cabs, and, farther down, the run of drab, international-style office buildings burning lights in every window. As he waited, with the back of his chair pushed up against the wall of a bank, a man wearing a sweat suit dropped a handful of coins into his lap. "Hey!" Joseph called out, fumbling to gather the money. "Come back here!"

The man turned around. His narrow, sharply defined face was a shade lighter where his beard grew, and he had an athletic build, all arms and knobby elbows. "I beg your pardon," he said.

"I don't want your money. I'm not who you think I am."

"Give it to someone else," the man said. "I don't need it." He pivoted sharply and continued along the sidewalk.

"But I said I'm not who you think I am!"

Joseph counted nearly a dollar in change. He put the money in his pocket and slumped in the chair, resting his head on the worn leather back. It was eight o'clock, and he had to wait another hour, watching through half-open eyes, before Laura Vannoy emerged from the restaurant, accompanied by a young woman.

The pedestrian traffic was lighter now as Joseph followed them up Connecticut Avenue, wheeling at the slow, leisurely pace they seemed determined to maintain. Joseph was trying to decide whether to remain on his side of the street and leave them alone or to cross over and confront them. He watched himself in the windows of the buildings, his wavering, imprecise form, the wheels flashing light. He passed a beggar displaying a rough-hewn square of plywood that detailed his tragic circumstances, but stopped long enough to forward what the man in the sweat suit had given him. He rolled in front of the Mayflower and felt the electric heat emanating from the marquee. Bugs swarmed in the golden air, some landing on Joseph's legs and shoulders. He closed his mouth to keep them out, and for some reason recalled the oil painting of his mother's that hung over the fireplace, *Eating Flies and Bugs*. The doors opened, sending a blast of air into the street. It was nice under the lights with the cool breezes from the hotel blowing against his face and arms. If not for the activity around him he believed he could have slept here, cold and hot at once, aglow beneath the marquee.

When he looked back across the avenue, he spotted Laura and her companion walking toward him, hurriedly now to beat the flow of traffic coming from both directions.

"Sir, you're blocking my entrance. If you don't mind . . ." It was the doorman, dressed magnificently in a silken uniform with braid and epaulets and a cap with shadows of sweat around the smooth leather band.

"Is your last name Mayflower? Do you own this hotel?"

A porter carrying overnight bags led a couple of businessmen around Joseph and through the doors.

"Please. Why don't you be a gent and move out of the way."

Joseph pounded his feet against the chair's leg supports. "I'm paralyzed, for heaven's sake."

". . . Sir?"

"Don't you dare say 'sir' to me again," Joseph said, then sped away. He got only as far as the alley entrance before Laura caught up to him.

"Darling, is that you?"

"No."

"My god, what happened . . . what happened to—"

"Nothing, nothing happened." He lifted both legs and shook them. "Look at this. I'm fine."

The young woman with whom she'd crossed the avenue was talking to the doorman at the hotel entrance.

"Then why are you in that awful chair?"

"It's my father's, it isn't mine."

"But why are you in it?"

"I really can't explain why," he said. "You can go now, Laura. Thanks for your concern."

"We were walking home. It's Amelia, darling."

Joseph looked back at the girl standing under the marquee, her hair stirred by the air coming through the open door.

"Whatever you're feeling, Joseph, and I don't want to guess . . . but whatever you're feeling . . ." She crouched in front of him and took his hands in hers. "Would you like to meet her now? It would mean a lot to me."

"She'll think I'm crazy."

"Yes, darling. I'm sure of that. But it's still the polite thing."

Joseph turned to get a better look at the girl. "She's lovely, Laura. She's all grown-up."

"Sometimes I can't believe it myself." She matted Joseph's hair down and he offered a quiet smile to show his approval. "Amelia," she said, "come meet someone, baby. It's Joseph. It's my friend I told you about."

The girl walked up and said, "Hi, Joseph. How are you?"

"I've heard a lot about you, Amelia."

"Same here," she said, pulling back strands of hair which the wind had blown into her mouth. "Practically all I hear about anymore, Joseph, is you. Truly."

Just as her mother had that day in the lobby of the *Herald* building, Amelia made a stunning first impression. In her cool black dress and heels she might have passed for a woman twice her age, and yet her piercing black eyes shone with the innocence of one just beyond childhood. Perhaps she'd gone a bit too heavy on the rouge and mascara, but that, Joseph had noted, seemed to be the fashion among most teenage girls these days. As if to detract from this less delicate aspect of her appearance, she was chewing a prodigious wad of bubble gum, and doing so with a vigor Joseph found almost athletic. He liked her immediately.

"Did Mother tell you about the café?" she said.

"Something, yes."

"Yesterday we called on maybe five restaurants," Laura said. "Today, after Amelia got out of class, it was at least twelve more. Show Joseph your menus, baby."

Amelia opened her bag and removed the cache. After a quick count she announced: "Fourteen."

"And that doesn't include the rental properties we stopped by first. How many of those did we see, Amelia?"

"About . . . oh, Mother, I don't remember."

Laura tapped Joseph on the arm. "Did Cameron Yates talk to you yet? He said he would."

"Talk to me?"

"He heard through the grapevine, I suppose, that we'd decided to sell our share of Louie's, and he sent a reporter over. He was sleazy, Joseph, a real weasel if you know what I mean. I told him you were the only person I'd talk to and shipped him home with his tail between his legs."

"Since when do weasels have tails, Mother?" Amelia said.

"Since I wanted them to," she answered.

"There's really no need to pander on my account," Joseph said. "I can handle Yates fine without your help—I have, in any case, for the last ten years now."

"I wasn't pandering, Joseph, and you should be nice."

"You really should," Amelia said.

Laura started digging in her purse. "All I told him was that I was a fan of yours and wanted you to do it. I pretended not to know you, and who cares if he saw right through me? I wouldn't be swayed, and he spat and stammered and beat what I assumed was his desk. Finally he said he'd think about it."

"I'm quitting the paper," Joseph said.

Laura chose to ignore this remark. She had removed some money from her purse and handed it to Amelia. "Baby, I'm going to visit for a while with Joseph at the restaurant. Think you can make it home okay?"

"I can walk."

"No. I'd worry. Let's get a taxi." She stood at the curb and called a cab over. "I shouldn't be late. Now give Joseph a kiss and tell him how happy you are to meet him."

"I really am," Amelia said. She braced herself against the arms of the chair, leaned forward, and kissed him on the cheek. "You're just playing around tonight, right, Joseph?"

"Right," he said.

"The chair and all, I mean."

"Just playing around."

"Don't be late," she said to her mother, and wagged a finger. "And don't you let her be late, Joseph."

"So long, Amelia," he said. "Nice meeting you."

Laura was quiet as she watched the cab climb the busy avenue. "Should I have invited her? You don't think I was rude or anything, do you, darling?"

"She seemed fine."

"I had a premonition I'd see you tonight, I swear it. Fourteen restaurants, Joseph, fourteen cups of coffee, fourteen bowls of either popcorn or peanuts. And guess how many times I had to hear waiters say 'Enjoy'?"

"Fourteen?"

"Yes, darling. Fourteen exactly."

Presently she stood behind the chair and started to push him across the street. "Where are we going?" he said.

"You look like you could use a good, hot meal. Am I right?"

Until now he hadn't realized how hungry he was. "A bowl of matzo ball soup would be nice."

"That's to start, though I'd never eat any myself—lord, how I hate that stuff. We'll follow with a salad and then graduate to Laurie Jane's garlic chicken. *Petto di pollo sorpresa*, we call it in the restaurant trade. Have you ever had it, Joseph?"

"No, sorry to say."

"I invented this version myself. And not to brag or anything, but it became one of Louie's most popular dishes. He even put a box around it on the menu—probably the nicest thing he ever did for me."

"Come on now. That's no way to talk about the dead."

"It is when it's Louie Vannoy," she remarked. They had reached the entrance to the restaurant. "I guess since you can't walk we can't use the revolving doors. Hang on a second." She pulled open a side door and clamped it open. "Here we are," she said. "You ready for me, Joseph?"

"Ready," he replied.

She backed him through the door and into a dark, near-empty lounge. A couple of men were drinking at the bar.

"We have an elevator, but I think I'll take you down the stairs. We'll make a grand entrance. Is that okay with you?"

"Whatever you want."

"Need a hand, Mrs. Vannoy?" It was the bartender.

"No, thank you, Billy. I want to do this on my own."

Halfway down the stairs a busboy offered to help. "Let me do it, Leonard. Really, I want to."

At the foot of the stairs there was a small waiting area cluttered with ersatz leather couches and armchairs. The maître d' walked over and bowed before Joseph. He was a small man with a bushy mustache and the broad, muscular shoulders and tapered midriff of a bodybuilder.

"Long time no see," he said to Laura.

"Yes, well, I met this hungry man, Charles—met him there on the street. Do you think we might feed him?"

Charles bowed again. "Right this way."

He led them to a table in front. Louie Vannoy's dining room had always reminded Joseph of an airport terminal—same overemphasis on space and order, same drab color theme, same inadequate lighting, and same generic posters of exotic cities on the walls. Tonight there were few people.

"This satisfactory, Mrs. Vannoy?"

"It's up to Joseph." She leaned forward and looked at him. "What do you think, Joseph?"

"You're the boss."

"Then we'll sit here."

The waiter arrived and Laura ordered the meal.

"I'll pass on that salad," Joseph said.

"Forget the salad, Howard." Her hand was resting on Joseph's. "Anything to drink, darling?"

"No, thank you."

"I'll have sangria and 7-UP, please, Howard." After he left she said, "You don't mind my calling you darling, do you?"

"I don't know."

She looked hurt by his reply.

"I mean it sounds weird to me, Laura—like how they talk in old books and movies. No one's ever called me that before."

"Then it's a good thing. With me you need to feel like everything's new. We'll start all over and be like children again, Joseph. Whatever we do will be for the first time."

A different waiter arrived with her drink and large pewter bowls of pickles and bread.

"Do I have to call you anything?" Joseph said.

"Call me whatever you like."

He took a small fist of hot bread, broke it in half, and buttered it generously. "Is Laura okay for now?"

"Laura's fine, darling. It's my name, after all."

Howard brought the bowl of soup and Laura fitted a cloth napkin in Joseph's collar. "Are you sure you don't want anything to drink?" she said.

"Water's fine."

When Joseph reached for the spoon she grabbed his wrist, stopping him. "Let me do it. Please. You don't mind, do you?" She took the spoon and broke the matzo ball into pieces. "Ready?" she said, holding out a spoonful. "It would make me happy to do this."

He opened his mouth and she fed him. "Too hot?" she said.

"Perfect. Would you like some?"

"No, thank you."

Joseph had almost finished eating the soup when he noticed that there was no one but them in the room. "We have it all to ourselves," he said.

"Yes. Isn't it romantic?"

Later, after Howard served the entrée, Laura took a knife and fork and sliced the chicken into small pieces. There were steamed spears of asparagus as well and she cut them in half.

"I love food," Joseph said. "Do you love food, Laura?"

"I do, darling. I love it."

After dinner the man named Charles pushed Joseph to the elevator and helped him in. "It was a pleasure serving you," he said, then punched the up button. The car opened to the lounge, and Laura rolled him out onto the sidewalk.

"I've dreamed about you," he said. "Twice now."

He might have declared his love, she looked so startled. She raised a hand to her face. "Joseph, how sweet."

"I dreamed I was in this same chair and you took me out to a street on Capitol Hill and told me to get up and walk away from it. And when I finally did, I could never catch up to you."

"Was it a nightmare?"

"It scared me. I chased after you, I ran as fast as I could, but I never got very close."

Suddenly she stopped, walked around the chair, and stood a few feet in front of him. The light from a traffic signal colored her face green, then yellow, then red, and a city bus roared by, splashing bolts of blue and white. "Let's try it," she said. "I'm here and I'm waiting and I promise I won't go anywhere."

"It was just a dream."

"Darling, if it scared you . . ."

He stood and, tugging at the pleats, straightened his pants. He was too embarrassed to look at her. He took a step forward and she did, too. He took another step and she was in his arms, pulling him close, her face pressed hard against his chest.

Joseph didn't get back to Logan Circle until after eleven o'clock. He had completed the tour from Louie's to the front steps in the wheelchair, and now his upper arms and wrists cramped from the effort. He stood and his legs were dull and sore, his rear tingly. He climbed the steps and entered the house, calling his father's name as he flipped on lights in every room. Woody was nowhere to be found. Joseph checked the second floor but he didn't turn up there either.

Finally he walked outside and into the park, his heart beating almost painfully in his chest.

Since it was a weeknight there were no streetwalkers or dealers out. Men were asleep on the benches, hugging bottles, sheets of stained newspaper covering their heads, and a woman in rags was lounging under a tree, picking at her shins and ankles. Her feet were swollen and discolored, and hair grew thick and coarse on her legs. As Joseph approached he could smell her infected feet.

"I'm looking for my father," he said.

She stared at him and smiled. "Hello."

"My father. He's a man in his sixties. He might've been wearing a baseball cap."

She was insane and he knew it, could see it in her small red eyes encrusted with dirt and mucus.

"I was wondering if you've seen him. He likes to sit on that porch over there." Joseph pointed to the house. He saw the wheelchair standing at the foot of the steps.

The woman took what she'd been holding, a flea, and tried to put it on him. She slipped her hand under his pants leg and he pushed her away. "I wish you wouldn't do that," he said.

The park smelled of sour wine and urine, and trash littered the walkway that encircled the statue. Joseph drifted over to the rubble of the burned apartment building. Wherever he stepped, black ash wafted in the air and dusted his face. A derelict with a rucksack slung over his shoulder was going through the debris, kicking it with heavy, unlaced boots. Joseph smiled and nodded to show he meant no harm. But this seemed to enrage the man. He grunted and kicked harder at the ground, upsetting more ash and coloring his already filthy pants.

"I'm just out looking for my father," Joseph said. "Don't mind me." Since so many homeless had flopped in the old building, he wondered if the man considered this piece of ground home. Had he come to reclaim something?

Finally Joseph crossed the street and reentered the park. He located an empty bench near the statue, brushed some dried bird droppings and scraps of paper off the seat, and lay down. Through the elms he could see the midnight sky, the stars a nest of perfect things, the moon a bleached sliver. But when he closed his eyes he saw something else. Laura Vannoy was standing before him with open arms, colored lights flashing across her perfect face; and now she was saying, "I'm here and I'm waiting and I promise I won't go anywhere."

About an hour later Woody rolled up and threw a blanket over him. "Didn't want you to catch cold, son," he said, moving from one end of the bench to the other.

"I wouldn't've," Joseph said.

"You might've."

"No, Father. I'm telling you I wouldn't've."

Joseph closed his eyes and was starting to drift off when Woody nudged him awake. "I brought you something." He put a box of crackers on the bench. "Some saltines. I could heat up a can of soup in the house if you're really hungry."

"God, no."

"What about some fish?"

"Go back to the house, Father. Or wherever it was you were hiding. I'm tired and I like being by myself."

Woody wheeled around and looked up at General Logan astride his proud, stepping horse. "If you're upset, it's your own fault. You started all this when you took my chair. You left me here alone with no way to get around."

"I went for a ride and when I got back you were gone."

"I wasn't gone."

"I looked everywhere."

"Not up on the third floor, you didn't."

Joseph pictured Woody in the hot, dusty rooms, boxes of books standing floor-to-ceiling, Cleo's discarded canvases stacked haphazardly against the walls.

"I was looking at your mother's paintings. I climbed the stairs using only my arms, every inch uphill. What a workout. I was thinking we should hang them again. They're not so bad as I'd thought. In fact, they're really pretty good, son."

"Average," Joseph mumbled.

"They're great is what they are. Your mother was a genius."

Joseph dropped his feet to the ground. He put his face in his hands and began to massage his eyes. "A saint, maybe. She might have qualified for that. But no genius. I really don't remember her being that smart."

"She had her qualities, your mother." His voice cracked and for a minute he couldn't continue.

"You should go inside, Father."

Woody turned the chair around, his back to Joseph, and gazed again at the statue. "I'd rather talk, son. A good talk, and serious."

Joseph lay back down, stretched his arms up over his head, and pulled at the weeds under the bench.

"I've been watching you. It's not only this park here I watch. Nothing escapes me. Not even you, Joseph."

"You'd've made a good Doberman pinscher, Father."

At the far end of the circle a couple of men were arguing, not loudly. Woody stared at them for a while. "You never asked how it happened," he said.

Joseph flung the blanket to the ground and sat up tall. "I never asked because I was afraid to. I didn't want to upset you any more than you already were."

"I dozed off at the wheel is what happened, I dropped right off."

"Yes."

"I suppose it was lunch in Georgetown that did it. We'd stopped at Filomena for Italian and she wanted wine. In the car we were sitting right next to each other like kids do. She had on this perfume I'd bought for her birthday. I remember her dress was red satin. It was a beautiful day, cold but sunny. No one should have to die on as fine a day as that."

"It's all right, you know. The state police told me all about it. Don't feel as if you have to do this."

Woody rolled to the foot of the bench. "They tell you anything about the shoes?"

Joseph shook his head.

"Nothing about how I got thrown from the car and my shoes stayed behind?"

"No, Father."

"Then allow me." He opened the box of crackers and took a handful from one of the tubes, holding them flush and square like a deck of cards in his hand. "When I got thrown from the car my shoes stayed behind. They were on the floor under the gas pedal and the brake, just stuck there. I understand this is rare. When a person's shoes come off, a cop later said to me, the head of the person they belong to generally comes off with them. He said I was the luckiest man he'd ever seen."

Across the park the bums were arguing more violently now. One dropped a bottle and it broke and splattered on the sidewalk, and after some screaming they both fell silent.

"Who am I to walk around in shoes," Woody said, "doing what I did to your mother?"

"Then walk without them, Father."

"Here," Woody said. "Eat a cracker." But he didn't offer any. He put them back in the waxed-paper tube and closed the box.

"I had a pretty big dinner," Joseph said. "But give me a couple. I'll eat."

Woody was hugging the box close to his middle.

"Father?"

"What?"

"You offered a cracker." He sat up and put his hand out. "Better give me one before I change my mind."

Woody took some out and they sat watching the statue and listening to the homeless mumble in their sleep. Every now and then Joseph glanced up at the sky through the trees.

"How'd you like the chair ride, son?"

"It was nice but noisy. You need some oil."

Woody seemed pleased. "An interesting perspective, that chair. Everyone seems so tall." His old voice was back and the dry, cowardly flutter had vanished.

After eating an entire tube of crackers, they decided it was time to turn in for the night. Joseph placed the cracker box and the blanket on Woody's lap and pushed him all the way to the house, then backed him up the stairs.

"Kiss me," Woody said, once Joseph had carried him to the bed in the sewing room.

Joseph leaned over and pressed his lips against his father's forehead. Then he kissed him on the mouth.

"You have her lips," Woody said, looking at the portrait of Cleo on the wall.

Joseph had closed the house for the night and was climbing the stairs when he heard Woody shouting from the sewing room. "A genius, your mother. Do you hear me, son? A genius!"

◢ *Nine* ◣

In the morning Marissa and her husband came over with a bouquet of flowers and a box of doughnuts. Fred was walking on crutches, shuffling along flat-footed, and with every step seemed on the verge of crumpling and falling down. He spent more than five minutes crossing the short lawn to the veranda, Marissa clinging diligently to his arm.

Neither Joseph nor Woody had expected Marissa to be accompanied by her husband. Although Joseph had suspected that this day would eventually come, he dreaded the meeting between his father and Fred Christiani, fearing it might become heated and confrontational. Woody's confessions in the park the night before promised a breakthrough in his recovery, and Joseph worried that any more excitement might hinder his progress or, worse, deepen his resignation.

Except for the crutches Fred's appearance was unremarkable. He had a slight, almost skeletal physique, and his small, square face radiated cheeriness, even though he was probably in pain. His manner suggested patience and intelligence, both of which, Joseph knew, would be required in dealing with Woody.

The men shook hands on the veranda as Marissa, adopting a studied, formal air, used full names to introduce them. "Woodrow Burke, I would like you to meet Frederico Christiani." Her accent was gone and Joseph found her demeanor off-putting and more than a little inappropriate. She placed one hand on her stomach, the other on her lower back, and bowed at the waist. "Woodrow Burke's son, Joseph Burke. I would like you to meet—"

"Hello there," Joseph said, cutting her off. "Nice to have you over. Woody and I have heard a lot about you."

For a short time the three men watched Marissa, as if awaiting her next introduction.

"Call me Fred," her husband finally said, a generous smile softening his sharp features.

"And me Woody," Woody said. He relieved Marissa of the flowers and doughnuts and rolled back to the kitchen.

It took a while to seat Fred comfortably at the table. Joseph carried the crutches to the utility room and stood them against the door. He could feel the sweaty warmth on the rubber hand and underarm pads. The smooth wood along the upper stock was stained brown from handling.

Woody had made a pot of coffee and Marissa poured cups all around. Joseph dunked a doughnut into his, leaving an iridescent scum on the surface.

"So you hurt your back, huh, Fred?" Woody said after the silence had grown long and burdensome.

"It is nothing serious. It feels stronger every day."

"Was it a fall?"

"I was putting in a light bulb over the lavatory." His mouth was full of doughnut and he had a hard time speaking. "I fell down and could not get back up."

Woody reached for another doughnut. "I guess you heard I'm paralyzed from the waist down."

"Yes, I did, Mr. Burke. And I am sorry. You have my deepest sympathies."

"I had a couple of tingles some time ago but lost them both. They came and they went like a goddamned thief in the night."

"Yes, but a tingle, I would suppose, means hope. I'd take that as a positive sign, Mr. Burke. You must be encouraged."

"I am," Woody remarked. "From what my doctors tell me, however, it may only be the ghost of something."

Marissa said, "What you say, Woodrow . . . ghost?"

"Yes, my love. Ghost. You see, nerves and muscles have a memory just as the brain here has a memory." He tapped the side of his head. "And, of course, the heart has a memory. Don't let anybody ever tell you different."

Marissa got the coffee pot and refilled everyone's cup. This morning her skin, generally a hearty nut-brown, was sallow and colored charcoal-gray along the jawline. Her hands were steady, though, and Joseph figured that the longer everybody sat peaceably together, the more relaxed she would become.

Woody leaned back in his chair. "It's no secret," he said, "that I've been a difficult person to get along with these last months since my wife died." He raised an eyebrow to Fred and folded his hands. "Has Marissa told you?"

Fred glanced sharply at his wife, his face heavy with sorrow. "She said you were deeply grieved."

"It's my remembered heart, the one I mentioned earlier. It acts up, Fred, it behaves badly, instructing me to do things I otherwise wouldn't."

Fred watched Woody closely.

"For example . . ." Woody said, stifling an urge to laugh. "Pardon me a second." He swallowed more coffee and shook his head listlessly. "May I speak forthrightly, Fred?"

"That would be best."

"I'm afraid I've been showing undue attentions to your wife. I've been taking her nursely diligence as affection. All my fault. The reason for this is probably reflexive. In all my life I had never been with anyone but Cleo, and the touch of your Marissa brought her back. I found in her hands something I thought forever lost to me."

Fred smiled again. "I understand that two people thrust together . . ." He stopped and gazed into his coffee cup. "It can make for a difficult situation."

Marissa walked to the sink and poured her coffee down the drain. "I have told him everything the truth, Woodrow. You must not take blame. I did not discourage it."

"Once again," Woody said, sounding warm and paternal and completely understanding, "it was my heart trying to remember. I intended no harm by it."

"No harm done, Mr. Burke. I assure you."

"I may be in a chair," Woody said. "But I'm no different from any other man. Truth is, I may be worse."

"What do you mean by 'worse,' Mr. Burke?"

"That I've been around longer than you people. The nerves, the brain, the heart—imagine all they've got to remember." Woody was watching Marissa at the sink. "Come over here, my love. Sit with us. Everything's okay now. Fred, you're a fine boy. I like you a lot."

Fred laughed, then seemed to turn serious again. "I can see everything is going to be all right," he said.

Woody unbuttoned his shirt. "Marissa tell you about these, Fred?" He revealed the scars that crossed his upper chest. "Keloids, they're called. Until the accident it was a word entirely unfamiliar to me."

"Oh, yes," Fred said. "Keloid." He pointed to his crutches and Joseph retrieved them, then he stood and pulled the tail of his shirt out of his pants. The whitened top of an appendectomy scar showed above his belt.

"Now there's one to be proud of," Woody said.

Fred stuffed his shirt back in his pants and Joseph put the crutches against the door.

"On the night of our honeymoon," Woody said, "Joseph's mother and I compared scars. All I had then was a tiny bump on my elbow but she kissed it and blew on it and told me that no more pain would ever come to me, not while she was alive."

Joseph could feel his heart hammering in his chest. He stood and wiped his palms on the front of his jeans.

"My son's embarrassed because he wasn't expecting any of this." Woody laughed. "He thought we'd fight over Marissa but you don't feel like fighting me, do you, Fred?"

"We won't fight," Fred said to Joseph. "It is nothing."

"He's a newspaperman," Woody said. "You should know that about him before anything else. It explains a lot."

"I write obituaries," Joseph explained.

"We in this house have been known to belittle his work and pretend it's somehow undignified when in fact we couldn't be more wrong. It's an important service, very necessary. For most people it's the first and last time they ever get their name in the paper." Woody, watching Joseph, seemed truly proud. His appetite was such that he gobbled down two more doughnuts, quickly. "See his lips, Fred? See the peaks and valley on top?"

"Yes."

"He got that from his mother."

Woody wheeled away from the table and down the hall to the sewing room. Marissa cleaned up the droppings of doughnut glaze on the table.

"Why don't you sit down and take it easy?" Joseph told her. "It's almost over."

"I don't mind," she said.

At last Woody returned holding Cleo's self-portrait. He rolled up to Fred and handed it to him. "See what I'm saying? Look at her lips and then look at Joseph's."

"Oh, yes," Fred said. "Of course."

He gave the picture back to Woody and Woody stared at it for a long time, saying nothing. He didn't seem saddened by it, although his smile had faded and his eyes looked empty. "This woman . . ." he muttered, but was unable to finish the thought.

"Anybody want anything else?" Marissa said from the sink.

"Nothing for me," Joseph answered.

"No," said Fred.

Woody raised his hand. "I do, I want something." Cheerful once again, he lifted the painting over his head for everyone to see. "While I have you all here, would you mind helping me hang her pictures back up?"

"Certainly not," Marissa said.

"Poor crippled Fred and I can sit in the room and watch. Joseph, you don't mind, do you?"

Joseph and Marissa spent the next half hour hauling the paintings down from the top to the bottom floor. Joseph's head ached from all the coffee and he was perspiring so much that by the time they finished, his shirt was wringing wet. Marissa, on the other hand, was full of energy and seemed to be enjoying the job. After hanging each picture, she kissed Fred, then Woody.

If Fred minded his wife showing affection for another man, he didn't show it. "We should get together more often," he said at one point, slapping Woody on the back.

"And next time bring the kids." Woody was so excited he seemed prepared to arrange an outing for the afternoon. "Do you fish, Fred?"

"I haven't in years."

"Joseph and I've been planning a trip to the Potomac. You're welcome to join us."

"And me?" said Marissa.

"Sure. I don't mind bringing a girl along. Hey, Joseph, do you mind bringing a girl along?"

"Not at all. I'd like that."

"And my Sonny and Louise?" Marissa said.

Woody turned back to Joseph. "What about the kids, son?"

"That'd be great."

After the pictures had been hung, and the walls were once again crowded with color, Woody led everyone out onto the veranda. The men shook hands and Fred announced that he was feeling better now and would descend the steps without any help. Marissa started to protest, but in no time he was halfway down. When he reached the flagstones Woody whistled and clapped his hands.

"You were very decent to them, Father," Joseph said, waving as the couple drove off. "You were even charming, I'd say."

Woody pushed up to the banister and watched as the car cruised up Rhode Island Avenue. "Take me in, son. I'm tired now."

Joseph rolled him into the den, lifted him out of the chair, and carried him back to the sewing room. He put him in bed.

"I made a fool of myself today," Woody said.

"Not at all, Father. You were wonderful. You reminded me of the man you used to be."

"It's all right now. It's over."

"Fred liked you. He saw what a good person you can be."

Woody held his hand up to shield his face from the ceiling light. "Did you know, Joseph? Did they tell you? He went and made her pregnant. Marissa said so last night on the phone."

Joseph sat on the edge of the bed and took Woody's hands in his.

"He saw me winning, son. I was making her love me."

"Oh, Father," Joseph said. "It's time to stop this, both of us. Mother's the one you loved."

"You think he hurt his back screwing in a light bulb? Let me tell you something, son. That was the act of a desperate man. I was winning and he saw it." Woody covered his face with his hands. "I've lost another," he said, sobbing now. "The heart doesn't remember. The heart forgets like everything else."

"No, Father," Joseph said. "You only wished it would." And he stretched out beside Woody in bed, his arms wrapped firmly around him.

At noon Joseph walked to the *Herald* building. He had taken great care in dressing, hoping to look his best. He thought it important to make a good final impression. If they didn't remember his work as a writer, he wanted them to remember how well he wore a suit.

At the Obituary desk, both Nate and Tinker were occupied on the telephone; neither so much as glanced at Joseph when he sat down at his desk.

"If I may say so myself," he announced, "Death Row has never looked so dead."

Alfred, clearly, was dejected. His eyes were swollen and his suspenders were hanging down to his knees.

"What's wrong now?" Joseph asked.

"Urban rage," he mumbled.

"Yeah? What about it?"

"Yates killed it. He said it stank."

"Yates might've killed it, but I'd bet the farm he didn't say it stank. He wouldn't say that about your work."

"More than once he said it. ' "Urban Rage" *stinks,*' he said. 'It stinks, fat man, *stinks.*' " Alfred put his feet up on the desk. "I wanted to tell him he was the one who stank, what with his hands up on his head all the time and his sweaty goddamn armpits showing."

"Let me tell him for you."

"My problem, Joseph, all mine."

"I've come to quit, so it doesn't really matter what I say around here anymore."

Alfred laughed. "You're starting to remind me of the guy who cut his penis off to keep from getting his girlfriend pregnant."

"Are you saying I'd stay on if I had a choice?"

"Urban rage," Alfred said, "is losing your dick to save your ass. Of course you'd stay, Joseph."

It was lunchtime and the newsroom was beginning to empty. People walked by, talking in whispers hushed and secretive, and it all made Joseph's insides churn. They weren't in church, after all, no matter how hard some higher-ups worked to convince everyone that the *Washington Herald* was a temple of worship, a sacred place. Now they all watched stone-faced as Cameron Yates approached from the other side of the room, a covey of underlings at his heels.

"Urban rage," Yates grumbled, approaching the Obituary desk. "You stank up the joint, fat man." Then, spotting Joseph, he wheeled around and started tapping the wall with his fist. "How are you these days, young man?"

"Doing pretty good, Mr. Yates."

"You want to get some lunch?"

"I've come to resign, sir."

Alfred was laughing again. "Joseph's like the guy who cut his penis off to keep from getting his girlfriend pregnant."

"Shut up," Yates said, then turned to Joseph. "Let's meet in fifteen minutes. We'll sit in my office and have a chat."

Joseph shook his head. "Nothing to say, sir."

"You'll meet me," Yates said more forcefully, his fist hammering the wall, "in fifteen minutes." Then he quickly strode away.

"He probably just wants to see it in writing," Alfred said, once Yates was out of sight. "Here. . . ." He typed something onto the blank screen of his terminal and hit the print button. "One sentence is all you need. I've been working on a resignation letter of my own."

"You'll never quit."

"Well, maybe not this week. Too many neat people kicking big buckets." Alfred got up from his desk, walked over to the printer, and ripped off a single sheet of copy. "I, Joseph Burke," he read aloud, "hereby resign my position as staff writer for the *Washington Herald* newspaper."

"Give it here," Joseph said, yanking the paper from Alfred's hands. But that wasn't what he'd written. "Dear Joseph," it said. "Please don't leave me here alone."

"If you go," Alfred said, "what will I do?"

"You'll do what you've always done. You'll eat too much and break pencils. You'll look after Nate and Tinker. You'll rejoice whenever someone famous dies. You'll complain about not being able to get a date with anyone."

"I'll get fatter and lose more hair."

"That, too," Joseph said. "But you'll be fine. I know you will. You're the best newspaperman in this whole building, Yates included. I'm not worried about you, pal."

Alfred pulled up his suspenders and fitted them over his shoulders, then straightened his tie and cleaned his glasses. "May I have a word with you alone in my office?" he said, holding Joseph by the arm. "There's something I suddenly feel like getting off my chest."

They walked side by side to the canteen and stood in front of the candy machine. Alfred whispered, "I did it, Joseph. I made them up."

"You made what up?"

"The quotes in those stories however many years ago. The libel suits, remember?"

"I do. But is that supposed to change anything?"

"I'm not the great newspaperman you apparently think I am. So don't ever say that to me again. It only reminds me what a fraud I've been."

"You're my friend, Alfred. You'll always be my friend. And no matter what you may think of yourself, I know the kind of newspaperman you are."

"The lying kind. The kind who deserves every piece of shit ever crammed down his throat. Death Row, for example."

"There's something I figured out only recently, Alfred. And it's that some mistakes are too awful to forgive, so we have to forget them. We have to pretend they never happened. Because if we don't, they come to define who we are." He put some money into the machine and pulled a lever. "You never made up quotes and you never libeled anyone, did you?"

"No," Alfred said, taking the candy.

Nate Thompson stepped into the room, blocking the entrance. "Hate to disturb you," he said, "but there's a story on the wires about a top executive with the Met dying of heart failure this morning. You want me or Tinker to take it?"

"Someone with the *Mets?* That's baseball, Nate. And New York baseball at that. See if anyone in Sports wants to handle it."

"Not Mets, Alfred. *Met.* As in New York Met. This guy was a big gun with the opera, my man."

"Hear that, Joseph? Someone with the New York Met." He clenched a fist and punched the air. "Did I or did I not say a lot of neat people were walking around kicking big buckets?"

"Does that mean you'll handle it?" Nate said.

"You're goddamned right I will," Alfred said, pushing past both men on his way out of the canteen.

Cameron Yates arrived in Obits a few minutes later. Joseph had fully expected Julian Bihm, the house attorney, to attend the meeting as both a company mouthpiece and a witness in the event Joseph became belligerent and threatened to appeal to the Reporters Guild for support, and he was surprised now to see that Yates had come alone. But then, as the old man began to cross the newsroom, Joseph trailing, a dozen or so brownnosers suddenly converged from every direction and tagged after him.

One, a cartoonist, asked if Mr. Big knew why the Mexican had thrown his wife off the cliff.

"I wouldn't know," Yates said.

"Tequila," the man answered.

Yates stroked his finely chiseled, prehistoric jaw. "Tequila, did you say?"

"*To kill her,*" the man said. And everyone but Yates laughed. "What else?" he asked the crowd.

"This is regarding Jakki," an Op-Ed writer said. "Over the weekend I cooked all the dishes in her new book—every one, to be honest, except those that called for eels, which I just couldn't find anywhere. I finished at about ten o'clock Sunday night. My husband and kids and I ate so much, we thought we'd pop."

"Pop, did you say?"

The woman held her ground. "I loved the book, Mr. Yates. I mean, it was as riveting as the Book World review said. I would also venture to say that it has immortality in it."

The crowd began a lively discussion about Jakki Yates. It seemed everyone had read her book, some closely enough to have memorized recipes. "It should be mandatory reading in all the schools," the writer said. "And not just in home-economics classes, either. It's that compelling."

Yates picked up the pace and left all but Joseph behind. He whisked past his secretary in a tweedy blur, saying nothing, and slammed the door shut.

"I said we'd meet in fifteen minutes. How long'd it take?"

Joseph checked his watch. He was subtracting the extra time spent crossing the newsroom. "Right around fifteen, sir."

"Right around or exactly?"

Joseph consulted his watch again. "Right around, Mr. Yates. Because it's been almost eighteen minutes since you suggested we meet. Take away the two it took to get here . . . If you want to be accurate, sir, we're closer to sixteen."

"Shit," Yates said, and kicked the trash can next to his desk. "I like being *exactly*."

Joseph found himself sweating, even though it was cool in the office. He felt slightly claustrophobic. Antiques crowded every inch of living space: delicate woods polished to a satiny glow, rare pieces of porcelain on chest-high pedestals, rugs stretching wall to wall. Decorated to suit Jakki Yates's tastes, the room contained none of the objects that had filled it only a few years ago, when fifth wife Helga, a German beauty, had assembled chrome and black-leather furniture and paintings by noted abstract expressionists.

Presently Yates removed his jacket and placed his small feet up on the typewriter stand. Under the glare of several high-wattage lamps shining overhead, his nose appeared larger than usual, his eyes as small and mysterious as a pig's. He folded his hands, placed them on top of his head, and chuckled smartly to himself.

"What's funny?" Joseph said.

Yates, laughing harder now, needed a moment to compose himself. Then he said, "So you really think you're going to leave us, do you, son? This place that is your home?"

Anticipating a reprimand, Joseph was more than a little disarmed by the question. He smiled uneasily and looked away. "I've decided I've done enough time here."

"My lord, son. You make it sound like a prison sentence."

"No sir. You've made it feel that way."

Yates lowered his hands and rested his elbows on the desk. Joseph hadn't meant to be short; it had just come out that way.

"We missed you at the funeral," Yates said directly. "We looked for you, I should say. Royston was pretty broken up about it. I'd never seen him cry before."

Joseph shouldered the sweat on his face. He imagined the scene,

Mary lying on a bed of satin, the senator weeping inconsolably by her side; but then he saw Charles Percy Frady with the crystal-bead rosary and big red face. Frady led to the self-portrait of his mother, and he felt his will weaken. He doubted he would be strong enough to say what he had to.

Yates laughed again. "What the heck are we getting all depressed about anyway? I didn't invite you here to discuss Mary Peden. That's got nothing to do with it."

"To be honest, sir, I thought maybe you were upset with me for not tipping off anyone here about the sale of Louie Vannoy's restaurant."

"And you'd decided I was going to chew your butt out about it, didn't you?"

"Yes, I did."

Yates was shaking his head. "This Laura Vannoy, this widow, she's a tough customer, Joey, real savvy behind that Southern belle veneer. It's not everybody tries to tell Cameron Yates how to run a newspaper." His hands returned to the top of his head. "Was it because you slept with her?"

"I beg your pardon."

"We're adults. Let's be square with each other. Is that why she wanted you to write it? Because you fucked her?"

"I didn't *fuck* anybody, Mr. Yates." He pronounced the word as if it were a peg he was trying to drive into the ground.

"You're getting upset, son. Don't do that."

"If there's one thing I learned during my years at the *Washington Herald* it's that a writer should never fuck a source." Joseph started for the door, barely avoiding a pedestal exhibiting a white porcelain bird. He honestly hadn't been offended and wasn't at all certain what he hoped to achieve by leaving so abruptly, but then Yates's voice, wild and plaintive, reached him from across the room.

"Listen," he said. "I'm sorry we got on this fuck business, okay? I didn't mean it the way it sounded. Sounded too much like I wanted to peek at the notches on your dick, didn't it, boy?"

"Mr. Yates . . . ?"

"I think it would be a mistake if you left us, I really do. The other day in the men's room you said you'd do anything to get out of Obits, and now I'm willing to give you that chance. Come back and sit down and talk to me."

Joseph looked through the glass wall at the newsroom. He could see Alfred standing at near-attention beside his desk, as if prepared to extend a full military salute.

"Hear me out now, son." Yates pointed to Joseph's chair. "I've got a proposition to make. You'll like it. It involves a close friend of yours."

"Alfred?"

"No, son. Jennifer. Jennifer Eugene. We've decided to make her assistant managing editor in charge of the Magazine. She's earned it by doing good, honest work."

"If good, honest work were all it took, Mr. Yates, Jennifer would have had your job a long time ago."

Yates chose to disregard this remark. "After all these years we decided she deserved the slot. It's her show now. And she wants you as a writer." He was almost babbling, making no effort to restrain his enthusiasm. "And frankly, son, I think the section needs you. You made a mistake and were disciplined for it, but you're too valuable to all of us at this newspaper to continue wasting away in Obits. Time to move forward."

Joseph walked back to the chair and sat down. "Mary Peden dies, her ex-husband buries her, and a day later Joseph Burke gets his job back. Forgive me for not seeing the obvious, Mr. Yates, but what's the connection here?"

"Forward, son. We're giving you a break."

"Why me? Why not Alfred? He's the better man . . . the better writer. And God knows he'd like out of Obits."

"Jen specifically asked for you."

"*Jen,* did you say?"

"She says she doesn't want him. And I can't blame her. He's like a ballplayer who can't swing the bat anymore. The rewrite guys have to sit on everything he turns in. And this rage piece of his was the worst garbage I've read in years."

Yates turned in his chair and faced the newsroom. Alfred was still standing as close to attention as his body would allow.

"Look at him, Joseph. And this is another thing. He's just become unpresentable to the public. Would you talk to that man if he knocked on your door?"

"I would, Mr. Yates. Yes. But maybe that's the difference between you and me."

"We both know it's not called Death Row for nothing. People like Alfred go there for a very explicit reason."

"And what is that?"

"To recognize the fool error of their ways," Yates replied. "And to pay for them."

"To pay for them?"

"To die."

"And what about people like me?"

"People like you, son . . . people like you go there until the coast is clear."

"What does that mean?"

Yates didn't answer.

"Please, Mr. Yates. What does that mean?"

"Suppose they found a note, Joey? That Mary Peden had left a note? No will, no diary, no videotaped testimony. Just a little . . . a note. It's really none of your business. But she did ask Royston to ask me to patch things up for you here."

"That's insane."

"She was a troubled lady, Mary. One minute she could despise her husband for dicking most everything that moved, and the next feel kind of responsible for it. I don't expect you to understand. Because I'm not sure I do. But one day Mary Peden could take a pretty-boy reporter like yourself and use him to publicly humiliate her husband. She could do it with malice aforethought, aware of the irreparable damage it'd cause, and you'd never know it bothered her in the least."

"Are you saying . . . ? What are you trying to say, Mr. Yates?"

"This note, by the way, it came on pink stationery, full of instructions. Do this, Royston, do that. Say this, Royston, say that. For every apology there was a declaration of love, all to him. You're right, son, it is insane—you might even say *fucking* insane. But this I know. Number one, Mary Peden loved her husband, loved him in spite of everything and perhaps even because of it. And number two, she used you, son, like most folks use a hank of toilet paper in the morning." Yates stood in front of his desk and leaned his rump against it. "So what's it gonna be?" he said, his voice bolder, more agitated now. "Are you ready to get with the program or not?"

Joseph's heart felt as if it had lodged in his throat. The air was warmer than before, and the room closed in on him. "Every morning," he said, "I get up out of bed and I think, 'You're thirty-three years old, Joseph. And your life is going nowhere.' Thirty-three is young, I will concede that. But I feel as if I'm running out of beginnings, Mr. Yates. I mean, how many times can one person start over again?"

"How's that?"

"When does it all stop? When do you become who you are? Is there a point when it just happens?"

Yates shrugged his shoulders. "Math never was my thing, son. I'm a newspaperman."

Joseph, convinced now that he had lost him, decided to continue anyway, for himself if not Yates. "I come to work and step off the elevator and I say, 'Last year thirty-two, next year thirty-four. The year after that thirty-five.' And then I tell myself—this is it, Mr. Yates, this is the real killer—I tell myself, 'Just be half the man your father is, Joseph, and you'll really be somebody.' "

"Half of who?"

"It's something my mother used to tell me about my father—back before she died."

"Your mother died?"

"In October."

"And your father . . . who is your father?"

"Woodrow Burke."

Yates shook his head. "Never heard of him."

"Well, he's heard all about you. God knows I've told him enough." For some reason thinking of Woody put Joseph at ease; he felt better now. "I'll turn in my letter of resignation as soon as I can get it typed," he said.

"You're no quitter," Yates said, more as a challenge than a fair appraisal.

"I quit a long time ago. We both know that."

"Not you, my boy. Never. I know your kind, it's in the blood. You're like me. You always loved it too much."

"I loved it, all right. I loved this business, I loved the life." His eyes returned to Alfred. Why didn't he sit down? Was he standing in support of Joseph? Was this his way of demonstrating his love? His loyalty? What?

Joseph said, "You know how it is, walking through the newsroom, Mr. Yates, with all the telephones jangling and the VDTs lit up and the smell of coffee and ink? Don't you love that? Feeling that you're really a part of something and it's important and you're important? I know I did, I loved it. And I'll tell you what else. Nothing ever felt better to me than seeing my byline in print and the words *Washington Herald Staff Writer* beneath it—*nothing.*"

Yates started writing on a memo pad.

"I loved you, too," Joseph said. "You seemed so much bigger than the rest of us, the way you strutted about. If you didn't laugh at our jokes, they weren't funny. And if you didn't like something we wrote, then it wasn't good."

Yates ripped the slip of paper off the pad and held it out to Joseph. "This isn't the company shrink, son. This one's a close personal friend of mine—"

"Is it hard being so much better than everyone else?"

"Look," he said. "If you don't want the job . . ."

"Imagine, Mr. Yates, how I felt when I learned that my wife, the woman I loved, was sleeping with a boy who worked here at the paper, a person I saw every day and whose job it was to sharpen my pencils and bring me my morning cup of coffee. Imagine how it felt to know that everyone I came in contact with was watching me for signs of . . . what? Pain? Humiliation? 'Poor Joseph,' they all said. . . . *I heard them!* 'Poor Joseph. Why does he put himself through it? Why does he allow it? Doesn't he have any pride?' "

"You want an answer?"

"I know the answer. Mary Peden gave me the answer, Obits gave me the answer. I let it happen because I thought I deserved it . . . because I thought I had it coming to me. I had failed her and failed myself. But do you know what, Mr. Yates?"

"Talk to me, boy."

"The only thing I'd done was love the wrong person—something you've been through at least five times yourself. I thought I would never get over it, but lately I've found—and this is what amazes —lately I've found that I have."

"Remarkable," Yates said, a sardonic grin spreading across his face. "Good for you, boy."

"I had to say all this, you understand?"

"Whatever." Yates stood before the bird on the pedestal, blowing against the glass box that encased it. "Fucking dust," he remarked. "You think it's hard finding good talent, Joey? Try finding good help."

"You're really not very big, are you, Mr. Yates?"

"What did you say?"

"That you're really not so big. You're silly if anything. Mr. Silly. Silly and old. Your tweeds are silly and your office is silly and you have a silly wife."

Yates turned his pig's eyes on Joseph. Blood pooled darkly in his cheeks and he appeared deeply wounded; but after a moment his expression changed and he looked happy. It was as though he'd suddenly remembered who he was, and to whom he'd been speaking. He was Cameron Yates, the most famous newspaperman in the world, and Joseph Burke was an obit writer who seemed determined to talk himself out of employment.

Yates, leaning forward, resumed his examination of the porcelain bird. He cooed, then said, "I may be silly. But at least I still have a job." Presently he began to wipe the glass box clean with the tail of his necktie. "You're fired, Joey."

They walked into the outer office and stood looking at the newsroom. Joseph half expected Yates to strike him with one of his enormous weight lifter's paws, but already it appeared that he'd turned his attention elsewhere. He was bemoaning the fact that his secretary, still on her lunch break, wasn't around to do something about the dust on his prized bird. "The woman's a prima donna," he remarked. "But she's got tits out to here." And he fixed his hands some two feet in front of him.

"I'll have my desk cleaned out in an hour," Joseph said. "And I'll turn in my credentials downstairs."

"Take your time," Yates said. "Take two hours if you need it. Take all day." He sucked in his stomach and tapped against it lightly. "I didn't miss that crack in there about Jennifer, by the way. A lot of people call her that, you know?"

"Call her what?"

"Jen."

"Yes, a lot do."

"As a matter of fact, I seem to remember having heard you call her Jen once or twice yourself."

"That's true," Joseph said. "I have."

He considered divulging his knowledge of their love affair, but Yates, perhaps anticipating such a disclosure, beat him to it. "Of course," he said, laughing in his heroic way, "I'm the only one who gets to do it while he's fucking her, aren't I, boy? Call Jennifer Jen, that is."

"Yes, Mr. Yates. I suppose you are."

As Joseph crossed the newsroom, he checked his watch and noted the time: 12:34. This was the moment he finally shed his old preoccupation with defeat and set out anew. Or so he now told himself.

At the Obit desk, Alfred Giddings raised his hand and completed his salute, clicking his heels together as he did so.

It took Joseph about an hour to clean out his desk, a job that might have required half as much time had he not been overwhelmed by colleagues who'd heard the news and come to say goodbye. The list of visitors included friends from Joseph's days on the Sports, Lifestyle, and Magazine staffs, some of whom hadn't spoken to him since his fall from grace. Apparently it was safe to converse with him now, and they came singly and in groups, heralding his contributions to the craft of journalism, praising his integrity as a reporter.

"We'll miss you, Burke," declared Bobby Capstone, the same Sports editor who'd ignored him at the elevator a few days ago.

"Dear Joseph, let's lunch sometime," said a writer for Lifestyle, a woman with whom he had exchanged not a word in the last eighteen months.

Alfred said, "Where are my hip boots when I need them?"

"How's that?"

"The bullshit's getting awfully deep in here."

After the visits stopped, Joseph transferred the contents of his bottom and largest desk drawer to a cardboard box. These were files containing clippings of all the obituaries he had written, a total of some two hundred. "There's a whole neighborhood of dead here," he said.

"More than that. You've got a town." Alfred rifled through the folders. "A small one, but I'd say it qualified."

"And I'd bet you've written a whole city by now."

"Yes . . . yes, I have. Giddings's Metropolitan of the Dead, I call it. And I find it somewhat biblical, Joseph. One city comes and another goes. It's just too bad I've been stuck all these years writing about the one going."

Joseph was reading an obit from ten months ago. It was about a man who'd died of natural causes. Not a word of it was familiar, not even the decedent's name. "Does the earth really abide forever?" he asked.

"Yep. The earth and the silver-haired lion. They go on and on."

"He'll die, too. Give him ten more years and another twenty-three-year-old bride."

"Yes," Alfred said. "Give it to him." He sat before his computer terminal and punched up a file. "I haven't shown you this yet, have I?"

The obituary was slugged "Yates" and ran a hundred column inches, long even for that of a U.S. president. It was topped by the byline of one Alfred C. Giddings III.

"Age and cause of death still undetermined," Alfred said. "I suspect he'll die here in the newsroom, though. And when he does, the buzzards'll finally be able to pick him apart. They'll come from every department—his honor guard, led by the shameless Jennifer Eugene. And for every time he didn't laugh at one of their jokes or comment when they praised his wife, they'll take something. A finger, a toe, a strand of silver-blue hair."

"And what'll you take?"

"His penis. Only to prove that he wasn't any different from anyone else."

Everything was packed now, but Joseph was in no hurry to transport it home. In fact, he didn't want any of it and would never come back to claim it. What place in his life would he have for a town of dead anyway?

"You taking the nameplate?" Alfred asked, handing it to Joseph.

"No. You keep it."

"It's not my name," Alfred said, and stuck the plate in Joseph's coat pocket.

"Walk with me to the elevator," Joseph said.

Once they had passed the copy aide station, Joseph turned around to get a final look at the newsroom.

"You'll be better off," Alfred said.

"Sure I will."

"No more deadlines."

"I know it."

"No more dead people."

"Nope."

"You really should be glad, Joseph."

"Yes," he said. "I really should be, shouldn't I?"

6 When Joseph reached the lobby, there was a crowd waiting for the elevators, and he immediately spotted Jennifer Eugene. She and another woman, a cartographer with the Art department, were standing in back near the security desk. Joseph tried to slip by unnoticed, but Jennifer grabbed at the sleeve of his coat and called after him. "Where ya goin', Joseph? What's the big rush?"

He walked quickly, hoping to distance himself from her. But she was shouting, "Hey! Wait up there. Wait for me!" as she chased after him onto Fifteenth Street.

It was hot and muggy outside, the sidewalk crowded with people returning from lunch. Joseph cut through them and started in the direction of Logan Circle.

"I'll follow you home if I have to," Jennifer yelled. "Joseph!"

He glanced over his shoulder as he crossed the street. She was struggling to navigate a grate that had clawed one of her heels. He finally stopped in front of the Madison Hotel.

"Why are you running away from me?"

"I wasn't running," he said.

She refitted her shoe. "What's the matter? What have I done this time?"

He began to answer but then didn't have to. He watched as her expression soured, then relaxed. Her lips were slightly parted, her eyes filled with tears. She knew.

"Can I go now?"

"Who told you?" she said, turning away.

"Does it matter?"

"To me it does."

"Then you'll understand why I won't say who. Because I can assure you, Jennifer, it matters to him."

"Was it Alfred?"

Joseph leaned against the building. "You could name everyone who ever set foot in the newsroom and I still wouldn't say."

A car emerged from the underground parking garage next door and turned into the traffic, tires screeching on the pavement.

"Go back to the office," Joseph said. "I'm sure all your friends are waiting around to congratulate you."

A breeze was blowing, lifting her hair off her shoulders. "He's not as bad as you think," she said.

"He's married, Jennifer."

She took a step closer. "Yes, but he's still not as bad as you think."

"He's probably worse."

"He's passionate and intelligent and exciting. He's got a wonderful sense of humor—"

"No, he doesn't, Jen. The man's lost it. He's gotten . . . I don't know . . . the word *daffy* comes to mind. I'm sorry, but he's become a parody of the guy we used to know."

"He's still a great newspaperman, Joseph. You've got to give him that much."

"He promoted you, didn't he?"

She punched him lightly on the arm. "And what about you, hotshot?"

"I just quit, Jen. Or he fired me." He shot a thumb back at the *Herald* building. "Something happened in there."

She didn't say anything.

"Mary Peden left a note," Joseph said. "Did he tell you?"

"I think I knew."

"All this time I thought it was just something that happened, it didn't mean anything. But it turns out that wasn't the case at all." He pulled the nameplate out of his jacket and tapped it against the palm of his hand. "Your boyfriend says she used me to get at her husband. Poetic, isn't it?"

"I'd appreciate it if you called him by his name."

"In there—in his office—I kept thinking about my father. You're driving along and next thing you know you've piled into a culvert on the side of the road. Everything that ever mattered is lost. Same thing happened to me once. I must've fallen asleep." Joseph laughed and looked up at the sky.

"He tells me he's going to leave her. They haven't been getting along."

"Argue, do they?"

"They've been sleeping in different rooms."

"Then maybe you two can get married. You're a little old for his tastes, but let it never be said that Jennifer Eugene didn't know how to kiss some powerful ass."

"Be that way, Joseph. Be cynical. I don't care, I honestly don't. I've worked in that place long enough to know . . ." She was gazing across the street at the *Herald* building. "Our relationship has nothing to do with this promotion. I'm not the whore you apparently think I am. And I've got absolutely nothing in the world to feel bad about."

"That may be so," he said. "But I'm not the one to convince on that score."

After she was gone, he went into the Madison and bought the New York papers at the newsstand, then sat down to read in the lounge while busboys in starched red jackets cleaned the tables. This was where he and Laura Vannoy had come to talk the day her husband died, and in her honor, and because he was suddenly feeling sentimental, Joseph ordered a screwdriver cocktail, extra heavy on the juice.

That evening after dinner, Joseph hiked from Logan Circle to the apartment building where Laura lived. He walked slowly, enjoying the last of the day, and by the time he reached the Dresden the arches of his feet were cramped and his thighs burned all the way from his kneecaps to his groin. He ascended a short flight of steps, shuffled into the lobby, and presented himself to a woman stationed at the front desk. "Mrs. Vannoy, please. It's Joseph Burke calling."

"Is she expecting you, Mr. Burke?"

He lied and said she was.

She watched him over the top of her glasses. "Very well, sir. Just a moment."

He waited as the woman rang the apartment. "A Mr. Burke to see Mrs. Vannoy." She paused and surveyed him again. "Yes, certainly. I'll send him right up."

"Thank you," Joseph said.

The woman told him the apartment number and directed him to the elevator. "Good evening, sir," she said.

Amelia answered the door. She was wearing a paisley silk robe, an enormous gold *V* wrapped in filigree on the pocket. Her hair had just been washed and she was running a comb through it. "God, Joseph, you really are tall, aren't you?"

"Tall enough," he said.

"Where's your wheelchair?"

"Didn't you hear? I got mugged at Dupont Circle and the assailant sped off with it."

"What a riot," she said, plainly unimpressed. She stepped back to let him in. "Mother's not here, but you're welcome to wait. It might be a while, though. She thinks she's found it."

"You mean the building for the café?"

"What else? It's become her whole, entire mission in life, not counting you, of course. Last night we stayed up till two o'clock trying to come up with a name. I wanted something chic and Frenchy like Café Vannoy but she wouldn't hear of it. I think she's settled on Laurie Jane's."

"Laurie Jane's, huh? Now that's sure to pack them in."

"It sounds pretty awful to me, too. The agent who's been helping us said you can take the girl out of Mississippi but you can't take Mississippi out of the girl. Anyway, the building has no electricity, so Mother took along a little transistor radio, a Coleman lantern, and one of those long-handled flashlights. She also brought a tape measure to measure for curtains and stuff. I told her she should bring a cot and some mosquito netting and just camp out there. If I know Mother she's walking every little inch of the place now, picturing this and that."

"Do you know the address, Amelia? Maybe I can catch her."

"Sure. It's over in Adams Morgan, not far from Kilimanjaro, that dance club. It's a redbrick building, kind of down on its luck. You know how Eighteenth, U Street, and Florida all come together? It's right around there." She took another step back. "Don't you want to come in, Joseph? I can make some coffee or tea or something. And it would give us a chance to talk. I've got questions, you know."

"Maybe some other time."

"Try to talk her out of Laurie Jane's, will you?"

"I'll do my best," he said.

He was starting to leave when she said, "Hey, Joseph. I really do like you better tall."

He took a cab to Adams Morgan and the area Amelia had described. Around the corner from the dance club he located a building with a real estate sign advertising a lease/purchase option tacked to the front. A few doors down, there was a Salvadoran restaurant called El Tamarindo, with people lined up outside waiting to be seated. Although the windows of Laura's building were blackened, a cool yellow light glowed along the edges. Posters announcing rallies for various peace and antigovernment groups papered the facade and broken glass littered the entrance. Joseph stepped through the line of people and banged on the door. He tried to peer through the dusty black glass. "Hey, Laurie Jane," he called, endeavoring to affect a Southern accent. "What ya got cookin' in there, girl?"

When the door opened he was instantly blinded by the cruel beam of a flashlight. She moved it over his face, then away, and then another light filled his vision, this one coming from directly behind her. It caught her hair in such a way as to leave him momentarily breathless.

"Oh, Joseph, it's you," she said, and draped her arms around him. The tinny sound of music reached his ears; he spotted the radio standing on the floor next to the lantern. "I thought maybe it was someone waiting outside. How'd you ever find me, anyway? Did you call and talk to Amelia?"

He began to answer but she stopped him, pressing her mouth against his. "Don't tell me. Let's pretend you were out walking and discovered me here. Can we do that?"

"Okay, Laura. We can do that."

"You'd walked all over the city and drifted into Adams Morgan and finally you saw my light in the window. Then when you got closer you heard my radio. You knocked on the door and I opened it and you knew your search was over."

"That's exactly how it happened," he said. And they kissed again, longer now.

Dust streaked her face and neck and Joseph could feel the sweaty dampness of her back, the cloth of her T-shirt clinging fast. She laid her head against his chest and took his hands and started to move with him across the room. "It feels like we're dancing," she said. They swayed in the polished light, the sound of the lantern a gassy whisper, the radio full of noise. "We *are* dancing!" she said at last.

"Yes. I think we are."

They dipped and whirled until the song ended, and then she said, "Dear Joseph. What's it like being you?"

"It's interesting."

"How do you mean, darling?"

"Just that," he said. "I'm rarely bored."

She looked at him. "Do you think you know me, Joseph?"

"I don't know if I do or not."

"Do you want to know me?"

"Of course I do. And I will. I plan on it. But let's not worry about that just yet."

"If I'm pushy, darling . . . or if I talk too much or say things that seem simple and not what an educated person would say . . ." They had stopped moving but she was still holding on. He could feel her trembling in his arms. "I never even finished high school, you know. Tenth grade is as far as I went."

"What does that have to do with anything?"

They were standing in darkness at the rear of the room, and it seemed to Joseph that her joy in seeing him had washed away. Her breathing, in any case, was labored now, and she felt heavier in his arms.

"Just don't let me get in the way of whatever it is you're looking for," she said at last.

"Laura, what's gotten into you? What's wrong?"

"I don't know," she said. "I really don't. But just before you got here, I was sitting on the floor looking all around, trying to decide whether I wanted this place, and I guess I just saw it for the dump it really was. The ugly old everything about it finally registered, and it hit me that only a fool from Point Cadet would think she could feed hungry people here. Only a fool, darling. Only a fool."

He looked around. "It's not so bad."

"All of a sudden I was that little girl again, Joseph. I was Roy and Tina Cobb's girl lying on the beach with the sun in her face. The light wasn't artificial like it is now, but bright and hot as it was then. And the girl had a baby already and there wasn't a chance in the world that she could ever give it anything. There she was, though, trying to convince herself how wild and unfettered she was, when all along she knew she was nothing if not scared. It made me so sad, darling. And I just cried like I hadn't since I don't know when."

"Why don't we go for a drink? What about Café Lautrec, Laura? You want to go to Lautrec? It's just up the street."

"I didn't start out being a bad wife," she said. "I just ended up one."

"That's done now. It's over."

"When we were still together, I'd look at him and think some mistake had been made. What was I doing with this person? I'd wake up and look at him and think I really must have done something wrong way back when I was a girl, because God was punishing me now—this was what I got for thinking I belonged anywhere but behind the counter of some dime store all day, going home at night to my double-wide trailer and fat, lazy husband and dirty, screaming kids."

"Laura . . . ?"

"Did you ever hear he bragged to everybody about all his girl-friends? At lunch in the restaurant he'd do this. He'd brag. Him and his buddies would sit around, smoking their big cigars, and he'd tell one story after another. Not just about them, either. It got back to me that he'd said things about me."

"I honestly didn't know the man."

"I can't tell you the embarrassment, Joseph. It wasn't that I coveted him, or that I even cared to keep him mine. It was that he made me believe I didn't amount to anything in this world. He had come, the prince, and rescued me, he'd saved me from myself. That's what he always wanted me to remember."

"Stop talking for a minute, Laura. Catch your breath."

"Do you think I need saving, Joseph?"

"God no," he answered.

"The day we buried him you'd've thought I was at the 7-Eleven buying a jar of beans. That's about how emotional I was. I guess in my head I'd buried him so many times that when the real thing finally came, there was nothing to it."

This time when he reached out to embrace her she didn't move away. He backed up against the wall, pulling her with him, and put his mouth against her forehead.

"I'm tired," she said. "I'm tired of thinking of myself in a way I know really isn't me."

He ran his hands through her hair and tried to get her to look at him. "I'm tired, too."

"Tell me you forgive me for being dishonest."

"There's nothing to forgive."

"Tell me anyway."

"Okay, then, I forgive you, Laura. Now settle down."

She pushed him away and he saw that she was crying again. She walked toward the front of the room and said something but all Joseph heard was the noise of the radio and the lantern and the people outside on the sidewalk.

He followed her to where she was standing by the door.

"I didn't even make a good widow," she said. "My day finally comes and I blow that, too."

He was watching the light play across her face. He pulled the loose collar of her shirt over the point of her shoulder, and he kissed her there, tasting salt. She held him, her fingers grappling with his belt, and he felt her unzip his pants and push her hand in. She tugged at his belt once again and his pants slipped down to his knees. He heard his buckle scrape against the floor.

"You're beautiful," she said, touching him. "You're the most beautiful thing I ever saw."

He took her by the wrists, raised her arms up above her head, and removed her shirt. He helped her take her brassiere off and tossed it on top of the other clothes.

"Shouldn't we go get our hotel?" she said.

"Whatever you want."

"The Mayflower. Isn't that the one we promised?"

He fell to his knees and pressed his face against her belly. A still, small sound came from her lips and he felt her hands in his hair, her nails hard against his scalp.

"Here," she said. "Let me." But he didn't stop, he couldn't. "Joseph? Come on, baby. Let me take this off."

She unbuttoned her shorts and dropped them to the floor, and then she removed her underwear. He placed his right hand behind her, cupping the thick, round muscle, and brought the left between her legs, the wetness warm on his fingers.

"What about everybody?" She was looking toward the door.

"Who?"

"Everybody, darling. Outside."

And he remembered the people awaiting their turn at El Tamarindo. He could see movement through the blackened glass.

"Aren't you worried they'll hear?"

He eased down to the floor, his back against the cinder wall. The concrete was cool and gritty on his legs. "Come be with me," he said, holding out his hands. "Laura."

"But if they do . . . what if they hear, Joseph?"

His hands were on her hips, guiding her toward him. He watched her face as she lowered herself onto him. Her eyes were only half open. She placed one hand at the base of his penis, pressing against his scrotum, the other on the wall to support herself. Once he had entered her she began to rock backward, then forward, a hungry, frenetic motion. He was suddenly aware of her odor. He felt her breath against his ear.

After they were finished, they lay on the floor a long time. Her breathing was slow and steady and he figured she was asleep. He wondered what to say to her. "Did I tell you I quit the paper?" he finally whispered. "Maybe you could give me a job at your café. Do you need someone?"

She didn't answer. He put his face in her hair and smelled dust mingled with rosewater.

"Do you need me, Laura? I'm asking. Because if you need me, I'm here."

He was about to say something else when suddenly she shifted in his arms, not much. He looked down and saw her eyes open, a smile only now forming on her lips. "Because if you need me . . ." he said again.

The next night Joseph had another engagement in Adams Morgan, this one with Alfred Giddings and Leander McNeese. He left Logan Circle at nine o'clock and took his usual route along avenues that led to monuments standing dark in the night, beneath trees only half as tall as the buildings they fronted. He liked the sound of his shoes on the pavement, the wind on his face. It was a relief, though, when he reached Eighteenth Street and saw the brightly lighted mural of Toulouse-Lautrec, because now Joseph's feet and legs were sore and he welcomed the cool of the café.

As he'd hoped, he had arrived before the others, giving him time to catch his breath and enjoy a whiskey alone. A noisy clutch of happy-hour diehards was seated on the terrace, laughing over wine and yellow candlelight. He chose a place inside, a table near the door.

"Scotch," he told the waitress, a woman he'd never seen before. "Does Charlotte still work here?"

The woman nodded sullenly.

"Is she here tonight?"

"She's working the other end of the room. Want me to get her? She's in the kitchen."

"I'll see her when she comes out," he said. But even as he spoke, Charlotte was striding across the dining room, balancing platters of food on a tray. She had not seen him. She served a table and went to the bar. The waitress told her something and Charlotte walked over to his table. "Didn't expect to see you ever again," she said.

"How are you, Charlotte?"

She smiled and gave no reply. She seemed embarrassed to have encountered him again.

"Mac should be along any minute. We're having dinner."

"Good for you," she said. "Growing boys need to eat." She drummed her pen against the cork lining of the tray.

"Did I do something wrong?" he said.

"I'm just not interested anymore. It's plain as that."

"Not interested in what?"

The bartender, a middle-aged woman with long black hair, was calling for her to pick up. Charlotte cursed under her breath. "Do I have to spell it out for you?" she muttered.

"Is it sex you're not interested in?"

"No, not that."

"In men?"

"I've really got to go." But she didn't. She held the tray flat against her belly and leaned forward, her mouth close to his ear. "I like girls now," she said. When she stood up straight again, she was nodding as if to convince herself. "It's true, Joseph. I swear it."

The woman behind the bar called out more insistently now.

"I really have to go," Charlotte said.

"Let's talk later."

She put her mouth against his ear again. "Joseph, do you know if Leander has gotten his results yet?"

"If he has, Charlotte, he hasn't told me."

"Doesn't matter," she said. "It's girls for me."

The first waitress brought his drink and gave him a copy of the menu. While he was reading, Leander and Alfred came in. "Here," Joseph said, but they had already seen him. "They're with me," he told the waitress. She looked disapprovingly at both of them. "What's wrong?" Joseph said.

"Nothing."

"Where's Charlotte?" Leander asked the woman. A camera hung by an embroidered strap around his neck. It was a 35-mm Nikon with a flash attachment.

"That's all hers back there," the waitress said. "You guys move or stay put, one or the other."

Before Joseph could say anything Leander had gathered the menus and was leading them to a table in the rear of the dining room. Charlotte was nowhere to be seen.

"Could you bring us something to drink?" Leander said to the waitress.

"I thought you wanted Charlotte."

"Bring us something to drink," he said. "Anything. I promise a generous reward." A bunch of daisies in a glass jar stood at the center of the table, and he took one, twirled it by its stem, and lifted the blossom to his nose. "Joseph Burke here has bravely chosen to withdraw from the rank and file," he nearly shouted. "It's time we lift a toast."

Joseph noted the fuzzy black shadow growing on Leander's chin and around his mouth. Although his hair wasn't much longer than when he'd last cut it, a red, ink-stained rubber band held a spit of hair high and tight against the back of his head, the makings of a new ponytail.

"Still mad at me?" Leander said to Joseph.

"About what?"

"Fantastic," Leander said. "I like a man who forgets."

The waitress brought them whiskeys, the same as Joseph's. "Let's make this sonofabitch count," Leander said. He put a ten-dollar bill on the woman's tray, raised his drink, and tapped it against the others. "To love and obits," he said.

"To love and obits."

They drank and then repeated the toast, Alfred leading the cheers. "May we never have one," he said.

"An obit, that is," Joseph remarked.

Finally Charlotte emerged from the kitchen, carrying a large dinner tray stacked high with food.

"What a woman," Leander said. He stood and snapped a picture, the flash filling the room with light. "Hey, honey. Try to look a little less disgusted next time."

She swept by him, her face twisted with rage, and attended to a table of young women near the piano.

"Guess what?" Alfred said to Joseph.

"Don't make me."

"Mac still hasn't gone for his test results. He says he just couldn't do it. He wanted to, really he did, it's just that he couldn't."

Leander began to laugh and drum the table. "You boys ready to hear a story?"

"Why don't we wait awhile?" Joseph said.

Alfred yawned, feigning indifference.

"After Joseph and I dropped by the Red Cross the other night, I decided to take a few days off—"

"He never listens," Joseph told Alfred.

"Not when he's got a story," Alfred said.

"—I was hoping to clear my head, you understand? But at home I was a nervous wreck, pacing the floors. Then yesterday afternoon I found myself working some wood in the bedroom. It was very therapeutic, and pretty soon I felt better. I had all the saws going, the electric hammer and drills, and what was it I found myself building but a goddamned coffin."

"Of course you were," Joseph said. "Everybody's building them these days."

"You know," Alfred said, "that girl over by the piano keeps watching me. I can feel her eyes undressing me." With a discreet wave he indicated someone in the party Charlotte had served.

"Let me tell my story, fat man."

"Funny," Joseph said, "but I thought she was looking at me."

"Let me finish, goddammit." Leander reached over, put his finger in Alfred's drink, and swirled the ice around. Once he'd gotten Alfred's attention, he licked the finger and dunked it back in the whiskey.

"God only knows where that's been," Alfred said. "Take it, Mac. If you want it that bad, take the sonofabitch."

Leander lifted the drink and took a long swallow. "So I've got oak planks all over the place," he said, "and I'm really working—sawing, nailing, sanding, all that carpentry shit. I work until maybe two in the morning and I've got the body of the coffin built but no lid. And, of course, at this stage it looks just like a boat. You could take it out on the water, I think. So that's exactly what I set out to do. I lift it on my back and descend the stairs to the street."

Charlotte arrived with a basket of black bread and scoops of butter in a ceramic cup. "Ready to order, gentlemen?" She was trying to appear professional. She listed the specials from memory, then sucked in some air, clearly taken with herself.

Alfred and Joseph told her what they wanted.

"If it's okay with you," Leander said, "I'm not eating tonight. Only more of this." He raised the glass of whiskey.

She left for the kitchen and he said, "Where was I?"

"I don't recall," Alfred replied, "because I wasn't really listening to a word of it."

"Same here," said Joseph.

Leander chewed on a piece of bread and thought for a moment. "Okay. I remember now. I was down on Eighteenth Street with my coffin that looked like a boat."

"Oh, yeah," Alfred said. "You were, weren't you?"

"Anyway, there's an old man sweeping the sidewalk in front of La Fourchette, and he says to me, 'Where ya going, Mac?' And I say, 'Boating. What's it look like?' "

"You ready for another drink, Joseph?" Alfred's eyes were riveted on the woman near the piano.

"Don't gawk, for heaven's sake," Joseph said. "They get spooked when you gawk." He buttered a chip of bread.

"So I walk and walk. I walk down by Foggy Bottom and George Washington University, the boat braced against my shoulders, then down below the Whitehurst Freeway. When I finally reach the bank of the Potomac, the sun's coming up and it's orange in the trees and on the water, and orange on all the birds flying overhead. I can see orange crew teams moving along the river, paddles stroking the surface with hardly a ripple, and what do I do but get in and chase after them."

"This has to be the nuttiest one yet," Alfred said.

"Nuttier than the one about the transvestite waitress at that diner in New Jersey?" Joseph said.

"Way nuttier."

"—and as I'm floating downriver, pulled by the current, it occurs to me that the only real difference between a coffin and a boat . . . the only real difference is a lid to keep the light out."

"And the worms," Alfred said.

"Snakes, too," Joseph said. "Got to keep the snakes out."

Leander sat gazing at the flowers. His lower lip had begun to tremble, as had his hands, and sweat glistened on the downy whiskers around his mouth.

"Look at that," Joseph said, rubbing his arms. "You've gone and given me a chill, Mac."

Leander cleared his throat and dried the perspiration on his face with a napkin. "And so it's six in the morning," he whispered, "and I'm floating past the Washington Harbour and the Watergate and the Kennedy Center. And then past the monuments to all those dead men nobody really remembers anymore. And it comes to me that by being here, that by being adrift in the early morning on my orange river—"

"She's looking this way again," Alfred said, tapping Joseph's arm. "Tell me I'm wrong."

"I think it's Charlotte she wants," Joseph said. "She wants wine. Check out her glass, pal. Empty."

Leander had begun to cry. "Coffin or boat," he said now. "Positive or negative. Yes or no."

"God, Mac."

"Let him go, Alfred. Let him go."

Leander was sobbing and there was nothing anyone could do about it. Everybody in the restaurant watched. They put down their food and drinks and stared in bewilderment. And then all of a sudden he began to laugh, or to do something that resembled laughter. It was a hard, violent thing, as painful to watch as the crying, and tears fell. Then, when he'd had enough, he slapped his hands against the tabletop, rose to his feet, and called for another drink. "Whiskey, Charlotte! Whiskey!"

"Maybe you should go to the men's room." It was the first waitress, pointing the way.

"Only if you come with me," he answered.

"He was faking it," Joseph told the waitress.

"Not very funny," she said.

Leander removed the camera from around his neck and handed it to Joseph. He pointed to a button on top. "Press there," he said, sitting back down. "Take my picture as I look at this moment. I'll buy more Calvados and invite you over. We'll have a slide show and sit on the roof and count the stars."

Joseph did as he was told and then gave the camera back. It would be a picture of a handsome, dark-haired man with a smile on his face, tears wet on his cheeks.

"Coffin or boat," Alfred said, sounding only mildly amused. "That was really clever, Mac."

A few minutes later Charlotte served the meal and another round of drinks. "Did something happen?" she said, and placed another basket of bread in front of Leander.

"Mac just told a story about boating down the Potomac River," Joseph said.

"You should've called me. I love to sail."

"Yeah, well . . . maybe next time, Charlotte."

"Can I get you guys anything?" She looked at her notepad. "Because if there's nothing you need—"

"Just do us one more favor," Joseph said.

"Anything."

"Don't say 'Enjoy,' Charlotte. If there's one thing I can't stand, it's when a waiter says 'Enjoy.' "

She put the empty glasses on her tray. "Hope you like it," she said. "Is that better, Joseph?"

Halfway through the meal, after he had eaten all the bread and finished both his and Alfred's drinks, Leander reached his arm across the table and dunked a finger into Alfred's onion soup. "You don't want this, do you, fat man?"

"Take it," Alfred said, waving his hands. "You want it that bad, Mac, take it, take the goddamn thing!"

Across the room a jazz trio began to play, weary-eyed men dressed in white slacks with satin stripes along the outer seams and pink tuxedo shirts buttoned to the collar. The piano player announced the arrival of the tap dancer, and the little man hopped up on the bar and tipped his bowler hat to the crowd. As everyone applauded, the band picked up the tempo and the man danced across the satiny wood. People sat on the stools below him, some still drinking cocktails, others eating food, and he disturbed none of them. The quicker his feet moved, the more noise the crowd made. By the end of his first number everyone was shouting for more. The man held his hat against his chest and bowed in gratitude, sweat gleaming on his face.

Leander stood and checked his camera. "I don't have it," he said. "I found out tonight."

"But just a while ago you said you'd chickened out again."

"I was lying, Alfred. I tested negative."

"I suppose a toast is in order," Joseph said. But he didn't offer one.

"It's like having a new dick, isn't it? I'm not sure I'll know what to do with it."

Alfred was staring at the dancer on the bar, through glasses fogged with tears. Leander lifted a hand to his lips, kissed his fingertips, and placed them against Alfred's mouth. "I'm going to live," he said, then walked across the room and introduced himself to the table of women near the piano.

"It looks like Mac really is back," Joseph said.

"Yes, I think he is." Alfred removed his glasses and wiped them on the tablecloth. "And it looks to me like he's gone and moved in on our girl."

They watched as Leander took the woman's picture and whispered something in her ear. She had long black hair, thick and kinky, and he examined it admiringly, holding a hank of it in the palm of his hand.

"If I could be anybody," Alfred said, "it'd be Mac."

"There isn't anyone else," Joseph said.

A few minutes later Leander returned to the table and knocked back the watery dregs in Alfred's glass. "Turns out all along she was watching me, boys," he said. He wheeled around and met her gaze again. "Hate to suddenly leave your retirement party," he said to Joseph. "But I'm sure you understand."

"Not only that, Mac. I sympathize."

"Sit down," Alfred said. "You're not going anywhere."

"What do I tell Charlotte?" Joseph said.

"That I went sailing. Don't mention the coffin."

After Leander left the restaurant, his new friend in tow, Joseph drank what remained of his whiskey and said, "Tell me if I got this right, Alfred. Our buddy McNeese learns that he's not going to die after all, and an hour later he goes to a bar, picks up a total stranger, and takes her home to bed."

"I think that about covers it."

Joseph ignited a cigarette, using the candle on the table. "Do me a favor, pal. Don't ever let me be surprised by human sexual behavior again."

"You can count on me," Alfred said.

They had coffee and dessert and Charlotte brought the check. She had been in the kitchen when Leander left, and now she watched the door as if awaiting his return. "Where do you think he went? Was he feeling bad?"

"He had a date with the sea," Joseph said.

"One of you ought to tell that boy to keep his thing in his trousers," she said, "before he makes somebody trip."

Joseph and Alfred split the bill and started for the door. The trio was taking a break now, sitting at a table on the terrace, smoking cigars. Outside Joseph breathed the hot air and checked the sky for constellations. City dust was blocking the view, and hardly a thing could be seen.

"Joseph ..." It was Charlotte again; she had followed him and Alfred out into the street. "Joseph, can I have a word with you?"

"Sure."

Alfred groaned wearily, walked over to a parking meter, and leaned against it.

"Joseph ..." Charlotte twisted the tail of her wine-stained apron. "Joseph, I was wondering if you ever thought about that time."

"What time is that, Charlotte?"

"That time ... that night at your apartment on Connecticut Avenue."

"Ah, yes," he said. "Sure I think about it."

She had wrung her apron into a knot. "Have the test, Joseph. Please. Do it for me."

He laughed and put his hands on her shoulders. "Charlotte, you just don't get it, do you?"

"I don't really like girls, Joseph, you know that. I mean, of course I like them, but not that way."

"I made a decision about something," he said. "From here on out I only sleep with the woman I love."

"What woman?"

"The woman I love, whenever I fall in love with one."

She looked whipped and miserable, the wind wild in her hair. "You're just afraid to give it up, Joseph."

"To give what up?"

"This," she said, pressing a finger against his chest. She looked past him. "Who's he, Joseph? The fat guy."

Joseph turned and waved at his friend. "That's Alfred Charles Giddings III. He's the best damned obituary writer the *Washington Herald* has ever known."

"Better even than you?"

"The man was a legend before I even knew what an obit was."

She unknotted the apron and smoothed it out. "He seems nice. Let me meet him." She was tracing over her lips with the tip of her tongue. "Introduce me, Joseph."

"Alfred, come say hello to a friend of mine."

Alfred shuffled over, hands working the change in his pockets.

"This is Charlotte, the finest little waitress in D.C. Charlotte, this is Alfred, mayor and only living inhabitant of Giddings's Metropolitan of the Dead."

Alfred folded his glasses and put them in his shirt pocket, forcing them in among a colorful forest of No. 2 pencils. He and Charlotte exchanged a long, lively handshake.

"Charlotte, Alfred here was just saying he could use another drink, weren't you, Alfred?"

"But Joseph—"

"You want a drink, Alfred?" she said. "I'd be happy to get it for you."

Joseph could see the fear in his eyes. "Alfred won a Pulitzer Prize, Charlotte."

"Won a what?"

"His father's a millionaire," he said.

"Yeah?"

Alfred finally ambled forward, Charlotte holding his arm. They were as far as the door when he wheeled around and walked back over to Joseph. "I love you," he whispered, leaning in close.

"I love you, too, pal."

"No," he said, shaking his head, "I *really* love you."

Then he rejoined Charlotte, offered his arm, and escorted her through the swinging café door.

6 Instead of taking a cab home, Joseph walked down to Laura's building and stood in front of it, watching the headlights from passing traffic play across the facade. It was late and El Tamarindo was almost empty. A waiter was sitting outside on the curb, smoking

a cigarette; another stood in the restaurant's open doorway, leafing through an underground newspaper. Gypsy music spilled into the street.

Joseph stepped up to the window and tried to look inside. Everything was dark now. The broken glass at the entrance had been swept away and some of the fliers and posters taken down. He smelled a faint trace of ammonia.

He was about to leave when he noticed some writing above the door. It had been scrawled in heavy ink directly onto the frame, and done so rather fancifully. CAFÉ COEUR, it said.

"Pardon me, sir," Joseph said to the waiter at the curb. "This building here. Was it a restaurant?"

He shook his head. "A grocery."

"It wasn't a café?"

The man flicked his cigarette away and stared at Joseph. "For years and years," he said, "it was a grocery. Nothing else."

Joseph nodded and looked up U Street. Fifteen, twenty minutes it would take to walk home, half that if he ran.

"Do you speak French?" he asked the man.

"*Un peu*" was the response.

Joseph gazed back at the writing above the door. "Then could you please tell me what *coeur* means."

"*Coeur?*" the man said. He placed both hands on his chest. "*Coeur* means heart, my friend."

Joseph thanked him and started running along the sidewalk, arms and legs pumping wildly. His calves and buttocks throbbed with pain but that did not deter him; neither did the possibility of being stopped by a police officer suspecting criminal mischief. Presently Joseph cut over to the middle of the street and chased after its unbroken center line. He ran past a firehouse and under a traffic signal burning green. A car was turning right onto a side street and he flew by it, his jaw relaxed, his eyes unblinking.

The hour being so late, there were few people out to see him, and this he regretted. He had begun to shout Laura Vannoy's name, and what a spectacular sight he must have been.

◈ *Ten* ◈

One day, about two months later, Joseph was awakened before dawn by shouts of laughter from the floor below. He quickly put on his robe and slippers and rushed downstairs. In the center of the den Pete Peters stood swirling a snifter of brandy; Woody, wearing his cap and sunglasses, was sipping from a pewter flask, his box of fishing tackle resting on his knees.

"Get dressed," Woody said. "Our day has come."

Peters removed a ring of keys from his pocket and held it out to Joseph. "To my pickup truck and bass boat," he explained. "I hear things've been popping down near Daingerfield Island. You boys'd better not even think about letting me down."

Joseph wasn't ready for this but his head was too muddled to devise a plan of escape. "What about the others?" he finally thought to ask. "I seem to remember your inviting Fred and Marissa. You said they could bring their children along."

"It's you and me, son. No one else." Woody turned to Peters. "Look at him, Pete. Look at my boy's face." He laughed. "Joseph's gone and fallen in love."

"That's good," Peters said. "Falling is usually how you get there, paying out the ass how you get out."

Joseph knotted his hands and pressed them against his eyes. "This isn't love, for heaven's sake. It's sleep."

"He's out of his head in love," Woody said. "He's in a daze around the clock. You tell him hello and he says goodbye. You tell him to eat and he does the dishes. But I honestly can't blame him. You should see this woman."

"Let me tell you about love," Peters said. "There's nothing like it for about two months and then one morning you wake up, walk into the bathroom, and there she is, sitting on the toilet. I swear that ruins it every time."

"Cleo never did that," Woody said.

"All wives do it. Women use the toilet the same as men."

"Well, she might've done it but she was such a goddamned genius I never caught her at it." Woody wheeled over to Joseph, patted him on the thigh, and winked, out of sight of Peters. "You don't remember ever seeing Mother use the toilet, do you, son?"

Joseph shook his head. "Not my mother."

"She was special that way," Woody said. "Her body just didn't function like everybody else's."

Pete Peters, at least, seemed convinced. "What a woman," he remarked, then took a taste of brandy.

Another hour passed before Joseph and Woody were ready to depart. With Peters's help they packed half a dozen boiled eggs, cheese sandwiches wrapped in waxed paper, a couple of chocolate bars, several bags of pistachio nuts, a thermos of black coffee, a gallon jug of distilled water, and a fifth of bourbon. Joseph secured the food and fishing equipment under an Army-issue tarp in the boat. He then carried Woody from the veranda out to the truck. "Bring the wheelchair, please," he called back to Peters. "God forbid we forget that."

Reluctantly Peters obliged, grunting with each step.

"I just thought of something," Joseph said, sliding his father's legs over. "I've never pulled a boat before."

"I figured you'd try to get out of this some way," Woody said, still clinging to the flask.

"Just take your time," Peters said. "If the rig starts to swing, don't panic. She'll right herself."

"Is that all I need to know?"

"No, not nearly. But it's all I plan to tell you. If you boys don't leave soon, you'll get stuck in morning traffic. On top of that, the bass are starting to feed right about now. You haven't time to waste."

"Now don't go getting all Navy on us," Woody said, and unstopped the mouth of the flask. "After all these months sitting on my butt I'm sure as hell not gonna be rushed now." He swallowed more whiskey.

The sun had risen and Joseph could see strands of gossamer floating atop the grassy park lawn. Under the trees people were beginning to stir, shedding their blankets of yellowed newspaper.

"Why don't you drive us?" Joseph asked Peters.

"I got a book to write. Morning's when I'm most inspired."

"You couldn't take some time off? There's room in the boat."

Peters was shaking his head. "I also got a wife."

"A big, mean wife," Woody added. "You should see her, son."

Joseph pushed some of the trash off the seat, settled in behind the wheel, and started the engine. He spent a moment studying the dashboard. "Mr. Peters," he said, "thanks for letting us borrow all this. It was very kind."

"You're more than welcome, young man." Peters reached inside, opened the glove compartment, and removed a magazine. "Have you seen this? It came last night in the mail." He turned to a page in front. "Look at this. You're famous, Joseph."

It was the column called "Don't Ask Andy . . ." situated below a small black-and-white photograph of Andrea Troy.

"Let me hear what it says," Woody said.

"Please, don't," Joseph protested.

"Then give it . . ." Woody yanked the magazine from Peters's hands. " 'And who has Laura Vannoy been seeing lately?' " he began, reading by the light on the dome of the cab. " 'None other than Joseph Burke, recently fired obit writer for the *Washington Herald* and plaything of the late Mary Peden, former wife of the distinguished Senator Royston Peden of New York.' " Woody paused and shrugged his shoulders. "Tell me something I don't know."

"You started it," Joseph said. "Go ahead and finish."

Woody held the magazine under the light again. " 'Sources say Burke, ex-husband of sexy new mom Naomi Richard-Verdooth, has started work on a novel about his experiences at the *Herald* and is helping Vannoy establish yet another hole-in-the-wall restaurant in Adams Morgan. Don't ask Andy, but these two won't last past the Redskins' first playoff game when star running back Michael—' "

"Enough, enough," Joseph said.

"That's all there is anyway," Peters remarked, taking the magazine from Woody. "Unless you want to hear about black football players having their way with white society dames."

"Miscegenation," Woody said. "Now there's a two-dollar word for you, Pete. I can go get my Webster's if you want to check it."

"Nope. I trust you."

"Tonight when you come by for the truck and boat," Joseph said, "we'll have some fried fish ready for you, Mr. Peters."

"I'm expecting no less than a feast."

"Let's go, Joseph," Woody said. "It's time, son."

"Should we drive you home?" Joseph asked Peters.

"I'll take a cab. Easier on everybody that way."

"Well, goodbye, then. And thanks again."

"Goodbye, Joseph." Peters tapped Woody on the shoulder. "And goodbye to you, Wood man."

At last they left, moving far slower than the posted speed limits, and taking up both lanes. Joseph spent more time watching his rear in the sideview mirrors than the road ahead, and once, drifting into oncoming traffic on K Street, Woody let out a whoop to get him back on course. A hundred yards later he said, "Pete Peters wouldn't know when fish eat from when they shit." He hit the whiskey again. "Don't rush it, son. We'll get there when we get there."

Joseph was driving on Vermont Avenue in the direction of the White House. Up ahead was Lafayette Square. He was feeling more relaxed now because no one was behind him. In the park protesters were camped on the sidewalks, some standing beside flimsy folding tables and distributing pamphlets to passersby. Their banners and

posters contained, among other things, painted and photographic images of firebombs, aborted fetuses, and atomic missile silos.

"We'll have to stop somewhere," Joseph said. "I need to call Laura.
She was expecting me this morning."

"Does Laura fish, son?"

"Don't know. Never asked."

"Then ask. It'd be something to look at if the fish don't bite. Tell
her to bring Amelia, too."

Joseph turned onto Pennsylvania Avenue.

"But before you do all that," Woody said, "let's go for a ride and
look things over. Let's celebrate."

"Celebrate what?"

"Let's go see the sights, son."

"At this time of day?"

Woody held the flask before him, swirled its contents, then took
another drink. "Take me to Glenwood Cemetery, Joseph. I want to
see your mother."

Joseph braked and pulled up next to the cement barricade in front
of the White House. "What did you say, Father?"

"Cleo and then the fish. One must have priorities."

After Joseph succeeded in making the block and freeing himself
from the congestion, Woody beat a fist against the glove compartment.
"I'm awfully sorry," he said, "but you're gonna have to stop, son."

"Need the bathroom?"

"Nope," Woody said. "My flask is empty. I'll need that fifth you
put in the back of the boat."

Joseph didn't dare pull over until they'd reached Logan Circle,
familiar territory. "I don't mind your getting drunk," he said. "Just tell
me if you feel yourself getting sick."

"You think I'm drunk?" Woody said.

"I think you're getting there."

Joseph stopped the truck in front of the house, rushed inside, and
dialed Laura from the phone downstairs. At first excited to hear his
voice, she fell silent at the mention of his proposal.

"We've packed a lunch," he said. "And Woody's in some kind of mood."

"Amelia can't swim, Joseph. And what if we had an accident? I don't know about this."

"There're life vests," he said. "We'll all have to wear one."

"Will you bait my line? I've never been good at that. I've never liked it."

"The bait's artificial. Plastic worms."

"No bugs? Are you sure?"

"Positive. If you decide to come, meet us at the marina by the Pentagon. It's just off the George Washington Parkway. Father and I have one stop before we get there, but it shouldn't take more than an hour."

"And where are you going, darling?"

"To see Mother," he said.

Under way once again, Joseph and Woody drove through the Shaw neighborhood and turned left on Lincoln Road. Now that they were only a few minutes from the cemetery, Joseph felt more confident behind the wheel. They would make it without incident, they would be all right.

Banners advertising burial and cremation sites stretched between iron poles in front of the cemetery. Financing was available to qualified buyers, they said. And for a limited time only you could purchase two plots for the price of one.

"Whoever heard of a cemetery touting bargains?" Woody said.

"Rare times, Father."

"Rare indeed."

The cemetery didn't open until eight o'clock, half an hour's wait. "Shall we stay or push on?" Joseph said, stopping at the entrance. He put the truck in park and cut off the engine.

"I don't mind the wait. Your mother's been waiting for me to come pay my respects for more than half a year now." He shrugged. "What's a few more minutes?"

Joseph rolled down his window to air out the cab. The morning breeze was moist and sweet; it quickly cut the sharp whiskey smell. "Have a snort, son," Woody said. He held out the flask. Joseph took it and drank, spilling some down his jaw and onto his shirt. It was hot going down and for some reason made him sneeze. He drank more and sneezed again.

"Whoever heard of someone allergic to whiskey?"

"Just keep drinking, Father. We'll see how allergic you get."

Woody capped the flask and put it in the glove compartment. "I'm hungry, Joseph. Get me an egg."

"Come on, Father. Give me a break."

"Get me an egg. I'm the one crippled."

Joseph stepped outside, ambled around to the back of the boat, and climbed up on the wheel well. Woody was watching him through the back window, his mirrored sunglasses reflecting Joseph's every move.

"This look all right?" Joseph said. He took an egg out of the paper sack and gave it to Woody.

"Better if there were salt and pepper handy."

Woody peeled off the white shell and took a bite. "Still warm," he said, admiring the steaming orb. Bits of yolk dropped onto the seat and appeared to melt into the fabric.

"I hate boiled eggs," Joseph said. "They stink."

"They stink until you're hungry." Woody removed another from the bag and offered it to Joseph. "Do it for me, son."

"No, thanks."

"Eat it now. It'll make me happy."

Joseph leaned closer to the door. "I really don't want it."

Woody peeled the shell off, working quickly. "Look how perfect it is." He placed it on the seat next to Joseph. "Look at it, son."

"I told you I don't want it."

"But look at it. Look how perfect."

The superintendent was right on time opening the gate. Dressed all in khaki, a riding cap fitted snugly on his triangle-shaped head, the man resembled an overgrown Boy Scout. A fat chain of keys bounced against his hip. "Going fishing?" he said to Joseph.

"We're here to see Cleo Burke," Woody said.

"Her grave," Joseph explained.

"Need any directions, stop by the office."

"I know where she is," Woody said.

Glenwood had forty-eight acres crowded with almost forty thousand dead. The road they took wound through the hilly park, past imposing mausoleums standing red and dusty beneath enormous shade trees. "I haven't seen the plots since we bought them fifteen, twenty years ago," Woody said. "But I remember they're near the old chapel."

Joseph gazed out at a yard studded with stone markers, most of them ancient and weathered, some overgrown with weeds. "Seems like they could take better care of this place," he mumbled.

Woody was pointing to a spot a short distance from the road. "It's there."

Joseph pulled over and stopped the truck on the grass.

"They've put down the stone," Woody said. "Can you see it?"

"What . . . ? Oh, yes. I see it now."

Joseph walked around the truck, positioned the wheelchair next to the door, and put Woody in it. Woody felt cold to the touch and he was trembling. "You want to go there by yourself or you want me to push you?" Joseph said.

"You can push me."

Joseph struggled to wheel Woody through the soft, high grass. He turned the chair around and pulled him backward, dodging markers. He tried to keep from walking on the graves, but with Woody in tow this proved impossible. Joseph's neck bulged with thick, knotted cords and he felt his scrotum draw in tight.

"Are we there yet?" Woody said, his voice small and weak.

"Not yet. We're close, though."

"How much longer?"

"Another minute," Joseph said. "Maybe less."

"Thirty seconds?"

"Count. Count to twenty and we'll be there."

The stone was so large that her name seemed overwhelmed by all the granite. Joseph had picked out the suit of clothes for Cleo to be buried in, had chosen the self-portrait to stand for the visitation, had observed the coffin being lowered into the ground, but only now—seeing her name on the tablet, and the dates of birth and death, and the words MOTHER and WIFE inscribed on the lower half—did it seem final and real.

"Cleo is dead," Woody announced, as if he too had at last come to believe it. "Dead," he said again.

Joseph sat on the grass and let the sun warm his face. He picked a tall, stringy weed and chewed on it. The black shapes of trees towered in the distance, high above the chapel. Nothing he could do or say would make things any easier, so he kept quiet.

"Whenever you're ready to go," Woody said after a few minutes. He pushed the cap back on his head.

"We can always come again," Joseph said.

"It isn't far."

Joseph rolled him back to the truck.

"It was my fault," Woody said.

"It wasn't anybody's fault." They had reached the truck and Joseph was lifting Woody into the cab. "Think about the nice things, Father. Think about the good."

"Okay."

"Remember what love there was."

"All right, son. I'll remember the love."

But Joseph could see the pain in Woody's face, the creased forehead, the redness of the eyes. He was doing his best not to cry. "I'll only think about the nice things," he said now. "Nothing else. Nothing but the good."

Later, on the road to the marina, Woody said, "Next time we'll have to bring some shears or something."

"Good idea. Those weeds were pretty tall."

"Some flowers'd be nice, too. Remind me."

They were crossing the Fourteenth Street Bridge when Woody took the peeled egg off the seat. "Take a bite," he said to Joseph. "Come on."

"I'm driving."

"Here. . . . Take this half, son."

Joseph finally ate the egg, tasting it more in his nose than in his mouth. "Are you happy now?" he said when he was finished.

"Yes," Woody said. "I'm ecstatic." And he took another egg out of the bag. "Don't you love an egg in the morning, son?"

"They're really horrible, aren't they?"

"Here. Eat another. Do it for the Wood man."

6   At three o'clock that afternoon they were fishing along the east bank of the Washington Channel, drifting slowly toward the Maine Avenue fish market and the Capitol Yacht Club. The Jefferson Memorial, not yet visible from the boat, was less than a mile away, squatting beside a body of water called the Tidal Basin. Nothing had been biting at Greenleaf and Buzzard points, or anywhere else for that matter. They had agreed to try a spot just past the Washington Marina before retiring for the day.

"Baby, will you put a little more goop on my back?" Laura Vannoy said. "I'm afraid I'm starting to burn."

"Who's 'baby'?" Woody said.

"Amelia," Joseph answered, and clumsily cast toward the shallows. "Don't get fresh, Father."

Joseph was standing on a deck at the bow of the boat, and Woody was sitting behind the steering wheel in the stern, his wheelchair folded and lying next to him. Laura and Amelia, wearing bikini tops, jogging shorts, and rubber sandals, sat on the bench seat in the middle. Not once had they tried their luck with the lines Woody and Joseph had prepared for them. Although the outing had begun with inflated expectations, it seemed unlikely that anyone would land a fish now. After hours without even a nibble, the anglers had lost all hope and had even begun making alternate plans for dinner.

"We could try down by Old Town," Woody said. He meant Alexandria, Virginia, several miles to the south.

"Is that where all the fish're hiding?" Joseph said. "I've been wondering."

"Why don't we park somewhere and have a cold one first?" Laura said. "Maine Avenue's full of restaurants."

"You don't park a boat, Mother. You dock it."

"Then let's dock it," she said.

"A little longer," Woody said. "Just a little longer."

They motored past the fish market, the yacht club, and the marina and eased in close to the pilings of a bridge. Joseph's cast landed yards away from the desired spot, but he had long since abandoned any pretense of knowing what he was doing. Also, he found it hard to concentrate with Laura sitting so close by. His eyes invariably returned to her, the smooth, shiny swell of her bosom, the flat belly, the downy blond hair that grew at the very tops of her thighs. Likewise, Woody was focused on Amelia. Since first meeting some six weeks ago, the two had cultivated a bond that had initially upset Joseph. He had feared that his father, still looking to fill the void left by Cleo, had transferred his affections from Marissa to Amelia. But as the two of them were often heard to say, Woody had taken the place of Grandpa Roy Cobb, dead a good ten years now, and Woody had discovered in Amelia a grandchild. They had brought as much energy and enthusiasm to these roles as Joseph and Laura had to theirs as lovers. "We can't seem to get enough of each other," Woody liked to say.

Joseph cast again toward the pilings and began to reel in. He watched as Amelia rubbed tanning oil onto her mother's back, her small brown hands massaging Laura's shoulders, and missed whatever it was that had struck at his line. Earlier he'd gotten snagged and thought it a fish, but this was nothing like that. He'd felt this one in his gut.

"Be patient," Woody said. "It was probably just a little one. A big one wouldn't play with your line like that."

Joseph felt the muscles in his shoulders tighten. His head hurt and he wished he hadn't drunk his father's whiskey. "Big or little," he said, "it'll be a miracle if it comes back."

"Be patient," Woody told him. "Miracles happen." And he and Amelia looked at each other in the knowing way of conspirators.

"But I don't think there's anything here—"

"Quiet, son," Woody snapped. "Fish have ears, they hear better'n you and me."

"Fish don't have ears."

"The hell they don't."

As they floated closer to shore, the sound of traffic overhead echoing across the water, Joseph spotted a colony of crudely constructed shelters in the shadows beneath the bridge. There must have been twenty of them, all made of warped pieces of plywood, battered tin sheets, and once-transparent strips that now were cracked and green with algae.

"Sometimes I can't believe this is America," Amelia said. "Pity the people who have to live like that."

"Amelia, not so loud, baby. We're trying to fish."

Amelia lowered her voice. "It's the nation's capital. It's where the president lives. It's where all the laws are made."

Suddenly Woody sat up in his seat and pointed. "Good lord," he whispered. "It's there again. Look at the water churn."

Joseph, however, was gazing at the huts under the bridge. "Anybody home!" he called. "Hello!"

"Not so loud," Woody said again.

As Joseph watched, blocking the sun with the flat of his hand, a woman crawled out of one of the huts. Her hair was coiled in braids down to her shoulders, and her clothes were brown with dirt and sweat and fell loosely over her thin frame. She was soon joined by others, men, women, and children, about twenty in all. They stood near the bank of the river and stared in silence.

"Do all you people live here?" Amelia said.

No one answered. The first woman dropped to her haunches and flailed at the water with a stick.

"I can't believe this is America," Amelia said again. "That it's the nation's capital."

"Maybe it was just my imagination," Woody said. "Maybe I'm seeing things. Maybe the water never did churn, after all."

He had begun to reel in again when a strike whipped his line and turned the tip of his rod toward the water. "Joseph! Hey, Joseph! I got it, I got one!"

The fish was headed for the pilings, pulling the line taut, making the reel scream.

"Get the net!" Woody was saying. "Get it ready! Come on, somebody. Don't just sit there! Help!" And suddenly he rose to his feet, Woody did, standing tall on both legs, looking as strong and athletic as he ever had.

"You did it, Father," Joseph said quietly. "You did it."

"I did it," Woody answered, stepping forward. "I got a fish, son. *I got a fish!*"

"Oh, Woody," Laura said, her eyes bright with tears. "Look at you. Will you just look at you?"

"I caught one! I finally caught one!"

"It's a miracle," Amelia said. "It's a miracle!" She stood and embraced Woody, heedless of his battle. "I'm so proud of you."

Joseph netted the fish and lifted it wild and flopping into the boat. Woody removed the hook and held the fish up by the bottom of its mouth. It was a bass, about three pounds. Its head had been cut against the rocks near the pilings and its eyes were bleeding. It was a pretty fish, though, a good fighter. Woody, still standing, kissed its swollen side and turned it in the sun.

"You want to touch it?" he said to Amelia.

"No, thank you."

"Here, Joseph. See what it feels like."

Joseph grabbed the fish and studied its iridescent flesh, though most of the color had faded by now. "Glorious," he said. "Absolutely glorious."

At the stern of the boat Woody took the wheelchair from under the life vests and tackle box, hoisted it by the handles, and threw it as far as he could into the water. It landed only about ten feet away, and after it settled, one of the wheels was visible above the surface.

Woody, careful to keep his balance, stepped toward Joseph. "Give it here, son. Give it back."

Joseph handed him the fish, and before he could do anything to stop him, Woody bounded over the side of the boat and flopped into the water.

"Oh, God!" Laura shouted as Woody went completely under. "Do something, Joseph! Save him!"

Joseph was preparing to dive into the channel when Woody suddenly popped up, standing in water no more than three feet deep. His baseball cap had come off and was drifting, tumbling toward the pilings.

"Woody, you scared me," Amelia said, clutching her hands to her breast. "That wasn't funny."

"Come back now," Laura said, holding her arms out to him. "Here. I'll help you."

Only now did Joseph see that Woody was still clinging to the fish. Its mouth was open, and its gills throbbed scarlet. And it seemed to have more fight than it did before.

"Let's get going, Father," Joseph said. "We'll need to hurry home and get you some dry clothes."

"I want to feed them," Woody said.

"Feed who?" Joseph said.

"I want to feed them, son." And Woody started trudging through the water on his way to the shore and the people congregated there. "I want to feed them, I want to feed them all."

"My heart," Amelia said. "Mother, you should feel my heart."

"Father . . . come back here! Come back, Father!"

The people near the huts had begun to walk toward Woody, some entering the water and wading out to him. Woody was struggling to reach them faster now, his knees pumping against the current. He raised the fish above his head and let loose with a wild Tarzan roar that echoed against the bridge and beat back down the channel. A flash of sunlight bounced off the surface, spitting a million sparks, and Joseph was momentarily blinded. When he could see again, it was as though he were looking at fireworks, his father the brightest of all.